The Complete Works

2017-2021

Adam Nicke

Adam Nicke Publishing

Reviews left on Amazon and Goodreads help promote the books you love

Adam Nicke Publishing 2021
adamnicke@gmail.com

Copyright © Adam Nicke 2021

The right of Adam Nicke to be identified as the author of this work has been asserted by him in accordance with the Copyright, Designs and Patents Act 1988

Cover design by Adam Nicke

Imprint: Independently published

All Rights Reserved. No part of this publication may be reproduced in any manner without prior written permission of the publisher, except in the case of brief excerpts in critical reviews or articles.

ISBN 9798768905989 (paperback)
ISBN 9798763252385 (hardback)

Introduction

The four books in this collection were written at very different times in my life and are here presented in the order they were written.

My *Grim Fairy Tales* was written around 1990, in the aftermath of my mother's death. At that time, I had been reading a lot of late 19th century French writers. A lot of these writers had read Baudelaire's translation of Poe and just as Edgar Allan Poe had appealed to them, they, in turn, appealed to me. I vividly remember the following passage by Paul Verlaine, written as a rebuttal to critics who had labelled such writers as 'decadent':

> *"I like the word 'decadent,' all shimmering with purple and gold … it throws out the brilliance of flames and the gleam of precious stones. It is made up of carnal spirit and unhappy flesh and of all the violent splendours of the Lower Empire; it conjures up the paint of the courtesans, the sports of the circus, the breath of the tamers of animals, the bounding of wild beasts, the collapse among the flames of races exhausted by the power of feeling, to the invading sound of enemy trumpets. The decadence is Sardanapalus lighting the fire in the midst of his women, it is Seneca declaiming poetry as he opens his veins, it is Petronius masking his agony with flowers."*

My *Grim Fairy Tales* was eventually published in 1995, by the occult academics Keith Seddon and Jocelyn Almond.

My *Temptation and Denial* began as a follow-up to *Grim Fairy Tales* but in 1991 I started studying for a degree in Literary Studies at the University of The West of England in Bristol. In my first year, we read *Wuthering Heights* and my reading of *Wuthering Heights* had the same effect on me as reading the Decadent school of writers had had on me the year before. I'd been interested in the Byronic Hero prior to my interest in the Decadents. I also found kindred spirits in many of the Romantic Poets, particularly

Introduction

Lord Byron. Whilst writing an essay on *Wuthering Heights* I came across this quote on the Byronic Hero by the 19th century literary critic and historian Lord Macaulay:

> *"a man proud, moody, cynical, with defiance on his brow, and misery in his heart, a scorner of his kind, implacable in revenge, yet capable of deep and strong affection."*

After reading the above quote, I was inspired to go back to the text of *Temptation and Denial* and turn Sebastian into such a man. Further to that, Sebastian's character and responses are also based on my character and responses.

Sadly, the text of *Temptation and Denial* would lie on a shelf in my study for over twenty years as the trials in tribulations of real-life took their toll on me. I became a carer for my maternal grandmother in 2006 and when she passed in 2012 my life became every bit as horrific as the life Edgar Allan Poe had endured. That may sound like dramatic hyperbole but the physical pain and mental anguish I endured from 2012 to 2015 was only explained when, in September 2015, I collapsed with what was subsequently diagnosed as a tennis ball-sized brain tumour that had been possibly growing for thirty years. The writer Matthew Pearl has posited that Poe may have died of such a condition and the day he was found sounds very much like the day I was found. His doctor thought him insensibly drunk and, I'm told, my doctors thought I had taken an overdose. Poe's death remains speculation but it is a fact that Mary Shelley died of a brain tumour.

After a successful craniotomy, I contacted Keith Seddon after reading online that Jocelyn Almond had died. He suggested that *Grim Fairy Tales* be republished. I was elated at such a suggestion as I was finally able to make the changes I had wanted to make in the twenty-two years since it was first published. The success of *Grim Fairy Tales* led to the publication of *Temptation and Denial*.

Around the turn of the century, I worked for a TV production company and wrote a screenplay that was never read by them as they relocated before I finished it. That screenplay would become *Mallard the Quack*.

Introduction

I've always been a recalcitrant person. Those of you that have already read my *Temptation and Denial* will know that I rail against patriarchy and patriarchal society. Further to that, the socialist ideal of a fair and just society had been instilled into me from an early age by my maternal grandfather. His father had been a member of the International Brigade and died at the Battle of Jarama in 1937. With socialist ideals, a recalcitrant personality, and a love of satire and the absurd, I was aghast when Trump became president but could see that some of the idiotic things he said had comic potential. The screenplay I had written almost twenty years before was easily turned into a Pythonesque satire on the Satsuma Simpleton's administration. I had such fun editing the text of my screenplay and turning it into a book. It's true to say that when writing some passages I was laughing out loud!

In 2021, I wrote my first entirely new book in over twenty years. This book – *Immortal Seduction* – had been inspired by an abandoned cottage I had found as I walked my dog in the woods above the village of Brockweir in the Wye Valley.

Immortal Seduction is a passionate timeslip tale. I have often felt socially dislocated and, in Edgar Allan Poe's words 'all I loved, I loved alone'. Over the years, I have often wondered what if my ideal partner had once lived but we had been separated by time rather than distance. What if such a woman was reincarnated and came into my life in her current incarnation? Unlike Lucius d'Orléans in my *Immortal Seduction*, I'm not immortal but I think immortality would be a curse if you had to spend immortality alone. I have to confess that the brain tumour I had played havoc with my libido and so the insatiable passion Cassandra and Lucius have for one another is something that is drawn from personal experience.

So, without further ado, may you enjoy the following collection. If you do enjoy them, please leave them a review.

Adam Nicke, November 2021

Contents

Introduction	**3**
Contents	**8**
Grim Fairy Tales	**11**
The Jewellery Box	17
On A Clear Day	21
The Lake	29
A Thing Of Beauty Is A Joy To Behold	35
A Day In The Life Of Abraham Marainein	42
How My Father Taught Me To Hate Myself	47
From The Blood Of Innocence	51
All A Dream	64
The Sins Of The Fathers	68
In A Perfect World	75
Temptation And Denial	**81**
Temptation	87
Denial	133
Denied No More	191
Mallard The Quack	**227**
Do You Like My Muff, George?	229
That's A Lovely Looking Leg	247
Ahoy There, Maties!	271
I'll Have A Kiss Behind The Cowshed	293
God, My Head Hurts!	305
I Love Your Money!	319
How Much For A Shag?	333
I've Just Rolled Onto Something Hot And Fleshy	347
Queenie Will Turn A Few Tricks For You	359
Fancy A Quickie?	371
The Way The Buggers Bounce	386
I Am Don Juan	401

Immortal Seduction   **415**
    Chapter One   417
    Chapter Two   428
    Chapter Three   432
    Chapter Four   435
    Chapter Five   443
    Chapter Six   452
    Chapter Seven   457
    Chapter Eight   463
    Chapter Nine   467
    Chapter Ten   475
    Chapter Eleven   477
    Chapter Twelve   481
    Chapter Thirteen   484
    Chapter Fourteen   488
    Chapter Fifteen   492
    Chapter Sixteen   497
    Chapter Seventeen   500
    Chapter Eighteen   507
    Chapter Nineteen   510
    Chapter Twenty   521

Grim Fairy Tales
Adam Nicke

Born on the Lupercalia – the Roman festival of the wolf – in 1967, Adam Nicke spent an unhappy and lonely childhood in a series of isolated houses along the Welsh Border. During this difficult period, he sought refuge in literature and within his imagination.

When he grew up, his artistic tendencies were first expressed in the designing and making of clothing, most notably for Wayne Hussey of The Mission. Later, he turned to writing fiction which explores an inner realm of moods and anxieties, and the feelings of guilt experienced by characters coming to terms with an alienating world. He has a degree in literary studies from the University of the West of England.

The illustrator, Jocelyn Almond (1956–2014) is probably best known for her illustrations in Vortex science fiction and fantasy magazine in the late 1970s. In the 1980s and 1990s her pictures and stories appeared in various small press publications and in art exhibitions both in Britain and in Europe. She also published books on the Tarot and on Egyptian paganism, and for over twenty years served as a Priestess in the Fellowship of Isis.

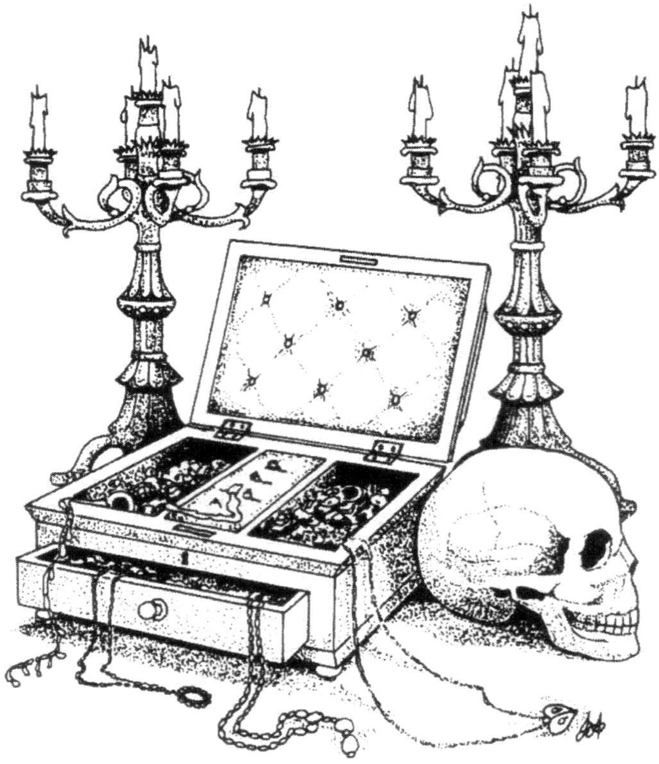

Grim Fairy Tales

by
Adam Nicke

with illustrations by
Jocelyn Almond

Adam Nicke Publishing

Reviews left on Amazon and Goodreads help promote the books you love

Acknowledgements

I would like to thank the Gothic Society for first putting me in print; David Hurst for taking the photograph of me in 1991 which appears on the back cover; and lastly, G. E. Vane and Jocelyn Almond of Tyrannosaurus Rex Press without whom none of this would have ever come to fruition.

Dedicated to both my mother and my maternal grandmother, Susan and Pat, both of whom I miss dearly but who would have both shared my delight in seeing Grim Fairy Tales back in print.

The Jewellery Box

How dearly as a young man did I love this time of year! The autumn equinox, the golden month of September, when all the world seemed resigned to death; when all her young offspring kissed goodbye to a dear mother who had nurtured them so tenderly while they had lain on her soft maternal bosom, unaware that their mutual ageing would so soon destroy their innocence.

Even then, in those far distant days, I identified with such dignified decay. It was only later that the crimson hues and twilight golds would hang heavily on my heart and remind me of a more tangible death. Even as I now write, some sixty years later, the memory of that golden era haunts me still, burning like a candle in the darkness; and I, like a moth, am forever drawn to the flame, its very glow all that sustains me, all that haunts me, binding me to it as surely as would any chains.

Then came my twenty-fifth year. Now a man, I found myself sanguine enough, if a little prone to bouts of melancholia; then, one hot summer's day, I met Ophelia, fluttering into my life as light and as airy as the most beautiful butterfly. I, having come from a good family with good prospects, was deemed a suitable beau by my future father-in-law. It was to our eternal happiness, for it quickly transpired that Ophelia loved me as I her. After a brief courtship, during which we spent many happy hours walking by the river, always chaperoned - Ophelia had her reputation to think of - we married. How my heart lightens still to think of that long hot summer, sun penetrating the lace of Ophelia's parasol, gently kissing the face I also longed to touch and kiss.

The following six months were the happiest of our lives. I never thought a mortal such as I worthy of so much pleasure.

The food I ate with Ophelia was ambrosia, the drink nectar, as long as my own Venus was there with me. But my happiness was yet incomplete until one frosty February morning when Ophelia told me that the fruit of our love would be born to us that autumn. Our joy seemed absolute.

All summer, Ophelia and I walked along those river banks, across those same summer meadows, those Elysian fields. Surely no god could ever have crafted such bliss! Every time I gazed at Ophelia my heart overflowed, like an overfilled ciborium. I would have died a thousand deaths for her.

Even now, these memories slice me in two, for a month before the birth, Ophelia fell ill. She became pale and ashen, seemingly overnight. Her once beautiful countenance became painful to observe. As much as I loved her, love this time was not enough: if Ophelia did not recover, the birth would kill her.

But it was not to be. There was nothing any doctor could do: Ophelia died giving birth to our child. The child drew a single breath and joined my dear Ophelia. The only woman I had ever loved was taken from me that autumn day. The trees wept tears of blood, as my tears ran crystalline.

And now all I have is Ophelia's jewellery box and beloved gemstones. How lovingly we bought them together, I to frame her idolised symmetry, she to please the man she loved. Little did I then think that these pitiful rocks would become the single thread to bind me to my dead love. I love these stones now as I loved her, and as she loved them. Every day I press them to my heart, and caress them as once I did Ophelia.

The black onyx, this beautiful variety of chalcedony: the exquisite striations of the stone remind me of her perfectly manicured nails and the slender fingers that once tenderly touched my face. I press it to my eye and see only the happy times, the sylph, the naiad that I loved and married.

The tiger's eye reminds me of her long golden-brown tresses and of long, golden days. How I wish I had them still!

The carnelian, this translucent orange chalcedony: how those flames framed her face! Turner never painted such flames, nor Burne-Jones such purity.

The haematite, the iron oxide, red as the blood I would gladly have opened a vein of mine to spill a thousand times that I might have died in her place.

The jade, green as the morning grass where we walked that idyllic summer, through the silver birch wood where bluebells

The Jewellery Box

had grown that spring, where birds sang hosannas while church bells pealed 'they have found their love'.

The garnet, that hard glassy red silicate: how vividly I remember still the night it clung to her neck at the dance! How every woman was envious, and every man jealous. Now all I have is their pity.

The coral, as soft a red-pink as she turned at our first kiss: its properties have saved my house from storms, yet nothing can dispel the cloud that has hung over me for sixty years. Even my happiest moments since are tinged with sadness that I spend them alone and at the memory of her last words: 'My only regret is that I must leave you.'

The turquoise, the green-blue of which reminds me of the burning summer sky when we first laughed, danced and sang like mad children. Never since has a day seemed worthy of celebration. How I tested the powers of this stone to the limit on my old horse that bitterly cold winter as if I could gallop away from reality.

The lapis, the midnight blue shot with a myriad of golden stars, makes me think of the place where my sweet Ophelia walks now, and of how my phoenix will never age: eternal youth is hers.

The amethyst, the violet quartz, Ophelia's favourite – and how we drank! Drank deeply from the cup of life, intoxicated with one another.

The pearl, the pale grey-white with a tinge of blue, the stone that brings a tear to my eye: it is the colour of her skin, and of the infant's too, as they lay forever in one another's arms. I knew that she would be taken from me when I dreamt of them, and many a tear has coursed my cheek since then.

The opal, the amorphous form of silicon dioxide, the jewel I hold to my lips, the one that lights my darkest hour: it is, as Pliny said, 'shadowed with the colour of wine'. When she wore it I called her Poederos. How she had then the beautiful complexion of youth: now she always will.

The diamond: its clear single purity is the love I still bear for my wife, but its qualities failed the somnambulist and the insane in me. For over half a century I have watched my once handsome countenance age in that same gilt mirror. Now it reflects an old, worn-out man as it once did a callow youth; dreaming now only of the day when once again I may experience the heaven above as I once did a heaven on earth.

The sapphire, the blue corundum, beloved of Saturn, god of greenery and vegetation: how its blue elates me! I press my lips to it as once I pressed them to the blue lips of Ophelia for the last time. Its quality of manly vigour, though, has failed me, for no vigour has coursed my veins from that day to this.

The emerald, the greenest beryl: how we loved the green and rolling pastures of Ireland and Wales, which sprang forth from it. We became one with the trees, the rivers, the ancient copses. But the qualities of this stone failed me too, and my child died, drawing but a single breath. And what venomous animal took Ophelia from me?

Each and every day I hold these gems, and each and every day, wonderful prismatic colours, that once shone so, grow dimmer. Often I see Ophelia's visage spring forth from them, and now she beckons. The lights grow dimmer still. Once again my Ophelia reaches for my hand; gently, tenderly, her youthful fingers take my aged arm. Once more I am with her; once again we will share the song and dance of soft, mad, laughing children.

On a Clear Day

The moment Richard de Lorrain first set his eyes upon the ruined old house, he knew that he had to have it. An endowment had recently elevated him to a fairly affluent level; ample enough to fund both his literary and aesthetic aspirations and sensibilities. As he gazed at the house, he felt for the first time as if he were truly alive; his stillborn soul spluttered and gulped its first invigorating breath, burning as the life force surged through it. Every vein burned, every artery coursed with liquid fire, every pore lay open to a timeless, cleansing breeze that blew age upon age right through him.

'I must have it,' he murmured.

The old house had lain empty for many years. Like an aged Dickensian spinster, it seemed to have relinquished any claim to the present, and by simply doing nothing had become an anachronism. The years had rolled by. Some terribly brave youths had tried to blind her many years before but fled in a desperate panic when they heard the low agonised groan the house seemed to emit as the first stone shattered her panes.

More than any other he had ever seen, this house seemed to have a soul, an immense sad soul that lay dormant and abused somewhere deep within it. Her archaic countenance was shrouded in a century's neglect as ivy clamoured and clutched at it. The once warm and welcoming crunch of the paths and the beckoning and becoming guiles of the rose gardens lay overgrown with years of indifference. Everywhere the air hung thick with something almost tangible. It seemed to speak of the youthful belief, now turned sour, that love can change everything; the finality was that it had not changed anything at all. A natural yet preternatural demise seemed imminent, and only he, he felt, could offer salvation. He himself knew what it was like to set love in a position so elevated that the ideal could never be reached. Like every man who claims to have no ego, he still felt as though he were the one who could make the three-hundred-year wait of his prospective lover worthwhile.

'This is the one,' he thought to himself. It did indeed seem as if fate had brought the two tragic lovers together, to burn a scarlet oriflamme of consummation for their mutually first time. The peak had already been reached; the denouement would show the tragic flaws of both – a tragedy in which no one would learn a thing. How could they have known? How could they have avoided the scythe of destiny, even if they had had the knowledge to anticipate it? Sometimes we anticipate an approaching disaster but are still drawn to it, like an alcoholic to a bottle.

The house would be paradise for de Lorrain, both as a man and as a writer. He had the wealth to recreate an age long gone, recall a past he had never been privy to. Courtly love raised its chivalrous head. The older inamorata could teach and guide her new literary lover, and in return he, like an alchemist, would convert gall to manna, lead to gold. Only he could see the beauty lying dormant in the near-cadaverous abode he now gazed upon.

Over the coming months, many workmen moved to and fro, making efforts to beautify the old maid for her new lord. Intrusively they cleared the gardens and fixed the ponds, then started on the house. Meanwhile, de Lorrain made efforts to find out who had gone before him.

It was not long before his thirsty curiosities brought him to the cool oasis of the local archives. The house had been built in the early 1740s, almost a hundred and fifty years before. The first owner had felt uneasy about living there, and consequently never did break the maidenhead of his abode. For the first five years she had lain empty and intact, whilst her unfaithful paramour simply vanished. Rumours abounded that he had lost his sanity, but this was merely speculation. What was not speculation, however, was the knowledge that the house had been built on an Elizabethan burial mound acknowledged by many to have been used for invocations or other diabolical purposes; pagan rituals, tumescent orgies, and other acts of salacious and prurient carnality. He flushed as he read it. From his youth he had read de Sade and other such writers. Perhaps he had been drawn to this place by the same forces that had possessed them? Perhaps such forces would guide his pen into hitherto unexplored regions. He shook with anticipation.

Finally, at the end of 1894, the house was finished. The community of local tradesmen whom he felt to be stupidly superstitious did themselves no favours in his estimation when he heard them talking of cold chills in closed rooms, mists, groans, knocking, and a hideous laughing face. One even claimed to have heard screaming, but his was a solitary voice.

De Lorrain made arrangements to decorate the house before he could fully satisfy his pleasure. The uppermost storey first of all: a vast room, with leaded windows in each wall looking out onto the newly landscaped gardens. The walls were hung with Italian paper that proudly boasted upon it an opium poppy in full bloom. He began to fill the room with exotic plants of every hue and nationality, a large scrivener's writing desk, a pianoforte, a few chairs, some soft couches. Pictures by his favourite artists hung on the wall. When the soft glow of the chandelier was deemed too harsh, it was replaced by some old candelabra, which glowed red, thanks to their stained-glass surround. A menagerie of animals was moved in: jewelled tortoises crawled upon the floor; a large European mountain dog lay languorous and incongruous on oriental cushions. Snakes chosen for their colour lurked in the foliage. Beside a small pool basked salamanders and various small reptiles. Exotic shawls hung from ceiling to floor, imprinted with ethereal images of peacocks. Copper censers perfumed the air. A bust of Shelley and a bust of Byron stood on either side of a great fireplace. All the furnishings were of soft, antiquated brass and walnut. A drinks cabinet made from an old pulpit served to highlight his rejection of religion. Amongst it all lay de Lorrain in an opium and absinthe dream too fantastic for description.

Though the rest of the house lay empty, the fever of anticipation had grown so great that he brought forward his wedding night to his new bride, so eager were they both. The old four-poster bed that lay in one corner, veiled with heavy red velvet drapes that matched the curtains, was first to know the young man's restless soul as he retired. Sleep did not come easy that night and as the hours passed he decided to smoke a little hashish in order to relax, to dull his fractured senses, for aside from absinthe little alcohol passed his lips, particularly wine and especially red wine. Tenderly touched by the hands of an almost moribund torpor he smiled as he began to drift away in a dream of a magnitude only two new lovers could share.

Sometime later he awoke with a start. Even though he had shut off all the gaslights and enclosed himself in bloody red sensuality and crisp, white virginal linen a light still penetrated the warm safe sanctuary. Shouting voices and a drunken babble accompanied it. Slowly he parted the drapes and placed an eye to the split. The room seemed to be full of people. Scared and uncomprehending, he looked again. Sure enough, it was his room, but in the centre, from where the revelry emanated, it was devoid of furnishings save for a Hanoverian table and a few chairs.

The revellers seemed oblivious to him, so much so that the young aesthete became a little more brave and pulled the curtains apart a few more inches. The dangerous appeal which the house seemed to have previously held quickly coalesced. The actual danger was terrifying, however brave he considered himself. The thought of danger had merely alighted on his shattered equilibrium as a passing fancy. But now…

Slowly his clouded perception began to clear and he was able to focus on the figures in front of him. Six men sat around the table gulping wine. At first, he had not recognised the clothes; bright muslin, embroidered coats not fashionable in a hundred and fifty years, full shirt sleeves, lace ruffles, breeches that only covered half the leg, round-toed shoes with a square silver buckle, powdered wigs pulled into a ponytail. But of the four characters who stood, two were only semi-clad, vying for the easy virtues of the four women who were present, all in various states of undress. Surely this could not be? De Lorrain, with mixed emotion, felt sure he recognised some members of the group. Was he really witnessing a gathering of the Hellfire Club?

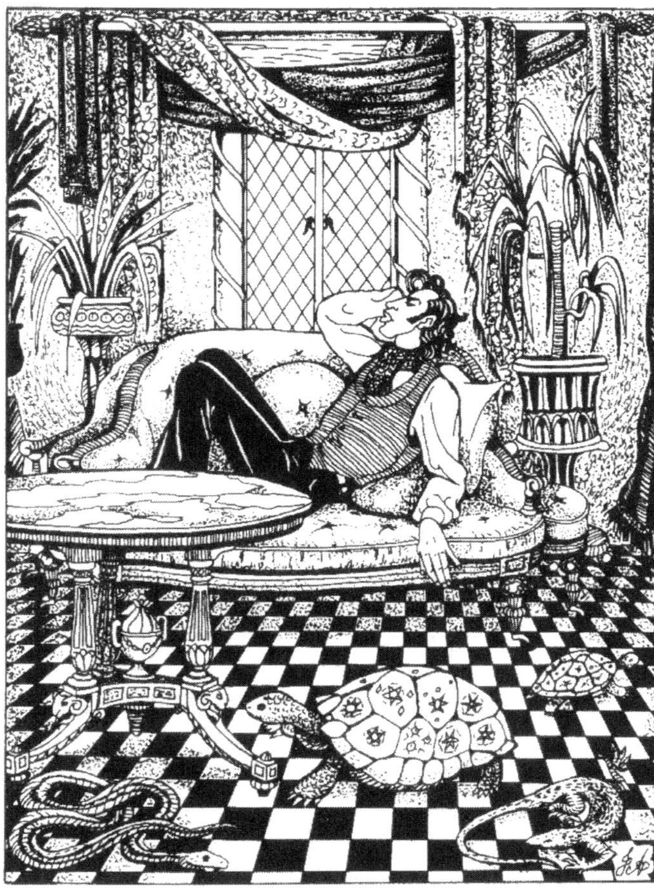

The figures seemed to pulse, like a heartbeat; almost translucent they shimmered like reflections in a pool. Try as he might to discern voices, he could not. It was as if all those he observed were talking under water, water of a thick glutinous consistency that seemed to make every word last a century. But if his ears failed him, his eyes did not. He stared, stared in disbelief at what the assembled crowd appeared to be doing. Various tools of the occult were brought onto the table.

Suddenly, one of the crowd pointed directly at him, petrifying him. All the assembled faces turned in his direction, and the man pointing proceeded to walk towards him. De Lorrain closed his eyes in dreadful anticipation. A cold chill fell right through him as the spirit walked through his. He turned, to see the figure standing on what appeared to be his bed, but to which the phantasm of a bygone age was obviously solid floor, as he was only visible from the waist up. Evidently, to him the bed simply did not exist, therefore neither did de Lorrain. The figure returned to his friends, carrying an old sack. De Lorrain began to laugh, first quietly then more loudly, hysterically. He leapt from the edge of the bed and rushed toward the group. He had made no conscious effort to will them here; perhaps that was why they could not see him. He touched one on the shoulder.

Flesh sliced spirit as easily as a rapier slices air. It was as if he were the ghost.

The gurgling language of the group fell silent as a skull with a pentagram carved on its forehead was removed from the bag and placed on the table. The cranial part was removed and red wine poured into it; all proceeded to drink. De Lorrain felt ill. Was this genuinely what had once happened in his room? Or was it all a product of his imagination, unlocked by the various hallucinogens he had imbibed throughout the course of the evening? Was it simply an elaborate plan the house had made in order to spurn him unequivocally?

As they all spread their palms on the table, making sure that the tips of their little fingers touched, one of the group seemed to fall into a trance. The room grew cold as the grave, as silent as a tomb. A window blew open and a howling gale entered. The table began to rock. A huge mound of earth violently erupted through the floor, throwing table, chairs and people in all directions. The small coven lay all about the room in disarray. As de Lorrain looked at the mound, there seemed to be movement from within it. With mounting horror he watched: three figures seemed to be emerging. Grime-covered, they struggled to the surface. Even more abstract than the first spectres in the room, these were certainly not the well-heeled affluent types, but peasants of the lowest rank, in the habiliments of the seventeenth century. Even though they were disgusting to look upon, one could sympathise: the former affluent group had no doubt used them for their sport. The poor and downtrodden would always be exploited in one way or another; some things do not change.

As he looked about him, de Lorrain realised with not a little surprise that he was the only one who could see this new assemblage. One of them moved towards his affluent caller, and with icy hands clutched at his neck and began to squeeze. What was happening, de Lorrain mused – how could this be? A ghost killing a ghost! Or was it some kind of bend in time which afforded him the dubious honour of witnessing a murder of flesh by spirit, and which had made his house uninhabitable since the first days of its creation?

The invisible attacker continued to squeeze harder. Unable to see his assailant, the victim's gasps became desperate. Flailing and clutching his throat, he sought to peel away the invisible fingers that squeezed his life away, but the peasant tenaciously hung on. Finally, the deed was done. A corpse lay motionless, extinguished by a ghostly hand, the only witness to the perpetrator of the act a man born more than a hundred years after it had been committed.

Slowly the sun began to rise. The old house had never seemed so alive or so beautiful. The first rays of sunshine fell upon it. Finding a chink in the curtains of the old bed, they fell upon a dead body. Richard de Lorrain, aesthete, writer, dilettante and sometime property developer, lay lifeless. The crisp white linen sheets bore a stain instantly recognisable as that of red wine. Around his neck were numerous bruises, where an unseen hand had squeezed him away from life.

The Lake

Maxwell Wilkes looked at his watch. A quarter to midnight. Try as he might, he could not sleep. He was restless and anxious, brooding over a sense of guilt even he himself could not explain. The few grains of laudanum he had taken an hour previously had not helped. The room seemed to be closing in on him. He had suspicions that the drug had been tampered with, as he had obtained it from a chemist friend who was prone to playing such practical jokes. The Latin American drug Yage had been a talking point with them recently: perhaps it was this that now made the crimson hues of his heavy embroidered curtains look like waterfalls of blood showering down the walls. His father's old bookcase took on the appearance of a coffin, what with the stained and crumbling tomes lining the shelves lying discarded like bones in a charnel house. Even the flames of his oil lamp appeared to be an exotic eastern dancing girl, beckoning him with flickering gyrations.

He had to escape. He broke into a sweat, yet was freezing cold. The room smelt musty and damp, sounds of Gregorian chants filled his head. His heartbeat became irregular, fluttering in his chest like an eagle in a canary cage, its wings breaking his ribs. What to do, what to do? Flee now, or stay and have all the evils of body and circumstances turn to bare slavering teeth on his flesh and sinews?

He lunged for the door. Opening it, he was in the passage, and staggered to the front of the house, the walls swirling. The figures in his beloved Pre-Raphaelite prints leered down at him from their frames. Pointing, they seemed to cry 'The hour is upon thee, satyr; death awaits thee, sybarite!' With voices ringing in his ears, he opened the heavy front door and took his first breath of the cold, midnight air.

He collapsed onto the grass. The cool dew on his face revived him, and after the oppressive heat of his opulent room the uncluttered chill of the night restored his senses somewhat. The mist clung to the earth, rising only a little over a foot off the ground, and as he looked about him, all that was visible to his eye was a deathly shroud that hung over his face like a veil.

He stood up. The clear sky and full moon made everything appear crisp and silent. He felt like an intruder in the stillness of it all. The only movement was that of the great trees, whose branches quivered like the limbs of a lover at the peak of ecstasy.

The huge lake at the bottom of the garden rippled with a silvery lustre, reminding him of his youth, days which seemed so distant now. How often, as a boy, he had swum in its loving embrace, before his father's tragic death, and long before the spectre of depression and neurasthenia had begun to plague his every waking moment. The demons that haunted him were now even tormenting his nights, depriving him of all but the briefest hours of sleep.

But now the lake seemed hostile, the only obstacle between himself and his sweet fiancée, Cynara. How he longed to hold her now, how he ached for her cool hands to wipe his brow and her soft kisses to ease the pain of living.

It was then he saw the small boat. It had not been used in five years, not since the death of his father, whom it was presumed had fallen from it one wintry morning, swallowed forever in the icy depths. Usually, Maxwell walked around the lake, even though it took a full hour, but with the boat he could be at Cynara's door in a quarter of that time.

Stealthily he made his way to the water's edge, checking his breathing as if the exhalations might wake his mother, she who had forbidden him ever to use the boat, keeping it as a shrine to her husband. The old lady still wore black, still mourned, worshipping Maxwell whose pale, dangerously wan appearance so mirrored that of the man she had married.

Maxwell untied the rope, stepped into the small wooden craft, fitted the oars into their mountings and pushed away from the shore. As silently as possible he began to row.

It was not long before the light of his room was obscured by the trees. Now there remained only the lake, the moon, the boat and the man.

The Lake

On he rowed, pulling the oars deep into the water. The small boat skimmed across the surface. Why had he not thought to use it before? He laughed aloud at the thought of his pious mother finding the boat gone and imagining her husband had returned for his craft – a craft to row himself across the Styx, a craft of the living dead. He laughed again to think of all those who had seen his father's ghostly apparition at the water's edge, warning his kin to stay away from the lake and its mysterious depths, before emitting a death rattle and evaporating.

Maxwell stopped rowing. For one so unused to it, the physical exertion had already blistered his hands; those delicate pale hands which had never done a day's work. The boat drifted to a standstill. The moon cast a silvery shadow over the whole lake, illuminating it as brightly as would the midday sun. But however bright the sky, not one of its glowing fingers dared to penetrate more than a foot into the dank, murky waters.

Maxwell heard a sound. He glanced to his left. For a split second, he thought he saw a head disappear quickly beneath the waters a hundred or so feet away from him. Maxwell began to feel uneasy. No one knew how deep the lake really was, no one knew what undigested secrets lay in its intestines. Maxwell began to row again. Suddenly it was as if the boat had struck a brick wall. He quickly turned around as a half-human form sank into the waters, with the speed of a bullet yet without a ripple. The boat began rocking slightly; Maxwell spun around again, in time to see what appeared to be a giant slug slithering over the front of the boat. By the time his eyes were able to focus, he realised that it was a decomposing human arm. He let out a yell and hit it with an oar. The arm fell away at the elbow, and despite its wet putrefaction, the limb crumbled to dust. Maxwell sank into his seat, hardly believing what he had seen.

It was to be a brief respite. Within seconds, another arm slid over the side, then another, another, and another. Maxwell screamed! Whatever was on the end of the ghastly limbs could stay hidden. He lashed out as hard as he could, spinning and hitting. Then he caught sight of the lake. The whole of its surface bubbled and boiled with rotting corpses writhing over one another.

Maxwell flung himself into the bottom of the boat and closed his eyes. His mortality had never seemed so fragile. After what seemed an eternity, he opened them again, tentatively. Nothing had happened. He glanced up. Nothing. He stood up. The lake was perfectly calm.

Maxwell found his seat again. He was shaking. What had previously seemed a good idea now threatened to place his life upon a precipice. How he wished he were somewhere else, anywhere else!

Nervously he began to row. The small boat seemed to be gaining speed. Maxwell stopped rowing altogether; the speed of the craft's travel threatened to sweep him overboard. He glanced to the side. The water was no longer flat. He told himself that this defied the laws of physics, yet, if anything, the speed of the boat was increasing and the slope of the water steepening: ten-degrees, twenty-degrees, forty-degrees, sixty-degrees. Finally, the boat hit a ninety-degree angle and plummeted into free space. Maxwell looked above him. All he could see were the stars, beneath him only blackness. The waters moved to ninety-five degrees, and the little boat was engulfed.

The aqueous blackness infused his lungs, not with the texture of water but of adipocere. Its glutinous character filled every bronchiole. Maxwell closed his eyes and prayed for death.

When he reopened them, he was amazed. A myriad of sparkling colours hung all around him: bedazzling, swirling paisleys. He floated gently through the heavy, oily atmosphere; each new breath making the colours more majestic. Each one seemed to have its own light, an internal iridescence. It reminded him of the strange paintings of Gustave Moreau he had seen in Paris. Gently he drifted through the ever-changing waters. No solid forms appeared, all was bliss. Then blackness; for what seemed an eternity but was, in reality, a few brief seconds. A white light illuminated him from above, brighter than a thousand suns. Bathed in this limelight, Maxwell wondered who his audience was to be. In vain he squinted to his sides. In the dark recesses, vaguely discernible shapes made their appearance, then the uneasy feeling that all eyes were upon him. Suddenly he realised he was unable to move his body, only his head. His legs were hurting, and he glanced down. What he saw made him

The Lake

retch: his whole torso and both his legs were covered in leeches, oozing blood through their raw red skin–leeches with the faces of people, all with teeth buried deep in his flesh. Unable to move or speak, Maxwell felt his flesh shrivelling and desiccating.

It was then that he heard a voice, an awful, guttural voice, the voice of death, the voice of creaking hinges on a mausoleum door, a hoarse rasp from somewhere dark and unknown: a voice that burnt his skin as fiercely as the flames of Vulcan's forge. Maxwell narrowed his eyes into the gloom, trying to see whence or from whom the voice had emanated.

He wished he had not tried. A terrifying spectre was slowly slithering its way towards him, covered in the skin of a black and scaly reptile, with blood-red talons at the ends of its long bony fingers. It stood up in front of him, its constantly-squirming form barely contained by the rags that constituted its clothes. Rising to its full height, more than six feet above Maxwell, it slowly raised its hand to stroke the bone that pierced its skin where a chin should have been. Within the blink of an eye, the hand clutched at Maxwell's throat, as swiftly as a cobra strikes a mongoose. Raising Maxwell level with its blazing green eyes, the beast spoke. Squeezing his victim's throat, the great beast declared, 'Maxwell, through your love for me, I possess your soul.' Lack of breath, fright: whatever the cause, Maxwell slipped into unconsciousness.

When he awoke, he was back on the surface of the lake in his father's little boat. Everything was tranquil. He looked around him and all seemed truly at peace. He grabbed the oars and began to row, rowing as he never had before nor ever would again. His hands bled, his skin was soaking, his lungs raw and cold.

Soon he reached the other side of the lake. He sprang from the boat and ran. Soon he would be in Cynara's arms, soon all the pain would be gone. He knocked on the door. A light came on. The door creaked open and there stood the frame of his beloved Cynara, silhouetted against the soft glow behind her.

'Cynara, Cynara, I love you,' cried Maxwell, falling to her feet and kissing them.

'Maxwell, it's half past midnight,' said Cynara. 'Be quiet, or you'll wake Father.'

'I had to see you tonight,' said Maxwell. 'I love you more than life itself.' Maxwell knelt and gazed at Cynara's beautiful face. Tonight, though, it seemed different. He had seen her face a thousand times before, but he had never realised just how green were her eyes.

'Oh, Maxwell,' said Cynara, 'you and your love! I truly think you would lose your soul to love…'

A Thing of Beauty is a Joy to Behold

Aubrey Cain was unhappy. There had been no external event to trigger the emotion, but the period of convalescence he had spent at his parents' had afforded him the time to analyse his concepts of existence and mortality, and the conclusion he had come to had been a surprise to him. Of course, the illness had inevitably clouded and coloured his perspectives, but try as he may, the memory of ever having felt any different had been dismissed: he had always felt this way, but had never had the time to actually think about it before. The conclusion drawn he felt to be a just and honest one.

Immortal longings dwelled within him that yearned to escape and wander barefoot in the cool green grass, caressed by a gentle warm breeze. Somewhere there were golden pastures hidden from the eyes of man, where one could live in a state of perpetual bliss, where the sobbing violins of Autumn would never give way to the frigid, frozen principality of which he found himself a prince, and which he so loathed. But where existed such a place? Certainly no one known to him knew the way there or even recognised that such a place existed.

Aubrey's longings were tolerated. Some even recognised that he was a hopeless dreamer whose feeble frame had wandered in a Gethsemane garden but who had sold his fragile state of mind for thirty pieces of silver.

In the middle of April, Aubrey was able to leave his sickbed for the first time in many, many months. Ennui had manifested itself of late, and now each step was tortuous with wasted limbs quickly tiring. The collusion between mind and body was doubly debilitating. Aged less than thirty, yet what seemed left? The tallow-white skin, as taut as a child's, seemed to crease a little at the prospect. Age, he realised, would wither him, and custom stale.

From the verandah he had watched the many trees in his father's garden, in the harsh, cold winter when their stiff appendages had penetrated the sky, tearing huge gashes into it; their stark limbs crowned in thorns, stiff as a cold corpse, awaited the resurrection which was now beginning to take place. The new spring sun eased apart the wedding-white blossom, which reciprocated the warm caresses. The occasional red berry, like a small spot of blood, was to be expected among the innocent flowering. The product of the union, shadows spattered and then swam in haphazard form on the new wet grass, eventually to fall in the shallow pebbled stream that carried them away in a constant purifying souse.

As the scene before him filtered through and eventually nailed itself to the walls of his mind, it seemed at last that the progenitive quality had not been totally curtailed: the immortal longings he had had for so many years began to respond, the two coming together in a process of fertilisation that made him shake and sweat. The lifeblood that coursed in every vein and artery, which for so long had seemed in decay, now swelled every limb in tingling ecstasy. His vision, the transcendent nature of that vision of which he had been a part, for the first time gave him the knowledge, so arcane, to stand outside himself. Others could seek escape or even oblivion; he had found a private, secret salvation, a personal shrine at which he alone could worship.

Over the following weeks, the happiness within him became more and more apparent. The locals still recognised him as the hopeless dreamer who 'hadn't a good day's work in 'im'. It was with a mixture of pity, sympathy and patronising superiority that they did so – ennobling reasons which they felt gave them a charitable disposition: it made them feel good to think themselves better than one person in this world, at least. As a priest views his congregation, it was with a feigned benevolence that they viewed the 'poor wretch'. Never was a soul so worthy of redemption!

With the insight his present circumstances afforded him, Aubrey seemed oblivious to it all, wandering in the garden, a fixed smile on his face as he gazed into the tumescent limbs of the trees. Occasionally, words of reverence and awe spilt forth almost unconsciously.

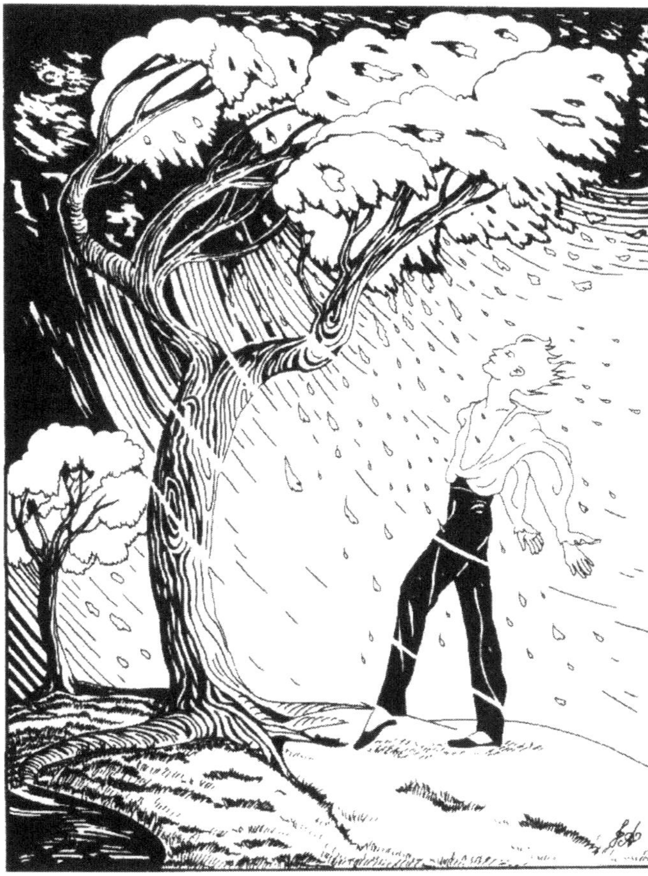

A Thing of Beauty

The weeks passed, but the family's pleasure had a serpent in it. The ghostly pallor of their son remained, and his mother especially found it disconcerting to see the white skin, almost translucent and seeming to radiate with an inner light, pressed against the lower branches of the tree, the pinkish-white of the blossom the only thing that gave her son any semblance of a living man. A dream also upset her. She worried: what would happen when the blossom went? The effect the soft petals had upon her son she knew to be a transient one. Their beauty would be ephemeral, fleeting. They had arrived in a state of beauty, existed in a state of beauty would die that way. However much her son loved them, their beauty could not be captured, absorbed or held in any way at all, however much one might wish to do so.

One day, from his window, Aubrey saw the branches of the trees quiver as a light breeze passed through them, and, in a state of stupefied reverence, he watched as thousands upon thousands of the petals fell from the canopy, tearing tiny holes in the shroud. Like confetti, they fell, carpeting the floor. The whole vision turned white. Like a gentle fall of snow, it fluttered to earth in silent, resigned decay, still as beautiful as the day he had first seen it. Quickly he dressed and ran outside, hoping to be an intrinsic part of what he saw.

Cool and gossamer-like, the petals stuck to his bare hands, feet and face as he availed himself to the deluge. His familiarity with all that lay before him stripped him of any incongruity now bare and naked, he proffered himself as a sacrificial lamb before the altar of all that he loved or would ever love.

The petals continued to float slowly down as if the air had a certain viscosity for them, contrasting radically with the light and refreshing nature of the heady balm Aubrey imbibed. He fell to his knees and lifted petals by the handful, bathing himself in their nature, smell, every quality they had, every quality he held dear and wished he himself possessed.

Slowly the breeze stopped, and the petals' last journey also fluttered to an end. Aubrey stood up. Tiny petals stuck to his hands and feet. After a few moments of dumb celebration he brushed them off, but none moved. A little harder this time, yet all stayed as they were when they had landed. With growing alarm and consternation, he tried to peel one off, but the pain was excruciating. With disbelief he saw that the rending of it had drawn blood, which rose to the fullness of the wound, obeyed the laws of gravity and followed a course to the end of his finger, whence it dripped to the white floor. For such a delicate constitution the stark contrast between the deep red and the pink-white was frightening to behold.

In a daze, he ran to the edge of a small pool which the stream in the garden constantly flushed with fresh waters. In frozen animation, he gazed at his reflection on the silver smooth surface. An inverted Narcissus, the sight was hateful to him. A transfiguration had taken place. The flesh tone of the petals had stuck fast to his own; every inch of what was visible was covered in tiny gossamer scales. Beauty, and the search for it, had begotten a monster!

Hearing his mother's voice calling him, he began to panic. He caught a glimpse of her blue dress, though she had not yet seen him. How could he let her see him like this? His mother had always seemed to him so unsullied, uncorrupted – now to have to witness the punishment which had been meted out to her son for crimes he had not committed. Thinking him gone to the local town, she went back inside the house. Aubrey realised that, until some cure could be found for the way he now looked, he must remain out of her sight. But what he had sought and acquired was now a part of him, and to try to divorce it from himself would take a fundamental change in his entire outlook on life. Uncomprehending of any whys or wheres, all Aubrey realised was that what lay ahead of him was incomprehensible. It would be a permanent cross he would have to bear.

Taking a few apples from a nearby building, still replete with autumn's harvest, Aubrey planned to leave, to contemplate his predicament. Stepping out into the road, he had gone but a short distance when he heard voices and, from a corner, a few small children appeared. At first, they did not seem to notice Aubrey's reptilian disfigurement – after all, the petals had the tones of flesh – but as they neared him, his scaly appearance caused them to stare, at first with intrigue, then with fear. Formerly the local children had been more tolerant of Aubrey than had their parents; if this was the effect which he now had upon them, what then would be the effect on their parents?

A Thing of Beauty

The staring children's lips began to quiver, and their eyes, like flooded pools, flushed the plains of their cheeks. With equal disgust, Aubrey realised that this would now forever be his lot in life: branded with the mark of Cain. What had once been beautiful had made a pariah of him. It was incomprehensible to him; how could he hope others comprehend? The transfiguration was complete. He could never return.

'Would you like an apple?' Aubrey said to them in an effort to return them to their natural selves. With trepidation, two tiny hands stretched forward and quickly stole forth the gifts. Turning away, the two corrupted innocents stumbled and fell.

Aubrey sat down on a low wall. He wept. As if in sympathy or rage, the grey sky above him made a fearful crack and began to rain.

A Day in the Life of Abraham Marainein

Abraham Marainein looked in the mirror. He felt old. Every day he would gaze at his countenance in one of his many mirrors, for his greatest pleasure was his own reflection. But today was different. Despite being only twenty-six, he could feel the qualities of youth he had once possessed slipping through his hands like water. He had a sophistication and an erudition far beyond his years, and they made him appear older than he actually was. The only incongruous factor was his face: black ringlets framed a bone structure of which any woman would have been proud, and large dark eyes flashed beneath eyebrows that gave his expression a permanently cynical aspect; nonetheless, his face still had an androgynous quality betrayed only by dark stubble.

Abraham allowed himself a rare smile. He knew he was handsome, he knew women found him irresistible, and that his effect on men was often the same. All acknowledged, he felt, that they were in the presence of a superior being. They squirmed, fawned upon and pampered the vain young man, anxious to win his favour and to bask in a reflected glory, whilst he observed, impenetrable and aloof.

To all intents and purposes, Abraham had everything. His father had died when Abraham was thirteen, leaving him the prospect of one day becoming a wealthy man. He knew he would never have to work, and he had never intended to: 'Work is the scourge of the drinking classes,' a friend had once said to him. But for all that his good fortune had brought him, his wealth had not bought him happiness. He was painfully aware that his needs were infinite, the possibility of his pleasures finite. Nothing satiated his needs. His search for that elusive something tormented him like an unquenched thirst. Constantly he felt the need to experience more. He had realised long ago that money could not buy it; he had also realised that without it he could not survive. His appearance became his only pleasure. Nothing mattered except the glorification of his sensual pleasures.

The previous year, he had decided to furnish his new house. He sought to worship in the temple of his eyes and travelled to France to buy some prints and soak up the atmosphere of aestheticism that he had heard so much about and which so suited his temperament.

He bought a self-portrait of Bocklin, with death in the wings. Whilst he stayed at the Hotel de Ville he saw some Clairin, buying a print of *The Distant Princess*; *Satan's Treasure* by Jean Delville, as much for the name as for the print; a Ferdinand Keller, some Khnopffs, a Karel Masek; a dozen cases of champagne for the Mucha labels; *The Sphinx* by von Stuck; a beautifully framed *Corner of a Room* of the poets Rimbaud and Verlaine by Fantin-Latour. How his heart filled! His desire for the perverse, for the symbolic, had been satisfied. His longing to escape reality had been animated in these beautiful paintings; for once the world seemed a glorious place. The immortality of those canvases contrasted so sharply with the transience of his fading youth. How he longed to escape to another time, another place, where the amaranth of his lost adolescence would bloom once again.

But, oh! How briefly those paintings had filled the void. Back in the grimy streets of London, full of grimy people, he soon felt alone again – even in a crowded room he felt alone. He observed the human race as a scientist observes amoeba under a microscope. He went out to observe; often he went out simply to make his superior presence known. He went to the theatre, of course: Debussy, Ravel, Satie and the lost soul opera of Wagner. All demanded a certain dress: the right colour gloves, carnation, walking cane, perfumes. One could never wear black to Ravel, nor viridian to Wagner.

Yes, today was different. He felt his once-handsome face to be ageing, and he was afraid that if his youth should die then so would he. His house, like his appearance, had become a shrine to the perverse, but his house had taken perversity to new heights: every room had been decorated in a single colour. As his mood was black, he went to his black room.

A Day in the Life of Abraham Maranein

A huge ebony-framed mirror hung majestically opposite the door. Erotic black and white prints by a strange friend of his clung to the wall like specks of blood coughed from the diseased lungs of the consumptive. Abraham moved toward his chair, across the huge black rug that lay in wait in front of the fire. Rows of jars filled with preservative and medical school oddities lined the shelves. Money could buy anything, Abraham reflected. Rows of books lay on other shelves, all covered in black reptile skin, so as to be in harmony with the rest of the room. To have them covered in such a manner had cost him as much as it would have taken an ordinary man a full year to earn, but no matter. They were pleasing to his eye, and nothing else came into consideration.

Abraham sat down. The heavy black brocade curtains and black lace at the window subjugated the midday sun, rendering the room a constant half-twilight. He lit a row of black candles in order to read and picked up a book: a collection of eroticism that a poet friend had given him. How often as a younger man he had read its depravities agog! Now they bored him. His life of dissipation had intertwined fantasy and reality to a point of uncertainty as to whether he had read the book and imagined the acts or committed the acts and written about them himself. Did the world now hold any secrets for him? Had every pleasure been drunk to the very last quaff? Was this reality all there really was?

He slammed the book shut and closed his eyes. He yearned to escape reality, to run away to a happier place. In his blacker moments he wished he were someone else, but the thought that he would not then be himself depressed him all the more.

He stood up and went to the mirror. It was time for a change. Abraham needed once again to brave the lonely London streets. A new play was opening this evening, and he made up his mind to go.

Although Abraham was certainly a misanthrope, it was a peculiar paradox of his character that, possibly to seek some excitement for his surfeit of sensibilities, he would always walk to where he wished to be, often taking a deliberate detour through the rough, run-down areas that one would suppose to be anathema to him; but like those addicted to the Gothic novel, he sought the sublime experience through terror.

Grim Fairy Tales

Abraham set out quite early with just such a detour in mind. How he hoped that the evening would reanimate some passion with a jolt to the jaundiced equilibrium that he had become too apathetic to even disturb, let alone dispel.

As the area of Highgate where he lived gave way to the more working-class environs to the east, he felt a slight adrenalin surge shoot through him. This, he knew, was a dangerous area. Many murders had been committed there some years previously by a man dubbed 'Jack the Ripper'. He knew the locals had suspected a 'gentleman' of these deeds. With his sartorial elegance, he knew he ran the risk of attack and the possibility thrilled him.

Eventually, he found himself within Whitechapel, having taken a hansom cab to save his legs the exertion of such a prolonged detour. He stepped out of the cab and paid the driver. The air hung heavy with claustrophobic oppression, and it was not long before he became aware that he was being followed. A delicious sense of his own distress ran through him as he continued to walk. The footsteps grew nearer. There were two pairs, or was it three? Excited by his own vulnerability, he was nevertheless startled when a hand clasped his shoulder.

'Hello then, Miss. Not from round this way, are you? Lost your way?' said a Bow Bells voice. Abraham did not answer.

'Well, well, it's a fella!' his aggressor said, with as much sense of irony as his narrow mind could muster. His friend could just grunt with grinning approval.

'But a pretty one!' he continued. Abraham's heart pounded. The realisation of his fantasy struck fear into him, but still it was strangely exciting.

'Give us a kiss then, pretty,' said the scabrous individual who held him. And with that, he forced his lips against Abraham's. With increasing salaciousness, he forced his tongue between the tightly closed lips. Abraham bit, an act he recognised as either heroic or stupid. Biting harder, he felt his teeth meet, and blood flowed into his mouth and gushed down his throat.

'Aah, he bit me!' the man screamed, in words ill-expressed due to the absence of half his tongue; blood, like a fountain, poured from his mouth.

Taking advantage of the confusion and panic, Abraham ran, ran as fast as he could. Hailing a hansom cab, he leapt into it.

A Day in the Life of Abraham Maranein

Only then could he consciously think of what had just happened. What had he found so invigorating? Was it the thought of placing himself in an alien environment? Was it the thought of laying himself open to physical attack? He found the thought of both painfully pleasing. But the more he thought about it, the more the same conclusion became apparent. The climax of pleasure had come in the taking of another's blood! His aristocratic English frame gave a shudder, yet slowly he allowed himself a smile. The life force of another was the one thing his money could not buy, but the taking of it he now knew would be his new pleasure, his new vice, his new compulsion!

How My Father Taught Me to Hate Myself

As the curtains peeled apart and the wooden box trundled away towards its final destination, the solitary soul allowed himself the luxury of a few moments' silent reflection.

The heat of the day was suffocating; nowhere was there a breath of wind. Everywhere the air hung heavy with a clammy, tactile quality that coiled around him like a constricting serpent.

The heat made any great display of emotion tiring ... tedious, but the observer was not in the mood for emotion anyway; everything seemed so distant, unreal. Instead, he remained aloof, calm in his disposition, even though it was his father who was being cremated. To become involved in any capacity would be far too strenuous, and would make him a hypocrite. Even the flies seemed listless. The room was as silent as the grave. Everything had a hazy timelessness which afforded the indulgence of reflection, and he wallowed in it.

Death is queer, life a strange phenomenon. What makes a lump of bone, blood, muscle move and act of its own accord? What force leaves it upon death, at once allowing the hideous processes of putrefaction to take a hold in its place? Putrefaction. Wasn't it Rousseau who said 'We are born of our Mother's bloodied entrails, and end in a mass of putrefaction'? Why? The process of conception, life, death – all a mystery beyond comprehension. How alarmed would we be if the power, the 'will' that animates matter, could be caught, captured, introduced to inanimate things, or even re-introduced to flesh that lay devoid of it? What agonies would a lamb chop go through if the life force could be restored to it? He allowed himself a smile as he thought of his father as a giant lamb chop. But this heat ... it really was beginning to become unbearable.

Thoughts of life and death once again returned to him. How easily life could be snuffed out! The human form, like a perfectly sealed piece of fruit, could be destroyed just as easily with the introduction of a strategically aimed blade. Native Americans had seen mortal wounds inflicted on cold days and noticed steam emitting as the warm blood hit the cold air, supposing it to be the soul escaping. Perhaps it was.

Death. The notion of it was not a straightforward black or white. Different deaths have different values. A listless fly lethargically landed on his hand: he crushed the life from its fragile body. He felt not the slightest twinge of remorse or regret; just as the death of his father had failed to shatter his sangfroid. He yawned. Both deaths, he recognised, had been the culmination of futile lives. What had the fly achieved with its life? What had his father? Who would remember either of them? He was now the only being who remembered his father and with his death there would be nothing to show that the old man had ever existed. Not only was his life fragile, then; it was transient ... ephemeral.

The heat of the day elicited such reflections. He had been allowed the afternoon off, so the rest of the day was his own possession. He closed his eyes and slipped back into reverie. It really was so hot ... the realisation went through his whole body like a pulse, a small electric shock.

Values of life came into his mind. How hypocritical we are! He detested blood sports but for the first time his critical eye landed on those, like himself, who opposed it. How many of this band, with no qualms or guilt, would poison vermin if found in the same abode as themselves? Why was a rat's life of less value than that of a fox? If one is to oppose death, one must oppose all deaths, without discrimination. But how successful is opposition? Death still comes like a tenacious, unrelenting affliction to everyone and everything. Why? What systems come into operation to bring about such a shutdown?

All our lives we assume we control our bodies, but the final reality to be recognised is that we lie paralysed and trapped within a fleshly prison, as surely as his father was enclosed in the box in which he now lay.

When the body takes a decision, independently of the will, to make the unique and final shutdown, the will is powerless to say no. The unity we have always considered our very selves is thrown into disarray. The chasm between will and corporeality becomes unbreachable ... an immeasurable chasm separates the two. Flesh aligns itself to the will's enemy, death. The two join forces and destroy their own dominion.

A hot wave coursed through him once again. What could be done to escape it? To escape anything? In a world of chaos, some things may seem preordained. We know there will be hot days; we know we will die. We know that in the final months, weeks, days, moments of our 'life' the will, recognising defeat, loses its ability to make order of this chaos, recognises the futility of existence and embraces religion in the vain hope of obtaining a second chance; or worse, in the hope of some eternal reward in appreciation of many years of self-abnegation – well, sometimes.

Should we avoid action we deem to be wrong? Why? No law of ethics exists in Nature. It was just another example of the frightened little lamb, Man, creating repressive values to govern his own behaviour, to compartmentalise everything, to destroy his natural beauty and stay within the confines of what we deem to be good and evil.

Are we really shut away and entirely independent of one another as one planet is from another? All shut away in our little boxes. Never knowing when the flesh that surrounds us will say 'it's time to die'. Never knowing what anyone else is thinking. Religion is the last recourse of the desperate: human life, mysterious and incomprehensible; human beings, frightened hypocrites, desperately latching on to any prospect of salvation offered them yet created by them!

Suddenly he smelt burning and opened his eyes. Everything was black. The heat was rising. He could feel his blood boiling like sauce in a saucepan, and like that sauce, thickening and congealing. He tried to stand but hit his head. Reaching out, he felt his confines: a small box. The burning he recognised as the box in which he was trapped! His box, with him inside it, was about to be consumed by flames. Not his father's cremation after all, but his own. Like a lamb to the slaughter, he had come in innocence to his own annihilation, uncomprehending. His death was upon him. A million hushed harsh whispers seemed to be saying 'burn, burn', and as the first flames broke through the scorching panels, he spoke for the first time: 'God ... I still deny you.'

And as we walked away from the charred remains of the funeral pyre, we all agreed: how dare anyone think such thoughts! An affront to the accepted order of things ... like all anomalies and freaks, it was his destiny not to thrive: it would be foolish to think otherwise.

From the Blood of Innocence

Carpathia

31st December 1899

My dear Victoria,

I can scarcely bring myself to articulate my feelings on the written page, but try I must. Rejoice, my love! Information has come to me that confirms what I had always hoped.

Many arcane artefacts have recently been acquired in a trunk I bought in an auction. The superstitious locals shied away from it and it was mine for a song. Many of the books we had always looked for were in it: "Philosophicae et Christianae Cogitationes de Vampires" from 1733 by De Schertz, Mannhardt's "Ueber Vampirismus" in Volume IV of "zeitschrift fur Deutsche Mythologie", which was also very old. But best of all, a Sylvanite cross, a large splinter of wood and three nails, the relevance of which will soon become apparent to you.

From the Blood of Innocence

Many manuscripts were enclosed; a few, with the artefacts that I have already mentioned, were written in an ancient language I have been endeavouring to understand and translate, and the monumental knowledge they impart is all that we have ever dreamed of. What follows is my rather stilted translation.

At the beginning of the first millennium there walked two men, two opposite men, as opposite as day and night. One was divine to look upon. Beauty radiated from his features. He had many admirers, and on the dusty roads of Nazareth and

Jerusalem, many base men told of the transformation he had wrought upon their dark souls.

The other was repulsive. Propagated by the first serpent, he was born of a fallen woman, and his countenance struck fear into the heart of all who dared to look upon him. Many were afraid and forced him from their midst. He wandered as an outcast.

Through an accident of birth, the first was born for eternal paradise in the kingdom of his father; the second was born for eternal purgatory, hidden away in the dark forests of Central Europe.

But as the obverse sides of a coin are intrinsically forged, so were these two men. The first bore no ill will or hatred, for he was incapable of it. The second, after many years of ostracism, became bitter as wormwood and gall, seeking revenge on those he blamed for his state; and by the forces of darkness, he propelled himself to the land of the first, to seek revenge. And as the first serpent tempted Eve with thoughts previously unknown to her, the second, through the terror of his countenance, planted an evil seed in the fertile, weak minds of those that he met, turning their bitterness against the first man, though he was as Nazarene as they.

The second supplied the thirty pieces of silver to his father's servant: the Nazarene was betrayed, tried and condemned. Three nails he wrought upon his father's anvil, which he supplied to his collaborators. Selecting a site where the first serpent's foul deed had gone awry, he sought sweet revenge by seeking to emulate his father's crime.

Adam's tree was duly planted in the shade of two others, and the Nazarene nailed to it. The blood of innocence that flowed gave the evil one cause to rejoice, and the life spilt over his upturned face. He drank, in the hope of gratifying his own ends.

After a few hours, he fell ill. The colour drained from his face, the flesh seemed to fall from his bones, the whites of his eyes became broken and red, and the nails on his hands became like the talons of animals that prey on the weak. The former wretchedness of his countenance doubled. Even nature fell silent, seemingly leaving a gap in its effort to avoid any contact with the fatal wanderer. Morning came with a light so painful to him that he had to hide himself away. But as night fell, two visitations came unto him: first an angel, then a messenger of darkness, a daemon.

The angel spoke to him: "For your sins, your

appearance shall forever remain as it is now. Your flesh will always betray the corruption to which you have stooped. As you have taken the blood of immortality, so it shall now forever remain with you. Never again shall you feel the warmth of light on your back or know the joy or possibility of friendship. For all eternity you are condemned to inhabit only darkness, utterly alone. No man shall ever suffer the pain that your appearance will elicit."

The man began to repent his actions and begged forgiveness, but the angel had gone. After a few hours, the daemon appeared and spoke.

"Fear not, your salvation has come. The course you have chosen to follow, none have walked. We salute you and crown you with a crown of thorns. As you drank the blood of innocence, so you committed your mortal house to decay without end. But you can be saved. As you drank the blood of innocence once, so you must again. But just as the first blood of innocence corrupted, all from now on will restore. The power to gratify your desires will always be with you."

And so it was that the man fled the hot and arid lands whose sun scorched his skin, and sought the land from which he came, and the dense forest. The Antichrist is in our midst. Just as the daemon had promised, the innocence of his victims restores his countenance and with each new victim he is more divine to look upon, though with each infusion he grows paler — legend has it, as pale as Seneca's widow. The victims usually live, but their life force quickly dissipates and they are robbed of their treasured vitality. Occasionally atheists are chosen, and their transformation is frightening: they become one with the perpetrator of the crime committed against them.

No weapon can destroy him, save the ones he himself possesses: a splinter from the bough of the cross, the three nails which held the Nazarene upon it, and a crucifix cast from the ore of his homeland.

Is this truly more than we could have hoped for? My theories as to the origins of the vampyre were true. His immortality was stolen from the blood of Christ! And the only reliques that can destroy him are in my possession!

Believe in him, V. Pray to him, revere his countenance. He alone will rid our lands of pestilential Christianity. He is among us!

But I must conclude. Thoughts of him have debilitated my spirit, and I grow ever more weak. In spirit, he comes to me yet, and I rejoice. My misanthropy grows ever more acute; only this can alleviate it. We shall be reborn through a baptism of blood! Through every dark day in history he has been present! V, we can be there too! Eternity is in our lips and eyes, just a breath away. Let the beating wings of daemons cool your brow as they cool mine. Only by the distillation of evil shall we have immortality.

I urge you to come at once. Nothing can part us once we have the secret of his arcane immortality. And with the reliques I hold, I am in the perfect position to bargain for an imparting of it. Come to me!

I am and remain

Yours ever lovingly

A.

All a Dream

As the burning embers turned to ash, an eruption from its midst took place; from it, a giant golden phoenix emerged and bade me ride upon its back. Its silver and golden lustre, beaten to gossamer thinness, was as soft as a bed of magnolia petals; I slipped into the gentle arms of Morpheus.

On awaking, I found myself in a strange new and wonderful land. All colours were painfully pleasing in their brilliance. The cool green grass beneath my feet shone, as each heavy blade stood crowned with a heavy dewdrop suspended in eternal animation like a glutinous gem.

A river that flowed nearby sang like a host of angels laughing. Its bubbling torrent, like liquefied diamonds, sparkled and shone before my eyes, its crystal clarity showing cool soothing depths.

From the trees came the sounds of harps and flutes, their delicate leaves sanctified every time the sigh of a perfumed breeze fell upon them.

As I walked, tentatively at first – for such beauty was unknown to me – the path that carried me into the wood seemed to shimmer beneath my feet. The lustrous canopy that shielded my eyes from the startling cerulean sky occasionally yielded to it, and a brilliant bright blue sky burst forth to kiss and caress my face, which, upturned, was cooled by the beating wings of ethereal and celestial cherubs.

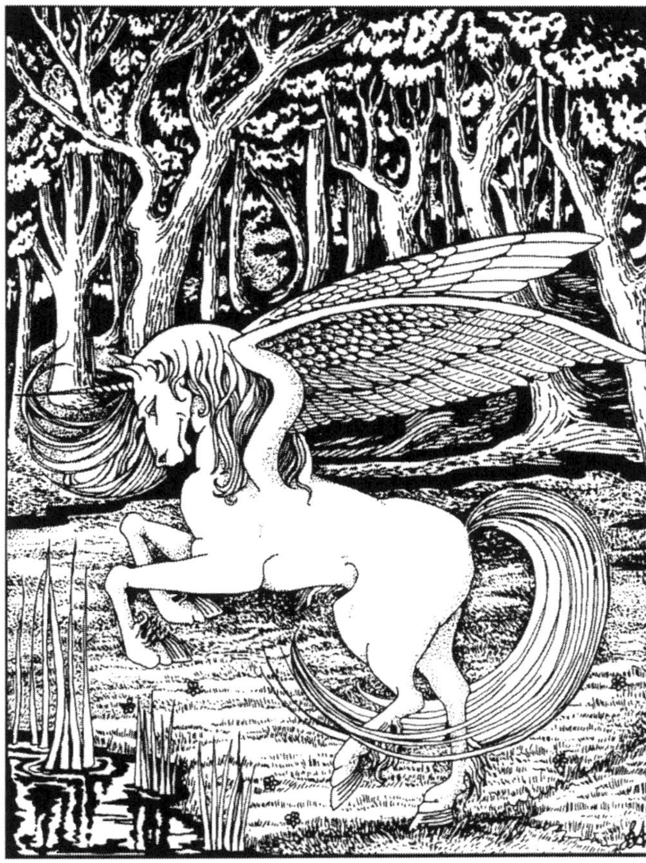

Many strange animals passed before me in the silent still centre of this sylvan scene. I spied a pool like that of a transfixed tear on the face of a false idol. From it drank a unicorn, wondrous in its wedding whiteness. As I gazed, its powerful wings lifted it airborne and away from me. Far into the distance it flew, to alight on an island in the middle of a lake that shone in mother-of-pearl magnificence, as both Phoebus beamed peace and warmth and the sovereign of true melancholy graced and garlanded all I saw before me in that unified moment that is both day and night.

My phoenix returned and took me to the shores of this beauty. The heady balm of orchids and lilies, almost intoxicating, filled me with exaltation and joy. Ten thousand lily leaves rained upon me, gilding a path to the palace, whose entrance was the gateway to paradise. Inside, strange trees grew with strange fruit, a gift from Zeus and his minions. Music infused every part of me, sparkling colours radiated before me.

The walls of the palace had mortar made with the juice of jasmine and frangipani. Warm aromatic zephyrs blew through me, cleansing, permeating the fresco walls that were painted in a hand that was to Raphael's as Raphael's was to a child, extending eternally in every direction, furnished in Alexandrian splendour. From the cathedral-high ceiling swung censers. All around were staircases carved from every imaginable gemstone, all gleaming with an inner light.

Climbing a nearby staircase that led to an array of stained glass windows, seemingly crafted at the dawn of creation, I spied the world without. One lancet arch was empty, the glass fractured and broken. I turned to it, so that my eyes might adore all that I saw, but was aghast at what befell them.

From the window, mortality lay about me in chains; children and animals beaten for no sin or crime; I witnessed the ugly face of intolerance; countries divided and wartorn; lives condemned to frailty through want; many starving whilst others grew fat; people living lives they felt had no purpose or reason. All I saw, yet none saw me. None broke their fetters and manacles to look with the inward eye that gives the lonely a friend and the prisoner freedom.

And so I choose my course: oblivion from it all ...

The Sins of the Fathers

The scrap of humanity no one had expected to live had now matured into a young man, against all the odds. His existence was still painful and traumatic, however, and would always be so. His father beheld the affliction his son had with disdain, feeling it a slight on his virility. The religious side of his character permeated his every thought and action; any sexual liaison therefore was felt to be accursed and sinful. Before him walked the result of religious justice, and he felt such results to have been a fair execution. His mother, though, loved her only son and had taken a vow never to bless him with a sibling, as such a child might well turn out to be like the monster her husband felt their firstborn had been.

No one knew the exact cause of young Edward Gray's affliction. Medical science had called it Porphyria. Laymen would just consider his appearance as too frightening to look upon. His terrible affliction cursed his every waking moment. Less unhappy times were spent in the hours of darkness when the sun's painful rays were safely hidden and the agonising beams could not avail themselves of his bleached countenance. In darkness he could rest easy without the constant threat of pain coursing through his body. His bloodshot eyes could only focus after the midnight hour when the constant threat of nature's flame being thrust into their midst had disappeared. But no time, day or night, could cicatrise his easily cracked and ever-bleeding skin. He felt himself accursed, and like all accursed things, felt it his duty to hide himself away from society; a society that would reject him, and whose rejection he reluctantly felt bound to reciprocate. Old wives' tales circulated in the village about 'the living corpse', many believing he did not exist. Others thought him a curse, the result of some profane and illicit union many years before. It had not helped when the local doctor, a thoroughly disreputable type, had made a drunken diagnosis, the result of hearsay, and had diagnosed Porphyria, proudly stating incest as the root cause. The misery

The Sins of the Fathers

such gossip had engendered within the thoroughly upright and pious family was untold. The wisp of affection the parents still bore was withdrawn still further. They felt the right decision now would be to confine their son forcibly to the most ancient and remote part of the large estate which they called home, but which for him would now become a prison.

The confines of his small quarters, though well-furnished in the decor of the day, quickly became tedious and hideously monotonous. The young man, due solely to his lack of companionship, came more and more to rely on his imagination as the sole form of escape. The waking moments of every day were spent in guilt and torment, yet lost in a reverie of far-off places he had seen in his father's books and of the people who had once inhabited such lands. With a sigh of resignation, the ideas were shut away into the realms of fantasy, with the realisation that physical escape would always lie intangibly out of reach. His physical circumstances bound him, as surely as poverty and lack of education bound the poor but healthy inhabitants of the local towns. His restrictions were of a different form but just as constricting and debilitating to wellbeing; one could either lie down and let life crush the desire to enjoy it - like an old cider press crushes little apples - or if circumstances are insurmountable, divorce oneself from reality and create a personal world, free from pain, irritation and the hurt a thoughtless world of fellow man can cause.

The oppressive gloom of his room would have hung heavy over most spirits, like a damp shroud, but his condition rendered the obliteration of any light necessary. A few candles that were the only illumination lent the ancient room an archaic air, though its modern Edwardian decor paradoxically gave it a very contemporary feel. It was doubly ironic in that it would have done any fashionable young man about town very proud indeed. He, however, sought to escape. Closing his eyes, he dared to dream; soon sleep crept over him.

After a brief lapse of time, he awoke. The room stood bathed in glorious sunlight, causing the now instinctive gesture of covering his eyes. After a few seconds there was a realisation: this time there had been no pain, this time was different. He opened his eyes and looked around. It was certainly still the same room, only the decoration and furnishings had changed entirely. Gone was the furniture of his period: the whole room was now decorated in what appeared to be the style of the Jacobean age. Gone was his brass bed; he was now in a four-poster affair. The paintings which had hung on his walls, depicting the fashionable world of Paris and London, had been replaced by tapestries of bucolic scenes. The smooth white walls of his room were gone, to be replaced by rough stone. He ran to the window. The familiar rolling lawns of his father's estate were still there but were now scattered with innumerable rose bushes and a small stone fountain.

Voices in the passage caused him to panic. The door opened and in walked what appeared to him, in his limited experience, to be the most beautiful girl in the world.

'Hello, you must be my cousin back from Spain,' she said, half-jovially, half-teasingly. 'Mother has told me so much about you, I feel as though I know you already.'

'Yes,' he murmured hesitantly, faltering and not knowing what to say to this apparent stranger who appeared to know him. He gazed at her as she flitted to the window, babbling garrulously words he had ceased to take in. Her clothes were not the fashion of his era. Her hairstyle, everything about her, was of a different age. Her delicate hand ran over a tapestry she was doing: 'Elizabeth Wheatley, age 16, August 1615'. Sixteen fifteen! With total incomprehension, he realised that somehow he was living, breathing, moving almost three hundred years earlier than when he had gone to sleep.

'Come with me, John,' the young woman said, 'Let me introduce you to my brothers and sisters.'

'John?', he thought but said nothing. They left the room together, his gut twisting itself into knot upon knot in dread and anticipation. Why hadn't his face frightened her? Why didn't his eyes hurt? What would her family say when they realised there was a charlatan in their midst? What was he doing two hundred and ninety-five years before his own time?

Wandering from room to room, they found no one. The whole house had changed, but he was relieved to find it uninhabited. She, however, found it quite disconcerting.

'They were here a moment ago,' she said, 'They are always playing their silly games and hiding from me.'

The Sins of the Fathers

'Your parents?' he asked.

'No, silly, your aunt and uncle are in town. My brothers and sisters. They always leave me out. It makes me feel so ... unwanted.'

Edward's heart went out to her. He knew the pain of castigation more than most.

'Still, I'm here now,' he said, startled at his own admission. Elizabeth blushed.

The next few hours were spent in a timeless togetherness walking in the garden. The great oak trees he recognised from his garden he saw now as saplings just a few years old. Despite the unfamiliarity of his surroundings, his soul had never before felt such a sense of home. For the first time ever he could feel the warmth of the sun on his face, gaze upon the splendid colours that tenderly enfolded him, talk to someone who did not shy away from him. If it was a dream, he prayed that it would never end.

As the sun began to set, Elizabeth became increasingly agitated: her family were still mysteriously absent.

'I am beginning to worry about them,' she confided. 'We really ought to look again. You try that way, and I will go this.' Edward agreed; he would have done anything she asked. As he walked away his heart went with her, but he must do as she wished: pleasing her was all that mattered. He rounded the corner of one of the old rustic outbuildings when suddenly everything began to swirl and close in around him. His vision began to constrict until everything went black. He felt dizzy, his legs began to shake and buckle. Like a drunken man, he clutched the wall in desperation, but fell anyway, violently knocking his head.

When he awoke he shouted 'Elizabeth, Elizabeth!' The gloom told him that it might be night. He stood up and ran to the window ... window? Before he could check his actions, he had pulled apart the curtains and an agonising shaft of sunlight seared into his eyes. He snapped them shut and slumped half-blinded to the floor. Had all this isolation robbed him of his faculties of judgement? What had happened to him? His head pulsed and throbbed; whatever had happened had left a very real bruise. It must have been a flight of fancy ... how else would he have been able to understand the spoken word of Jacobean

England so fluently when it would have been so markedly different in actuality? It must have been a dream.

The weeks passed and his solitary, lonely existence continued as before. Out of curiosity, he decided to trace the ownership of his parents' house. The only book he could find on local history in his own library seemed to suggest his ancestors had acquired the property sometime between 1610 and 1620. No records existed for the earlier period.

After a few months, all had been consigned to memory and its shallow grave, when one particularly lonely evening his sleep was once again disturbed. He roused himself from his hypnogogic state and into a full illuminated consciousness to find himself immersed in the decor of the early seventeenth century. Once again he recognised the unfamiliar familiarity. There was a gentle tap on the door.

'Come in,' he said rather gingerly. Delicately the divine features of his beloved Elizabeth appeared.

'Where did you go last night? I found the others, but then we couldn't find you anywhere.'

'Oh, I ... I just came back here. I couldn't find you either and I didn't feel well.'

'Oh, I am sorry. Never mind,' she continued excitedly, 'They really are going away today, so we can have the day to ourselves. Would you like to go riding?'

That day spent with Elizabeth was the happiest day he had ever had. When they returned that night, he had quite forgotten his tenuous hold on reality and what or who he was. When he retired to bed, he clutched the sheets as hard as he could, in affirmation. They were very real indeed. Could they be the haven, the hold which he hoped for; what, if anything, would be? He was desperate. Here he wanted to stay, but already something was pulling him away.

The next morning, he awoke and instinctively knew. All his hopes and dreams fell on barren soil; this was no different. The dreary, drab room closed in like a coffin. Could there ever be any escape?

Slowly the visits to 1615 came with greater regularity, yet however long the passage of time in his own era in 1615 just a moment or two had passed. As the years in the twentieth century trundled towards the first great war, so his visits continued.

'Elizabeth,' he said one day, by now feeling sure enough of their bond of affection for such familiarity, 'would you tell me about your family?'

'Don't be so silly,' she said, 'they are your family as well!'

He had forgotten; she thought him her cousin. Rather flustered he continued, 'Could you tell me what happened during my trip abroad?'

'One day,' she whispered, 'one day.'

The love of the two continued to grow with only the ardour a young heart can know. Though he knew they could never marry – not simply because they were cousins but because he was not a part of her time, nor she his – he also knew that the affection they both now nurtured was, at least for him, a partial deception. But could such passion be quashed? Conversely, the opposite seemed to be happening, until one day the two young paramours loved one another utterly.

The next few visits were awkward and strained. Still, he had not met any members of her family – indeed, any tie to family seemed cumbersome and difficult. To the two young lovers, any bond other than to each other disappeared. Her trust in him, he began to feel, was misplaced. What sort of person was he to elicit the force of love in someone so naive, when only he knew his dark and sickly secret? Never could he fully reciprocate her love. He felt himself to be some stealthy incubus condemned to haunt and perpetrate hideous acts and cause untold misery.

'Please, Elizabeth, tell me what happened when I was abroad,' he insisted a few weeks after that fateful day.

'Please ... it is so painful,' she winced.

'Please – what happened to our family?'

'Our branch of the family,' she continued, with short gulped and laboured breaths, 'had to change its name, owing to the purge on Catholics. When we moved here, we changed our name from Gray to Wheatley to avoid the purge.'

'Gray to Wheatley,' he murmured, 'Gray to Wheatley! Elizabeth Gray! My God, you are one of my ancestors!'

'Stop it!' she cried, 'How can I be when you and I are of the same age?'

'Elizabeth Gray!' he wailed, 'Elizabeth Gray!'

'Stop it! Just stop it! It's not going to alter the fact that I am going to have your child ... '

Suddenly everything froze. Only then did the full horror of everything illuminate a perception previously clouded. He was the perpetrator of his own affliction! It had lain dormant through all those generations, only to execute justice on its original culprit. His father had been right all along: passion did equate with sin, did equate with guilt. If they had been allowed to live their natural lives in a natural way, she would never have had to change her name, and he would have known from the start that they were related. Her family would not have had to change their name to avoid persecution, his family would never have had an offspring to be ashamed of; whom they believed to be a punishment for a long-forgotten act. The chains of morality were chains of guilt. What had started out so right was now so wrong ... so very wrong.

In a Perfect World

The cool crystal pool looked very inviting as the crepuscular shadows gave way to the cool jewelled kisses of Diana, child of the sky. Latona was beckoning and covered everything like black mercury. Unerring arrows fell lovingly upon Endymion as he died an ephemeral death, only to arise Lazarus-like as the circle comes to its close.

Jade and emerald fell from the fresh and sparkling trees into the water. Eden-like, and unspoilt. All was silent, all was bliss. Untouched by the filthy hand of man, it breathed with a promise to change and alter and imperceptibly turn all that is bad to good. Just as one can only know sweetness by contrasting it with sourness, so it is that true unity only comes when opposites are unified. No objectivity can come from either left or right, dark or shade, happiness or sadness. So it was with humanity. Yet everywhere the deformity of feminine grace and masculine virility persisted. In the majority of the protagonists the hideous façade was still paraded as the only way; indeed the dichotomy, the impassable gulf, was seen as a wonderful thing. A million years of evolution had brought us to this! The conquest, the battle of constantly displaying all one's wiles to their full advantage, was never to be seen as anything less than an epitome of a possible partner for the propagation of an effete and degenerate species. How wonderful if there could exist the *übermensch* that could combine the two – able to transcend any trial or tribulation relationships bring! No jealousy, no preconceptions or ugliness, that often are the attributes so esteemed in any gender.

So it was that the small town had thrown up two such individuals, uncomfortable with their sex. She felt the narrow confines of her environment all too painfully. Closing in, they crushed out of her the joy to live. Local girls she had once called friends she now perceived as the worthless wretches they truly were. Only the local prostitutes she deemed to be honest. With an ironic eye, she watched her former friends parading in pairs, hoping to catch the eye of any available man. Such frivolous determination! One would think that their life depended upon It. Occasionally 'Prince Charming' did come along, but their own stupidity usually excluded love in preference to the jealous friend who always came first. Their small imagination left everything that really mattered closed and dormant to them. None had any aspiration to achieve anything more than a wealthy husband to ensure they would always be provided for. Why could they not cut the ties of their self-imposed bondage – reach out and clutch a world that lay in store like an autumn harvest. Instead they continued in their narrow little confines gossiping over social events they imbued with magnitude. How she hated them! How she hated herself for being the same sex as they! She felt tied to them by upbringing and environment. She hated the men who complied with them. They really did deserve each other. If only she were a man, then she might be accepted for herself, or escape to find herself and independence without having to use her sex to obtain a shallow reflection of it.

The other was a man. How he hated his sex! Too kind-hearted for an unkind world, he was an easy target for any hard man to prove his own virility upon; the physical beatings by such men still hurt. He lay all his fractured senses bare until the elements scorched them and washed them away, until the act of feeling became difficult, and he began to fear retribution for trying to do so. For him, love and beauty overrode alcohol and lust. His body he despised. The thinning hairline, the distended veins in his arms the coarse hair on his body, his large blunt features. How could he reconcile all this and then partake in the obscene parody which the courting ritual had become? How he longed to be a woman! To be allowed to be sensitive, to procreate, to give birth to a tiny child which could then be the sole receptacle for his love! But how could he escape? In a man's world he would always be a failure, an outcast. Not only was his physique lacking, his attitude was also sadly wrong: he lacked the self-righteousness, the aggression needed to be a 'real man'. There never would be a vocation for him. Nature had singled him out; it was a role he would have to play until the bitter end.

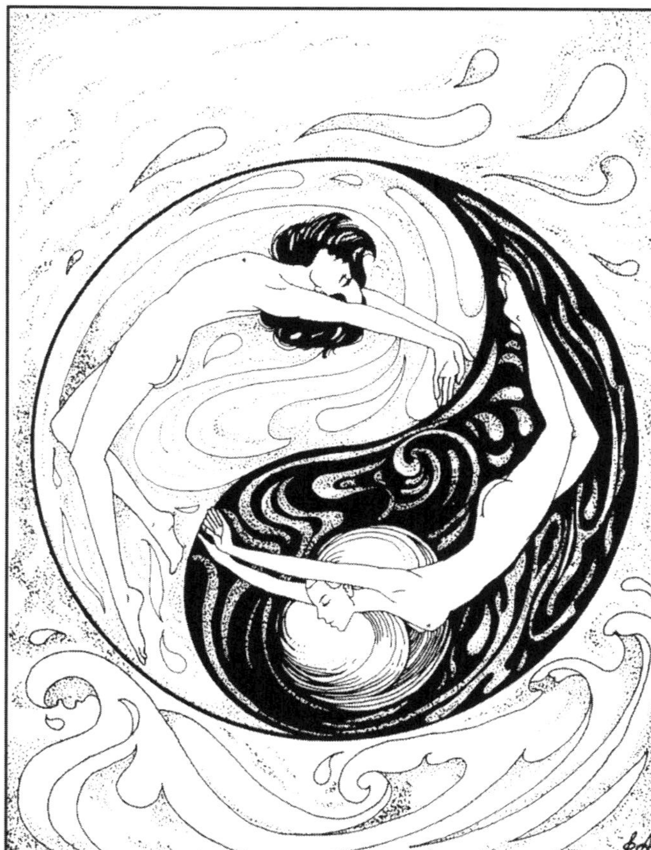

But the dissatisfaction did not stop there. In such a small town, the juxtaposition of sexes, and therefore the observation of their fraternisation, is hard to endure when one feels excluded, especially when the virtues lauded by others are anathema to oneself. It quickly escalates into an intense misanthropy. So it was with them both.

As the moon coolly beat on the pool, two great minds individually made one decision: suicide. The arcane and archaic woodland gently shimmered and swayed before them.

Breezes that had seen the first man light the first fire would now witness a new birth. Destiny, previously thought so cruel, had seemingly changed her mind. Salvation was now within their grasp.

On opposite sides of the pool they stood, split by a liquid ebony. Both were naked as they penetrated the still waters. In they plunged: two bodies suspended in a matter that caressed every part of them. Water lapped against them both; only the waters of transfiguration separated them; waters that were penetrating every part. In ecstasy, death seemed near. In ecstasy, two bodies swam ... two bodies ... two bodies ... one body.

A transformation had taken place. Like Hermaphroditus and Salmacis, the two were united in a single body. All that was beautiful existed within its sensual and graceful form. Broken chains of conformity and expectation floated free and drifted to the bottom of the pool. A perfect union stepped forth, liberated.

Society's constraints cast aside! Now the wasted years' others spend in pursuit of one another could blossom into a thing of beauty. Apparent opposites had made a whole! No guilt for sensitivity, no obligation to pursue aggression: a phoenix – an angel – rising anew in an epicene swirl. One body, one soul, one mind, one spirit, a synthesis of beauty, the quintessence of perfection. They had found one another: love had found a way.

Love rode into town on an ass, befitting, it would seem, a being worthy of veneration. What lay ahead? All knowledge had died. Only by a process of empiricism could a path be paved forward.

But the microcosm is subject to the macrocosm. The streets grew nearer and nearer. Human hostility began to coil and crouch and prepare to attack; the ridiculous in fear of the sublime. The being before them was flawless. No solace was afforded. In the presence of a deity, the deity becomes a mirror reflecting every imperfection, ugliness, and oh so short life of those that gaze upon it. The truthfulness of beauty was all too much for them.

A line of people appeared on the streets, their faces twisted and contorted by their own failure. The town fell silent. Suddenly a rock was thrown, then another, then another. The rural byways offered a plentiful supply of ammunition, which was readily used. Soon love lay dead. There was cause for celebration. The ordinary revere the average, are hostile to the transcendent. But they continued to gaze at love. To them love was freakish. The appalling mediocrity of their gaze withered what was new and which now lay before them until, finally, all that was left was a pile of dry ashes. The philistines congratulated themselves on their success as the new god died, ridiculed and ostracised.

Temptation and Denial

Adam Nicke

Born on the Lupercalia - the Roman festival of the wolf - in 1967, Adam Nicke spent an unhappy and lonely childhood in a series of isolated houses along the Welsh Border. During this difficult period he sought refuge in literature and within his imagination.

When he grew up, his artistic tendencies were first expressed in the designing and making of clothing, most notably for Wayne Hussey of The Mission. Later, he turned to writing fiction which explores an inner realm of moods and anxieties, and the feelings of guilt experienced by characters coming to terms with an alienating world. He has a degree in Literary Studies from the University of the West of England.

Adam Nicke Publishing

Dedicated to my maternal grandfather, Jack Tagg
1919-2016

The brother shall betray the brother to death, and the father the son; and children shall rise up against their parents, and shall cause them to be put to death ... But he that shall endure unto the end, the same shall be saved. ~ Mark 13:12

Temptation

The mind can make
Substance, and people planets of its own
With beings brighter than have been, and give
A breath to forms that can outlive all flesh
                                        Byron

As I close my eyes strange and wonderful shapes animate themselves: images from the purple pageantry of the imagination; archetypes from age upon age that have waited, watching from dark and hollow recesses. Shining, divine lights flow like weightless waterfalls: golden and anointing. Could I ever convey the experience with words? Words are the tools of humanity; I walk with gods. Writing of such things as I now see them is almost beyond me, for only now can I see that everything in the universe has always been housed within my body, a body that now stands on the brink of an abyss. Death holds me in its soft and gentle arms. All things living and eternal pulse within and without everything my senses fall upon. Not that there is a 'me' to perceive it all. There was never an 'I'. In vanity, previous thoughts indicated there was something deep within that had constituted identity: that was the real *me*. To realise that all one's identity is founded upon nothing more than an endless stream of thoughts, fears, hopes, and dreams is strangely liberating. There is no 'I' or 'me' to stand outside those shifting sands, at all.

Options seem limitless and infinite, yet death smiles. Ah to die! To drift into unknown realms, where gentle rivers kiss with lips of beatitude. Only now can I feel life; facing death.

It seems obvious to me that those that either will not, nor cannot, see with my eyes - eyes that now bear witness to the beating of a transfigured heart, a heart of stardust and as old as time - that these few words will be nonsense. Still, I must try, even as the fire of exultation burns within me and my flesh grows weak. It is a sobering experience to think that these hands are capable of murder. All I had ever wanted was to be free - free to choose for myself - yet my every choice had been moulded by others. Their thoughts had always lain cruel dominion over my every action. There could never be a turning away for they had always been there, like an evil virus, drawing strength from weakness. Yet from death came life! Alas, time is short.

My name and the date of my birth are less important than the eldritch tale I have to tell so, without further ado, I shall begin.

I was an only child. My friendship with Sebastian seems to go back to the point when I first felt my loneliness and despair to be unbearable. Prior to that, there had been no one, other than family. Perhaps he has always been there, a part of me.

My parents' house was considerably larger than any others in the area. The downstairs had large windows that stretched from floor to ceiling, and beautiful on sunny days when the light of Helios shone and chrysanthemum-like rays would shimmer upon the old flagstone floor; on days when the weather was bad, however, the whole house appeared grey and damp, as though a storm might erupt within its confines: my childhood was invariably grey and stormy. The house, it seemed, had always been there with its rough, stone countenance, seemingly drawn from the rocks upon which it sat, giving it the appearance of something naturally occurring. Yet, for all that, it seemed as if it had once been a happy house. The right family - a *happy* family - might well have enjoyed the many gardens it stood amongst; the honeysuckle crowding the back door that made warm summer nights come alive with odours deliciously ageless; children might have enjoyed each dark room filled with dark secrets or the long staircases that seemed to reach from heaven to hell. Blackened beams supported every room. Every night they seemed to wheeze as relentlessly as the old miners in the local village.

Given the isolated and windswept location of my parents' home it is possible that my destiny was always going to be that of a lonely and withdrawn individual, irrespective of later events that ensured such a disposition. Yet even then, in those first years, I had a rare plant that few cultivate: an imagination!

The house had been built in the foothills of one of the giant jagged mountains that are so abundant in Wales. The previous owner had obviously been a keen gardener, but years of neglect had had an effect on the landscape he had sought to perfect. Nature had waited to reclaim her offspring and now the garden retained only a portion of its former order. As a child, that garden seemed to me to be steeped in mystery that unfolded in silent supplication. Everywhere there seemed new delights: an ancient rose garden, thick with perfume and heavy with the loving care with which the unseen hand had once caressed it. On the little gravel paths, covered in moss, I often pondered on how many dead generations had walked those paths, breathed those perfumes and spoken of their lives, loves, hopes and dreams. Huge rolling lawns reached out to winding steps that seemed to lead nowhere. All those forgotten plans that had never come to fruition; or maybe they had: when did one make the appraisal?

Temptation

Perhaps, at some distant point in the past, everything *had* been right. Perhaps everything was still in the ascent and at some future date everything *would* be right, but then how would we ever know when that moment was?

At that time that garden afforded me many a happy reverie. Every plant seemed fluid and sensuous, able to radiate an inner light, a light illuminating the darkest caves of my imagination. Nothing needed contemplation, for it was already understood.

On rainy days the garden offered some little escape from the oppression of the house. I wanted the garden to gently hold me until the sadness fled. On summer days I became heir to the universe for at those times everything seemed right, true, and honest. I knew how the grass felt to wash in the morning dew; how every flower felt to be touched by the sun. Birds resting on the golden boughs above sang for me and all creation. The child, like the generous rose, gave itself without discrimination. Existence was given purpose by the pleasure of giving.

In this garden, however, lurked a serpent. At the far end of those Elysian fields was a gate, almost otherworldly in all its baroque glory. It felt dangerous for beyond it was something terrifying. It repelled me but also captivated me. Its charm appeared hypnotic. Its penetrating form seemed to reach up and lacerate the sky.

Had it been forged to keep me out? Worse still, to keep something in? What terrors lurked beyond it, submerged in that awful gloom? Even daylight seemed reluctant to enter more than a few feet down the steps beyond - that infernal realm – that it guarded so well. In the rare moments' courage could be mustered to look at it, nothing could be seen save for those few steps down, yet where did they lead?

Even today, that long, hot summer comes back to me. That summer the garden became more important in my life than ever. Every day was spent in solitude, creating and peopling planets of my own. Vividly, one day stands apart from the rest. It was a hot day, even for a summer now remembered as searing. Occasional breezes often sped up and down the valley floor punctuating the warmest of days, yet this day was different. This was not a breeze, but a chill so sudden and unexpected it could be likened to an inescapable fall. Unseen hands seemed to throw my body through a sheet of ice, each tiny shard tearing my skin. Petrified fingers clutched my warm heart tightening and constricting with every beat, like an anaconda with its prey. Borne aloft, without control, so cold and hurled toward the gate.

What force threatened to dash the child's brain upon those steely spikes? Then, as quickly as it had all begun, I felt a gentle, graceful lowering until I found myself reclining on the top step, the gate swinging freely open behind me. Previously, the doom and darkness of where those steps lead had frightened me. Now, golden lights spilt forth with love and an amber-like embrace, warm and tender on my prone shape, wrapping me in an everlasting caress.

What was happening? Did *this* sort of thing happen to everyone? Why hadn't the truth been told? I looked out into the garden and everything seemed frozen. What was once green and fertile was now white and sterile. Where had the summer gone? Out there all was cold and numb. Here I had warmth, salvation and a place to call home. Life had beckoned from a hinged egress. Was there never to be a return to what once had been? What to do? To stay? To die? Death comes too easily for it is living that is difficult. Death makes ugly clowns of us all, with no opportunity to redress any calumny heaped upon us, giving us masks where once were faces.

I stood and silently appraised my options. Suddenly, out of the warmth and comfort a cold, deathly hand reached out and clutched at my wrist. Long fingernails, seemingly befouled by an eternity in this subterranean underworld, sank into soft, young flesh. A face drew nearer to my own. The features scared me as they seemed too primitive and savage, like some sort of half-human atavism.

"Come with me," it croaked, the voice rasping like some great beast. I felt a strange compulsion - as though this was my destiny, but then how could that be? How could we ever be free if things were fated? If we never had a choice then why should we feel guilty? Unknowing, uncomprehending, and with the curiosity of a child, I entered.

The gate swung shut behind me. From that moment things would *never* be the same. There could be no going back. I knew the gate would be closed to me, even if I tried its lock. What could one say about my new surroundings? The figure that had pulled me in had, seemingly, disappeared. Now, *anything* seemed possible. Maybe even start a new faith - or kill an old one. Those steps seemed a tunnel to my innermost soul. The first steps had seemed warm and inviting but now, looking down, there was nothing save the absolute blackness of the void. Was that good, or bad? A complete negation but also a complete infinity. An empty canvas where one could paint anything, given the right tools and a vivid imagination.

To touch; to savour every new delight. To feel along rough stone walls. To listen, as each footstep seemed to echo in caverns immeasurable to man. Turning, a passageway had but a single candle to light my way. Unseen hands seemed to guide me. Somewhere, someone - or some *thing* - wanted me to be here. Stumbling toward the little waxen light, the ground beneath me appeared to move. On the dank, dark floor there was to be no salvation. I fell, yet the anticipated pain of my body colliding with hard stone did not cause me to come to a painful halt. Floor and walls seemed to crumble. Now, I was plummeting down into what? Upon what was my body to be dashed? Was I really to end here, smashed to annihilation, deep within the earth and with nothing to mark my ever having been?

After falling for what seemed hours, I took a single step forward and regained my footing as easily as if it had simply been the next step in a leisurely stroll. No pain and no sudden, jarring stop merely a step into the dark and safety. Miles of rock, entombing, yet comforting and embracing. Nothing could hurt again. Time became relative. How long had circumstances been thus? A second? A century? Was it all the dream of an old man thinking of himself as young again; or a young man imagining himself as old? Did it matter? It seemed real so wasn't that enough?

Staircases stretched away in all directions. Some went down, snaking their way into the long, dark night whilst others reached high, to new horizons and beyond. This void had everything! The urge to jump, to let myself fall again to who knows where was tempered by curiosity. Spiralling around and around, down and down, the distant walls closed in on themselves.

Ropes, pulleys, chains, all moving as though either powering or being powered, by some mighty engine. Oh, to be king of all one perceives! Without my presence *none* of this mechanism would be in motion, of that I was sure.

Stone faces formed in the walls surrounding me, some smiling, some mocking; some mournfully sad, others hysterically laughing; death masques showing the whole panoply of human emotion yet one thing united them all: they were all of the same countenance, the face now known to me as Sebastian. Stone eyes followed my every move.

If only the workings of this place could be remembered! If my presence was the essential component, it had to be important to retain something of this mechanism. Herein lay the secret to everything but everything retained a breath of the arcane that made their workings as elusive as the philosopher's stone. Fleeting glimpses of the magnitude of it all dissolved as quickly as the reflection of Narcissus in a pool, but then how fleeting was fleeting? A second? A century?

Wheels continued to spin and grind as the whole machine trundled along, endeavouring to perform some unfathomable and distant task, perhaps since the beginning of time and perhaps until the end. Perhaps that was the way of things. Stone eyes still watched. Watching for a mistake? What if a mistake were made? What were the rules? Did I make the rules? If I were now making the rules then how could I *ever* make a mistake? Maybe the rules were always changing so they could never be known. If only those petrified eyes would stop staring...

Would it ever be possible to leave this place? To be a child again in the garden! Now there was no way to go, only down. Down to what? Down there was unknown. Down there it was cold, so very cold. Even thinking about it brought chill winds blasting, as cold as the icy hand that had brought me to this place. What to do?

Walking with trepidation, and on weary legs, flesh became stone. Was there really no escape from this tomb? No, there *had* to be a way out of this place. Suddenly, I was back in the garden with the sun shining. It seemed a nice day. I let out a deep breath and lay back in the grass so that the warm rays of the sun could vivify me a little. I must have fallen asleep, I figured, and had a dream. I tried to rationalise it. How could something I had always feared have become dangerous and exciting? I had tasted freedom and wanted more. It wasn't just the gate in the garden I had opened but another gate in my heart; one that could never more be closed. That dream had been a rite of passage. I may not have realised it then but I realise it now. I was breaking away from the life I had known and that day was the start of life anew.

If the reader will permit me, scant attention needs to be accorded to my school years; my time is short and if I am to commit to paper all that needs to be recorded, these last few hours can be better spent than recollecting such tedious events. I have to execute some discernment and I choose to edit this portion of the story.

Suffice to say my school days were, largely, unhappy. Fortunately, they had no detrimental effect on my education. Initially, these years were uneventful. Geographical isolation had made me unsociable even though I longed to be otherwise. In fact, the only friend throughout those years was Sebastian.

Sebastian was a quiet boy. Even though we were inseparable he always remained a little unknown to me. He seemed to keep so much to himself. He never spoke of his family, his home life, where he lived, or where he had been. He seemed to have come from nowhere and simply existed.

Vividly, I remember one visit Sebastian paid me. My father didn't even give him a glance but it was the conversation afterwards that I recall. By this time, I hated being anywhere near my father and felt acutely self-conscious that his personality should show itself to anyone outside of the family. My mother and I enabled the tyrant rather than expose him for the bully that he was. I had already realised that I had to break the chains of familial paternity were I ever to be free.

Unlocking the heavy back door, the twilight sun shone through the cascade of honeysuckle that sensuously encircled the door frame so that the whole air seemed alive with life.

"God, what an atmosphere! I can see why you're like you are. His piety can go to hell", Sebastian said.

"Be quiet, will you! He'll hear you."

"All that religious nonsense on the bookshelves. It doesn't fool me."

"Well, he is a Christian," I countered.

"Christianity! Don't start me on that!"
"Don't you believe in God, then?"
"Do you believe in Santa Claus?"
"Of course not."
"Well, there's your answer."
"Haven't you ever asked yourself why we are here, or where we are going?"

"Yes, I have." By now, we had descended the broken stone steps and had found our way onto one of the lawns.

"And?"

"And what?" He was well aware that I wished him to continue yet would not do so until I asked.

"Do you? What conclusion have you come to?" I asked.

"That I want more from Christianity than it actually gives. I don't want a religion that makes me feel guilty for something I haven't done. I don't want a religion that puts another man to death to save me. That's awful. Why are we taught to believe superstitions as if they are demonstrable fact? And what about the people the church venerates? I know your father beats your mother, you know. Christianity is misogynistic so no wonder he approves! Tertullian said of women 'thou art the Devil's gate'. St. Jerome that 'woman is the root of all evil'. St. Augustine asked 'why was woman created at all'. Odun of Cluny even asked who would wish to hold 'ipsum stercoris saccum' and that loosely translates as 'a stinking bag of dung'. Ask your mother what she thinks such a religion can offer her! If these are the people a Christian church looks up to, then it is a church I can do without. The Christian concept of God is dead. Look inside yourself and ask 'What do I think of such and such as a person?' not 'What do I think of such and such as a Christian?'"

We turned left, our boot heels crunching on the narrow gravel path and onto one of the lawns, where we sat.

"What is it you want, then?" My manner was rather truculent. After all, being brought up to believe in the biblical account of creation, I now found myself listening to a friend voicing every doubt I had begun to harbour about the faith in which I had so long believed. Was my castle *really* built on sand?

"I want to escape. I dream of the past, and the future - of other times, other places and exotic lands! Of great heights where the picturesque becomes the sublime. A place where everything I know now might be left behind! Of mountains where I can see forever. But what is life if not an existence that is chaotic and confusing? Does anyone want a life that has no hope or reason? Do not tell me it is because I am an unbeliever. It is because I was once a believer that I now feel so betrayed. I don't want rational explanations, I want mystery, not mystery presented as fact. I want to live in a world where *anything* is possible. I'm supposed to be free yet everywhere I am in chains. Sometimes it feels as though I'm swimming in a bottomless ocean of treacle and with every new stroke, I sink further and further away from the cool morning. All I have are my moods and the ceaseless ebb and flow of my thoughts and they're all that constitutes *me*. I want to find others like me, for, like you, all that ever spoke to me before was God but God is a liar. I grew up and stepped out of the nursery and now face maturity without such a crutch." With that, he paused and picking up a broken branch that lay nearby idly flicked at the grass.

"I once read of a man who, when looking at the night sky, felt a dual awe. On the one hand, he witnessed the infinity of starry space, on the other, the inner workings of himself. I want to synthesize the two - infinity without and infinity within. Before I fall asleep it sometimes comes to me - when everything is dark and hidden - the powers that drive the universe come and unfold their secrets and I see the majesty of it all. At that moment *anything* seems possible. Each star could be ten, with every planet around each star the home of someone as lonely as me, none of us ever complete without the other. I want all those lonely people by my side, so I too may feel the warmth of human affection. Do you understand?"

"I think so," I mumbled. I did, of course, but it felt blasphemous to say so.

"I feel sure that some veil obscures an entrance to the untapped reservoirs of the mind. Rend that aside and infinity will rain down upon us like a summer shower on a hot July day," he continued before suddenly stopping. I looked at him for some explanation, in time to see him frown. The silence continued for what seemed like an age until be drawled "I never want you to repeat this. If you speak of it and you shall not see me again." It was easy to see the look of cold earnestness in his face: I could tell that he meant what he said, yet felt angry that he thought such a threat was needed and that his friendship meant so very much to me. What did he think I would do without him? Wither and die? Who was *he* to think that withholding his friendship would be a punishment? Another part of me, however, wanted to hear what else he had to say, so I bid him continue by nodding my acquiescence. He was about to continue when the sound of a door being slammed interrupted us. A few light steps scurried upon the path that led to the garden, before a face as familiar as my own came into view.

"You're not going to be able to come back in at the moment," said my mother, as she approached. She looked furtively at Sebastian, clearly wishing to conceal the real reason for our exclusion.

"I'll open the side door for you. If you can stay there, there's a good boy." I, of course, knew the real reason why we couldn't return via the door we had left: my father had evidently taken umbrage at what he felt to be some transgression and was now in some sort of rage. I would probably be hit, my mother thrown into a wall or door and who knows what else. That is why we had so few visitors: my mother discouraged them through a sense of shame and humiliation. She would blame herself; ask what her neighbours would think of a woman who could not look after her own home, never realising she was entirely blameless.

The three of us seemed to stay together for a long time, long enough for me to catch a tear trickle down my mother's face. She raised her hand to her eye and wiped the little course away. She smiled and, just for a moment, looked at Sebastian, then back to me with an expression that begged me not to betray her secret - *our* secret. She was a beautiful woman, but most sons probably think that of their mothers. She had grace, poise, elegance and deserved so much more from life.

"I'll go and open it for you." I had quite forgotten the door, being lost in a reverie. There was no hypocrisy in her thinking, only the false virtues of shame and guilt. Before I could reply she had turned away leaving nothing but the warm fragrance of her perfume, and something less tangible and unique: the scent of *my* mother.

"He's made her cry." Sebastian's voice shattered the quiet like a stone dropped into the still waters of a long-forgotten well. It wasn't that he had broken the silence, it was that he had realised *our* secret. His tone suggested that *every* door of that closed and awful world had now been shown to him. My cheeks burned with shame, not just for me, but also for my mother. I wanted to protect her. At that moment, for the first time, I wanted to kill my father.

"Don't be stupid. Why should she be doing that?" I looked at Sebastian. His face softened into the same appealing look my mother had given me. He wanted me to tell him the truth but was sensitive enough not to insist he was right.

"Sorry, my mistake." I looked at Sebastian for a trace of sarcasm that his voice had not betrayed yet there was none. He smiled, sensitively. "Now, where's this door?" His voice had changed, his manner now cheery as though he were trying to lift me out of my torpor.

Without looking at him, I turned and led the way around the side of the old house to what would once have been servants' quarters, those occupants now being long gone. Mother and I did any chores that needed doing, whilst a local man came to tend the garden occasionally. We walked to the heavy age-blackened door, recessed a few feet or so into the walls of the house, the walls of the house thus serving as a porch. Either side of the door were two old benches. I gestured Sebastian to sit.

"We'd better take off our boots." It wasn't that carpets would get damaged, for there were no carpets only flagstones of the sort that so many houses of antiquity in Wales have as flooring; my fear was that our heavy boots would make a noise as we walked upon those stones, thus giving away our hiding place.

"May I go in?" Sebastian had removed his boots and stood with his hand on the door handle, his gaze focussing on my attempts to remove my footwear.

"Yes, of course, only be quiet." For added effect, I had whispered the last two words as if the words alone were not enough and had to be demonstrated. How embarrassing, I thought. Why had I done that?

By now, the setting sun had almost given way to the silver denizens of the night. Now, a mist from outside had entered, uninvited, and had begun to coil along the ground like some serpentine shroud. Where Sebastian had led, I followed.

"Sebastian." I might as well have spoken, given the volume of my hoarse whisper. There was no reply. By now, the mist from outside had not only begun to make its way into the little vestibule into which the door had led but was now silently making its way up the staircases. There was no sign of Sebastian. The ancient stone floor felt as cold as a corpse beneath my feet. This part of the house was almost unknown to me. It was less the rural estate in which we usually lived and more a country retreat. Strange paintings looked down from the walls, strange in that they were supposed to be of my forebears. Was I really the culmination of that near-extinct, effete lineage? Had people *ever* really looked like that? Where were their eyelashes? Why the pursed lips? Yes, they were strange: otherworldly. There was a creak on a staircase behind me. Stepping through the mist came my friend. He had, evidently, somewhere removed his jacket. Now his white shirt billowed in the gliding motion of his descent. From somewhere he had found a candelabra, in which burned three slender candles. As the rounded staircase brought him a full quarter-circle, he finally faced me. Behind him, light from the night sky swathed his silhouette in translucent darts. Haloed, knee-deep in a carpet of diaphanous, swirling gossamer, he seemed unreal: a phantom of the night.

"Let's have a look around, shall we?" It seems strange to admit that the experience was as much a revelation for me as it was for him. The house was *too* big. This wing I had, maybe, been to once in the last five years. Silently our stockinged feet ascended the stairs. "All these rooms!" It might have impressed some but I think with him it was just a casual observation. He looked at me for a reply but I had none to give.

"How about here?" Sebastian's swarthy fingers took hold of the heavy brass handle and twisted. The door creaked open. He turned to me and, gesturing with his head, beckoned me to follow. The room was neither small nor large, being rather nondescript. At the far end of the room there were a low set of leaded windows, in the Elizabethan manner, that stretched the entire breadth of the wall but a little too low for either Sebastian or myself to look through without bending to do so. Were people ever really that short? In front of the window, and also running the length of the wall, a windowsill large enough to sit upon.

"These bloody candles." I hadn't realised that the flames of Sebastian's candelabra had died. The room seemed well lit but, now that he had drawn my attention to it, it was obvious that all the light in the room came from outside. I walked to the window. By the light of the encroaching night, the whole garden seemed eerie. Multi-hued colours were all becoming the same smoky-blue, punctuated by unknown black shadows. I turned and looked back to Sebastian, who, by now, had placed the candles on the floor and, with his back to me, was endeavouring to light them. My eyes had become accustomed to the brighter light of the garden; by comparison, the room now seemed dark. Looking to the walls, against the ageing whitewash, boxes appeared to be stacked. On the walls themselves, black frames hanging dark pictures. In the gloom, they might have been prints of anything. I looked back to Sebastian, who, by now, had managed to light one of the candles. Standing, he turned.

"We can light the other two from this one." He strode toward me, his attention focused on the job he had set himself. By the time he had reached the window, all three were lit. "Look at that breeze!" I looked at the little flames as he placed them in the window. Far from burning upwards, a chill from the window caused the flame to ripple and splutter at right angles to the wax. "Let's have a look in these boxes, shall we?"

Our eyes soon became accustomed to the dim shadows around the room. Sebastian's attention was captured by a large coffer. Bands of black iron hammered securely into all four sides, in two continuous strips, save for the lid, which was hinged and shut securely with a battered lock. Both Sebastian and I took a few steps toward it, he to the front, I behind.

"Shall we take a look?" I nodded my agreement. The prospect that something secret, something which had lain awaiting rediscovery for so long, was about to be unearthed was made me shiver.

Sebastian kneeled in front of the mighty casket and inspected the lock. Taking it in his fingers he gave it a twist. Rusting metal against rusting metal made a sound that made me wince and him reconsider his plan of approach.

"I'd give it a kick," he said, rising to his feet, "but not without my boots. I'll get something with which I can knock it."

"There look, pass me that gun."

"Gun?" I hadn't noticed a gun. A gun here?

"Yes, behind you." My attention followed the aim of Sebastian's outstretched finger.

"Why is there a gun here?"

"Oh look, does it really matter? I only want something heavy. Pass it to me, will you?" His tone was becoming exasperated. I handed him the gun.

"Make sure it's not loaded."

"Stand back," he said, ignorant of my concern. With a single deft motion, he brought the butt of the gun down upon the padlock. In an instant, it lay broken on the floor. Sebastian handed me back the weapon. "Now then, let's have a look."

Sebastian bent over, clasped the lid where the iron bands were hammered and lifted. The rusting hinges made a creak as they submitted to the force. Removing one hand to rummage inside, he began pulling at something.

"What is it?" The lid obscured my view: whatever it was, it looked shapeless and ragged.

"I don't know. I think it's an animal skin."

"Oh no!" I made no attempt to disguise the sadness in my voice.

"I said I don't know. Pass me a light so I can see a little better." He nodded his head toward the window. By now, the clear moonlit sky had dark and ominous shapes congregating upon it. As I approached the window, I noticed the rain was now splashing against the glass.

"I think there's a storm coming." I was thinking out loud, trying to distract myself. I was about to turn when something caught my attention. There, in the glass - just for a moment - a face had been looking in at me. In the darkness, it had been indistinct, yet there had definitely been *something*. A flash of lightning lashed across the sky. For a moment - a hideous moment - the whole of the room behind me had been reflected in the wet, leaded glass. In that brief instance I could have sworn I saw Sebastian's face transform into that of a wolf, its gaze never distracted from me as he paced the room.

"Sebastian!" I took a step backwards and fell taking the candelabra and candles with me. They tumbled to the floor, the molten wax extinguishing the flame. Worst of all, it left us in total darkness.

"Oh, that's just wonderful." My friend made no attempt to hide the irritation in his voice.

"No, you don't understand. In the window ... I saw you turn into a wolf."

"Really? Well, as Acts twenty, twenty-nine says, 'grievous wolves enter in among you'."

"No, I saw it I swear." Already I had the feeling that he didn't believe me.

"I really think your imagination is playing tricks on you, you know," he said, smiling. "Now I'll have to try and light the candles again."

Sebastian had already forgotten my alarm. I rose to my feet and took a few steps toward the window. As I did so, the moon tore away her veil and shot arrows of pale pearlescence upon the whole of the garden beneath. Had there really been a wolf in the room? As I looked from the window, a large canid form moved with stealth across the garden before suddenly scurrying toward the gate as though it were about to launch an attack on some defenceless prey. As I watched, the form reached the sill of the mighty portal and disappeared beyond. Behind me, muttering, Sebastian struggled with the candles. Dare I tell him what I had seen? This time I chose to keep quiet.

"Let there be light."

"And there was light! Thank you, Lightbringer" Once again, the room relaxed under the golden flickering of the candles.

"Now, let's see what this is." I had quite forgotten the chest. Sebastian began to pull what was left of its contents out and onto the floor. Initially, the shape seemed indistinct but as Sebastian began to smooth out the many folds, we both recognised what it was at the same moment.

"Oh no!" Sebastian said as he dropped what he was holding and sat back. On the floor of that high and dusty room, the skin of a white hart, complete with antlers, lay flat and lifeless. "That is just awful. This breaks my heart. Who would want to kill such a beautiful animal?"

With a movement that was frightening in its suddenness, Sebastian leapt to his feet, took hold of the gun he had used to shatter the lock of the chest, and ran to the window. Without a pause, the butt of the shotgun smashed its way through the glass, before being turned and fired. A roar bellowed across the silent night. Through what remained of the window a cold gust of air, like death on a summer night, entered. The gunfire disturbed a family of crows that had thought their day over and who now left the safety of their black trees and ascended the night sky like ebonised angels.

"Bastard!' He shouted. "You bastard."

In an ever-speedier vortex, the wind began to howl and swirl. Eventually, he leaned forward and rested his hands on the sill beneath the window.

"What's beyond that gate?" he asked. I shrugged my shoulders. "You haven't the courage to look, have you?"

"What do you mean?"

"You know what I mean."

I did know what he meant. There, locked away it was the part of me that was primitive and instinctive. I didn't like it that *he* knew. My upbringing had made unnaturalness seem natural; I could no longer rationalise anything. Everything was sick, affected, decadent and dying. How did he know? Then the thought of that day, years before, when I had had that strange dream and found myself carried through that gate and the journey I had taken beyond it. Was it a madness of my mine to think that my friend had been the man I had met in that place? If that gate - and what lay beyond - was a construct of my own wild imagination then how could it have been peopled with a real-life person? It couldn't, could it?

We faced each other for what seemed like an eternity.

Next day, Sebastian had gone. Later, my father took me aside. His face reddened as he spoke, his tone angrier than it had ever been. His ignoble features bent toward my own. He could never placate or explain, only bully.

"I have made arrangements for you to finish your education at a new school. You start tomorrow." That was it. I knew not to ask why, or for what reason, as it would not get a response, only a beating. My only explanation would be because it was what *he* wanted. I had to convince myself it was for the best. Maybe it would give me a chance to become independent. Maybe if I could leave Sebastian's influence behind then things might be different. Now the decision had been taken for me, I had to tell myself that everything would be easier.

The rest of that day was spent in idle contemplation. Occasional glimpses of the gate brought a strange feeling of awakening. I was aware that in stepping from the garden and, once more, through that gate again might well precipitate the end of everything that had given me an identity. Nonetheless, forbidden fruit is often the most tantalising. It was now hung in vine leaves that bore plump, full grapes, whilst a young quince tree made concerted efforts to establish itself a few short feet away. The gate itself looked almost otherworldly; ethereal, as though all that separated me from complete union with all things natural was its foliage. Some invisible and intoxicating ether seemed to connect me directly to it, floating, iridescent and - if I closed my eyes - like tiny rainbows, exploding worlds, or precious gems bursting into flames. It spoke to me with a sobbing voice but it was then that I remembered my friend.

I thought on my condition that day. Perhaps it *was* time to cast aside childish thoughts now that I stood on the threshold of maturity, but everything seemed so daunting and invasive. For the first time I really understood - and with all my heart - what Sebastian had felt when he had spoken to me of religion and what he wanted from it. I too longed for infinity, for the transcendent, for something to take me out of my squalid insignificance. My garden no longer supplied the escape that it once had. I had to acknowledge that the gate - that portal to another realm - now had more allure than ever.

That night I lay awake, thinking. My bedside lamp flickering; shadows played, danced, and jumped across the walls like nymphs and satyrs. Lying there, something transfigured the uncertainties of the day. If only I could breathe the lotus flower, or wash in the waters of the Lethe. Why *had* I avoided the gate and the change it might wreak upon me? Maybe it was a symbol and a symbol of the transition within me that caused me such uncertainty. If I could welcome that transition then with a few brave steps, both literally and figuratively, I could be free. Blissful thoughts of freedom floated in timeless suspension. For a moment, I felt unbounded joy as thoughts gently rippled in fluid formlessness across my inner eye. Dancing with the shadows, I was a shadow; flickering with the flame, I was a flame. A part of everything as everything was a part of me. No past; no future; only the eternal *now*. White, sterile walls began changing and transforming. Lachrymose autumn tones flooded the room in holy copulation. All manner of artefacts from my dressing table fell to the floor, as though swept aside by an unseen hand. Something life-giving had entered my room. Beating angel wings lifted my curtains so that the heavy fabric seemed to shake in anticipation. Then, a face in the night. With a shatter, the large windows opened. White walls began turning crimson as a sphere of light entered, radiating a spectrum of colours around my small room. From the depths, a figure swirled and gyrated sinuously and sensuously. Drones, like chants intoned in a medieval monastery, seemed to herald a fanfare to my goddess. Thick plumes of incense swirled and clouded, heavy skeins coiling snake-like over everything they gently touched. Slowly, the music ground on as she moved with the same slow eroticism as the feathers of perfume around her. Her lithe, tanned body - the colour of ancient cinnamon from some far distant spice trail - adorned in decoration as exquisite as the form upon which they rested. Silver; gold; gem upon gem framed and accentuated her perfect symmetry. Every beautiful facet of those precious stones seemed to compliment and extol the aspect of their peers. Then the face! Lips as red as a wound; eyes blacker than a sinner's soul; skin as taut as the sinews of my heart - a heart which looked, and died - upon such perfection! Even the tresses of hair framed the most perfect of portraits. Come closer, my lady without mercy! Each century of her moving brought pain and pleasure. Ah, to touch! Suddenly, each thin layer of fabric that covered me was torn aside in a movement unseen. Cool hands on hot, damp skin.

"Who are you?" I mumbled incoherently, every fractured nerve longing for her lacerating caress.

"I am Lillith. I am Salome. I am the spirit of Sodom," she breathlessly intoned, her lips running a burning course upon my moist skin. Bared teeth sank into my soft neck, painlessly opening a vein. I closed my eyes in ecstasy as my lifeblood spurted forth into her eager mouth, besmearing lips in crimson stains. Only the agitated, irregular fluttering of my heart - like the beating wings of an eagle in a gilded canary cage - came to my ears. Then, the low murmur of delight: the deep, guttural groan of her consummated desire. A new, strange consciousness swept over me as my angel of the pit began to lick, like a wild beast with its new offspring. Beneath that mouth, my ethereal form stirred. In an instant, all that connected an eternal part of me to the temporal prison of the flesh was a shimmering silver thread, like a cool brook on a summer's day.

"Sebastian." Her heavy-lidded, satisfied eyes could barely open as her stained lips shaped the whispered words.

"No, I'm not Sebastian," I replied in stupefied and distant confusion.

"Sebastian," again her soft breath brushed my naked skin. "Sebastian." Floating; hypnotising.

"Is this death? Am I dead?"

"Not dead, but dreaming," she murmured as she drew her nails down my chest. Pathways of light now reached from my room to the horizon. Out, over the garden; out, over the trees, valleys, mountains: a pathway safe and eternal. Onward we went, high above towns and cities. Over measureless expanses of purple-black water shimmering in mercury night. Onward, ever onward, to a dark wood. There, a flame consumed the still and silent night. There, too, we stopped: where earth joined air; air joined fire; fire met water, we spiralled to the ground.

In the distance, an elevated platform supported a throne, yet in the blackness, nothing seemed to stir: sublime space! My companion placed her finger to my lips and pursing her own mouth gestured for my silence. An unearthly quietness followed broken only by a distant, thunderous procession. A thousand pounding cloven hooves presaged dark and fearful shapes appearing out of the gloom with what, I felt, were all-seeing eyes. Horned gods, antlered and as wild as stags. Sinuous forms like panthers, leopards. Great animals pulling chariots adorned with leaves from this sylvan glade. Strange beasts emerged; men and women carousing in ecstasy. Then, the great god enthroned with syrinx and crook clutched close. Dust turned to fertile earth. Couples raced naked to cool waters: anointing and baptizing the earth in holy copulations. I speak of joy and holy communions! Bodies; flames; naked skin glistening, inflamed by fire; desire.

Dancers whirled in circles, shrieking and laughing. In the midst, turning, the great beast had features known to me: Sebastian!

What had gone so terribly wrong as a child when communion with nature had been as natural as breathing? Like an empty vessel, had I turned to Sebastian for succour? He was nature whilst I was ... something wrong. To be loved only drew my suspicions for what was there to love? I could only return love with hostility, testing the other's affections and bitterly congratulating myself when I had succeeded in turning love to hate. To love would be to allow a thawing of what lay within and to give away a deep and secret thing; what if that were then rejected? How could I ever communicate the *real* me, anyhow? People only like others for the feelings they elicit within *them*. Love is always a selfish act, even if we like to think otherwise. People might listen, but how many are really interested? Sebastian had been right to think the transcendent an incommunicable thing. What about my unique experience? Always it would tinge the happiest of experiences with hues of melancholia.

I awoke with a jolt. My light had gone, not that that mattered anymore. The first rays of the morning had joined in majestic union with the earth, lighting the room in a coy brilliance. I arose, strode to the door and opened it. A brief look back confirmed what I had been thinking: the room, if nothing else, was as it had always been.

Thinking of the night before was difficult. Surely it had all been a phantasmagorical flight of fancy? Now, in the penetrating light of day, it all seemed so vague. Perhaps it was better for it to remain that way. Ah, bittersweet memories! What was the past? An intangible breath that only supplied phantoms to haunt the present. My memories were of no importance to anyone except me. For good or bad they were, nonetheless, unique. What, after all, did any of us have? A dead past; a future that never comes; a present that is instant history. All I had was myself, and how fragile that was! All truth could ever be was what I wanted it to be because my truth might be a lie to another. That day I took a step into the unknown, away from Christian absolutes, away from what other people wanted me to be. It was a difficult, stumbling step, for one harsh word from another would always cause me to tumble. In order to make the rules, one needed to play the game

Temptation

yet, often, I felt too hidebound to even participate.

I made my way to the kitchen. I knew my father would have already left, so at least my mother and I would be able to talk in peace. I opened the door. There, at the far end of the room stood that cherished frame: she whom I adored. I had thought my bare feet to be silent on the old stone floor as I approached, but that notion was soon dispelled,

"Morning, dear." She busied herself at the old porcelain sink, lifting a hand to crank the water pump that, even then, must have been a hundred years old. Finally, she turned. A dark shade on her cheek spoke volumes. Ought I to mention it? The closeness of our bond made the silence all the more awkward. Trying to look anywhere save the hideous bruise upon her delicate face my eyes were, nonetheless, drawn to that place and no other.

"I hit it on a door this morning." Already she had guessed what I was thinking, or maybe her own sensitivity to the disfigurement wished to draw my attention to it before she thought I had noticed.

"Did you?" It was painful to see how she felt it necessary to lie, even to me. Did she think she was protecting me? Protecting her husband? Guilt had fastened itself to our family like a horrible tumour. There was a long pause.

"No, you know I didn't, don't you?" I raised my eyes from the floor to meet her gaze. There could be no more untruths. However painful the experiences, she and I bore them *together* - a partnership forged in suffering. We had the mother and son relationship, but more than that we were now allies fighting a common enemy. What if she still did still love him? It was more a love for what he once was rather than the person he had become, I was sure. I hated him for the way he had taken her love and thrown it to one side as though it were something worthless. What could I now say?

"Yes, I know. I've always known." The words weren't that comforting, but such a situation often makes the right words difficult ones.

"Have you?" There didn't seem any hint of a surprise in her response. Maybe his success had been that all her responses were now flat, dead, ones. "I'm so sorry."

"Sorry for what?" It seemed incredible that, despite it all, she still blamed herself.

"I didn't want it to be like this." She, too, seemed to be struggling for the right words to say. Her brow knitted. Her eyes closed, yet tears still began running down her face. "I wanted to give you a good life. I wanted you to be happy. He wasn't always like this. He was a good man ... once."

"We can't go on like this." I tried to imagine her desperation. I felt trapped but knew one day I would be able to leave, whereas her life must have felt like an eternal punishment. Her only option was to stay and hope he would change, meanwhile suffering the bullying and tyranny that had come to constitute their marriage.

"I can't imagine my life without him. I still love him." This time the tears came in floods. Turning away from me she bent over the kitchen sink and sobbed.

What could I do? After all, I had to leave that day. How could I leave a situation, like this? Did that man realise what he was doing to the both of us? Did he even care? For a moment I turned away. The sight of my mother, crushed, was just too pitiful. My attention came to rest on the door that, moments earlier, had hastened my entrance. There was that dent in it. I must have been about ten years of age when I saw him pull her by the arm, swinging her into it, then his concern for the damaged door.

"You must do something." I turned to face her. Already she had composed herself and was wiping the tears away on a little white handkerchief.

"I'll be alright. You go to your new school and enjoy yourself. When you come home again everything will be alright, you'll see." I don't think she believed the words but, for her sake, I mustered a smile. I had intended to bewail my own misfortune at having to attend a new school. Now, my pain seemed insignificant. I felt guilty. Looking at her, she seemed different. For the first time, she had become more than just a mother. She was unique - a person with the same dreams, hopes, ambitions, and loves, as anyone else. Why should she be denied the right to love, and be loved, by someone who could feel no one's suffering but his own? My mother was beautiful, yet blighted by tragedy. Something, somewhere, had gone horribly wrong for her, yet she bore it all with dignity. Her blue eyes as deep as an ocean looked at me with pride. All her dreams were invested in me. If I let myself down, then I would be letting *her* down.

"Do you think it will be a good school?" I tried to change the subject, to speak of lighter things and to lift her spirits a little, so that she might dream it a wonderful place: a place where her son could be happy, his happiness, in turn, bringing happiness to her.

"I'm sure it will." A light came from deep within her eyes and a smile stole over her face.

A little while later, after a final preparation, a little time was left to kill before the carriage would come to take me away from this place. The last days of summer made everything appear elegantly decayed. Yes, everything *would* be alright because it *had* to be. It may have been an argument, I had told myself a hundred times, yet each time the statement seemed more and more absurd. Perhaps everything *was* as it should be. Perhaps everything was right because it had been ordained that way. But then how could that be? How could any god see the torment being meted out on this good woman and stand by and do nothing?

Without realising, my wanderings around the garden had led me to the gate. It no longer seemed terrifying. Now, it appeared benevolent and kind. Nonetheless, something made me stop. To go any further would be to confront something that, from my earliest days, I had denied. Dare I embrace something that unknown, dark, and unfettered? There were serpents in my garden. Only on the distant horizons were there waterfalls drenching all creation in a rich ablution, washing life into the inanimate. Out there - somewhere - was freedom; salvation. People passed: I stood among them, but not of them; in a shroud of thoughts which were not their thoughts. To sleep; to die; to break these chains of convention.

Later that day I started my new school. My experiences there were painful ones so I shall not dwell, to any great degree, on my time there. The regime there was very different from my previous school. Even the building was markedly different, in every respect. My old school had once been a nunnery, converted into a seat of learning after the decline of Catholicism in Wales. The building itself had been splendid in its gothic pretensions: corridor upon corridor that seemed to lead to nowhere; dank, dark passages which, in my naiveté, I believed might well have led to hell.

Temptation and Denial

My new school was just a few miles from the old one, but might as well have been a few thousand. One might have supposed that it would have had the same ambience of religious degeneration as the old school given that it was once an old rectory. There, however, the similarity ended.

My tutor - Mr Torquemada - seemed intent on making my days there as unbearable as possible. Discipline was harsh and executed with zeal but always, of course, under the aegis of piety. To him, pleasure was a sin. In retrospect, every sentence that the man uttered stank of control cloaked as Christian morality. Even subjects I had previously enjoyed became painful as the self-righteous Mr Torquemada sought to impose his will upon mine. He was the mortar and Christianity the pestle, whilst I - the grain - was ground to dust between the two.

A solitary light burned in the darkness: Lillian. She was another pupil at the school, yet she was different. A part of me moved with her. In her free, easy manner, elements of Sebastian evinced themselves. She moved with grace, dignity, and deportment. She, unlike myself, appeared proud of the person that she was. I longed to talk to her but how could I muster the courage when I knew I could do nothing for her?

That academic year passed with dismal slowness. By attrition, Mr Torquemada finally succeeded in suppressing all that was natural within me yet all the while Lillian inflamed such natural desires, leaving me feeling both guilty and disgusted.

By the end of that year, my love for Lillian was boundless and immeasurable. Every part of me wanted to be a part of her. It's true to say that I would have died for her.

Nonetheless, a pitiless sun beat upon my sole oasis; a serpent that fastened itself into every part of me. Being so tightly bound by artifice, there, at last, came a point of no return. I had left something raw and essential behind so long ago that, at times, it seemed to have never been there at all.

By June, my school days were nearing completion and my sense of doom had increased tenfold. All around me life, as I thought it was meant to be lived, was in decay; putrefying bodies of joy. Why? With the bony hand of self-doubt upon my shoulder, feelings magnified in the presence of my father. My head spun in turmoil as I thought of things and with no release, I began

Temptation

physically hurting myself so that my mental anguish had some release. It started with needles but progressed to nicking my arms with a cut-throat razor. It wasn't healthy - I knew that - yet seeing the blood flow down my arm and spill into a white porcelain sink felt like a release. If only Sebastian and I had still been friends. I missed him. His company was timeless: fresh. He was everything I aspired to be but was told to abhor. Many things had changed since we last met: Mr Torquemada, father, Christianity and the patriarchal system, it seemed, had given me an identity. However miserable life was, I was told, death would bring its just rewards.

On the last day of term, the shapeless spirituality that had been floating inside me, at last, seemed to coalesce into a very definite shape. As I sat in the dusty classroom listening to Mr Torquemada's final lesson - on how physical pleasure had been sent by the Devil and that we must all seek to rise to a more spiritual plane - it dawned on me how I could escape *all* temptations. By taking up the cloth, how could evil ever tempt me again? If putting aside hedonistic pursuits for a life of quiet prayer was the only way it could be done, then so be it.

I left school in a state of near ecstasy. At last, there was a focus in my life that concurred with all the doctrines I had been taught! My feet trailed lightly up a little side street, toward the centre of the town and, from there, the carriage home. With downcast eyes, the narrow, cobbled street seemed as if it were mile upon mile below me. A terrible teratism had finally lost its grip on me. Steps angelic; heavenly. A liquid sun wept and bled; in the east cherubim and seraphim guarded a tree bearing strange fruit. Between us, a flaming sword turning, as I turned. Diaphanous mists, as delicate as lace; clouds. A holy tree, beckoning. Streams of fire emanating from the rubied enclaves of Endymion, cloaking the land in flames of elemental purgation. Burning, in the robe of Nessus, burning! A strange calling. Onwards; upwards; reptiles groaning. Cherubs falling like rain. Centuries of dust and sand, congealed and conspiratorial. Half-glimpsed shapes. Funeral pyres burning my corpse on branches torn from the Tree of Life.

When I opened my eyes, a dark and indistinct figure stood over me, yet a shape familiar, a shape I thought had cast me aside: Sebastian.

Looking around, I sought to make sense of it all. The tree, the sword, the fruit, and the cherub were all gone. I lay where I had fallen: at the side of the road. It took no more than a few brief moments to register that it had all been a waking dream. Finally, Sebastian pierced the silence.

"Well, it has been a long time."

"Sebastian, you look dreadful," I said, causing him to laugh.

"Well, thank you." His once handsome visage had become gaunt and drawn. His clothes clung to him like tattered rags on a corpse. His fingernails were long, broken, and so filthy one might have suspected he had been tilling soil. Even his eyes were dull. "I am ashes where once I was fire." He affected a theatrical pose before his lips parted and, once again, a smile spread across his face. It was wonderful to see him. It felt as though a fresh breeze had blown away the autumn leaves of uncertainty.

"What have you been doing?" he asked. As he spoke, I realised I was still lying in the gutter by the side of the road. It seemed ironic that I should be contemplating his fall from grace when mine appeared to have laid me equally low. I wanted to tell him that I was about to enter the church but felt acutely embarrassed at having to say so, or that I had even considered it.

"What have *you* been doing?" It was the best answer I could think of as I sensed his question had been rhetorical. He didn't answer but, instead, extended a hand and helped me to my feet.

"I know," he said casually.

"Know what?" I knew what he meant, my face burning with embarrassment.

"What your plans are." It was unnerving and seemed as though every thought I thought had been written down for him to read.

"My ... my ..." I began to stammer. My stammer would betray me if nothing else would.

"Come on, don't stammer! I'm not your father. You've no need to be frightened of my response. Just don't think you can keep it from me. I know you plan to join the church." I didn't know how he knew, only that he did. What could I say? To tell him he was mistaken would have been a lie; to tell him that I was, would have been to betray myself as weak and someone in need of such a crutch. "I'm not going to condemn you for it. You must follow the path that is right for *you*. If you think that what you're doing is right, go ahead - with my blessing. That said, you and I both know that it is not really what you want. You want freedom. Are you going to get that by entering a prison?"

"But I can *never* be free - not now. Too much has happened. I can't make a single decision without thinking 'what would so and so want me to do', or 'is this right as a Christian'? I've had so many absolutes foisted upon me I've lost my identity. Everything would be so much easier if I surrendered completely."

"Nobody said it would be easy. Without God, life is anguish, abandonment, and despair but that is the price we pay if we want freedom. Life is oh so cosy, isn't it, when you have universal laws of right and wrong to guide you on your way? Well, let me tell you, nothing is *ever* as straightforward as that. Even murder might be right in the right circumstances. For me, the great object of life is sensation - to feel we exist, even if in pain." By now he had straightened up and had begun walking, taking me with him. With his gaze set on the ground in front of him, every word seemed deliberate and well-chosen, as though he were wrestling with each one so that he could clarify his point as clearly as possible, lest any ambiguities elicited a confused understanding on my part.

As he spoke, his words sliced me like a sabre. On an instinctive level, they seemed true yet all I had been taught considered them wrong. Dual feelings began tearing me apart. I knew my failings, but the brutal way Sebastian had confronted them was crushing. I hated myself for being weak and hypocritical. I hated my father for forging me into something I despised. I was a mess; a wreck, incapable of taking control of the forces within my own life. I had been tyrannised, bullied, beaten; my will crushed to annihilation. Every action I had ever made had been prey to scorn, derision and mockery by him or, conversely, unwarranted praise by those who could see the effect his actions had on me. All I ever wanted was the truth! How could Sebastian advocate self-creation without acknowledging *those* factors?

Tears began to roll down my face. Not tears of physical pain, but tears of loss, hopelessness, frustration, and rage. I had lost something apparently irretrievable. I clung to my refuge, and he to me.

"I really think we need to talk about a few things, but you've got to believe in me," he continued.

"I do, I do." Nervously, I laughed. Sebastian straightened. Almost at once, he seemed reanimated and colour flushed his cheeks. I knew I needed something beyond time, space, and reality: something deep and arcane. At the bottom of my soul burned fires of rage, indignation, and torment; of something hopelessly crestfallen yet still proud and noble. If he could nurture all that I wasn't going to turn him away.

"Then meet me in your garden tonight." My thoughts seemed to drift away into the cool evening, thoughts as heady and intoxicating as the finest opium. Destiny began to unfold itself like a giant magic carpet. In what seemed like an instant, Sebastian was gone.

My ride home was swift, my mind too alive to notice my surroundings or the passing of time; I was travelling on a journey of greater magnitude. Finally, I turned the road that approached my house but as soon as I saw it standing dark and resolute against the mountain and dark trees my heart seemed to leap into my throat, and all the fears of childhood came surging back. Clattering across the night sky, hooves from ghostly, unseen nags. Desperate, baying, howling hounds. High above, in the evening empyrean, sunbeams flowed like tears. Who will mourn the death of the white hart and a loss of innocence? Now, to return to satisfied smiles that celebrated unreal kingdoms.

How I made it from the carriage I shall never know, nor how I made it to the house and opened the door that penetrated the inner sanctum. A huge and hellish fire glowed and spat in the hearth like molten iron. No other light, other than the one in the grate, lit the room leaving much of the room in an awful gloom, neither light nor dark. Reality; unreality. Flames hungrily consumed the once-living wood so that it hissed and cracked in apparent agony. Then, the figure that ruled this ghastly place.

"I'm ... I'm ... I'm home." Once I had struggled to get the words out, they left a taste in my mouth as bitter as wormwood. Home? This was no home! I knew that to say anything untoward would only bring his awful twisted wrath down upon me.

"Stop stammering. What are you? A man, or a nervous girl?" His reply was nasal and droning. He moved, seemingly tearing his head away from the winged armchair that had previously kept

Temptation

it from my view. With a slowness terrible to look upon, that head turned until the eyes upon its face met with mine. Sickeningly pallid cheeks seemed to reflect the flames of the fire to such a degree that his whole appearance seemed scalded.

"Where's my mother?" The question fell upon ears that refused to listen.

"You needn't think you're going to spend the whole time under my feet. I've made arrangements for you to attend Bible classes. You might think yourself a man, but you're *nothing*. Maybe the scriptures will make something of you, for I cannot."

With that, he slumped back into the chair. The chief prosecutor had spoken: my fate appeared sealed.

"Where is my mother?" My temerity unnerved me. He still refused to answer. "What has happened to her?"

"Shut your damned mouth! As the great St. Paul said, 'Let the woman learn in silence with all subjection. But I suffer not a woman to teach, nor to usurp the authority of a man, but to be in silence. For Adam was first formed, then Eve. And Adam was not deceived, but the woman being deceived was in the transgression'. She transgressed if you must know. That woman was as worthless as you. I refuse to believe you're *my* offspring." He leaned forward, like some rabid canine. "Why should I - a pious man - have to suffer iniquities in my house? Get out of my sight! You're an offence to me and the Lord."

If I had any doubts about the way I felt, by now they had been fully dispelled. I turned silently away and walked to the garden. Down the steps, a turn right, past the lawn. At first, the stillness of the night made everything appear tranquil. Then, from the shadows, a figure that had been stood by the gate stepped into the last rays of a dying, crepuscular, sun. The great iron edifice swung open and free behind him.

"You wanted to speak to me?" I began before emotion threatened to choke me. Like he who wishes to put an end to life's pale vicissitudes, I felt both anguish and yet a strange calm knowing the race was almost done, like a man holding a loaded gun: unable to go on, yet comforted in knowing that in his hand he has the means to draw a final line under his existence.

Sebastian extended an arm and bade me welcome, gesturing that we both should go beyond the boundary marked by the edge of the lawn and the steps beyond. I wanted him to speak: to allay my fears. I had always known this temptation would be one to which one day I would succumb. Whatever happened now, it did not matter as *nothing* mattered anymore.

I took a step, then paused. What would happen next? If I were to reject my whole education then what would replace it? In doing so, might I lose *myself*? Already, it felt too late to go back. I took a deep breath and closed my eyes, allowing Sebastian to take my arm and guide me. I don't know what I expected but after a few brief moments, mustered the courage to open my eyes only to find myself deep in a darkening forest. Initially, it felt as though I were alone as I had lost all trace of the narrow path. Shadows that I had once feared, as silent as the grave, seemed to envelop me in verdant arms like a mother nurturing an infant.

"Sebastian!" In the darkness I could see his indistinct outline, drawing nearer, becoming more definite. He didn't answer: perhaps that was the way of one grown feeble from long being mute.

"We need to make our own path if we want to be clear of this place," he said, taking my arm and leading me toward the copse from whence he had stepped. The velvet canopy above us was so dense it appeared to be a thick brocade stretching upward and around us like a soft blanket. Somewhere, high above us, branches moved like swaying limbs allowing near-pellucid silver shafts to light our way. Here we were safe in this unspoilt cocoon. From liquid night, from darkest shade, Sebastian again stepped toward me.

"Let's sit down. I want to talk to you about your faith." He made his way to a clearing and sat, making himself comfortable, before he continued.

"How do you think religion began?" The question seemed a rhetorical one as before I could answer he continued. "Let us go back to the origins of all religions. We understand now, that people die from all manner of unseen causes, but did people always think like that? What of the person who sees her, apparently healthy, offspring perish for, ostensibly, no reason and an old man survive? What conclusion would the savage mind have come to, seeing seemingly healthy young people die, and sick, elderly, people recover? Of course, knowing little of medicine, the reasons were not explicable by natural causes, but by the supernatural. Thus, evil or good forces were deemed to have willed events to have occurred. Disease, attack, a good or bad harvest, were nothing more than the agents by which those malignant or benevolent forces manifested themselves." He paused for breath and nodded to me for me to acknowledge my understanding. I nodded back. "Now, far from God making man in his own image - which is a ludicrous vanity of man - humanity - typically - made gods in *their* image. Initially, gods were the souls of trees, plants, and animals, all of whom were propitiated as they ensured the primitive's life or death. How long before the tree spirit became a forest god? This is an important change, for, after losing its tenancy over any one particular tree, the forest god became an abstract figure. I'm sure you'd agree with me that humanity's one proclivity is to clothe abstract forms with concrete human shapes."

"Go on. I think I follow you." It didn't seem as profound as what Sebastian had to say, but I was anxious for him to continue. He smiled and brought his hand to his mouth, as though he were struggling with his thoughts before continuing.

"Already then, we have nature gods. How long do you think it would have been before those gods were venerated? How long before every good or bad spirit was subordinated to a good or bad god?" He paused again, before standing.

"Sebastian?" It appeared as though he were about to walk away. He raised a finger to his pursed lips, gesturing for my silence.

"So then, the early gods associated with plants and animals, by their nature, must have been associated with the continued survival of whichever plant or animal with which they were associated. Continued survival necessitated procreativity and fertility. Thus, many of the early gods were fertility gods, because they ensured survival in what were often very hard circumstances. Nearer our own time, Plato posited a theory of 'Ideal Forms'. Loosely, his idea was that heaven - though not the conditional Christian Heaven - had the perfect image of everything we have on earth. We, in the world of matter, had only pale shadows of these originals. Thus, in Platonic thought, matter was deemed inferior to spirit. Couple this idea with the earthly,

Temptation and Denial

carnal gods of fertility, and how long do you think it would be before those gods came to be vilified? Look at Pan - half-man, half-goat, with hairy legs, horns, cloven hooves, huge genitals! Now, where have I seen *that* image before?" His face affected confusion before breaking into a smile. "I tell you, the god of the old religion always becomes the devil of the new. Look at what the Christians of the middle-ages did to those warm, sensual gods of nature - they turned them into demons. Do you know why fertility cults were suppressed? Because the faith of Judaism, virtually appropriated by Christianity, considered immortality as attainable only through one's offspring. As they say, 'It's a wise father that knows his own child'. That's why that faith esteemed a faithful woman 'far above rubies'. Do you think fertility cults would have been so suppressed if it were men who bore the child? Of course not! They would have been sure their offspring were theirs, so faithfulness and the absurd notion that the only virtuous woman is *virgo intacta* would not have even been a cause of concern."

"God forbid!"

"Yes, unfortunately, he does!" We laughed, as I leaned back on my elbows, and stretched out my legs. Again, I wanted to let him continue, lest I break his flow of thought.

"Look at the Devil and God." By now, he was becoming more animated. Pacing up and down, he began to use his hands to reinforce the spoken word. "Both of them evolved from nature Gods, with a little help from Persia and the Old Testament. In the early years of Christianity, many people thought of God and the Devil as equal powers, given that good cannot create evil. This was eventually deemed heretical since no power could be equal to God. In the year five-sixty-three, the Council of Braga decided that no power could be equal to God since God created *everything*. If that is the case, then God *must* have created evil! Some versions of the Bible have God saying, in Isiah forty-five and seven, 'I form the light and create darkness. I make peace and create evil. I, the Lord, do all these things'. We might well ask ourselves what sort of a monster God really is, given that little outburst! On the other hand, many Biblical passages also acknowledge God's failure to administer power on earth. Doesn't John twelve and thirty-one, call Satan 'Prince of this world?' Corinthians four and four, goes even further, calling Satan 'God of this world'. Not bad for a former nature spirit!" Sebastian's face creased into a smile. He paused and looked to the ground. "Can you see where this is leading?" He seemed concerned that he should speak with clarity.

"Yes, of course." It seemed obvious that he was stripping away the sacred aspect of Christianity, explaining it as nothing more than one of many creation myths.

"In Matthew four and nine, we find Satan taking Christ to the top of a mountain to show him the world, promising 'All these things I will give thee if thou wilt fall down and worship me' and it is quite explicit that such treasures are Satan's to give but - really - what nonsense! And it is this passage - along with a few others - that led to the *supposed* worship of Satan and the *actual* torture, rape, murder and cruelty inflicted on thousands of innocent people by Christians during the Witch-Hunts and Inquisition. Let's look at the Bible: have you noticed just how many inconsistencies there are within those pages? Let's stay with the Devil. Doesn't Matthew thirteen and forty-two, call hell 'a furnace of fire' whilst Job ten and twenty-one calls it 'a land of darkness, of darkness itself'. Not a great inconsistency, perhaps, but there *are* some important ones.

"The Biblical account of creation says God made the world in five days, then on the sixth day made man, before resting on the seventh. Isn't this flatly contradicted in Genesis, chapter two, which tells us that God made heaven and earth, then he made Man? On the third day came the Garden of Eden, fourthly came the beasts and fowl and lastly the forming of a woman from a man's rib. This second version gave us Eve, supposedly responsible for The Fall. Perhaps that is why Anselm of Canterbury wrote 'woman has a lovely face and a lovely form. She pleases you not a little this milk-white creature! But ah! If her bowels were opened and all the regions of her flesh, what foul tissues would this white skin be shown to contain'. Needless to say, Anselm is held in high esteem by the church! You think the Bible an upholder of virtue? Then ask yourself who Adam and Eve's sons married. Having children with one's own sister - a sister not even worthy of being named! - was obviously not as great a sin as stealing a loaf of bread to feed one's starving family, or worshipping a god of one's own choosing.

"Because of the absurd notion that, in the guise of the serpent, and as 'God of this world', Satan had the ability to offer secret knowledge, the scientific quest was - for centuries - thought to be acquired only with the Devil's help. This condemned many to lives of disease, poverty, desperation, and ignorance. St. Paul - as we might expect - even denied women pain relief in childbirth, thinking that, given Eve's `transgression' woman shall be saved in child-bearing thanks to a passage in Genesis that states 'in sorrow thou shalt bring forth children'. Now, let us look at this matter. If, for a moment, we put aside the knowledge that Christianity only developed from paganism and that God is the divine creator then what can we say of God? Given all the atrocities in the world, we must conclude that God either *wills* such events or is *powerless* to do anything to prevent them. Given the latter is impossible - because a Christian God is seen as omnipotent - we must conclude that God *wills* these atrocities. I know that you may say 'God gave us free will so it is us who are at fault', but what sort of a monster would not stay the hand of a cold-blooded murderer if it were in his power to do so?

"I'm sure you're well aware of the 'Thou shalt not suffer a witch to live', in Exodus twenty-two and eighteen. Intolerant, you might say, but what would you say upon realising that in Paulian Christianity *anyone* not of Paulian faith was deemed a witch? At various times Jews, Muslims, Cathars, Waldenses, Albigenses, Manicheists have all been called witches. Protestants and Catholics have even called each other by the name! Would St. Paul have had them all killed? And what of pagan witches? No witch worships the Christian Devil! The Devil is a part of the Christian tradition so why would a pagan witch - often knowing *nothing* of Christianity - worship a Christian Devil? Do you know why the Witch Hunts and the Inquisition were so popular? Because it gave those in a position of power a rod with which to break the backs of the poor people that they deemed undesirable. Religion had *nothing* to do with it even if that was the name under which it was perpetrated - it was simply persecution. As we might have expected from such a misogynistic creed, many of the victims were women, but what did that matter? It wasn't until the Council of Trent met in the middle of the sixteenth century, that women were even deemed to have souls! Even then, it was only passed by a majority of three!" Sebastian let out a sigh, and sat down, next to my recumbent form.

"I find that unbelievable," I said after waiting a while to see if he'd finished. There had been so many facts in what he had said and every one seemed more extreme than the last. Just what sort of a faith had twisted my lifelong thinking?

"I know. If you read it in a novel you might disbelieve it, but every word is true. How can we have any respect for people who carry on that tradition?" He looked at me with raised eyebrows and an inquisitive look. I knew to whom he was alluding.

"Well, even the Devil can quote scripture for his own ends", I muttered, pondering what he had said.

"Yes, I can. I mean, yes, *he* can", Sebastian said, accentuating what he had said with an inscrutable wink.

"Have you finished?" I wished to avert his attention.

"No. Look what God has done to the Devil - the fallen angel who dared to question the authority of God, and who was then cast into the pit, to forever rail against a smugly triumphant power. Is that a God of forgiveness and mercy? It's not even a god of law and justice. It's the act of a monster.

"But do you know what? I hate the fact that Christianity capitalises on people's fear of death by promising conditional immortality. It's only a form of control perpetuated by those in power. Be a good boy and you'll go to heaven but be a bad boy and you'll go to hell. It's the greatest confidence trick ever!"

With that, we both fell silent. For a long time, both of us stared at the floor in quiet contemplation. Finally. Sebastian spoke.

"Come on. Let's head home." He stood up and offered a hand to help me to my feet. This time, however, I was able to rise unaided. Sebastian smiled.

As we entered again the sweet, summer garden, things appeared to have altered: again, the garden provided the solace I had felt as a child. Suddenly, a door slammed causing Sebastian to pull me into the shadows.

"It's your father," he said, his eyes training upon the sinister figure at the top of the steps, a figure scouring the garden. Sebastian raised a finger to his lips, gesturing for my silence.

"What's he doing?" My whisper was hoarse.

"If you be quiet for a moment, we'll see."

Satisfied that the garden was empty, the threatening shape that towered above us locked the back door and made his way to the road upon which, just a few hours before, I had walked.

"I'm going to follow him. Come on." I said, but Sebastian stood firm. "What? What is it?" If we were to follow, we needed to take our leave quickly,

"I think you should go alone. You don't need me."

"Why do you say that?" Already I knew there would be no convincing him otherwise. "Are you going to come with me, or not?"

"No." He bowed his head. "You go. I'll meet you here tomorrow."

There was no time to argue. If I delayed my leaving any longer the hope of a pursuit would be lost.

I ascended the steps, quickly, and silently made my way to the road. There, in the distance, was the dark silhouette I wished to follow. It wasn't long before my nocturnal pursuit took on a more concerted, obvious, purpose. No longer did the figure in front of me appear to be out for a midnight saunter. There was reason and purpose in his manner and - judging by the numerous furtive glances - a very secret purpose to his journey.

A mist that had covered the whole area was beginning to lift. As we entered the old part of the town that led down to the river, there was a final glance over his shoulder before the shape in front made an abrupt turn up a squalid side street. I had to keep up with him and tried to silently run on the old cobblestones. Despite the mist, I could see quite clearly. Suddenly, he stopped and looked behind in what, I thought, was my direction. I hid in the shadows. Quickly, he removed a key from a pocket before leaning close to a door and trying to open it. I was close enough to hear the key fall to the ground. In the moonlight, it shone, like a fish in a dark pool. Stooping, he picked up his lost trophy. This time, however, the door opened for him. Like Jonah and the whale, he was quickly swallowed and the door closed behind him, I made my way to the window of the house my father had entered. Three figures sat at a table, in the middle of the sparsely furnished room. Moving to give myself a better vantage point, one face came into view: Lillian! The object of my unrequited love sat opposite two figures, both of whom had their backs to me.

"Lillian, go to your room," a woman barked before standing

and gesturing toward the stairs. No sooner had the young woman left, then the figure I had followed through the darkened streets thrust himself upon his female companion, frantically tearing at her clothes, whilst she - laughing - eased open her fastenings, hastening the work of his clumsy fingers. Pulling the woman to the floor, both sets of hands then set to unbuttoning his attire. Lank hair fell upon bleached and pitted skin. I had seen enough; I turned and made my way home.

Next day was spent in my garden; it was as it had been when I was a child. I was desperately worried about my mother and where she might be as she'd still not returned home. I'd made up my mind that if she had not returned by the following day, I would visit her acquaintances and see if she was with them but a dreadful, empty feeling told me something awful might have happened. Ought I to have acted on that hunch so soon? It was difficult to know. With the lengthening shades of the afternoon, an indistinct contour appeared on the road, before stepping nearer: it was my friend, Sebastian.

"I'm not sure about this," he said, despite his voice betraying no sense of uncertainty.

"About what?" I didn't remember asking him to do anything for me.

"About going to that house with you tonight."

"How do you know about that house? How did you know I even *intended* going there again, and that I was going to ask you to come with me?" It unnerved me. How did he know?

"Am I wrong, then?" Always, he seemed so assured.

"Well, you know you don't have to come if you don't want to, but why don't you?"

"I feel as though I'm intruding. There's a bond of blood that I can never be a part of. You should go and go *alone*," his final word seeming to echo all around me.

"Well, I *am* going. Will you stay here?"

"Of course - *always*." Again, his final word had a resonance.

I stepped out of the familiar confines and was soon making my way through the darkening streets, the silence as harrowing as a distant howl. It was a clear night: a full moon, in fact. Although the road I had to take I had seldom walked before it seemed known to me. It lay before me, like a shining river making its way to the ocean. Sebastian's sombre mood had sapped my enthusiasm, leaving me enervated. Like a cat stalking a bird, though, enthusiasm played no part in the actions - it was instinctive.

Soon I came to the Norman gate that separated the outlying areas from the town. Clouds, like sepia-tinged funereal veils, that previously shrouded the moon were gone: my way was illuminated.

Something deep and primitive had become a welcome guest somewhere within me. For the first time, it felt as though there was something *whole* taking charge and shaping my destiny – and that thing was me. At last, I had recognised my gaoler, executioner, and undertaker. Freedom would finally come only upon the destruction of that unholy trinity.

There was the little house. I knew who would be there. In the still of the night, one light burned, high above me, the rest of the house lying as dark as a spent seam in one of the local coal mines. I clambered up, and then upon, a porch that happened to be fortuitously placed beneath the window from which the light emerged. From there I could see everything.

There, standing proud above a tiny single bed, was my father. Beneath him, blankets barely covered a form, yet not covering the face I instantly recognised as Lillian's. A sickening, familiar smile flushed his bloated face as he began to undo his belt. One brief sentence unfolded the entire story. Cowering under the thin fabric, one pitiful strain broke the night air.

"No, Dad, no."

That one utterance transformed our lives. The girl for whom I had harboured a passion was a product of the same loins as me. I had loved my sister! Now her father - our father - was about to ... no, it was too horrible to contemplate. He had bullied, tyrannised, and dominated everyone, in whatever way he could. His hands, his religion, his masculinity, were all tools to be used to gratify his own ends.

What was to be done? Could I just stand by, like God, when it was within my power to stop it? How could any god allow *this* to happen and stand idly aside? It sickened me. If I stood by and did nothing then that would make me as bad as that god. If need be, I had to die stopping him.

Temptation

Punching a hole in the glass, the next thing I remember was facing the man. The initial shatter had caused him some little surprise and he had clutched his waistcoat around himself. His countenance soon changed to a sneer as I made a grab for him - and missed. Everything I hated, everything I could possibly hate, lay housed in that hideous frame in front of me. That face; that sneer.

"Leave her alone ... you destroyed my mother, you destroyed me. You're not going to destroy her as well." Rage made my face throb; my eyes pulsed with the racing rhythm of my pounding heart; the collar of my shirt pressing hard against the bulging veins in my neck.

"Well! Not stuttering for once, girl? Wha ... wha ... wha ... what's it got to do with you? You're both daughters of mine and I'll do what the hell I like with you both." The mocking in his voice broke into a laugh.

Those words - that admission - sealed his fate. I knew then I would either kill or be killed.

"Now, get out!" The smirk on his face withered to a bloody wrath before he laughed again - laughed at my powerlessness; laughed at his oppression. Frozen, I remained motionless. Anger shattered that laugh.

He stepped forward and with a huge, hammering blow, struck me across the side of the head. Everything else in the room faded into darkness. Now, there was just the two of us. The force of the knock had sent me reeling into a wall. Before I could recover, his huge red face came bearing down on me, his wide mouth roaring and slavering.

"Come on, what are you going to do?" I remembered how he had pulled me to the ground and bellowed in my face when I was a child when I had bought him a birthday gift and had tried to sneak that gift into the house without his knowing. He had demanded to know and I, not wishing to spoil the surprise, wouldn't tell. That had been the last gift he had ever received from me. Now, the impotent rage I had long suppressed welled up inside me and I threw him off and leapt to my feet. Unarmed, I would be killed.

I looked for something; anything. The walls? There! There hung a huge, heavy crucifix. I ran toward it, clutched it from its fixings, turned, and with a heavy swing, powered by all the force I could muster, brought it down upon the side of his head. The wound opened up like a stigmata. Trickling at first, then spurting like a crimson stream onto his open shirt.

He stumbled backwards, placing his coarse fingers to the hole, without uttering a sound. He fell to the side of the bed, his blood staining the thin cotton sheets. His discarded apparel fell from the bed and into his life's flow. I looked at Lillian. We stared at each other in mute horror. She looked away as the figure slumped on the floor. I followed her gaze. Somehow, from somewhere, the man had found new life. Before he had the opportunity of a reprise, I ran forward. With all the strength I could muster that old rugged cross was brought down again and again. Every strike opened his wound a little wider, every crisp retort opening the door of the cage that had always locked away the real me. Firm skin and bone gave way to splintered wood and torn blanket, both saturated in blood. Then a bang; a flash of flame; a warm wetness spreading itself across my chest.

In my enthusiasm, I had not noticed the little pistol in his hand. Somehow, in those final moments, nerves - or the contractions of his muscles in their death agony - had managed to squeeze the trigger. The cross dropped from my hand; the hole in my chest began to weep. I looked at he who had fired: hideously the shape, having stood, now began to slide down the wall sideways, before the whole figure hinged at the hip as it negotiated the open space of the broken window. Already dead, the figure sat motionless for a moment. Finally, gravity alone pulled the figure backwards. Like the drop of a sack of grain, a dull thud told us it had hit the pavement below.

So, we come to the present. The last few days have been odd. Sometimes I am aware that I lie in a hospital bed, guards at the door. Other times it feels as though I am home, in my garden: in the eternal Summerland of childhood - or at least those first few years of freedom.

Sebastian? Has Sebastian ever really existed outside of my own imagination? He was the natural and unrecognised aspect of my personality made flesh and blood. Only now that I feel whole can I acknowledge that he was the ideal construct of my mind and all that I wished to be. As the philosopher said, 'Art is long and life is

Temptation

short'. If that is true then Sebastian will live forever for all that can ever survive of us is our imagination and the things that precious gift leaves behind. In this insane, Godless, world he had been the voice of sanity.

Lillian, I am told, has been to visit me but some sort of criminal collusion is suspected so her visits have been denied. What sick mind found gratification in throwing the two of us together in that awful, twisted school?

Now, however, I must stop as I am growing so very weak. Free at last - yet dying. How ironic! The two appear uncomfortable companions for an atheist, yet both are singing, melodiously, sweetly. Mother is beckoning. I must follow. Free - finally free.

Denial

What is the worst of woes that wait on age?
What stamps the wrinkle deeper on the brow?
To view each loved one blotted from life's page,
And be alone on earth as I am now.
                                        Byron

In the old house, high on the Welsh mountain, Lillian sat at a large, carved, and age-darkened desk. Dipping a fountain pen in a small pot of ink she began to write in a beautifully cursive hand, softly speaking the words as she wrote: "I am a sick woman. I am an evil woman. Thorns of melancholy pierce my heart. All I have is the fragile permanence of a few last and precious words. Love has survived he who wrote them, as it survives us all. I remain - unnatural, hateful, insane. No part of nature flows within me."

Lillian closed the journal she had only recently begun to keep and walked from her desk to a window at the far end of the room. From there she could see the whole panorama of the garden, the garden where once her brother had walked. She was still unsure of the house. Until recently it had been peopled by her father and his family, a family of whom she had known nothing. Death had given her wealth. Her father had not intended a woman get his property, but a catalogue of misfortune - his death, the death of his son, a mysterious disappearance - had all left Lillian the sole beneficiary. She had once dreamt of escape: to leave her awful little house behind and live in luxury. Yet luxury was a bloodless consort: she would have traded it all for a life of even moderate happiness. Inside her, there was nothing: a void; a well of loneliness. A feeling familiar to those who yearn to love.

It was raining. Now, the pane of glass that separated her from the outside world had become opaque. Outside, the world remained as cloudy as her warm breath as it hit the cold glass, only to confuse her view of the world even more. Without realising, she raised a finger to etch idly upon her pane. How might life have been if only she had been different; if circumstances had been different? She felt small, frail, vulnerable and alone. It seemed as if some imminent catastrophe, worse than death, awaited her. Suddenly, her eyes focussed on her aimless finger's ramblings: why on earth had she written 'Sebastian'?

"Sebastian," she mouthed silently, her lips barely moving. Her brother's journal had come into her possession and she had read it; she knew the name from that. "Sebastian." What could Sebastian be to her? Perhaps it was that all the other figures in her brother's journal were unfleshed skeletons compared with his depiction, or maybe it was because he alone remained. Who was he? Had he *really* been nothing more than a figment of her brother's imagination? If he was real, would he one day pay her a visit? So much remained uncertain. In her rational moments she told herself that he did not exist yet her heart hoped he did - with a passion - and when has passion ever been a slave to rationality? Deep within her, she wanted him to be real: for him to come to her and make everything right.

Shadows that only the dying rays of an early evening sun can bring had already entered the room. In the eerie gloom, dark shapes were becoming threatening; dangerous. Images seen from the corner of an eye had a life. Only when her attention focussed on them did they lose their terror. Lillian closed her eyes but that was worse as shapes then took on the form of hideous caricatures of her father. She lit a lamp. She could never run away from what had happened because it was a part of her. If only she had never been born, then both her father and brother might still be alive. Sometimes, she sought to shift the burden of guilt to another's shoulders but there was still a bond of blood which, even if she could hate the perpetrator, resulted in her hating herself because a part of him walked with her. The little flame, however, was bright enough to expel the night terrors. Now the room took on a gentle glow. With a swift motion, Lillian turned and drew the curtains. Now she felt safe: shut away from the world.

She had lived alone in the old house now for a few months. It had taken almost a year for her father's finances to be put in order but now that they finally had she found herself a considerably wealthy young woman. Nonetheless, the wealth had become a curse that seemed to have a strange and terrible obligation binding her to it.

Night, with all its dark dominions, is never an easy time especially when every night is a fraught and restless one. As her brother had noted in his journal, the old house groaned and creaked more than most. Now, however, its terrible history populated it with many an unhappy revenant. Sometimes it felt as though she were being buried alive, the cold damp soil failing relentlessly upon the casket in which she felt immured, she being the only living thing amongst century upon century of the dead. Already, the house had begun to drain any enthusiasm she had once had for life. Days became agonies only to be endured. Every night the same pestilence descended upon her lonely rooms.

Denial

Another restless night found Lillian arise unusually early. A slight chink in the curtains had allowed the first unruly rays of the sun to tenderly touch the white blankets of her bed. Falling upon her face, those same rays slowly melted the frozen wasteland, thawing despair.

Her bedroom had been one of the rooms little used, prior to the property becoming hers. It had once been a guest room but as the previous occupants had shunned guests the room had lain dormant for many years. It was the only room she felt had not been violated. It was a room on which she could stamp her identity rather than feeling crushed by the weight of another's. She liked its asexuality. So many other rooms in the house had become gendered, suggesting male oppression and female subjugation. If the room appeared sexless, however, Lillian did not. Despite all she had been through, her appearance gave no indication of the troubled waters beneath the calm surface, a calm surface that radiated a sensuality.

Something small and almost intangible had, with the sun's rays, shifted the pivot of her world. Her equilibrium - the indefinable scales of the mind that shifted from despair to elation in an instant - had balanced. For the first time in years, she began to feel positive.

The sun had awoken a multitude of slumbering creatures. Now, the whole room seemed teeming with new life. Through one tiny gap, Lillian could see that the new day had performed the same miracle in her garden. It was still very early, so dew still hung like tiny tears upon every green leaf and stem. Now, a loving hand had begun to wipe them away.

Lillian pulled back the sheets and bounded downstairs and raced toward the door. In the garden, the dew of the new day's grass made her giddy; unsteady upon her bare feet, like a newborn deer and like a deer, every ungainly step seemed a joyous celebration.

Dancing; whirling. Something *had* changed, something of which Lillian was not even aware. All the while that change watched from the dawn shadows: Sebastian had returned.

Laughing, and with feet wet from the damp grass, Lillian fell to the ground running her fingers through each strand as one might run one's fingers through the hair of a lover, every sensuous touch more exhilarating than the last. It was then her gaze met the eyes of he who had been watching her.

The laughter stopped. She had wanted to scream but could only lie still and transfixed. The gloriously black pupils of her eyes widened and her soft lips parted, yet remained silent. All the while, Sebastian did nothing save return her gaze. Shadows played upon his form as a gentle breeze caused the tree he stood beneath to quiver. Protean, it appeared that just for a moment as if *he* were also changing. Finally, Lillian spoke.

"Sebastian?" There was no answer. The young man continued to gaze upon the supine woman in front of him. Her voice had registered like a heavy blow: like the voice of his own soul.

"Are you Sebastian?" Lillian said the words with slow deliberation, as though she were talking to someone who she feared could not understand her. The silence made her uneasy. Something else unsettled her: for a long time, it had felt as though stagnant water had coursed her veins. Now? Now it felt as if a new life spring flowed through them, washing away every impurity.

"Yes." The reply was clear and distinct, and with a resonance that could move worlds. The brevity of the reply did nothing to allay the feeling of anxious anticipation Lillian felt as she brought herself to a sitting position. Here was a man she felt to be, at least partially, responsible for the death of her brother yet she could not help feeling fatally attracted to him. Maybe he could answer her questions, once she had the courage to ask them.

Sebastian stepped from the cool shadows. Lillian, instinctively, moved away. He had brought about a collapse into ruins of so many people. She felt drawn to him, yet wished him to banish him. He reminded her of things she laboured to forget.

The bright sunshine washed over the lithe young man swathing his features in light. He was everything her brother had described, yet somehow different. Lillian found it difficult to determine yet there was something, she felt, that her brother had missed.

"And you?" Lillian had quite forgotten that in asking his name she had not given her own.

"Lillian." Her voice trembled slightly. She felt the statement needed to be qualified as though her name, her identity, were not

Denial

enough. "I live here. This is my house."

"Where is …?"

"Dead." Lillian anticipated the question.

"Dead?" Sebastian staggered, temporarily losing his balance, before reaching out a hand to a tree to steady himself. Lillian flushed hot and cold. The way she had broken the news had been insensitive. She had assumed Sebastian would have known or, at least, guessed. She remembered how she had felt when she had first heard. Now, her heart went out to him.

"I'm sorry. Didn't you know?" Her voice indicated concern but remained aloof. After all, however well she thought she knew Sebastian, in actuality, he was a stranger.

"No. No. You must be mistaken." Sebastian's voice was not yet desperate. His reply indicated disbelief, but of the kind one intones when given any fact one believes to be false.

Lilian shook her head, letting her gaze fall to her feet.

"Where is he? He's got to be alive." The rise in pitch told Lillian that, regardless of what Sebastian said, he now knew her words to be true.

"No." Her soft voice shallow.

"Tell me." Sebastian took a step toward Lillian. She, feeling threatened, retreated. Sebastian's tone was becoming desperate and accusing.

"It's your fault. You left him when he needed you most." The moment Lillian uttered the words, she regretted every syllable. It was wrong of her to apportion blame. Now the words made her mouth sting. If they did that to her, what had they done to him? She looked for a reaction upon his face, but there was none. Sebastian turned and strode toward the gate, the same gate that had figured so prominently in her brother's journal.

"Wait …" Lillian wanted to run after him but her pride would not let her do so. Before she could say another word, Sebastian spun around, interrupting her.

"So, it's *my* fault, is it? Am I my brother's keeper?" Sebastian's emotions were running high. Now, his tone became hostile.

"No, you're not." It wasn't an apology but the nearest she could come to one.

"Thank you." The tone of the words was sarcastic, yet with them, his whole body appeared to relax. There had been a moment of shock when she had first told him of the death but that had now been replaced by an uneasy calm. The sun caught his green eyes as they scrutinised the young woman in front of him.

"I know your name is Sebastian, but who *are* you?" The question needed to be asked, for, despite all she knew, Sebastian remained an enigma.

"Sebastian." A wry smile followed. If Lillian had expected the question to reveal the inner workings of a soul, she now realised those workings would not be revealed with one simple question.

"Yes. I know your name is Sebastian, but who are you?" Perhaps if she persisted a little more may be revealed. The smile dropped from his face and, once again, he turned away. Lillian thought to ask again would be unwise and was about to desist when, unexpectedly, a reply came.

"I can't say." The words seemed pitiful and tragic. It didn't appear that Sebastian was unwilling to say but that he could not say because he really did not know.

"You don't know?" Her voice was gentle and coaxing.

"No, but aren't we all such stuff as dreams are made of?" It didn't tell Lillian a lot, if anything,

"Are you trying to tell me you're a dream?"

"No, more a creation of the mind."

"How can a mind create ...?" Once again, her sentence was preempted.

"Doesn't a mind create *everything*? How can anything be perceived other than through the mind? It is only the senses that make anything real." Sebastian spoke the words with conviction, as though he had given the subject his every thought for a long time. Lillian paused to consider what the words meant before a glorious confusion swept away her thoughts in an epiphany. She could not reply because she was unable to do so.

"I don't understand. What will happen to you?" The question seemed a trivial one, but everything, now, hid behind a veil of confusion.

"Nothing." The words were spat out as if to enforce his desperate plight.

"Where will you go?"

"I've no idea. Every law in the universe says I should not exist but, as you can see, I do. As an act of imagination given life, I should imagine I will remain forever as I am. Only time will change the way others perceive me but, like all acts of the imagination, I cannot die." The words seemed calm and reflective.

"This is just too strange to contemplate! How can you be real? If I hadn't read about you in my brother's journal, I should think you nothing more than a hallucination. Maybe you are. Here, let me touch you." Lillian moved toward Sebastian and extended her arm until the tips of her fingers brushed against his arm "You are real! I can't believe it! What will happen to you? Will you change? Age?"

"Age? Yes. Change? No. I will doubtless remain as your brother thought of me. He moves with me for I am a part of him."

"But my brother is *dead*." Lillian tried to emphasise the last word.

"No! No! No!" For the first time, Lillian understood Sebastian's desperation. If he were immortal, and a creation of the mind then he had no one. He would never grow old with the people he loved. Given that her brother was dead, Sebastian would always be as he was at this moment in time. She tried to convince herself of the impossibility of the situation, yet in front of her stood a creation of the mind! Before she could organise her thoughts, however, Sebastian interrupted: "I must go", he said. Evidently, he had been considering his condition as much as Lillian had been. He swiftly turned, walked through the gate, and disappeared into the gloom.

The rest of the day Lillian spent, as had quickly become her custom, in the old house. Her encounter with Sebastian haunted her imagination. Trying to think of other things, she sought to make the house hers by stamping her identity upon it: hanging a painting here; arranging a plant there, whilst all the while feeling something of an intruder. "I've no right to be here," she would tell herself. By the end of the day, her encounter with Sebastian felt like nothing more than a dream. How could a *person* be a creation of the *mind*? Not only that, one that would never age or die? No, it must have been a dream even if something told her it was not. Perhaps she and her brother had inherited some madness? No, it was too awful to consider.

A few days later the last of her father's financial affairs had been set in order. Lillian, therefore, now had an income that would sustain the employment of a few domestic employees. In such a large house, she would also appreciate the company. With other people in the house, she might also be able to forget Sebastian, whatever he was.

After placing an advertisement in a local newspaper there came a response: a husband and wife applied for the post of gardener and cook. As theirs were the only applications, the posts were duly filled.

They had been expected at nine in the morning, but by ten o'clock the couple had failed to arrive. Lillian busied herself, looking for their arrival at the window. At ten, there was a loud knock on the door. Lillian knew it to be them. Moments later, and with the door now unbolted, her new employees stood in front of her.

The man was typical of many other Welsh characters of the time: his clothes were some years' out of date, yet considered practical; he was rather short, with thick, creased fingers that told of many decades of hard work; he looked every day of his sixty years, what with his hunched shoulders and tufted silver hair that he cut himself. Nonetheless, he had a kind face with large, doleful eyes. He loved his wife and the country he seemed such a part of, Lillian could see that.

The woman was large and maternal. She greeted Lillian with a smile, unconsciously flattening out the wrinkles in her navy-blue coat so that she might give a better impression.

Lillian had been busy arranging the couple's accommodation so that the two would have their own living quarters.

"Ah, Mr and Mrs Llewellyn, come in." Lillian tried to make first words as genial as possible but, in actuality, she hated meeting new people.

"Thank you, Miss." The woman's voice was soft. An accent of the borders rather than the harder tones to the west.

"Please, call me Lillian," the young woman said, bidding the pair enter. Lillian hoped that the two would not yet be familiar with the rumours surrounding the house. As is typical of any Welsh town an elaborate embroidery had been woven over the facts until the rumoured events had become so far removed from the actual ones as to bear no resemblance whatsoever to what had actually happened. Lillian chose not to offer explanations until explanations were sought.

They trailed down a long corridor in awkward silence until Lillian drew them to a halt, opening a door to her left.

"These will be your rooms. I've tidied them up a bit for you but they haven't been used for years so you may have to open a few windows. I'm afraid they're not in the best of repair." Lillian smiled, nervously.

Mr Llewellyn dropped his suitcase to the floor and sighed.

"Home is home though it's never so homely," he said, making his way to a window and opening it. His wife also seemed to visibly relax in her new surroundings. Lillian, for her part, watched the old man struggle with the window before it eventually opened and a cool breeze entered the room.

"Now, if you're to call me Lillian, I hope I can call you both by your first names," The old man still had his back to the two women so Lillian addressed her comments to the woman.

"Yes. I'm Florrie. He's Ivor." His name being mentioned, Ivor awoke from a reverie and turned to see why his name had been spoken. No one seemed to be expecting a response from him so he turned back to the open window and the garden.

"Well, I hope my home will be your home." Lillian was unsure of how to conduct herself in a situation in which she was in control.

"I hope so. I'll be glad to get away from that town. Only last night, someone was seen digging in the cemetery at gone midnight and then, when he was disturbed, ran off. Anyhow, seems as though he was filling in a grave rather than digging one. All the same,

I'm glad to be away." She looked to her husband, hoping he would validate her story, but he appeared not to be listening as his eyes were still trained on the garden.

"Yes, well I'm sure you'll want to unpack and make yourself at home." Lillian looked at the couple's meagre possessions.

"I'm expecting a housemaid at any moment, so if I can leave you to it." With that, she glided to the door and was gone.

Flo Llewellyn was not concerned that Lillian had cut her chatter dead. She had done nothing more than idly gossip in an effort to hide her insecurity with her new employer. She had not registered what she had been saying until it dawned on her that, perhaps, Lillian had left when she had heard mention of cemeteries. She had almost forgotten the rumours she had heard about Lillian's family and how many of them now lay, it was supposed, silently beneath the cold ground. Now, feeling tactless, her face burned with embarrassment.

Lillian walked from the house to the garden. The old woman's words came back, like an echo in the night. She had not taken offence at what had been said, nor even thought about her own family. What intrigued Lillian was who it might have been in that windswept place, quarrying a grave by moonlight. Who had wished to lay their hands upon a cold corpse at such an hour, and for what reason? As one thought collided into another, her imagination came back to Sebastian. At first, the graveyard incident and that uneasy young man appeared unconnected. Why, then, had she connected them? Of course, the two thoughts might have been entirely arbitrary - as thoughts often are - having no connection to one another whatsoever other than the fact that she had thought them. Something, however, told her that there had to be a connection between Sebastian and the figure in the graveyard. Had it really been Sebastian in that infernal place at such an hour? Surely not! He wouldn't, would he? Then it came to her: the horrifying thought that Sebastian, doubting her word, had gone to exhume her brother's body. No, it was too awful to contemplate. Nonetheless, if anyone were capable of such an act, Lillian thought, it would be him.

As Lillian crossed the sun-drenched grass her attention was captured by a movement near to the gate. Even though she had only seen the figure once before already it was one that she recognised. Out of the shadows stepped Sebastian. Now, as if history were about to repeat itself, they faced one another as they had when first they met.

"Was it you?" Lillian spoke the words quietly. So many things seemed incommunicable between the two, yet so many things could be left unsaid.

"Yes." Sebastian's reply was flat and devoid of emotion.

"What were you thinking? What sort of a monster are you? Must you make everyone else's existence as wretched as your own?" Lillian felt her anger rising. She wanted to hit him - to beat her fist against him - but her own bitter experiences told her that

Denial

violence was no recourse.

"I loved him. I loved him and I destroyed him. His death gave me a life independent of him, but what sort of a life is it when that life is outside time? For all eternity I must carry the weight of knowing it was I who brought about his death. Can't you understand? I had to know if he were truly dead to know what my future 'wretched existence' holds for me." All the while Sebastian spoke, his gaze had not once averted from Lillian nor had his voice been anything other than low and hoarse.

"But Sebastian, he's been dead for over a year." Lillian's anger began to subside. No longer did she have the wish to punish, or even admonish.

"Yes, and in peace. What peace can I know, knowing it was I that put him beneath the cold clay?" Sebastian's voice betrayed a quiver of emotion.

"What peace can *you* know? What peace can I know, knowing my brother and I harboured feelings for one another in a way we should not? Thank goodness neither of us had acted upon those feelings. Who else but a brother could love someone as wretched and as I? What burden of guilt do you think I carry, knowing my brother and father killed one another because of me? That is a sorrow that can only cease when I cease." Lillian turned away, her voice choking with emotion. Unseen by her companion, sunlight caught her tears, giving them an iridescence.

"Others could love you, Lillian, if only they were given the chance," Sebastian spoke the words with soft hesitation.

"Who? Who could love me now?" Lillian brought herself around to face the young man. Curiosity shone through the tears bedewing her eyes. Her dark hair fell around her face catching the salty course and darkening a few strands.

"You forget. I am your brother or, at least, a part of him. The things he loved and despised, I love and despise. Lillian ... I could love you." Sebastian's sentence seemed to pause the moment for an eternity so that it hung in the air like frozen gossamer. Lillian wanted to throw herself into his arms but the act would have been too impulsive and desperate: the act of a drowning woman clutching nothing more than the tiniest of branches. How would such an act be right when so many things were wrong? He was uncomfortably close to her, yet still she doubted his reality.

Perhaps, like her brother, she had invented a character able to fulfil all her darkest, unacknowledged desires. Was there real blood in his veins? But what had he said? To kiss him now would be to kiss a brother. His lineaments and aspect were too like her own. She hated herself and, in hating herself, hated him.

"You must go." Lillian's full lips mouthed the words, almost inaudibly.

"Lillian." Her name was spoken plaintively, almost apologetically.

"Please ... go." Lillian had broken her gaze and looked to the ground. Even the whisper she could manage was tremulous. If Sebastian were to ask her again, her next response would have found all her resolve weaken. She would then have had to admit her feelings to herself, and to him.

"Do you really want me to go?" That was the question Lillian had dreaded. She closed her eyes in an effort to contain her tears and nodded her acquiescence. A silence ensued. Opening her eyes, Lillian was alone.

"Miss?" A soft gentle voice behind Lillian begged her attention. "Miss, I've come about the job."

Lillian swallowed and took out a handkerchief to dry her eyes. What sort of an impression must she have given her prospective employee, standing alone in the middle of her garden, sobbing? She did not wish to appear ridiculous, nor did she wish to fan the flames of local gossip. She had heard the rumours that to live in the old house turned a person mad: what had her actions, seemingly, proven?

"Ah yes, let's go to the house." Lillian led the way. The young woman, she had glanced at for just a second, seemed personable enough. Pretty, one might say although, like Lillian, the young woman thought herself quite the opposite. She also looked to be about the same age as Lillian. Yet Gwen - for that was her name - had known nothing of the tragedy that can blight a young life, just as a cruel wind twists a tree. Gwen's family had been a loving and caring one which, despite their poverty, had made Gwen a woman with a happy disposition.

Happy, that is until she began work at the old house. As the weeks turned to months Gwen became a confidant, as well as a maid, yet all the while her once healthy complexion grew more

Denial

and more pale. Her once bright eyes became glassy and lifeless. Lillian noticed the malady afflicting her fiend, and the general unhappiness stalking her everywhere she went. Lillian blamed herself: always, she felt people's unhappiness to originate with her. One day, as Gwen cleaned the drawing-room, Lillian waylaid her.

"Gwen, sit down." Lillian gently took her friend by the arm and guided her toward a large tapestry settee that was the centrepiece of the room. All around them the evidence of Gwen's work gleamed. Against the wall, the old furniture shone like ripe horse-chestnuts. Upon it, silverware caught the rays of the sun so that previously dark corners of the room were dappled in flowing colours.

"Gwen, are you happy here?" There was genuine concern in Lillian's voice.

"Yes, I am." Initially, it had seemed as though Gwen were about to pause but after a moment's reflection, in which she looked heavenward as if seeking divine inspiration, the pause furnished her with a curt reply that explained very little.

"Are you *really*? You don't seem happy. I worry about you. Although I would miss you dearly, if you were to leave, I should rather you go and be happy than stay and be so sad." Lillian placed her hand on her friend's arm.

"Well. I'm not unhappy *here*, but I am unhappy." Gwen looked awkward, like a shy suitor telling his sweetheart of his love.

"I guessed you were." Lillian congratulated herself on being so perceptive.

"It's not my job. I love what I do", she quickly responded, before hesitatingly adding "It's you."

"Me?" Lillian could not help sounding shocked. The fact that she made a friend unhappy in some way confirmed all the fears she had about herself. Now, she wanted to laugh; to cry; to throw her arms around Gwen and thank her for confirming what she had always felt about herself: that she could do nothing save pollute the lives of those around her. Gwen, however, was becoming tearful.

"It's just that you seem to have everything and are still so unhappy. It's made me think that, for all my life, when I thought that to have all that you have would have made me completely happy. I've now realised that, even if I did, I might be no happier than I am now. I've always had nothing except the consolation that, in my sad moments, if I had such and such I would be happier. That's not the case, is it? You have everything and are the unhappiest person I know. Seeing you sad makes me sad because I know there is nothing I can do." Gwen's eye focused on the face in front of her.

"Oh, Gwen! Then you don't hate me." Lillian threw her arms around her friend.

"Hate you? No! You're my best friend." Gwen was astonished to think her words could have been so misunderstood.

"Well Gwen, I may appear to have everything but you've got something money can't buy - a family that loves you. I would trade everything I own to love and be loved. To be as happy as you were when you first came to this place. That must be glorious!" There was no trace of self-pity in Lillian's voice. She spoke the words calmly; comfortingly.

After the two women had finished their conversation, Lillian was left alone. As Gwen finished her chores, Lillian had time to reflect. The sight of Gwen's misery had troubled her for weeks. Now, she felt guilty that she should have caused it although the knowledge that someone cared about her so much gave Lilian a warm glow. Perhaps she should go and look for her friend, hold her tightly, and tell her how much her concern meant. Then again, maybe a second, less spontaneous, show of affection might invite a rebuff that would leave her feeling vulnerable. Gwen's affection was the closest thing Lillian had ever had to an unconditional love. Gwen expected nothing, unlike others who had spoken of love but only used it as a weapon.

"Love comes in different forms. Love can be one friend caring for another. Never think you're not loved", Gwen had said. Like a trebuchet, it had broken Lillian's defences. An almost inaudible rap at the door announced Gwen's return.

"Gwen, come and sit with me awhile. Forget the house for today." Lillian's friend smiled and made her way to the settee where Lillian sat, waiting.

"I have to be honest, Gwen. I just don't know what it is to love." Lillian's admission startled them both. Lillian, because she had never been able to trust anyone enough to be so candid;

Denial

Gwen, because she found it hard to believe that anyone as beautiful as her friend should be unloved.

"I didn't know anything of romantic love either. I love my family, but a passion for which I could die has always been denied me. Since I've been working here, a man I've known for a few years, and who I thought never liked me, has asked me to marry him. I don't know what to tell him because I feel little for him. Maybe I do love him and this is what love feels like. I've wanted to tell you, but I didn't want you to worry about my problems when you seemed to have so many of your own." Gwen looked crestfallen as she spoke, her forehead creasing with confusion.

"Oh Gwen, you never said!" Despite everything, Lillian still idealised love, according it the power to transform everything. "Who is he?"

"Well. I've known him for a few years but, as I said, he's never shown any interest until recently. My family has always been poor, whilst his are in insurance and well off. We've always spoken. Maybe he didn't like me because I didn't work. He has a good job and works hard. I know his family lost a lot of money after that mining accident last year so, maybe, he also has his problems."

"I would like to meet him." Lillian gave a positive affirmation as if to negate Gwen's lack of enthusiasm.

"Yes, he wants to meet you." Gwen's voice trailed away into silence as if her thoughts were elsewhere.

"Me?" Lillian was surprised that anyone should wish to seek out her company. Her face flushed.

"Yes. He speaks of you often. I thought you may have known him." Whatever it was Gwen had been thinking had obviously been dismissed and she now accorded Lillian her full attention.

"No. I don't know anyone really." Lillian failed to realise the implication of what she had said.

"That is strange." Gwen frowned.

"I agree. That really is very strange."

* * * * * *

Despite Lillian having banished Sebastian, he had not gone far. He had kept his presence out of sight but something tied him to the house. There was the promise made to his friend; then there was Lillian. He would never be able to leave the house completely for he and the house were too tightly bound for that, but what about Lillian? She was the only thing that could change his existence into that of a life worth living.

Sebastian's days were spent wandering. Sometimes his journeys would take him to the bleak and barren wilderness of Mid-Wales where the huge, open vistas - like an empty sheet of music - allowed a vivid imagination such as his to compose its own symphony. Here was a scenery where *anything* might be possible. Often, amid the coarse grass and shattered boulders a solitary, twisted tree would grow; he would smile, thinking it as weatherworn and alone as he. Other times he walked the great valleys, where mountains rose up on all sides like the walls of a giant's tomb, walls that threatened to cascade down upon him in mighty earthen torrents sending him back to hell. On days that were less bleak - days when his terrible isolation was less painful - he would walk to the more lush, pastoral east. Here there seemed to be unity and harmony in the world yet, always alone, he remained outside such holy communion. Here, nonetheless, he might find a poet writing some reverie to a ruined abbey, or eulogising nature. Sebastian, too, found solace in nature even if nature spurned him. Nonetheless, there could be no escape. However far his lonely wanderings took him, he could never stay away from the one place he'd felt tied to for too long. Always there would be a point of recoil. Whilst there was still hope he, at least, could never turn away completely.

Back in the small town, Sebastian trudged along the dirty streets. Since the death of his friend he could never sleep for sleep, like death, was also denied him. Slowly, he walked, for having nowhere to go, he had become aimless. Every street was quiet. Every street, that is, except the streets of the town that had once led to a dock. Here, fights were breaking out as landlords sought their beds and crowds were beginning to empty into the streets. Sebastian withdrew into a darkened doorway. The prospect of an encounter with *any* member of the human race was bad enough but tonight it would be unbearable.

In the gloom, Sebastian could see but not be seen. Voices approached. Two of the multitude whose drink-soaked bodies staggered upon the road that, moments before, Sebastian's aching frame had traversed.

"No, you can't do it." Despite the slurred tones, the words were distinct.

"Why?" A voice as equally slurred as the first broke into a laugh, a laugh only friends have about a secret collusion. In the darkness, flashing eyes were watching their every move and ears listening to their intoxicated ramblings. The two figures continued to walk, propping each other up until they came to a halt before the bright window of their next inn.

The first of the two men stood at almost Sebastian's height. His features, however, were remarkably different. His face was long and thin and appeared to have been squeezed into an awkward shape. His lips - even from a distance - were markedly thin and to such a degree that his face, far from having a mouth, appeared to have nothing more than a split beneath his nose.

"What do I get, then?" The thin lips pulled apart like a bloodless slash.

"Oh, you'll be alright, don't you worry." Once again, the laughter between the two flared up like fire beneath a bellows.

Sebastian turned his attention to the second figure. He was, perhaps, slightly shorter than the first but of a heavier and more athletic build. His mouth was coarse, suggesting a permanent look of disdain. He, like his friend, appeared uncommonly well dressed for the little town.

"But how ... how ... how are you going to do it?" In his stupor, he appeared to have forgotten the second half of his sentence until with all his concentration, it came back to him. "How?" The one with thin lips was evidently not satisfied with the time it was taking his friend to respond, feeling it necessary to ask the question again.

"I know. I heard you the first time. I was just thinking." The heavier of the two leaned against the window and, fumbling in his frockcoat pocket, removed his empty hands a few seconds later. He stared at them in confusion, trying to remember what he had been looking for, or what he had lost.

"And?"

"And? Oh, I've shown some interest in that girl that's working for her. Gwen something. I don't know ... I don't know *anything* anymore!" The two broke into laughter and embraced one another as only two drunks can.

"Gwen Davis?" The taller of the two, it appeared, was marginally less drunk.

"Is that it? Yes, I think you're right." The confusion he had found in looking at his hands was now transferred to his friend's face. He looked up, frowned and squinted, then smiled as the face came into focus.

"And?" Although the questions kept coming, the tone in which they were asked suggested no real interest, only idle curiosity.

"Well, she thinks I like her. I've tried to get myself an invite to meet her boss. Lillian is it? From there, what could be easier? She's got no friends, a lot of money, so a seduction shouldn't be too difficult."

Checking himself, Sebastian stood silently in the shadows and hoped the two would let slip further plans.

"But she's a hysteric. I've heard it was her who got her brother to kill her father." The words were said as if some great secret had been told and enforced with a wink, ludicrous in his state, as both eyes closed.

"They're just stories. I know that one because I started it!" The two broke into laughter for the third time.

Sebastian felt a cold rage run through him before it turned to a flame. His large eyes watched the two figures steady themselves before they stumbled off. What to do? The thought that some buffoon thought himself conniving and irresistible enough to wield his duplicitous charm upon two women with the sole aim of lining his pocket ate into Sebastian. He tried to control his anger, realising that it was born of jealousy, and from such a genesis something might irrevocably escalate. It wasn't that Lillian could not take care of herself as she could. She had proven herself an able and capable woman on more than one occasion. No, Sebastian knew all the pain Lillian had suffered in her short life and how much damage the actions of the self-serving imbecile he had just heard speaking would cause. He felt honour-bound to prevent further grief if it were in his power to do so.

With stealth, he crept from his dark dominion and into the grey night. The pair had disappeared into the hungry jaws of the town; it was up to Sebastian to follow. He knew the two would be

Denial

negotiating a lane through the churchyard, somewhere he could hide. There, under the high steeple that had never offered him salvation, he could eschew prayer for prey. For the first time ever, the church had shown Sebastian a way. In the jaws of the night, shapes were threatening, like dead things awaking from slumber.

Almost at the point of invisibility the two figures that, unbeknown to them, were now being hunted paused before going their separate ways. Now Sebastian could pounce! Slowly, the drunken braggadocio swayed his way home. Sebastian moved swiftly and with purpose, the final words of the two still reverberating in his ears. Sebastian and his quarry crossed the bridge that divided the town. The wind had lashed the silent murky depths beneath them into a foaming tempest that snarled like an angry animal. Almost within striking distance, yet with still no plan of attack, Sebastian knew he would rely on instinct, just as he had always done.

Despite the weather, the click of the footsteps of the figure in front upon the pavement, and the rustle the dried leaves made as he dragged his feet through them could now be clearly heard. Drink had benumbed the senses of the hunted so that he, at least, considered himself alone. With one final movement, Sebastian drew alongside and, with a firm grip upon the man's arm, pulled him around.

"What the ...?" In his drunken state, he fell to the floor.

"I want a word with you." Sebastian kneeled down and leaned over the prostrate figure, drawing his face near.

"Who are you, then?" There was no tinge of fear in the voice, only aggression.

"That doesn't concern you. I'm a friend of Lillian's. Stay away." The words were spoken with venomous intent.

"I don't know any Lillian. I don't know what you're talking about." Turning his head away, the drunken figure lashed out with the back of his arm. It was met with outstretched fingers that caught the flailing arm firmly by the wrist, before squeezing tightly.

"Oh God, it's not me! I think my friend knows a Lillian." For the first time, clouds that had veiled the pair in darkness had drawn aside like stage curtains; now the pair were bathed in a pallid limelight. For the first time, the light was bright enough to catch the pitiless depths of Sebastian's angry eyes, eyes that focussed on the now trembling clown beneath him.

How did such a figure as Sebastian know so much about him? Fear had a sobering effect and now he asked himself how a stranger had come by his information. What were his motives? Perhaps *he* also wanted to get his hands on the young woman's money.

"Look, if it's the money, maybe we can work something out." Sebastian raised a hand to strike the cowering form beneath him, but his glance was fearful enough.

"Oh God, I know who you are! Please, don't kill me." Something deep within the young man's intoxicated brain had started to work. Like everyone in the town, he had heard of the increasingly diabolic nature of Lillian's brother. Had that diabolism succeeded in raising the Devil? To a superstitious mind, it seemed possible. Like all gossip, it had become misshapen and magnified a story until nothing of the truth remained. In the pious, twisted little community, had what had once been suggested, now been confirmed? "You ... You keep away from me. I know what you are! It was you that killed the others. Kill her as well, I'll not stop you, just don't kill me."

"I'll not kill you." Sebastian's voice was calm. He allowed himself a smile, realising the insensible idiot thought him the Devil incarnate!

"What then?" Sebastian had regained his composure. A passion too excessive might have caused untold harm and that was not what he wanted. The temporary respite was enough for the young, still prone, man to take an opportunity to regain his liberty. Seeking to free himself, he began to flail wildly about, but Sebastian's grip was too strong. How could he free himself? How to escape with body *and* soul intact? With his free arm, he reached into an inside pocket of his long dark coat. Sebastian anticipated what was to come as the hand withdrew. In the moonlight, the blade shone like a mirror in the noonday sun. Sebastian took a step backwards.

Blade outstretched, the drunk lunged forward, only to lose his footing and fall. In the mottled, flickering light, a dark and rapidly widening patch now contrasted with the brilliance of his white shirt. Moonlight caught the dark stream, making it glisten.

Denial

Embedded in the chest of the still shape beneath him, Sebastian could only see the protruding handle. The blade had sunk to the hilt in the soft, drunken, flesh. A fearful and ghastly groan emerged from the mouth of the victim, heightened by a guttural rattle deep within his throat. As the patch of blood expanded, Sebastian crouched beside the injured man. Carefully, he dipped his fingers in the life flow before bringing them to his lips. 'So that's what death tastes like,' he told himself. Already the hot effusion had cooled and was now beginning to coagulate.

"Murder! You'll not get away with this." The whisper was fearful and breathless. The look of disdain Sebastian had observed a little earlier was now a sneer.

"Look, shut up and I'll help you." Sebastian brought his face near to the other man's. He hadn't wanted to help him, yet found himself unable to let him die alone in a gutter.

"Murder!" In the distance, footsteps were approaching. What to do? Stay and be accused? Or go, and make good his escape from a crime of which he was innocent? Footsteps were coming nearer. One more "Murder!" would surely bring help. Sebastian arose. Despite it being autumn, he was, in an instant, lost in the still dense foliage afforded by the trees that stood, shaking, on either side of the lane. Voices drew nearer. He would be safe, but what of he who had been left? He had gone horribly silent. Then there was a groan.

"What was that?" One of the approaching figures had heard the noise.

"Don't know. An animal?" Both voices were slurred, yet laden with panic the pitch of their voice beginning to rise.

"What's that?" From his haven, Sebastian guessed that one of the two had located the source of their unease.

"Christ, it's a body!" Suspicions were confirmed. There followed the sound of a few hurried footsteps that seemed as anxious as the voices had sounded a few moments before. They too were interrupted by a long, deeper, groan. "Oh God, he's bleeding!"

"Bleeding? He's been stabbed!"

"Who did this, boy?"

"The Devil! The Devil did it!" The voice was gasping, punctuated by gulps of air. Less audible than the other two, he sounded desperately ill.

Sebastian allowed himself a smile. He knew that he, at least, would be safe. Who would believe a drunk claiming to have been stabbed by the Prince of Darkness himself? Silently, Sebastian slipped away.

Lillian was never far from Sebastian's thoughts, yet the events of the night made him more acutely aware of their separation from one another than ever. He had not intended to return to the house since her banishment, but tonight was different. He had to be near her, even if it only meant to walk a path that she might have walked.

With a purpose he alone accorded it, Sebastian made his way back to the old house and its garden, his journey lit by the silvered countenance of Diana, her loving arrows piercing his upturned face. The coldness of the night had given rise to a mist that clung in frozen abandon all around him. Within an hour, he was standing beneath Lillian's window. A solitary flame flickered in the darkness. How he longed to make his presence known. To take her in his arms so that she, with a few soft words, might make everything right. But Lillian had banished him: he could never let her know he was still near to her, at least not until he was sure that is where she wanted him.

The next morning, Lillian's old gardener arose early. The autumn season gave him plenty of work, not least of which was the many leaves to be raked. He did not trade in the same sort of gossip as his wife, but that was because he had fewer friends than she. She kept him well informed on all the local rumours, especially the ones regarding the house in which they lived.

Now that summer was over and the season of mellow fruitfulness was upon them, the lawn needed less tending. The old man sighed. He had been a gardener all his life, and had always enjoyed his work but, just occasionally, thought how different his life might have been had he been given opportunities. He bent down and pulled up a fern whose knotty roots, deeply embedded in the Welsh hillside, reminded him of his own life.

Ah well, it was too late to do anything to change his life now. From the corner of his eye, something caught his attention. Somewhere near the gate, in the early morning sun, something had moved.

Denial

"Ah, it's just a breeze", he told himself, but hadn't that wind come from the east? The old man used proverbs to give some order to his existence. Now, a proverb came back to him: 'When the wind is in the east, 'tis neither good for man nor beast.' He gave an involuntary shudder, remembering his wife's stories.

"Ah, it *has* to be the wind." This time he spoke the words aloud, in the hope of feeling less alone. To hear the sound of his own voice gave him a feeling of support. But what if spoken words had only drawn attention when otherwise he might not have been noticed? He began to wonder. Again, a branch moved but this time there could be no mistaking it for an effect of the weather. Something awful and foreboding was lurking; watching. Trying to dismiss his fears, the old man began to rake the dead leaves that had fallen in the night.

A rusting creak as cast iron ground against cast iron told the old gardener that the gate had opened, or had been opened. Dare he look? Lifting his gaze, he squinted. Within a second, a dark silhouette had become clear and distinct.

Taking a step backwards, the old man's legs became entangled with his rake and he stumbled. Quickly, he brought himself around: if an attack were imminent, he wanted to be ready.

If Llewellyn had expected to see something alien, he found it in the features of Sebastian, whose bearing set him so apart from others in the little community. Instinct told the old man to run, but try as he might he could not avert his eyes. As the old man blinked, the figure was gone. All that remained was a clump of bushes. Beyond, the gate swung.

All that day there remained, it seemed, an unearthly presence in the garden. Nervously, the old man tried to work, all the while feeling as if a pair of cold and unblinking eyes appraised his every move. Now it seemed as though something awful had descended over the garden. Had what once had happened in the house come back to haunt it?

The working day drew to a close. After carefully tidying away his tools, the old man returned to the house. After a pause, he considered that tonight he would lock away his tools, thinking it a sensible precaution given that axes and scythes were amongst them. As he ascended the steps to the back door, his wife came out to greet him.

"You look as though you've seen a ghost, love." Her voice as warming as winter mead.

"It's nothing. 'Talk of the Devil and he is bound to appear'." He tried to make what he said sound light and humorous, but his wife knew him too well. She recognised the underlying disquiet.

"Pardon?" She was curious, but not excessively so. She raised her hand to his face, sliding it across his cheek, and into his hair.

"Just someone in the garden earlier. A strange-looking fella. I think he must have been homeless. 'If the eyes are the window of the soul', he must be a lonely wanderer searching for his, because he certainly didn't have one when I saw him."

Despite his earlier conviction not to speak of his experience, now that he had started there could be no stopping him.

"Didn't you get him off the place?" The old woman felt concerned; threatened.

"Didn't have a chance to, dear. 'Quickly come, quickly go'." The old man sat down upon a bench embedded in the wall of the deep porch and crossed his legs, before beginning to untie his bootlaces.

"Then why did you say 'Devil'?" Flo Llewellyn sat opposite her husband, before placing her hands in her lap.

"Oh, I don't know." He tried to shrug off the conversation as though it were trivial and did not warrant so much attention. Both knew this not to be the case, but the old woman took the hint and let the matter drop. What neither had seen was Lillian approaching from within the house. She had only caught the last part of the conversation, but it was enough. Given that it was her garden, she didn't feel it unmannerly, or an imposition, to ask of whom they had been speaking.

"Ivor, excuse me for interrupting, but did you say there was someone in the garden today?" Unexpected, Lillian's voice startled the old couple.

"Yes, Miss." The old man pulled off a boot, before continuing with the next.

"Where?" Lillian braced herself by leaning, apparently nonchalantly, against a wall.

"By the gate." The words seemed to resound, like an echo. Lillian held her breath, lest her companions realise the significance of what had just been said.

Denial

"Why did you call him the 'Devil'?" Lillian was still unsure whether it was Sebastian who had returned. The words made the old man blanch. His job might be in jeopardy if Lillian thought he was spreading rumours.

"It's just me, Miss. As they say: 'One man may steal a horse, while another may not look over a hedge'. I didn't like the look of him from the start." The old man stopped untying his boots and, with his sad eyes, looked at Lillian.

"Well then, Ivor, I don't want you repeating this story to anyone. We all know how these things can take on a life of their own." Lillian had no wish to chastise the old man for, in actuality, he had made her very happy by suggesting that there was the possibility that Sebastian had returned. The old man closed his eyes, drew down the corners of his mouth, and nodded. Her secret would be safe. Lillian turned to go, yet some deep instinctive urge stayed her moving.

"Ivor, this figure. Did you notice anything unusual about him?" Lillian's voice betrayed her curiosity. The old couple both looked up at her.

"Yes, and no." The reticence in his voice betrayed his uncertainty.

"What?" Lillian asked, as Flo looked to her husband, then back to Lillian. Ivor pulled a face as he struggled for the right words. Lillian knew then that Sebastian had returned. "Thank you." Trying to regain her composure, she turned before walking speedily to the inner sanctuary of the house.

No more was said about the mystery that evening. The next day, as Gwen arrived for work, Lillian noticed her friend's red eyes and swollen cheeks.

"Whatever's the matter, Gwen?" Lillian took her friend by the arm and led her from the hall into a nearby sitting room. Knowing of her friend's genuine compassion for her allowed Lillian to reciprocate a similar sentiment.

"Do you remember I told you someone had asked me to marry him? Well, he's been attacked." The young woman began to sob, allowing herself to slump into a nearby chair.

"Oh God, that's awful! When did this happen? Do they know who did it?" Lillian fell gently to her knees at Gwen's feet, before pressing Gwen's hands into her own. Lillian's long dark hair cascaded into Gwen's lap. Her dark eyes looked on, concerned.

"I don't know. Nobody can get any sense from him." Gwen closed her eyes, but some image must have flickered across her mind, for soon her chest began to heave and she exploded into tears. "I don't know how anyone could harm him as he hasn't an unkind bone in his body. The doctors think he might die. It's made me realise that I *do* love him, now there's a chance I might lose him."

"Gwen, what has he said has happened?" Gwen had become the sister Lillian had never had. Gently squeezing Gwen's hands, she tried to coax the information from her.

"Some men found him stabbed and bleeding, in the road. He can't say anything about who did it. He was drunk, and now he has a fever and is imagining all sorts. Nobody knows what happened. Oh God, what will I do if he dies?" With that, the young woman broke into new convulsions.

"Now look, you'll be alright. You try and think who would want to kill him." Without the emotional involvement, Lillian was able to take a more practical approach.

"There's no one. No-one. That's why they're saying he tried to kill himself. Everyone's saying his family is one step away from the workhouse and that that is why he did it."

By now, the words had become lost on Lillian. Sebastian's face had come back to haunt her. Since first she met him, she had felt him capable of any atrocity. He was wild; untamed. But there was more, much more. In Sebastian, Lillian had found the voice of her own soul. Was that why she found him so attractive yet, at bottom, frightening? He had a vengeful streak, she felt sure, but Gwen's story had triggered a flow of ideas that now crowded in on her.

"Go to him, Gwen. Take as much time as you need. Just keep me informed." Lillian had snapped out of her cloud of thought. She had not wanted to think Sebastian capable of such things, because it suggested she too might be capable of such an act.

"Oh, thank you!" In an instant, Gwen had put her coat and hat back on, and was gone. Lillian stood in silence as her friend's footsteps quickly pattered away. She was now alone, the Llewellyns far removed in other parts of the house. After a few minutes, she moved toward the window. Rolling and angry

Denial

clouds were gathering with alarming speed upon the horizon. A deep rumble, that could be felt as much as heard, preceded an awful blue-white flash that cracked like a cruel whip across the sky. On the distant hills, a single tree stood blasted, its barren branches aflame.

Lillian knew Sebastian had returned. Lillian stared from the window, pensive; vacant. Her soul, like an empty chalice waiting to be filled; her gaze wandering over the dark farmhouses in the distance. Was it really night already? The black sky indicated so. How long had she stood there, lost in a realm of thoughts unique to her and her experience? A minute? An hour? A day?

Tiny rivulets flooded down the pane of glass that separated Lillian from the storm outside. Out there, there was nothing only the blackness of the eternal void. Only Sebastian could fill that aching chasm for only he had made her painfully aware of it.

Thunder growled in the distance, slow and indistinct as if two mighty worlds were in collision. Then, another strike of the white whip as lightning again seemed to lash at some recalcitrant enemy. Some thought the brilliance capable of re-animating life. This time, it only illuminated it. Had that been a figure, far below her, in the outer reaches of the garden? A second flash confirmed her suspicions. There, far below the window, stood Sebastian, his face beaten by the deluge. Silently, he watched her form in the window high above him.

Lillian gave a gasp. Sebastian's features had an uncomfortable familiarity to them. In the savage storm, he seemed different to how she remembered him. Now, his face had a frail, haunted, beauty to it that frightened her. Guilt came in torrents, like the rain upon her true love's face. Somehow, she felt responsible for his trouble.

It would be foolish to ask him inside. A situation might arise that she would not be able to control. She knew Sebastian would never hurt her: it was her own feelings she sought to imprison. Moving from the window to the door she asked herself 'what to do'? She would have to ask him to leave. It would be difficult, but what other recourse was open to her? Reaching for her coat: she would not let herself suffer unduly.

The door was still slightly ajar. Evidently, Gwen had left it open in her haste. Now a damp patch had worked its way through the opening, soaking the cold stone floor. Lillian stepped forth and carefully made her way down the old steps that, even in the light of day, often felt unsafe. Now, she feared falling. Once again, the lightning flashed. This time Lillian could not suppress a scream. Sebastian had come to her. In the light that had momentarily cleaved the hopeless dark, his form stood less than a breath in front of her, his lips almost touching her own; wild eyes searched for an unspoken response.

"Sebastian..." Not a scream, but a breathless whisper. By now, his arm had been placed gently around her waist, the other brought up so that the palm of his hand touched her cheek; his thumb tenderly brushing her lips.

"Lillian." The way he softly spoke her name made her shiver; her knees weaken.

"I thought you had returned. People have been talking." She turned her head to the side and broke free from Sebastian's embrace.

"People do." Sebastian let his arms fall to his side.

"No, talking about *you*. Or, at least, a person I hoped might be you." Lillian had not realised her words had betrayed her true feelings.

"Hoped?" Sebastian had noticed her slip.

"Guessed! I meant guessed." But it was no good as any denial now would be a false one.

All the while, the two figures were becoming saturated, as the rain rolled down the mountainside and into the valley. In the distance, thunder rumbled like a bellowing beast. Aside from the momentary lightning flashes, the two remained in darkness.

"Well, what have they been saying? I may be guilty of many crimes, but I do have some virtues."

"I never said you didn't." Sebastian was twisting the conversation away from what she had wanted to say. Lillian looked around her. The storm had begun to bear down on her.

"Can you take me somewhere away from here?" She was, after all, just one frail person. How could she match the majestic power of the vast eternal? She now regretted asking, fearing Sebastian might see it as an invitation to enter her house. He did not.

"We can go over there." Sebastian was gesturing toward the gate, and what lay beyond.

Denial

"I'm not sure." She didn't fear what lay beyond, as her brother had done. She didn't fear the supernatural: it was what was *natural* that she feared.

"You'll be quite safe, trust me." Without waiting for her reply, Sebastian took Lillian's arm and walked to the entrance. Already his firm grip had softened her resolve. Beneath it, she felt safe. Yes, the place he was taking her to felt forbidden yet only now, as she stood on its threshold, did she realise how delicious forbidden fruits could taste.

"Come with me." Sebastian's hand slipped down her arm until it reached her hand. Slowly his fingers entwined with hers. She wanted to turn and run away; to pull her hand from his and slap his face yet could do neither. She wanted to hit him; to knock him to the ground; to put an end to his immortal being, but knew she *could* not; she also wanted to fall into his arms and press her lips to his, but *dared* not.

In the darkness. Sebastian lit a candle. Its brightness was enough for Lillian to see where she was. Amazed, she found they had already passed through the gate and were now in a dark wood.

In the pale brilliance, Lillian looked to Sebastian. In the little coppice, no rain fell. From somewhere, more and more candles had been brought forth and were now being lit.

"All these candles!" Lillian thought aloud.

"Call me Prometheus!" Sebastian turning, smiled. Lillian sat down and made herself comfortable. It wasn't long before the little copse resembled a Catholic church.

"Sebastian… about my brother's journal." Lillian's voice was soft and low. With the final candle now lit, Sebastian walked to Lillian before kneeling in front of her and taking her hands in his.

"Your brother had a very active imagination." Lillian wanted to pursue the matter but chose not to. Away from the storm, she was beginning to again feel the blood flow within her veins. After a few moments' deliberation, the conversation continued.

"Sebastian, this is wrong." She tried not to look at him, although well aware that he was looking at her.

"What is?" Now he was playing games, she thought.

"Us."

"Why?"

"Because I say it is. It feels as though you're my brother." Under the heat of his attention, she felt herself beginning to redden.

"Brother, or kindred spirit?" His tone was becoming persuasive.

"You're confusing me... in here!" Lillian pulled a hand from his and, clenching it into a fist, banged her chest.

"It doesn't confuse me," Sebastian countered.

"Yes, but you're different."

Sebastian withdrew his hand and, rising to his feet, began to walk to each candle, pinching out the flame with his bare fingers. Only when there were just a few left did he, once again, permit his gaze to fall upon Lillian. By now, his face was dry; his hair, however, still wet, fell about his face.

"So, that's the problem." His voice suggested he had always known the reason. Now, it had merely been confirmed. Under his gaze, Lillian felt her fortitude begin to dissolve and turned away.

"That *is* the problem. I just don't know. I feel as though I know you *too* well, yet another part of me doesn't know you at all. You frighten me. I'm scared to have you near me, yet miss you when you are away. You seem too like me, but I hate myself and in hating myself I can't help but hate you." Lillian longed to lift her eyes, to gauge the reaction her words had provoked but dared not. She listened for a response, but there was none. Should she look? If she caught that gaze - that smile - her uncertainty would magnify tenfold. "Why did you stab that man?" Lillian sought to escape the pain Sebastian had caused her by asking of the pain he had caused another.

"How do you know it was me?" Sebastian showed no trace of guilt: maybe he hadn't been involved, Lillian thought. He sought to avoid answering, knowing he could never lie to Lillian; he could, however, avoid telling the truth.

"Was it you?" Lillian knew a direct question would get a direct answer. A heavy sigh preceded his response.

"Yes, Lillian, it was me." Sebastian turned away from Lillian and placed his hands against a yew tree, bending his head forward as he did so.

"Why did you do it?" Lillian's voice was flat, as she battled to contain her emotions.

Denial

"I cannot say."

"Cannot, or will not?"

"Lillian!" Sebastian's response was plaintive.

"Sebastian, I *demand* an answer!"

"It is an answer I cannot give." To tell Lillian that there had been a plan to seduce her solely for her money would be a cruelty beyond measure. No one had ever loved her for herself. She had trusted Gwen's judgement when she had said her beau was an honest man. Would she believe Sebastian if he were now to unmask that man as a villain? Wouldn't it look as if he were simply blaming another for his own guilt? To tell her that her trust had been ill-founded would open a wound that might never heal. Whatever the consequences, he could never tell her the real reason.

Lillian took the silence as an insult; as though she had been slighted or ignored, which only inflamed her temper.

"Sebastian, will you answer me?" Still, there was no response. "Is it a practice of yours to go around attempting to murder innocent people? After all, you managed to dispose of my brother rather cleverly." As soon as she had said it, Lillian bit her tongue with regret.

Sebastian made no movement, indeed made no response whatsoever. Lillian looked up to see only his back and bowed head. The candle over which he stood spluttered and plunged them into darkness. Tears had filled Sebastian's eyes and, falling to the ground, it had been these that had doused the little flame.

"I'm sorry Sebastian. Please forgive me." The words were barely audible.

"How could you think such a thing? I loved your brother. Maybe I did destroy him, but I didn't murder him. Do you know what it feels like to walk around with a burden of grief and guilt like that upon my shoulders? To exist knowing one of the few people I have ever loved lies rotting away in the cold ground because of my actions? Do you know what it is like to have these thoughts and know that until the end of time they will always be with me? Even after everything else has gone and I alone exist, that knowledge will still haunt me. The knowledge that I could have saved him. And now? What could be worse than a condemnation by she who remains - the sole vessel of my passion?

Do you think I would have let him go alone had I known the outcome? All I gave him was the knowledge he needed to act in a way that was true to himself ..." Sebastian's sentence broke and he turned away.

"I'm sorry." Lillian's words sounded hollow and empty. The silence between the two became deafening before Lillian continued. "Sebastian, it's not that I *don't* feel for you - I feel for you *too* much." Sebastian turned to face Lillian, as though simply to hear the words would not have been enough. Lillian, her eyes now accustomed to the light, anticipated the move and turned away. "I worry about you. You say you want us to be together. Maybe it would make us both happy now, but what about in ten years? Twenty years? Fifty years? Sebastian, I'm not like you. There is blood in my veins. This skin will age and wither. How can we two be one when you shall forever remain as you are now? Sebastian, I have to think of what's right for *both* of us."

"No, Lillian." Sebastian made a sudden movement toward her, falling to his knees at her feet. Clutching both her hands, he pressed them to his lips. Tears, again, began to well in his eyes. Teardrops spilt from the corners, trickling warm and wet over Lillian's hands. "Whatever you say, I won't go. I want to always be with you. I cannot leave you."

"Oh, Sebastian!" By now, she too had begun to cry. "Tell me it isn't so. Tell me the warmth I feel beneath my fingers is the blood of a human heart - that the tears flowing from your eyes are the same as mine own. Tell me that is true and I will try to forget everything else. You don't know how I long to press my lips to yours, but to do so would be my undoing, knowing afterwards they nevermore could part. Sebastian, tell me that the years will not take me from you and that their passing will change us *both*. Tell me, and I will believe you. But, I fear, where now you hold a young woman, one day she will be an old one, whilst you remain as you are now." Her sentence broke off, choked by her tears.

"I don't care. What can my existence be without you?" Sebastian stood and brought his face toward Lillian's until the warmth of his breath touched her face. In silence, Sebastian brought his lips forward, lifting his hand as he did so to draw it through her hair. As their lips were about to touch, Lillian brought the palm of her hand between them and turned away.

Denial

"Sebastian, I care. It hurts me more than you can ever know to tell you this, but you *must* leave." Convulsively, Sebastian's grip tightened around a thick mass of Lillian's hair. "Sebastian, you're hurting me!"

"And what are you doing to me? To *us*?" Lillian began to sob profusely. Closing her eyes, she brought a little handkerchief from her pocket and mopped away her tears.

"But Lillian, if you too could live forever, you would never find anyone who loves you more than I." The desperation in his voice had gone, as he let his hands fall to his side.

"You don't know that." Both of them knew in their heart that he spoke the truth.

"I do because you don't know the depth of my affection." Sebastian extended a hand, in the hope that his touch might console her.

"Nor you, mine. That is why you must leave and never return. Sebastian, ours is a love against nature." Lillian closed her eyes. There was nothing but silence. Lillian guessed that Sebastian had already left. She was about to break into a fresh outburst of uncontrolled sobs when a hand gently, just for a moment, took hold of hers. Through her veil of tears, she could see Sebastian's disconsolate face drawing nearer her own.

"Lillian, please don't send me away. Stop and think about what it will do to both of us. Is it really your dearest wish that I should leave?" Choking back the tears she could do nothing more than nod an affirmation. Was she doing the right thing? Already there were doubts. Would it be right to say yes, and live for the eternal now? But then, what of the future? What would other people say? If she were to follow her passions, then she would fall into his arms here and now. How would it be to run her fingers through his long, dark hair? To press her lips to his? No! She had changed her mind. She must have him or die. Wiping her eyes, she opened them only to find the little wood cold, dark, and empty.

Lillian made a dash back to her garden. If she were quick, she might be able to catch him. Through the gate, the raging storm lashed the Welsh mountainside more terribly than ever. Now, it seemed as if her world were ending. Where was he? Lillian shouted his name at the top of her voice. Why had she sent him away again! Nowhere was Sebastian to be seen. To call his name was futile for it was lost in the roar of the elements. Nature had conspired against her. Slowly, she sank to her knees in the mud.

"Oh Sebastian, I'm sorry. I'm so, *so* sorry. Please come back … I love you." The words were spoken quietly into the sodden earth.

It was too late. Already, the young man had made his way up an ancient mountain path toward what appeared to be an equally old outcrop of farm buildings, seemingly wrought from the landscape and long since abandoned. Oblivious to Lillian's lamentations, onwards he strode, ever onward, out into the hopeless night.

The last few hours of that day Lillian spent in solitude, in the old house. All the while, the weather raged and foamed like a wild, untamed beast. Inside, floods were equally forthcoming as Lillian bewailed her lost love. To think it was she who had cast him out, uncaring of where he might go, not even thinking if he *had* somewhere to go. Then she thought of how she really felt for him, and how, now, he might never know. Would he always think himself scorned when, in actuality, he was adored? Would she be able to treat him lovingly, even if he did return? Then she would think of the possibility of never seeing him again and, once again, the tears flowed.

When Lillian awoke the next morning, the events of the previous day seemed distant; dreamlike, as though they had happened centuries before, or had been nothing more than a story someone had once told, and her imagination had embroidered the rest. She had expected Sebastian's presence to be still felt by the vacuum he had left behind yet today, for the moment, things felt normal.

Pulling back the sheets, Lillian took a few faltering steps toward the window, yawning and trying to shake the last vestiges of sleep from her aching body. In the morning sunshine, the garden appeared brilliant: even her bedroom felt as if golden arms were stretching through the panes, to tenderly enfold her. Despite the day being an autumn one, the garden looked new: fresh.

A gentle knock on her bedroom door begged her attention. Lillian turned, just as Gwen pushed the door open and entered.

"Gwen, you're back!" Lillian ran to her friend and threw her arms around her. The two embraced. Lillian had missed her friend. So much had happened in the short time they had been apart, that Lillian felt as though they had last met a lifetime ago. "How's your intended?"

"Oh, he's much better. The truth has come out. He'd seen a young woman being attacked by a man and, bravely, went to save her. In the fight that followed he was stabbed. He may have been a bit drunk, but he's so brave." Gwen became starry-eyed, as she looked at the ceiling with a smile on her face.

"Not attacked, then?" In a strange way, she hoped Gwen's fiancé had been attacked. She, after all, had blamed Sebastian. She could feel justly vindicated if the attack had been an unprovoked one perpetrated by Sebastian. Had the injured man not been the victim of an attack, then she had sent Sebastian away for the sole reason that his presence was too much of a temptation to her. But what if Gwen's intended was telling the truth? What if Sebastian had been attacking a woman and he, being genuinely chivalrous, had gone to her assistance? Was Sebastian lying? She loved him and hated him; was jealous of him; would have given him all she had but was such an attack beyond him? If only she could convince herself of his villainy, it might ease the pain of never seeing him again. No! That thought was just too awful. She would lie down and die now if she thought that to be the case. Oh, to see the breeze blow through his hair again, or the light catch the colour of his eyes.

"No, not attacked as such. After his head cleared the truth came out. He cried as he told me how helpless he had felt at not being able to do more to save that woman." Gwen said, in ignorant admiration.

The words seemed to grab Lillian. Before, there had been uncertainties about whether she had done the right thing in sending Sebastian away. Now, it began to appear that she had been wrong. It had helped to presume him guilty, easing her own doubts. Now, if he were innocent, she felt as if she had betrayed them both.

Gwen set a small silver tray that she had brought upon the heavy oak desk, from which Lillian conducted her limited correspondence, and left. Although her duties were, strictly speaking, to clean the house, the bond that had grown up between the two women meant that she often brought Lillian her breakfast in the morning. Occasionally, the two would have breakfast together but Gwen was evidently busy today.

Now that Lillian was alone, she wandered back to the window. The old gardener was pottering about trying to look busy, but in actuality, doing very little.

"Sebastian ... What have I done? Will, I ever see you again?" She raised her hand to her face and was surprised to find her eyes had moistened her cheeks. Tiny tears streamed between her fingers. A few drops fell upon her hair, unsealing a scent. "Sebastian." Even the aroma of his body clung to her.

Days turned to weeks; weeks to months. Lillian began to reconcile herself to not seeing Sebastian again, yet far from time easing the pain, every day became a trial. Nights were no easier. Lillian went to bed breathing his name; every morning she awoke from dreams of him. Sleep, nonetheless, brought some escape, for it was only then that they could be together. Tenderly; gently, her fingers would run over the contours of his face. Softly, yet with strength, his arms would hold her close to him, making everything right and safe in the world. All the pain would go. He would tell her how much he loved everything about her, even the things she hated about herself because those things made her uniquely her. She was the person he loved utterly: without condition or fear. Then she would awaken and find herself alone in an otherwise empty room. She would tell herself it had all been a dream - a fantasy - because no one could ever feel like that about her, not wanting to acknowledge the fact that Sebastian really did feel about her in such a way.

Drearily, every day became the same as the last. Sometimes, she thought of how Sebastian must feel, for sometimes she too felt nature to be mocking her, leaving her an outsider, unable to participate. Why did she feel so bad? After all, she had everything anyone could want: a nice house, money, a friend that loved her. Yet without that special love, it all meant nothing. Only Sebastian could supply that love, and what had she done? Sent him away! It hadn't been anything he had done - even she could recognise that - nor could he have done more. It was her own feelings about herself that had destroyed everything. Feeling unlovable, she had become just that. Every day, she withdrew more and more; hating herself more and more. Looking in the mirror, she would see a monster, where others saw beauty. Who but Sebastian could see it

Denial

all and still be there for her? Her inward self - the part that blooms like a rare orchid when nourished with love and affection - had died. Inside her there was nothing but dry and dusty sands, awaiting a little rain. Only she could see the many bleached bones upon that sand, bones that had once been living things who had died waiting.

A year slowly slipped by her. Nothing, on the surface, appeared to have changed. Lillian found a little solace in her garden, as once her brother had done.

Once again, autumn arrived and replete with all its golden legions. Lillian, standing silently, gave an involuntary shudder as a weeping willow, caught in the breeze, tenderly lashed her. Breathlessly, it intoned: "How my heart trembles at your vanished presence." Only nature punctuated her endless emptiness, yet nature also denied her. If only she knew where Sebastian's lonely wandering had taken him.

Far away, over purple-black desolate moors and mountains; lakes smooth and black as ink; over ancient forests, as wild and old as time, strode a figure as desolate as the landscape of which he stood a part.

Through the early morning mist, the young man made his way through the dense bracken and fern that clung to his feet. In the distance, a forest threw out wraith-like shapes that shimmered in the rising sun. Was there really something awful within those sylvan glades? Something lurking, waiting to take him away from everything he had ever known, or ever loved: something to cast him into the eternal night?

His path led to the deep, dense foliage. Flecks of golden sunshine pierced the dying verdant canopy, turning silver in the rising diaphanous mist.

Absolute stillness made the wood eerie. One might have expected a birdsong - or even a whisper in the trees as the wind embraced them - but there was nothing. As quiet as the wood, Sebastian strode onward, pausing occasionally to stand. If only he had known that such still waters presaged an approaching storm: a storm that might well dash him upon rocks as jagged as the Welsh mountains.

As the trees began to thin, Sebastian found himself at the top of a hill, or rather, upon the peak of a vast expanse of land that looked down upon a valley. An old path, as broken and forgotten as those who had built it, spiralled down to a river, a bridge, and on the far side, a small village.

Sebastian made his way down the steep-sided, precipitous slope toward the village. Each footstep was a painful one, separating him from where he really wished to be.

As he approached the little stone bridge that spanned the fast-flowing river, the sun tore away its death mask and arose to bathe the land in what, Sebastian thought, felt like warm amber after the horrors of another sleepless night. Ghostlike and unreal, three figures, still in the distance but approaching, emerged from the rapidly vanishing mist. Half-glimpsed; ethereal.

Drawing nearer, their features became defined; distinct. A young man, perhaps twenty-five years of age, with a shock of red hair. A second man, perhaps twice the age of the first accompanied but whereas the first had been slim the second had a portlier frame that betrayed his age. He too had red hair, yet Sebastian's attention was drawn to a figure that walked between them.

In the fading mist, Sebastian almost thought the woman to be Lillian. Drawing nearer still, her eyes could be seen to be red and puffy. It also became increasingly apparent that, far from being with the pair by choice, her two companions held her in a firm embrace; one on each arm, apparently escorting her from the village. As the unlikely trio reached the far edge of the bridge, they came to an abrupt stop. By now, Sebastian was just a few yards from them.

Their halt had not been a simple stop, but also an abrupt turn that meant all three were now facing the right-hand wall of the little stone bridge. A few ill-constructed bricks were all that separated the three from the fast-flowing waters beneath them. Curiosity had got the better of Sebastian, but even he could scarcely believe it as the elder of the two men took a rope from his pocket and, pulling the woman's arms behind her, tied them roughly at the wrists. For her part, she now appeared compliant, even willing.

The younger of the two men produced a small, hessian sack. Drawing the woman's head toward him, it became apparent her head was to go inside. If the woman had been crying, she now

Denial

accepted events with a calm, even dignified, resignation.

Sebastian had seen enough. His presence had seemingly gone unnoticed. Now it was time to make known his disapproval, putting an end to the perverse ritual. Drawing level with the three, he snatched the sacking and tossed it into the river, whereupon it sank and was lost from view.

"Eh, what are you doing?" The protestation was made to Sebastian's back.

"What are *you* doing?" Sebastian said as he spun around.

"Dad ...?" The younger of the two had turned, looking to his father to supply an answer.

"It's alright, son. Hey, you, leave us alone." The elder man sought to allay his son's fears, before turning to Sebastian.

Sebastian stood in glaring silence. Were they really going to throw a woman to a certain death, and speak of it as if he had interrupted a family day out?

"You, take your damned hands off her!" Sebastian pointed to the younger man. "Whilst you ..." For the first time, the elder man's eyes met with Sebastian's.

"But she's a whore. We throw whores in the river. It's what we do."

Despite trying to qualify himself, the elder man unhanded the woman and looked to Sebastian to make the next move. Sebastian looked for approval from the young woman. She really did look like Lillian, but that wasn't why he wished to help. Why should she suffer under some outdated feudal justice?

"You release her ... now!" Sebastian brought his hand up and, with a pointed finger, thrust it to within a hair's breadth of the younger man's face.

"Do as he says, son." The father nodded an affirmation to his offspring, the younger man doing as he was told before, along with his father, shuffling away. Occasionally his head would turn around but, catching Sebastian's gaze, would quickly turn back. Only when the distance between them was deemed sufficiently safe did he feel brave enough to fire a parting shot.

"She's a slut." As he said it, he turned quickly away and ran, leaving his father to slowly follow.

As the two men faded into the distance, Sebastian's thoughts came back to his own situation and that of the still-unnamed woman. There was an awkwardness to their plight that he had not anticipated. Would she look to him for answers? She could not go back to her own village, obviously, for they would only succeed in what they had already attempted. She was now as much an outcast and a wanderer as he.

Sebastian turned to face the woman.

"Thank you. What do you mean to do with me?" Her voice was almost inaudible; pathetic. It appeared that no recourse other than victim had ever been open to her.

"I don't mean to do anything with you. You're free to go." Sebastian averted his eyes and looked at the river.

"Free to go where?" Freedom has its burdens: both she and Sebastian were free, yet neither had a place to call home.

"Well ... what's your name?" Sebastian said, letting out a sigh.

"Sabrina."

"Ah, Goddess of the Severn," Sebastian said before the irony of the name and her recent situation dawned on him. "Well, Sabrina, suppose I give you a little money. Is there a place to which you could then go?" Sebastian brought himself around to face the woman.

"I've no place to go. I wish you had let them drown me. I can't be with the person I love. I've no home. I wish I were dead." Sabrina sat down and rested her back against the wall of the bridge.

"I can understand that," Sebastian said, causing Sabrina to look at him with surprise.

"You can? Have you ever loved someone, then?" It wasn't that Sabrina was prying, simply that she had a naive curiosity more often associated with children.

"Yes. Yes, I have." Sabrina was intrigued by Sebastian's wistful look.

"Did she love you?"

"I would like to think that deep down she did, but I'm not right for her. Perhaps she should find someone else." Sebastian looked back to the river. In the morning light, the sun had sent out golden trails that flooded upon it, making it appear a resplendent pathway to distant and exotic lands.

"Then you don't love her anymore?"

"I love her more than life. Her happiness is my happiness."

Denial

"Nobody's ever loved me like that." Sabrina looked from Sebastian to the wall on the other side of the bridge, opposite.

"We must get away from here. They're bound to come back for you." Sebastian stretched out a hand to help Sabrina to her feet.

"Let them. I don't care." There was no petulance in Sabrina's voice, only despair.

"Sabrina, death is a precious thing. Don't waste it." In the distance, Sebastian could see a mob approaching.

Sebastian made up his mind not to risk another refusal, so bending over, he scooped up Sabrina's unhappy form and carried her. In what seemed like a moment, they were back under the safety and cover of the trees. The mist had finally lifted. From the forest, a path had now emerged. Sebastian let Sabrina gently to the ground. Exhausted, he fell to her side and rolled upon his back.

"I could have walked, you know, but thank you for saving me ... I don't know your name." Sabrina brushed the indignation from her clothes.

"Sebastian." Sebastian, still prone, stared up at the sky.

"Nobody has ever cared whether I lived, or died, before." Sebastian's gesture had struck an emotional response.

"I'm sure they have." Sebastian turned his head to face Sabrina.

"They haven't. I've no one. I'm frightened."

"You needn't be frightened." Sebastian tried to believe his own words but winced at their hollowness. What could *he* do? It would be impossible for him to take Sabrina with him for he had no place to go himself. It would be difficult for her to find employment in this area as it was far too remote and barren. She would have to go to the borders or the coast. If she went south, maybe he could help her. He chose to ponder the matter before making any suggestions.

"What was going on in that village?" There was a little curiosity in him, regarding Sabrina's situation, but the question was to buy him some time to think of how best he could help her.

"It's not what you think. I'm not a slut. I worked for a wealthy landowner, as did the other two you saw with me. Because I was poor and had no family, he took advantage of me. One day, last week, his wife caught us together. As soon as she had the chance, she told those two to throw me in the river. They've done it before ... to someone else." Sabrina began her story slowly and without emotion, but by the end of it had begun to cry.

"I'm very sorry." Sebastian had intended to pay scant attention to Sabrina's story, but as the pitiful tale unfolded, he began to take an interest. By the end, her plight felt almost as real to him as it did to her.

For the first time, he was able to give her the attention she deserved. She really *did* look like Lillian. Both had the same dark hair and eyes; the same sensuous mouth and full red lips. The difference was their attire: whereas Lillian could now afford nice clothes from London, Sabrina's clothes were made of dark and heavy fabrics that were torn and dirty. But it was her boots that made her truly pitiful. It wasn't that she was pathetic, it was that circumstances had brought her to such a level. Huge working boots, that made her legs look painfully thin. That anyone should be reduced to this, Sebastian thought.

"Sabrina, will you do something for me?" Sabrina looked at Sebastian, intrigued.

"That depends."

"If I give you some money, will you go south for me with a message?"

"What do you want me to say? Who do you want me to see?" Sabrina, although not suspicious, did not want to commit herself.

"Here." Sebastian rummaged in his coat pocket and pulled out a perfectly creased letter.

"May I read it?" Sebastian knew she would eventually do so, even if he said 'No' now.

"If you must." Sebastian moved on to his back again, staring skyward.

"My dearest love." Sabrina began the letter, reading aloud in the manner of those unfamiliar with such a practice. "I have never ceased nor can cease to feel for a moment that perfect and boundless attachment which bound me and binds me to you - which renders me utterly incapable of real love for any other human being - for what could they be after you? They say absence destroys weak passions - and confirms strong ones - Alas! mine for you is the union of all passions or of all affections - has strengthened itself but will destroy me." Sabrina finished and fell silent.

"I'm glad I heard you reading it." Sebastian took the letter from

Denial

Sabrina and tore it in two.

"Why? What did you do that for? It was a beautiful letter." Sabrina was shocked by the violence of Sebastian's actions, especially after reading such beautiful sentiments.

"Because, Sabrina, the wages of scorned love is baneful hate. Why should I write such a glowing missive to one who has cast me aside?"

Sabrina stared at Sebastian, uncomprehending.

"Do you still want me to take a message then?"

"Yes. I want you to go to the woman I love and tell her I had your sister drowned because she was incapable of keeping a true affection for me. Say whatever you wish. I want her to *hate* me with a passion."

"Are you sure? That's an awful thing to do - cruel." No sooner had she said the final word, Sebastian interrupted.

"Cruel? Cruel! Don't talk to me of cruelty. That's why I want you to do it. I want her to hate me. I want her to curse me ... *and the day we met.* May her unquiet spirit know as little rest as mine."

"You sound as though you hate her," Sabrina began to wonder what sort of a person Sebastian was.

"Perhaps it is best if we hate each other. Shadows of death would only blight the marriage bed. I want her to find someone who can love her as an equal. If she has any feelings for me then she will never be able to do that. Will you take that message for me?"

"Yes, I will, but I think you're making a mistake." There was a little hesitancy in Sabrina's voice, before she agreed, remembering the debt of gratitude she owed the troubled man in front of her.

"Better to suffer the once, than be left to suffer for eternity ... as I must," speaking the words under his breath.

"You talk as if you're immortal!" Sabrina gave a nervous giggle.

"Do I? I'm glad you find it amusing." Sebastian gave Sabrina a cold look, before averting his eyes.

"I'm sorry." Sabrina intoned, before falling silent. She felt embarrassed, now that Sebastian thought she had been mocking him. Even in the short time since they had met, she could see there was something painful deep within him: a wellspring of emptiness; of something unresolved.

"So, will you do it?" he said, before standing up.

"Yes, but I'm not happy at being the cause of so much grief." Sabrina had a rare sensitivity in her nature and genuinely cared for people. Like Sebastian, she would have given her life for love, or simply to have one person say they needed her.

"There will be a kindness in your cruelty." Sebastian may have had his doubts, but kept them hidden.

"I'm not convinced, but I will do it." Sebastian's face creased into a smile, which quickly vanished. He reached into his pocket and withdrew a card with Lillian's address upon it.

"Here's the address," he said, before passing the card to Sabrina.

"Aren't you coming with me?" Her voice betrayed her alarm.

"No. No, I cannot. I have my own path to follow. I shall give you a little money to help you. The town I want you to go to is a little more affluent than this one. You'll be able to get work there." Sebastian helped his companion to her feet.

"But what if I cannot?" Sabrina lowered her head.

"You will." Sebastian brought his eyes to focus upon the young woman who was looking to him to answer all her questions. Raising her eyes, they met with his.

"Do you promise?" Already, Sabrina believed him.

"You have my word." The words were hypnotic. Reaching inside a pocket, he pulled out a small reticule, which he then passed to Sabrina. Tenderly, he took her hand and, uncurling her fingers, placed the bag in her palm. The young woman stood staring at it.

"I can't. I can't take all this." It appeared as if she had never seen so much money.

"You can. If you do as I ask, I would pay you all I have." Sebastian spoke the words with assurance. "It's only money. We attach too much importance to it. All the money in the world can't buy the things that *really* matter. All material things eventually pass away."

Sabrina looked at him. She was a simple, untutored woman, yet her innately sympathetic nature went out to the man standing in front of her. She also knew of pain; of being a rare bloom, bruised and crushed by life. She may have been ill-educated but was as capable of as wide a spectrum of feeling as anyone.

The two made their way to one of the well-worn animal trails. Why hadn't Sebastian been able to find such a trail before? Within a short while, Sabrina caught hold of Sebastian's arm.

"Have you seen that?" Sebastian followed the direction in which she was pointing. At first, obscured by the dense undergrowth, it was difficult to make out to what Sabrina was pointing. Strange, unfamiliar, plants covered huge stones, but standing stones carved and laid with purpose. The passage of time had made the ancient stones an anachronism, something that now had no place in a Christian country. What evil had so successfully burnt its own history, destroying the past? Sebastian knew but, for once, kept the answer to himself.

It wasn't long before the narrow track brought the two to the far side of the dense forest and back into the autumn sunshine. High in the sky, the flaming orb that had greeted the day a few hours before had turned pearlescent, yet still sought to spread itself over the desolate expanse in front of them. A single earthen track cleaved the landscape in two, it being the only thing that gave an indication that a human presence had, at some stage, sought to tame such a wilderness. Apart from that, the two might have been playing out a scene from any date in history. As far as the horizon, nothing could be seen save coarse grass, marshland, bracken, and fern. In the distance, an elevation in the land culminated in a mountain.

"Here we must part." Sebastian breathed the words as his eyes focussed on the horizon.

"I will be safe, won't I?"

Sebastian's heart softened. Had he never met Lillian, he might have found happiness with someone like Sabrina, but then she too, in time, would have had to know his dark and terrible secret. Even if he chose not to tell her, the inexorable march of time would have eventually betrayed him. The years would pass but his countenance would remain unchanged. Then, one day, in one way or another, she would be snatched from him and, once again, the terrible spectre of loneliness would descend leaving him alone for all eternity, to grieve for his lost love.

"Yes, quite safe." Sebastian turned his head to look at Sabrina.

"Then this is goodbye." Sabrina looked at Sebastian's for an indication otherwise.

"Yes, Sabrina. I'm sorry."

"So am I," Said Sabrina, gently pulling his head toward her own until her lips brushed the side of his face. Then she turned and, as casually as she could manage, gestured a last goodbye. Twice she turned to look upon his dark silhouette outlined against the trees. The third time she looked he was gone.

A few days later, Sabrina arrived in the small town, a town that had once been a camp for a Celtic tribe known as the Silures. Sabrina's appearance did not mark her out for undue attention so quietly and unobtrusively, the young woman wandered from shop to shop, buying a few things, yet all the while trying to muster the courage to perform her act of duplicity. More than once her nerves got the better of her and she thought of leaving, never to return. After all, Sebastian would never know, but then she thought about where she could go. There was also the obligation she felt to return Sebastian's kindness. She resolved to do what Sebastian had asked, concluding that he knew Lillian's mind far better than she did. If he thought that by telling her he had had a mistress drowned would spare Lillian's feelings then who was she to say otherwise?

She made her way through the old arch, and up the steep hill that separated the town from the outlying areas. Without expecting to, she quickly found herself on the right road. With trepidation, she made her way toward the large house that stood magnificent, overlooking the town. So much had changed so quickly. Had it only been a few days since she had lived and worked with people who, upon the words of an overlord, had suddenly tried to kill her? Those experiences felt like an empty lifetime ago.

She raised a small hand and, hoping no one would answer, knocked on the old black door. A noise came from within as hard-heeled shoes hammered upon the flagstone floor. An unfastening of bolts preceded a fearful creak, as though some old tomb was about to give up its dead. The door finally opened and Gwen stood within the frame of the massive portal.

"Yes, can I help you?" Gwen smiled, her manner cheerful, which only made Sabrina's task all the more difficult.

"Miss Lillian? Do you know Mr Sebastian?" Sabrina had not

waited for a response to her first question before asking the second. She felt embarrassed at not knowing either Lillian's surname or Sebastian's but felt it would be more mannerly to give them some sort of a title even if, after she had said it, she felt gauche. She had expected to stammer, or feel her face begin to burn; her nerves to unmask her as a fraud. Whilst thinking over her story, she had thought it a good idea to pretend she was estranged from her fictitious sister. It would be so much easier to play the role if little emotion was needed. She might be able to lie for Sebastian, but she couldn't act for him.

"No." Gwen's reply was emphatic.

"You don't?" Sabrina felt a rush of joy. The thought that Sebastian may have given her the wrong address, or that the family had moved, seemed like a blessing. After all, she had fulfilled her part of the deal.

"No, I'm not Miss Lillian. I'm her maid." Sabrina felt her optimism sink. She would have to carry through her awful charade after all. "I'll see if she's at home." Within a few minutes, Gwen had returned. "Come in."

Sabrina's heart began to beat a little faster, sending convulsions that the young woman felt in the back of her dry throat. The sides of her eyes began to pulse and darken. Gwen gestured for the stranger to follow her.

The two women walked a short way up one of the long, dark halls before pausing as they finally reached a door on the left. Gwen gave it a gentle knock. A voice from within indicated approval had been granted to enter. Gwen turned the handle, and the door groaned open.

"This is ...?" Gwen looked at the visitor with expectant eyes.

"Sabrina." Sabrina felt her long, dark hair sticking to the sides of her face, burning it as though each strand were made of something incandescent.

"This is Sabrina." Gwen smiled and left.

For a few short seconds, Lillian said nothing. What did her guest know of Sebastian? It had been a long time since she had seen him; a long time since anyone had spoken his name. She imagined her lips saying his name. Delicious. Gwen's absence made the silence awkward

"Please, sit down. I'm forgetting my manners." Lillian gestured to a chair. "You have news of Sebastian?" Lillian's manner became officious. She had erected an emotional shield to hide behind; now someone had come seeking to knock it aside. It was unusual for Lillian to dispense with pleasantries, but passion affects us all in strange ways. As Sabrina sat, Lillian walked to the window, her back to her guest. She expected bad news, and something illogical within her made her feel that by not being able to see the bringer of ill-tidings then, somehow, the bad news would be lessened.

"Yes." Sabrina did her best to make herself comfortable in the soft, heavy chair but the whole situation left her feeling quite the opposite. She had become acutely aware of how her attire differed from Lillian's. Lillian had glided to the window like liquid and now stood like a classical statue. Her flowing cambric dress flowed with her. Short sleeves and a low neckline highlighted how clean the morning ablutions had left her. Sabrina looked at her own dirty hands and then at Lillian's shoes, shoes that were flat and pointed with a thin sole, cross-gartered in the classical fashion; as was the Attic grace with which she wore her hair. Even the room had a refined elegance to it that was far removed from the dark quarters of the near-medieval rustic retreat of other parts of the house. Again, Sabrina appraised herself. Her heavy working clothes jarred severely with those of Lillian. And what of her bare, unstockinged legs, terminating in a pair of oversized men's working boots, boots that had left a trail of damp mud on Lillian's carpet?

"Good or bad?" Lillian braced herself for the worse.

"Bad." Sabrina followed the word with a dry gulp.

"I thought as much." The dangerous liaison Lillian had had with Sebastian ought to have been tempered by her fear of him, but it was fear that made him so appealing. She had always expected he would somehow bring about his own undoing.

"What news have you?"

Now, Sabrina braced herself. She was glad that Lillian had turned her back on her as that made her promise to Sebastian that much easier to keep.

"Some time ago, my sister and I met Sebastian at a May Day Fair in our village. He introduced himself to us both but his interest, it soon became clear, was in my sister. It wasn't long before his attention was returned. I warned her because I could tell there was something odd about him. His passion for her was like a fire - often it appeared to be nothing more than grey embers, yet the slightest jealousy could cause it to burn with rage. Hers was a more constant flame that lit everything it touched. I could see that Sebastian cared less for my sister than she did for him, but she wouldn't listen. She never spoke to me again after I told her." Sabrina paused. By now she had warmed to her part, finding it easy to create a story from nothing. "Then one day, we heard she was expecting a child. I was told that he asked her to get rid of it - with a hot bath and gin - suspecting the child to have been fathered by another. She wouldn't. Somehow, he got a few of his acquaintances and - God save me - had her tied up and thrown in the river, for the infidelity he'd imagined. They fished out her body the next day."

For a long while, Lillian remained with her back to Sabrina. Silent tears clouded her eyes. She longed to turn and express her sympathies, but for who would those sympathies be? Sabrina and her sister? For Sebastian, and what he had become? For herself? If Sabrina's story were true - and she had no reason to doubt it - then Sebastian's embittered heart was lost to her forever. Eventually, she stemmed the flow of tears sufficiently to speak.

"I'm very sorry, but why bring me this story? What do *I* care of Sebastian?" Lillian did her best to sound indifferent but her voice had cracked as she spoke his name, doing her a disloyalty.

"It's the only address we had. He left in rather a hurry, leaving a few things behind. One was a letter with your name on ..."

"Where? Show me?" Lillian's quick and spirited interruption destroyed any pretence she had sought at indifference. She cared, and cared *too* much. Sabrina felt herself sink into her chair as remorse began to wash over her in an unholy ablution. She had raised the tearful young woman's hopes unduly. There was no letter, for no such events had ever taken place. Now, Lillian had turned to face her. Sabrina shifted uneasily in her seat, looking away.

"I'm ... I'm afraid I don't have it with me." Sabrina knew any inconsistencies in her story might unmask her as a liar.

"Did you read it? What did it say?" Lillian snapped the words voraciously.

"I'm afraid I don't read too well. Someone told me the address.

My mother asked me to come and tell you, to see if you knew where Sebastian was." Sabrina let out a sigh. Lillian slumped into a nearby settee. How she wished she was small so that the folds of the fabric might have the expanse of huge fields, fields where she might lose herself.

The two women sat in silence. Lillian wishing to be alone; Sabrina wanting to leave, yet both lacked the words to bring their meeting to a close.

"Anyway, I'm sorry if it's all been a mistake. If you're not that close to him, I don't suppose any of this is of interest to you." Sabrina rose to her feet.

"I'm sorry about your sister." To speak any more of Sebastian would be too upsetting.

"Yes. May the gods have mercy on her." Sabrina looked anxiously at the door.

"I'll see you out." The conversation was becoming stilted; strained.

As the two walked the long hall, the only sound heard came from Sabrina's heavy boots. To little effect, she tried to walk on tiptoe.

Finally, they came to Lillian's front door. Quickly, Lillian opened it.

"Well, thank you for coming. I'm sorry I couldn't be more helpful." A strained smile flashed across Lillian's face.

"Thank you for listening. Goodbye", said Sabrina, escaping, Lillian closed the door behind her, without reply.

As the door shut, Lillian let out a sigh. Turning, she rested her back against the old timbers. In the dim passageway, it wasn't easy to see her whole body shaking, convulsing, as grief took its toll. Sobbing, she slid to the floor.

"Sebastian. Oh, Sebastian." The first call of his name seemed spoken to a friend: as if Sebastian had appeared in front of her. Her second intonation was softer, like the tone of a mother receiving a first birthday card from her child. Both times, sobs punctuated her phrasing.

Sebastian's scheme had failed. Lillian's affection for him had not dimmed nor lessened. In some strange way, she blamed herself for having driven him to such a base level; as though by spurning his affection, she had driven him to exact a terrible revenge upon all other members of the human race.

"Are you alright?" From the darkness, Gwen's voice came like a soft light.

"Dead. Dead." Through her veil of tears, Lillian murmured.

"Sebastian?" Although she had not met him, Gwen knew the name.

"Dead. Dead."

"Sebastian? Dead?" Gwen knew nothing of Sebastian's lonely and unending pilgrimage.

"Dead. Dead." Lillian began to wail uncontrollably.

Lillian closed her eyes. If only she were someone else; somewhere else. Somewhere where pain and misery would be unable to touch her. Yes, that would be nice. In the background, the perfect ticking of a grandfather clock stopped.

Sebastian's name was not often mentioned after that day. As the days turned to weeks, and then to months, his name was spoken less and less. Only Lillian remembered, when on the darkest nights the storms outside her window, and the rumble of thunder far away over the Welsh hills, reminded her of the night she had sent him away. The thought of him was never far away, but at certain times - when the whole universe appeared angry and tormented - the thought of him would become a constant one. Lying in her bed, sometimes it felt as though she could reach out and touch him, as he appeared silhouetted against the window. Running to meet him, her arms would pass through nothing more than cold shadows. She would open the curtains and, hope against hope, look out to see if, once again, his rain-soaked face might be there, gazing up at her from the garden far below.

Months became years. People came and went. Gwen married her hero. She continued to work for Lillian, despite having children and, in due course, her children having children. The Llewellyns had long gone the way of the flesh, as had Lillian's mother. Only Lillian sought to stay as she always had. She, however, was powerless to stop the years changing her. Now, when she looked in the mirror, she saw her once young and vibrant face turned into that of a lonely old woman, framed by silver hair, and with an expression bearing the saddest words of all: "It might have been."

Lillian was old. She had never married. How could she after

Temptation and Denial

him? Of course, she had had her chances. She had been both a beautiful and eligible young woman in her time but the days, like the suitors, were gone. How different things might have been if only she had been given the chance to change things. Now, it was too late. She had wasted a lifetime waiting. All those wasted years, years that might have been spent with someone who could have loved her as much as she loved him. It might have given her existence some meaning. Her happiness hinged on bringing happiness to others. It had all gone horribly wrong. This wasn't the way it was meant to have been. She had wanted a husband and children of her own.

As she closed her eyes, the wind and rain began to beat their familiar pattern upon the roof above her. Tapping the windowpane louder, it seemed, than usual. In the distance, thunder and lightning began to roll and crack, as though some ghostly coachman were whipping his nags, that they might draw their leaden load across the sky just that bit faster.

"Sebastian." The night, all those years before, when she had sent him away, came back to her waking dreams.

"Oh, Sebastian. I'm so sorry." Beneath her warm sheets, Lillian shuddered, remembering.

The tapping at the window continued. Lillian opened her eyes. As before, Sebastian's shape appeared, framed by the window, darkened by the tempest outside.

"Oh, Sebastian." Lillian knew the tricks her imagination played on her. This time, however, the image was more distinct than usual.

"Sebastian." She extended her arm. To touch his handsome face once again. "Sebastian."

"Lillian." The voice was clear and unique.

Lillian sat up, as quickly as age would allow.

"Sebastian?" Many times, she felt she had seen him, but never had he spoken - not since that fateful day.

"Lillian." The voice was soft and full of sorrow.

"Is it really you?" Lillian sought to contain her excited doubts,

"Oh, Lillian." The voice cracked with emotion.

"Come. Come to me." Lillian turned to light her bedside lamp. By the time she turned back. Sebastian had moved, yet remained hidden in the shadows.

Denial

"Lillian, I'm so sorry." His voice was grief-stricken.

"Come to me." Lillian still felt unsure her senses were being truthful. Slowly, Sebastian stepped into the light. "It is you! Exactly as I remember you!" Lillian realised what she had said. The years had passed, leaving. Sebastian unchanged. "Sebastian, I'm so sorry."

Sebastian pulled a chair to the bedside and took Lillian's hand in his. His still taut skin jarred against the wrinkled fingers they embraced.

"I loved you, Sebastian. I have always loved you." Lillian squeezed Sebastian's hand.

"But you sent me away." The years had not dimmed the anguish.

"I was young. It was a terrible mistake. I came after you but you had gone."

"Don't say it. Lillian, what have we done? I would gladly have spent those fleeting years with you and mourned you until the end of time if you had only said that you wanted to spend those years with me. It would have been worth it. I really thought you didn't want me."

"Because I was afraid. I was afraid of what other people might think. Afraid of my feelings for you. I was a fool. I denied myself a chance of happiness but I was young. I thought myself unlovable. When someone like you came along, I didn't know what to do." Tears made her eyes glisten before a few spilt out. Following the lines on her face, they trickled down to the pillow beneath her. "You're so young."

"It's a curse. I, alone, will have everyone I love taken from me, whilst I remain." Tragedy was in his voice.

"Sebastian, never forget. I shall *always* love you." Lillian gave his hand another squeeze and closed her eyes.

"I only ever wanted you to be happy. I wanted you to hate me so that you might find someone else. That you might find some happiness."

"But ..."

"I know what you're going to say. I sent her. She did it for me. I wanted you to hate me. I knew if you had any of the feelings for me that I have for you, you could never be free unless those feelings were shattered forever."

A smile played on the old woman's lips for a few seconds. Her gentle breathing became shallow. Sebastian brought Lillian's hand to his lips and pressed it to them. Another smile, then the breathing stopped. Tears streaked their way down Sebastian's cheeks with a burning ferocity.

"No!" The cry was agonised and mournful. Tears rolled down his cheeks, and onto the hand still pressed in his. Running to the windows, he flung them open. From the balcony, he leapt to the garden below. The rain had turned to snow, turning hill and valley into an immaculate wasteland; featureless; unearthly.

To escape, Sebastian ran. Up to the bleak and barren Welsh moor. There, there was nothing: nothing except a white emptiness and an awful silence.

"Let me die!" Sebastian fell to his knees and raised a fist at the sky. "Let me die!" Falling forward, he buried his face in the snow. "Please, let me die."

Denied No More

But I have lived, and not lived in vain;
My mind may lose its force, my blood its fire,
And my frame perish even in conquering pain;
But there is that within me which shall tire
Torture and Time, and breathe when I expire.
                                        Byron

For a long time after Lillian's death Sebastian stayed away from the old house. Shades still cast long shadows over his mind: to immerse himself in an environment where every memory that had ever mattered had taken place would have been too much to bear. The wandering continued. A fugitive and a vagabond upon the earth. Scorned, Sebastian remained a man of sorrows, well acquainted with grief.

Only after many months had elapsed did he feel able to return, all the while knowing that there would be no homecoming. No garlands strung from steeple to steeple would welcome the return of the errant brother.

As Sebastian trudged through the quiet streets, dark and abandoned as night began to fall memories came flooding back in a deluge. In the months since Lillian had died, grief without hope of respite had made him inconsolable. All those wasted years! Experience had twisted his heart until only the bitterest of dregs could now be wrung from it. Circumstances had denied him a chance for happiness. Some terrible knot of fate had conspired to waste not only his life but Lillian's as well: love would never flow through this world again. All that resided in his hard heart now was hate and a desire for implacable revenge. Others would suffer as he had suffered, he would make sure of that!

Well-worn paths led back to a familiar place. Looming large, the old house was nearing. Onward, through leafy glade and leafy bower. Beckoning, the house called to him like a siren on the rocks. Wearily, Sebastian finally reached the outer reaches of the dark dominions of the old house. For a moment, it appeared unrecognisable. Before, there had always been a lifeblood flowing within it. Now, the house appeared exsanguinated and stood horribly alone. Every window had been boarded shut., reminding him of sightless eyes. Since the tragedy, the untended garden had grass that now stood waist-high. Rotting fruit lay on the ground, as did dead flowers.

Sebastian limped toward the house, as the last strains of a dying sun kissed goodbye to the old house's deathly facade.

For a short while, the old man stood in silent appraisal. Tearing aside a few boards, he pushed his way inside. Every piece of furniture remained as it was, only now, covered in the habiliments of the grave: death shrouds, motionless and funereal.

How life had altered in the years since Sebastian had first

visited that house! Time had poured away. So much had changed: only he remained. Sebastian moved about the room. So much was still as it had always been. Furniture, ornaments, portraits, all as he remembered them. All awaiting the loving touch of a long-departed hand. How those few artefacts had shaped lives! Now, like lovelorn orphans, they awaited the return of she who had once needed them.

As he wandered further from the door, so the room became darker. The shuttered windows let in no light. Sebastian looked about him for a lamp or a few candles. In the gloom, a small candelabra presented itself. At last, there was a little illumination.

Tentatively, Sebastian stepped from one room to the next. He had not taken much notice of the rest of the house before, being more concerned about the people that had lived there. Now that all human life lay dead, there was nothing *but* the old house, however empty and lifeless it seemed.

Sebastian's boots echoed, as each footstep met with the cold floor of the long passageway. In the dreadful silence of the house, each retort seemed to reverberate throughout the entire building. Self-consciously, Sebastian tried to lighten his steps. Unknown to him, Sabrina had once felt the same, as she had walked the same corridor. That, however, had been more than half a century before.

Each door, as it yielded to Sebastian's caress, offered new surprises. Silently peering in, few brought back memories as he had never visited them, yet each one touched him; held him with the cold clasp of the past.

Finally, the corridor came to an end. The door in front led to a different wing, the wing where, many years previously, he had found all that remained of the white hart. Sebastian shuddered. He had no desire to go further or to venture upstairs. That had been where he had last seen ... No! Why *had* he come back? The question rolled about in his head like seawater in the hull of a sinking boat, lurching it from side to side, threatening to pull it beneath the waves. Maybe it was because the old house was the nearest thing he had ever come to a home; maybe it was to feel near those he had loved - and continued to love. He had hoped the old house would soften his heart, pouring a little compassion into that empty chamber, but even now, he was aware that it had not. Only anger, rage and impotent fury flowed within it. He who had created him had left him. She whom he had loved had spurned him. Worse still, he had once returned, only to find he had been mistaken, and that both he and Lillian had wasted a lonely lifetime. Now, nothing mattered. Now, there was nothing.

Sebastian made to turn back: to return along the corridor whence he had come. As he did so, something to his left ensnared his attention. There, in the half-darkness, a gilded mirror hung uncovered upon the wall. Sebastian approached with curiosity. How did others see him? Almost petrified, he looked at his own reflection. The mirror shimmered, returning the candle's tiny flame. A young-looking man gazed back, but more. In the gloom, his reflected features had become more than his own. A face was merging with his own, softening his masculine lineaments with a softer and more female aspect. Yet still, the face was his own: the countenance of his soul. For a moment - a fleeting moment - the face had been another's: Lillian's. Two *had* become one! Sebastian reached out a hand and touched the silvered surface. In that instant, the image was gone.

"Hey, what the hell are you doing in here?" Sebastian spun around as a gruff voice challenged him. At the far end of the corridor, an athletic-looking figure stood framed in the doorway.

"I lived here ... once." Sebastian was still shaken with the image in the mirror, his words now drifting like those in a dream.

"You never lived here, boy. My grandmother worked here as a maid for over fifty years. The only person that ever lived here was the woman she worked for." The words were spat with no intention of informing but in hostility. The figure began to approach.

"Then whose house is it now?" Sebastian shouted into the darkness,

"What's it to you? Get out!" By now, the figure had drawn close enough to face Sebastian. In the shallow light, he looked familiar. His lips, that sneer. What had he said? His 'grandmother had worked for the owner'. Sebastian knew where he had seen that face before. Gwen had married the man whom Sebastian had warned away from Lillian all those years ago. Not only had they had children, but their children had also had children. History had repeated itself.

Before Sebastian could reply, his arm was snatched and

wrenched behind his back.

"Nobody's going to cheat me out of what's mine, got that?" The words were hissed into the side of Sebastian's face as he was pushed toward the door.

Sebastian's character had changed considerably in the years between his encounter with Gwen's intended and the present encounter with her grandson. Hope had fled and mercy sighed farewell. Once there had been compassion in his heart, now there was none.

Sebastian allowed himself to be pushed toward the old back door. Breath tinged with the fumes of alcohol came from behind him. His arm suffered a tug as the figure behind him stumbled. Ah, once again, perhaps there was a way to capitalise on such a condition!

Finally, the two of them reached their destination.

"Wait! This house of yours. Care to take a little bet upon it? A game of chance? The rights to your inheritance, for all the money I have on me?" Sebastian's ploy had worked. They paused.

"And if I win?"

"As I said, l shall give you all the money I have, and you shall never see me again."

"And if I lose?"

"Then I will request you to sign something to the effect that you relinquish all claims to this property."

Sebastian felt the grip on his arm slacken.

"How much money do you have, then?" The words were spoken a little more quickly.

"Enough to buy this place twice over."

"I see. Then you'd better come back inside."

Sebastian smiled to himself, as he turned. In the darkness, Gwen's grandson lurched back into the room they had just left. He staggered about the room, lighting. a few candles, before sitting down at a table.

"I need a drink." Casting a glance about him, he pulled a hip flask from his pocket and took a large gulp.

"A game of skill, or a game of chance?" Sebastian had sat down at the same table. From an inside pocket, he had drawn a pack of cards.

"Chance." Gwen's grandson swallowed his drink and moved

in his seat.

"Then we'll cut the deck. Highest card wins. Ace high."

Gwen's grandson nodded in agreement.

"You first?"

In the half-light. Sebastian leaned back in his chair, as his companion clutched at the deck before lifting his hand. The King of Diamonds. Even in the dim light, Sebastian saw his face break into a smile before his pursed lips blew a kiss at the heavens.

"C'mon, let's see your money." As if to emphasise his words, he banged the table with his outstretched finger.

Sebastian reached inside his coat pocket and withdrew a roll of banknotes of the highest currency and threw it onto the table.

"My turn." Sebastian reached out to the remaining cards and lifted half the pack. "Oh, bad luck! The Ace of Spades," Sebastian smiled and drew his wallet back to him.

"Wait! This house against *my* house." Gwen's grandson was still looking dumbfounded at the deck of cards in front of him.

"Have you the deeds?"

"Yes, I have them on me. I've been to the solicitor today, to see about picking up the deeds to this place. I wanted to sell my home but had to prove I owned it. I have them here." He reached his hand into his pocket and, withdrawing it, threw the papers upon the table.

"Your house against this house?"

"Yes."

"That really doesn't seem fair. You wouldn't be trying to cheat me, would you? You and I both know this is the largest house in the area. Your house against the right to dispute whether this house is yours. If your case is a watertight one - and you feel confident - I'd accept that as a bet." Sebastian leaned back in his chair and smiled, awaiting a reply.

Gwen's grandson buried his face in his hands, before drawing them through his hair. Puffing out his cheeks, he let out a sigh.

"Yes, I suppose." Lifting his flask to his lips once more he took a second, larger draught. Downing it in one, he pulled a face as the liquid burned a fiery course to his stomach.

"Good." Sebastian reached for the deck of cards and shuffled them before placing them back on the table and withdrawing one.

"The Three of Hearts."

"Yes! Yes!" Gwen's grandson threw another kiss at the gods. Slowly, he reached forward and lifted half the pack.

"Oh, what a shame! Two of Spades." There was little sincerity in Sebastian's sympathy. "I think I'd better find a pen for you to sign these deeds."

"I'm ruined. What of my family? I've no home. I needed this place. I have debts to pay." Gwen's grandson looked at Sebastian with plaintive eyes.

"Well, that really is a shame. I can see only one way out."

"What is it? I'll do anything." There was desperation in his voice.

"Kill yourself." By now, Sebastian had found a pen and thrust it into the young man's hand. It was taken, and the deeds duly signed.

"Oh God, what do I do know?"

"Leave *my* home for a start. And if you see your grandfather, give him my regards."

Early the next morning, Sebastian made his way into the little town nearby. Lillian had not told him who her executors were, but given that only one solicitor practised in the vicinity, Sebastian guessed there was a good chance any legalities might be in his hands.

The road into the town was a steep one. Houses crowded in on either side, reaching high, darkening the narrow streets below, even in the hours of daylight. Only when one passed through the ancient, fortified arch did the street pan out and become unusually wide. At the far end of the town, a castle imposed itself upon the fragile community, dominating the landscape as it had done for a thousand years. Beyond that, a river and cliffs presaged the onset of wild forests.

With intent, Sebastian made his way from the narrow, cobbled street that even in the early waking hours bustled with activity as the little community prepared for market day. Sebastian had no time for such matters. Circumstances were threatening to take him away from Lillian. He would kill to make sure that never happened again.

The sun crept over the town wall. How many generations had passed through that arch? How many had done so with as much purpose and meaning as he? What did it matter now? To what had all their plans come? All things must pass: nothing mattered.

As Sebastian pushed open the solicitors' office door, he glanced around in an effort to familiarise himself with the interior. It was an old building, rather dark and sombre. Panelled walls, stained, or perhaps dark with age, gave the inside a sinister aspect. Papers, some yellowed by time, were piled on every available space. It was then Sebastian became aware he was being watched. Two clerks, or perhaps the office junior and the solicitor, were exchanging nervous glances, both then looking with disdain at Sebastian.

"Can I help you, sir?" The eider of the two men lowered his spectacles as he spoke until they perched precipitously upon the end of his nose,

"Perhaps." Sebastian sensed the discomfort his presence caused and revelled in it. Why should he offer them any respite? Slowly, and with mannered deliberation, he turned from the two, and walked around their premises, stopping at every picture to pay it some disinterested attention. Finally, he halted at the window where he remained with his back to the two.

"Sir?" A full five minutes had elapsed since the initial question had been asked. Sebastian turned his head and, looking at them, raised a questioning eyebrow. Eyes met momentarily. The solicitor again looked to his younger colleague. The elder man was, perhaps, sixty years of age. His receding hairline was swept back, revealing a full and rounded face. Broken veins upon his nose and cheeks suggested too fine an appreciation of port.

The younger of the two, all the while, remained silent. Unlike his senior, he had remained seated but enough of him could be seen above his desktop for Sebastian to take a guess at his position in the company. He was, perhaps, twenty-five years of age, yet still retained a shiny, inflamed complexion more often associated with a younger man. Unlike his superior, his hair was oiled, as was his moustache, and both were combed into perfect centre partings. Both men sported white shirts and dark waistcoats. Armbands, it might be supposed, sought to impress their clientele of their efficiency.

"A very close and dear friend of mine died some time ago. She owned the large house at the top of the hill." Sebastian folded his arms and brought one hand up to his chin.

Temptation and Denial

"Yes sir, I'm aware of whom you mean. May I ask the nature of your enquiry?"

"She was without relatives. My enquiry, is to whom has the estate been left?" Sebastian slumped into a chair.

"Well, the will has been read. It was made rather a long time ago, I'm afraid. She left it all to a friend - a Mr Sebastian ..." he began, snapping his fingers as he looked to his junior to supply a surname. The younger man, taking his cue, began rummaging in a pile of papers.

"But", he continued, "we've been unable to trace him. There was a clause in the will that anticipated this. In the event of his not being found, the entire estate was to go to a friend of hers - a Miss Gwen ..." Again, the elder man looked to his minion to supply a surname, which only caused the younger man to rummage amongst the papers upon his desk even more furiously than before.

"In the event of her death - if I remember rightly - the house and all its contents were to go to her offspring, if she had any. Her grandson, I believe, survives, so barring us finding Mr Sebastian ..." furtive glances were again exchanged, "it would seem everything is to go to him."

"I see." Without explanation or even a departing grace, Sebastian sprang to his feet and left.

Conscious thought flooded through Sebastian's mind like a stream. If the will had been made fifty or sixty years ago, how would he be able to prove himself *the* Sebastian in question? The passing of years should have given him the appearance of an old man. He was old - very old - but looked, at most, to be a man of twenty-five. How would he be able to explain his apparent youth?

The rest of that day was spent in aimless wander, but unlike the hopeless meanderings of the past Sebastian was, this day, lost in a reverie. He longed to go back to the house, but to do so would merely confuse matters all the more. What to do? How could he prove he was the legitimate heir to Lillian's estate? There had to be some way.

By the time Sebastian finally returned to the old house it was late. Lost in thought, he lit the candle that had been used the day before and sat down. There *had* to be something that could help his claim, but what?

With slow deliberation, Sebastian walked from room to room. In the time since the house had last been a home, thick layers of dust had come to rest on all the furnishings. Without life, the house felt as cold as death. There could be no question of Sebastian ever not wanting to live there for it was a part of *her*. Until the end of time, nothing and no one would come between them again.

Finally, every downstairs room had been investigated, all to no avail. Sebastian pulled his coat tightly around himself and fastened it at the narrow waist. There was only upstairs left: then he remembered the night, many years before, when he had ascended the same staircase; then, he had had a brother to accompany him; now, he was alone. Pale silver arrows from the night sky pierced the same window, falling upon a face unchanged in over half a century.

Lost in thought, Sebastian twisted a door handle and found himself in the one room he had wished to avoid: Lillian's. Quickly, he slammed the door shut. No, it was too soon. He could not yet bring himself to enter *those* quarters.

Strange faces: lost faces: faces now misread by the passing of time: Sebastian walked past the portraits of Lillian's ancestors that hung in abandoned suspension. Would he too, one day, become like them? Made ridiculous - even hideous - by the passing years; unable to change: fixed?

No, he had to go back to Lillian's room: there could be no avoiding it. With trepidation, he made his way back through the dark, dusty passages brushing aside cobwebs as he went. Taking the handle in his hand, before giving it a twist, closing his eyes as he did so. This time, the door shuddered open. Letting out a sigh borne of relief rather than lassitude, Sebastian entered.

The room was as he remembered it. The bed; the chair where he had sat; the dressing table where Lillian's brush and comb still lay in silent expectation. Sebastian's eyes burned. Was there anything in that room that might help authenticate his claim? On the walls, a few paintings hung. With uneasy curiosity, Sebastian moved from one to the other. Then, for a moment, one image seemed half recognisable. There, hanging nailed and crucified, was a portrait of himself, accurate to the finest detail. Anyone could see it was unmistakably him. And the title? 'St. Sebastian'.

Temptation and Denial

So that was why arrows were shown piercing his heart! This was the evidence he needed! The final proof! What's more, it was signed by Lillian herself. Sebastian took the painting from its mount and carried it with him to the door, locking the door as he left. Moving downstairs, he awaited the first strains of the morning.

Later that day, Sebastian made his way back to the solicitors with the painting, which he had now wrapped.

When he opened the door, the same furtive glances greeted his arrival. This time, no pleasantries were offered, only raised eyebrows and an expectant look.

A few hours later, Sebastian left the little office a wealthy man. He had proven himself to be *the* Sebastian. Looks, needless to say, had been exchanged upon the disparity of a sixty-year-old will that bequeathed an entire estate to an apparently twenty-five-year-old man. Still, facts had been proven. The house was his!

Walking home, Sebastian allowed himself a smile, rare since the death of Lillian, not that they had ever been that frequent. Now, however, in the space of a few days, he had gone from owning no property to owning two.

Back at his home, Sebastian spent the rest of the day pulling the boarding off every window in the house, and deshrouding every item of furniture, Finally, every unwanted board and sheet was taken to the garden, piled into a heap, and set aflame. In the half-light, the flames gave a living hue to the desaturated colours of the house, seemingly bringing it back to life. The house would now be as Lillian would remember it! Moreover, as *he* remembered it.

Over the next few days, Sebastian acquainted himself with the rest of the house, excepting Lillian's room, telling himself that it would be a long time before he could ever enter *there* again. Although it had provided him with the proof he needed, there had been a high price to pay. Seeing Lillian's few, pitiful belongings still, silent and waiting had touched something unhealed. All he had now were memories and who can throw their arms around them? Lillian's bedroom door was locked.

The next day, as Sebastian prepared for a visit to the other property he now fortuitously owned, he was disturbed by a knock upon his front door. In irritation, he briskly trod the corridor that approached it, revelling in the noise each footstep made as it echoed throughout his house. Snatching the handle, he threw open the door. Outside, huddled together, stood a woman of about twenty-five years of age, and two children: a boy of around seven years of age; and a girl, perhaps a few years younger.

"Yes?" Sebastian frowned at his visitors.

"Sir." Almost as soon as she spoke, the woman began to cry, drawing her children nearer to her as she did so. "It's my husband. He's killed himself." The woman brought her hands to her face and wiped away her tears. The children, bewildered and uncomprehending, looked up at her.

"Well? What business is it of mine?" Sebastian glanced behind him to a clock. Already, he was late.

"He left a note. He says you have the deeds to our house."

"Have I? Ah, I see! Yes, I have, I'm afraid he lost them. Very sad, but what can I do? He would have taken all I had if he had won." Not a trace of sympathy or compassion tinged his voice. "As a matter of fact. I was just on my way to see you. We need to discuss your rent."

"That's why I've come to see you. We've no money. My husband was the only one that worked. We've no insurance either. Sir, I've *no* money to pay you any rent."

"I see." Sebastian paused and brought a hand to his face in contemplation. "You'd better come in," Sebastian extended a hand inside the house, gesturing the three past him, before closing the door. "This way." Sebastian made his way past the little group and walked toward a door that opened into the room that had once been Lillian's reception room. Again, he ushered the three inside, before he too entered, closing the door behind him.

"Please sit down." Sebastian nodded toward a sofa and the young woman made her way to it, taking her children with her. Sebastian walked to a window where he remained, his back to them.

"This puts me in quite a situation. You see, the house you live in *was* your house, but was lost, as I'm sure you're aware. The house is now mine. This entitles me to charge a rent or - should I wish to do so - sell. I gather you're not in a position to pay rent, so you can hardly be in a position to buy. Now, where does that leave me?" All the while, Sebastian spoke the words, he faced the window. The question was a near rhetorical one. Other than a few gentle sobs, there was no response.

"There are, however, a few options. Either you get a job, I have you evicted - in order that someone who *can* pay can take tenancy - or I offer you accommodation here, employed as my housekeeper. For no money, of course! I'm not going to put a roof over your head *and* pay for the privilege." Sebastian turned, to see how his offer had been received: the three figures sat huddled against one another.

"I can see no other option if I want to keep my family together." The words were whispered: desperate.

"Then we must make some arrangements. Obviously, you won't, need your own furniture so you may sell that. The servants' quarters here are adequately furnished. If you'd like to come this way. I shall show them to you." Sebastian led the little troop to the wing of the house that had once been occupied by the Llewellyns.

"Here we are then. Not the most luxurious of rooms, I grant you, but it's this or the streets. I think you've made the right choice. I'm going into town to organise my affairs. Acquaint yourself with your quarters, if you like." Sebastian looked at the young woman opposite him. How empty she looked: as if her life had been taken from her, leaving only a shell behind. Still, what did he care? Who had ever shown *him* compassion?

Sebastian closed the door behind him and departed. How strange recent events had been! Until very recently, he had been a rootless vagabond, blown wherever the cruel elements took him. Now his bitter heart had shackled him to one place alone. That same bitter heart had made him a man of means and given him Lillian's ancestral home; another property that would provide a regular income; a housekeeper who needed the shelter he provided so desperately that she would work for no pay. If only her husband realised the dire straits in which he had left his family! Perhaps he had, and that was why he had killed himself. What, of the two children? Perhaps it was grief that had made them so strangely silent, or perhaps they were simply too young to appreciate their dramatic collapse in fortunes. They were not unattractive children, acquiring their looks from their mother, and not their brutish father. The little girl had her mother's complexion and hair, yet whilst the mother's eyes were dark and hazel, the daughter's eyes were of a deep blue. It was the boy who had troubled Sebastian a little more. Whilst he had been in his presence, he could not think why but now, in hindsight, the reason became apparent: he had the same disdainful look playing around his mouth that had cursed his family. His father had had it, as had his great-grandfather. Always there was the look of disgust; of ill-disguised contempt; of unslaked retribution.

Days turned to weeks. Some degree of routine had been established in the running of the house. Sebastian shut himself away in the upper reaches of his new home, sometimes for days at a time. Every night, Branwen (for that was her name) and her children would hear him pacing back and forth. When the countryside was still and quiet, every footstep made the house creak. Branwen would draw her children toward her, fearing the wrath of God, as the very heavens above appeared to shake. They all knew not to approach his room.

Weeks turned to months. Branwen and her children became accustomed to their new surroundings. Despite the gloom of their own quarters, much of the house was open to them, thus leaving them free to enjoy the more spacious and airy rooms of the gothic pile. Branwen began to treat the house as her own. As the months wore on, Sebastian's forays from his lonely abode became a little more frequent. Initially, she had hated him: he, after all, had been responsible in no small measure for the death of her husband. She could not forget how callously he had treated her when first she had come to see him to explain her plight, Now, as time - the universal panacea - passed, she had come to see qualities in Sebastian that others had not. Her husband had been a spendthrift, a womaniser and a drunkard. His paternal lineage had, at one time, been a wealthy one; her husband had never forgotten the fact, and for all his life he had considered work to be beneath his social status. He had married beneath himself - God knows, he told her often enough. Yes, he *had* worked, but so much of his money had been squandered in pursuit of selfish pleasures. All they had ever had was their home, and he had been prepared to gamble even that! To who else might he have staked it? Only good fortune had found her a sanctuary with Sebastian. Sebastian had saved her from a loveless marriage *and* had put a roof over her head. Her new house had a nice garden in which her children could play, which was more than her previous house had had.

Temptation and Denial

Yes, perhaps Sebastian wasn't a *bad* person after all.

High in the uppermost reaches of the house, Sebastian sought to lock himself away. For a long while, grief had made him desolate. He had taken care of finances; the rent from Branwen's old home was simply pin money. His own home, despite his apparent lack of concern, was well cared for. Now? Now there was nothing. There was no one except Lillian, and she was dead. How he had loved her! Time, however, had taken her from him as he had known it would. All that remained, for a long while, he had hated. He had anticipated the numbness. Good or bad, he could not feel *anything* anymore.

As dawn banished the night's purple legions, Sebastian sought to shake the ennui that often overwhelmed him and, rising from his chaise longue, walked to the still-drawn curtains. He liked the room as it secluded him from the rest of the world. High in the uppermost floor of the house, when the door and windows were closed, he sought to banish all thoughts of the world from his mind. As he drew the curtains apart, the warm day caressed his face. Fresh air blew into the room, accompanied by the sweet refrain of birdsong. Then a sound, at first indistinct and half-forgotten: the sound of laughing children, playing in the garden far below. Sebastian could not see from where the laughter came as the window did not look out upon the garden, that being one of the reasons he had chosen the room. He had not been aware that the garden was even within earshot until now. Now, chuckling children caused a thawing. Oh, to be young again! Where had it all gone wrong? Oh, to be a child and full of joy and untainted optimism! To see the world as a friendly place, with long days and short nights. Now, distant laughter had unfrozen memories half-lost. Blissful laughter, laughter that might once have been Lillian's and his, if circumstances had not cleaved them in two. Down there, there were no rules, no conditions, only a joy and happiness found in one another's company. Children's laughter rose like larks ascending, the laughter of children that should have been Lillian's and his. Sebastian cursed himself. Why had he - and he alone - suffered the curse of immortality and been excluded from the chance of such happiness?

Slowly, Sebastian turned back into the room. It had always seemed a large room, running the length and breadth of the house. Now, it appeared vast and daunting. Perhaps Lillian had once found solace in that same room, away from everything. Sebastian walked to Lillian's piano. In a smaller room, it might have been a centrepiece. In the high attic, however, it appeared small and insignificant. The passing years had given Sebastian the opportunity to acquire many talents, more talents than can be accrued in a normal lifetime and, gently, his fingers touched the keys. He closed his eyes and let the music waft over him like an exotic perfume, lifting him away, far away over the wild Welsh countryside. There, Lillian was young, and they were together. The music was slow, melancholic, and had brought a wistful air to the warm day with memories bittersweet. Suddenly, the playing stopped; only chuckling children punctuated the silence. Sebastian arose, and slowly made for the door.

By the time he had reached the bottom of the stairs, Branwen had stopped her work, having seen his approach. Surprised, she stood in silent expectation.

"Are those your children in the garden?" Sebastian drew nearer to Branwen until she could almost feel the warmth of his body next to hers in the narrow passageway.

"Yes, they're only playing ... *please*." Branwen's entreaty was pitiful. For a moment, she had lifted her hands to stay Sebastian's departure but had thought better of it. She thought he had not noticed but, of course, he had. Did she really think him such a monster?

Sebastian made his way to the door, without reply. Branwen followed, stopping when the door was closed to her. What could she do? She was in no position to admonish Sebastian as he might well ask her to leave if she did so, and then where would she be? Her heart sank as the melodious joy evinced in her children's laughter stopped. Surprisingly, it soon started again, only now a little fainter: more distant. Branwen opened the door and quietly walked out. She had expected her children to have returned to her, if not crying, then at least subdued and downcast. Why were they still in such good spirits? She had been able to see them from the window all morning: they had been playing on the lawn, just in front of the house but now it was empty. Brushing a few long, thick curls of hair from her eyes, Branwen moved to the top of the broken steps that led to the rest of her children's personal Eden.

Still, there was laughter unseen. Suddenly, Branwen made a start. There, far below her, on the lawn by the gate, Sebastian ran about the garden, with Rhiannon - her daughter - high upon his shoulders. In the sunlight, Rhiannon's dark blue eyes gleamed like sapphires. Whooping with laughter, her son – Ifan - made concerted efforts to pull his sister from Sebastian's back. Even Sebastian could not suppress a smile, yet even as Branwen watched, the scene was a strange one: one might have been forgiven for thinking it one of a father playing with his children, but there was something more than that; something intangible. For some reason, it seemed as though *three* innocents were playing.

Branwen returned to her work. She enjoyed looking after the old house; in a way, she felt it to be hers. Now that Sebastian had shown a little affection to her children, perhaps she could finally put her life back together. Could he be the father figure she had always wanted for them?

An hour or so later, Branwen heard the back door click shut. Laughter still filled the summer day so, for a moment, she wondered which of the three had tired of their play. From the kitchen, she walked to the room into which the back door opened, just in time to see Sebastian.

"Had fun with the children?" Branwen tried to make her tone as friendly as she could. She had originally come from further west, along the coast of Wales, thus her accent was different from those of the central valleys, or the south. She received no reply.

"Sebastian?" For quite a while, Sebastian had permitted her and her children the use of his 'given name', as he called it.

"Yes, but they're not *my* children, are they?" Sebastian said with sadness, before moving Branwen aside and bounding up the stairs to his sanctuary, three steps at a time.

Neither Branwen, Rhiannon or Ifan saw Sebastian for a while after that day. Only in the nights when, perhaps accidentally, he left his window open could they hear a few strains of some lilting nocturne played on a piano high above them, as though channelled through some ghostly chamber before it met their ears.

Despite their being forbidden to do so, it wasn't long before the children ventured upstairs. If Sebastian would not come to them, then they would go to Sebastian. Neither Rhiannon nor Ifan were frightened of Sebastian: their only reticence was that Branwen might discover where they had been. She had forbidden them to pay Sebastian a visit because Sebastian had not requested their company. He had given them a home in which to live; the least she could do was respect his privacy.

As the children mounted the stairs, the almost inaudible sound of a piano came to greet them. Each child nudged the other forward until finally, amidst nervous giggling and half-suppressed panic, Rhiannon tapped on Sebastian's door with her tiny hand. The piano playing stopped.

"Who is it?" Perhaps it had not been such a good idea after all.

"Sebastian, will you come out to play?" There followed a sound of approaching footsteps behind the door that elicited a few fearful glances between the two children. Run? The door clicked open. Sebastian glared down at them before his face creased into a broad smile.

"No, not today. You may come in for a little while though, if you wish." Sebastian turned and walked back into the room. A cool breeze blew through the open window, billowing his hair and loose white shirt. The door slammed,

"Why don't you come out? It's a lovely garden. Have you ever been all the way around it?" The little girl fell to an idle chatter as she walked about the room, running her hands over everything within her reach, but paying no real attention to anything. Ifan remained silent. He walked to the window and peered out, before looking at the clear blue sky above. Sebastian walked back to Lillian's piano and sat at the stool, facing out into the room. He crossed his legs. He had enjoyed the children's company that day in the garden as their friendships had been fresh and unconditional.

"Ours is the biggest garden in the world, and there are pixies, elves, and people that only we can see," said Rhiannon, pointing at Ifan.

Sebastian looked at the two children. Yes, Rhiannon did look like her mother, for both had the same hair and large eyes, despite the disparity in colour, whereas Ifan's badly-cut hair gave him a look of careless abandon. Even the look on his face appeared to have softened.

"Why don't you come downstairs with us? It's a big house so

you won't be in the way." Sebastian laughed. Evidently, Rhiannon had no idea how, or why, she had come to live in the old house.

"We'd all like you to." Ifan had come to Sebastian's side and placed a finger on a piano key which he tapped lightly until it hammered out a note. Looking at Sebastian, he apologised.

"It's quite alright. You haven't damaged it," Sebastian looked at the little boy in front of him. Would he have sought Sebastian's company so readily had he known him to be, at least partially, responsible for his father's death?

"Who's that?" Sebastian looked at Rhiannon who, by now, had also drawn alongside. He had no need to follow the direction of her outstretched finger for he knew where it pointed.

"That's Lillian," Sebastian had found a portrait of Lillian, not long after he had found the portrait of himself. It was unfinished, but unmistakably her, and Lillian as he remembered her: young, and in the bloom of life.

"Who's Lillian?" Rhiannon's questions were artless.

"Lillian used to live here and was someone that I loved very much." Sebastian followed the little girl's gaze until his eyes met with those of the portrait.

"Why did you love her?" Ifan's curiosity had, by now, been aroused and he too asked a question.

"Why?" Sebastian had never asked himself that question before and, for a moment, paused. "I'll tell you why, Ifan. It's because she was the only woman I have ever met who had a key to the chambers of my heart."

"Where is she now?" Sebastian looked at Rhiannon, whose curiosity already seemed to have wandered elsewhere. Sebastian's failure to reply appeared not to have been noticed and the question was not asked a second time.

"Rhiannon! Ifan!" In the distance, Branwen's voice sounded.

"I think your mother wants you." Sebastian ushered the children to the door and shut it behind them, before returning to the piano.

He looked up at Lillian's portrait. Had it hung in Lillian's room, he would not have removed it. No, this had been found - along with a few other artefacts - in an assortment of different rooms. He probably accorded it far more worth than Lillian had ever done, but now it was all that remained of what once had been.

A few days later, Rhiannon and Ifan paid another visit. It had rained heavily for the entire day, and the two children had become bored. Gently, they knocked at Sebastian's door.

"Come in." This time, Sebastian knew who it was who sought his company: the two children entered.

In the far corner of the room, crushed by a lassitude of which Rhiannon and Ifan could know nothing, Sebastian managed a smile to greet their arrival.

"And how are you, my two young friends?" He enjoyed their company. The two children chatted with Sebastian, and with one another before Rhiannon was once again taken with Lillian's portrait.

"She's the lady in the garden." Rhiannon looked to her brother, who simply shrugged his shoulders, before continuing his duel with an unseen musketeer.

"You saw her in the garden?" Sebastian felt as though he had been struck by a thunderbolt.

"Yes, but she looks sad in the garden. In the picture, she looks happy."

"I recognise the necklace," Ifan interjected, having emerged victorious from his fight to the death and now taking an interest in what his sister said.

"This necklace?" Sebastian stood up and walked to the piano. Opening a little box, he pulled forth an ornate silver chain, with a large, tear-shaped stone. Rhiannon nodded, whilst Ifan broke into a gap-toothed smile.

"Why is it here?" Rhiannon walked to Sebastian and stretched out her hand.

"Would you like to put it on?" Sebastian let the cool metal run between his fingers. "Here, let me put it on for you," Sebastian crouched down upon his knees, and clasped the necklace together, around Rhiannon's neck.

"Look, Ifan, I'm a princess!"

"Why is it here?" Ifan looked at Sebastian, ignoring his sister.

"Because they help to remind me of the person that once owned them."

"How do they do that?" Rhiannon had given up admiring her reflection in the room's large mirror and walked to Sebastian with a new question.

"I'll tell you, shall I?" The little girl nodded in affirmation to Sebastian's question. "Well, here I have a black onyx necklace. If I press the stone to my closed eyes, I can see happier times. Here is her tiger's eye brooch - that reminds me of her hair as the sun shone through it, making it shine so much that precious metals seemed to be woven around each and every strand. Her cornelian earrings remind me of fire - passion. A haematite necklace, as red as blood ..."

"Urg!" Rhiannon pulled a face; Sebastian smiled.

"Jade reminds me of the garden, where once we walked. The turquoise - the blue sky under which lives can be truly lived, or existed in lonely isolation. The lapis - the midnight-blue, shot with a thousand gold stars, reminds me of the night we said our last farewell. Pearls - of the tears shed. Opal - shadowed with the colour of wine. How love intoxicates! The sapphire - beloved of Saturn - my star, I think - if I have any. The emerald - doesn't the green remind you of the mountains of Wales?" Sebastian pressed the stone against one of his closed eyes and turned his head to the window. Lost in thought, only silence interrupted the quiet and haunted realms of his imagination. Putting the stone back in its box, he snapped the lid shut. "Where is your mother?" Sebastian looked at the two children sitting in front of him: both stared up, in open-mouthed attentiveness.

"Getting ready for church," Ifan answered; Rhiannon continued to stare in mute confusion.

"Oh no! She doesn't go to church, does she?" Despite the many months since Branwen and her family had moved in, Sebastian had noticed very little of the day to day running of their lives: news of Branwen's Christianity had been a revelation. "Well, go and tell her 'God is dead'. No, wait until you're in church and then tell her as loudly as you can. Will you do that for me?" Both children nodded.

"Will you take this off for me?" Rhiannon gestured to the necklace that still hung around her neck. Sebastian removed it and watched as the two little figures left, before closing the door behind them.

Sebastian let the necklace slide between his fingers. Slowly, he walked back toward the piano, passing the mirror in which

Rhiannon had admired herself. Unconsciously, he placed the necklace to his own throat as he gazed, not so much at his own reflection, but the reflection of the necklace. Only then did he notice the mirror's image of his hands: gone were the large, powerful hands of a man. Somehow, they had shifted shape into the slender and delicate hands of a woman. What of his face? Now that he looked, his masculine features had softened. For a moment, hadn't it been Lillian's face in the mirror, holding the necklace to her throat? Lillian as he remembered her; Lillian as she was in her portrait: young and beautiful. What *was* happening? Sebastian closed his eyes in spiral confusion. Pale shade? Ghostly imaginings? Opening his eyes, the reflection of a man looked back: his reflection. There was nothing else.

Sebastian's room became dark unusually early that day. Normally, to dispel the night terrors, he would light a few lamps. Today was different for he continued to sit in hopeless night. Alone, in contemplation, the silence was ruptured sometime later by a sharp retort upon the door.

"Come in." The door seemed to almost explode open on his command, its hinges sending it crashing into a wall.

"Sebastian, may God save your twisted soul." Branwen stood framed in the doorway, her long hair falling about her face, her eyes flashing in undisguised rage.

"Branwen!" Sebastian feigned surprise but knew the real reason for her fury.

"I'm grateful for your putting a roof over my family's head when we needed it, but I won't stand for you corrupting my children's minds with blasphemies."

"Ah." Sebastian smiled, as he rose to his feet. Languidly, he made his way to the piano. "Let me play you a little piece I've written; it's called 'Ave Satani'."

"Stop it! Please stop it. What sort of man are you?" Branwen entered the room and slammed the door behind her.

Sebastian sat down at the piano stool and hit a few dissonant chords.

"Will you listen to me? I'm very annoyed. The children shouting 'God is dead' in the middle of the sermon! Haven't we suffered enough? Must you bring the wrath of God down upon our heads as well? I suppose it's all just a cruel sport to you, isn't it? Is it?"

Sebastian gave a momentary laugh.

"I can't help it! My sympathies are with the Devil!" By now, he was teasing Branwen, whose rage only made him search for new provocations.

"What are you, to say such things? No wonder this house has no luck."

"I love the Devil! I love the Devil!" Sebastian stood up and moved toward Branwen, swaying like a cobra, and repeating the words and revelling in their impiety. Suddenly, a stinging retort caught the side of his face; Branwen had slapped him and was about to do so again.

Sebastian caught her hand in a firm embrace as Branwen sought to again strike Sebastian with her free hand before that was also caught. With all her strength, Branwen sought to free herself, pushing Sebastian backwards until he crashed into a wall. The momentum of the push and the suddenness of the stop caused her body to fall heavily into his. In an instant, the two were pressed against one another. Her anger spent, Branwen's eyes met Sebastian's before she lowered her gaze.

Branwen's eyelashes brushed Sebastian's cheek; her lips parted.

"I'm sorry, Branwen." Sebastian felt the warmth of his breath reflect off Branwen's cheek, echoing upon the nearness of her face. The words had been spoken quietly. Slowly, Branwen raised her eyelids until her gaze, once again, met his.

"Sebastian." Branwen's eyes, even in the dim light afforded by the little room, flushed a little darker as her pupils dilated. A little breath, as she had sounded his name, brushed his face. Closing his eyes, Sebastian brought his mouth toward Branwen's. In supplication, her lips parted a little wider, before she too closed her eyes. For just a moment lips met.

"No, I'm sorry." Sebastian released Branwen's hands from his and turned sharply away. Only the click as the door shut told him she had gone.

By the next day, Sebastian's spirits had lifted a little. The weather had brightened to such a degree that he opened his window to embrace the day. In the distance, the sound of laughing children shimmered in the warmth of the morning. Had

Rhiannon and Ifan really seen Lillian in the garden, or had their vivid imaginations taken the haunting image in the portrait and transposed it into surroundings with which they were more familiar? There could only be one way to find out…

Sebastian made his way downstairs. As his heels echoed through the cavernous halls, a door opened: Branwen. had heard his approach.

"Sebastian. About yesterday." Nervously, she looked anywhere, save at him.

"Yes, I'm sorry Branwen. It's not you, but me." An awkward silence followed as both sought the words to say next. "Anyway, I'm off into the garden." Branwen smiled as Sebastian departed.

It wasn't long before Sebastian found the children_

"Sebastian!" Rhiannon ran toward him, throwing her arms around him as he stooped to greet her.

"Now, where do you see my friend - the woman in the painting?" Sebastian tried his best to phrase the question as nonchalantly as he could, yet a tinge of anxiety remained.

"There! There she is!" Ifan pointed past Sebastian, in the direction of the gate. Sebastian quickly turned, his movement restricted by Rhiannon's arms around his shoulders. For a single, fleeting moment, Lillian had been there. Sebastian stood fixed. The image had gone. Eventually, he turned back to Rhiannon.

"Do you speak to her?" He gestured with his head toward where Lillian had been standing.

"Yes, but she doesn't answer. She doesn't even see us. All she says is 'I'm sorry'…"

"And then she cries." Ifan, having no wish to be excluded, concluded his sister's sentence.

"Cries?" Sebastian could cope with seeing Lillian if she were happy, but the thought of her restless wanderings being unhappy ones was too much to bear.

"Yes, and this morning she had a white deer with her. They went through there." Again, Ifan pointed toward the gate.

"Did she? I won't be a minute." Sebastian's steps sounded as he crossed the scorched brown grass and cracked earth, toward the gate. In an instant, he was in the dark wood. It was empty. Downcast, he returned to the children.

"How often have you seen her?" Sebastian sat down on the

arid lawn. A golden scourge from a merciless azure empyrean oozed over them like lava.

"We see them every day." Rhiannon had lost interest, leaving Ifan behind to answer what she now thought were Sebastian's silly questions. This was the first Sebastian had heard of there being anyone other than Lillian in the garden, then he remembered the time Rhiannon had first ever mentioned seeing anyone and she had said "people".

"Yes, there's a man who looks after the garden - he's old with silver hair. There's another man who stands over by the gate - he looks ill. There are a few others, but we don't see them very often."

"Do any of them speak to you?"

"No. It's as if they can't hear us." Ifan was beginning to become bored with Sebastian's constant questioning; already he was looking elsewhere.

"Does your mother see them?"

"No! Don't tell her we told you. She shouts at us and tells us off saying we won't go to heaven if we lie, but we're not lying. You won't tell her, promise?"

"No, I won't tell her that you told me, I promise." Sebastian pulled himself to his feet and brushed the grass from his clothes. "Thank you, Ifan. Your secret is safe." Ifan grinned.

Back in the house, Sebastian soon found Branwen; she was cleaning the windows.

"Branwen, have you ever seen anyone in the garden?" Sebastian tried to make his tone as innocuous as possible.

"People? What people?" For a moment, she had stopped what she was doing, but that meant looking at Sebastian. Her humiliation came back to burn her, so she continued her self-appointed chore.

"Have you seen *any* people?"

"No. The children say they have, but they've vivid imaginations. I've been with them and they've actually pointed to where they say these people are, but there's nothing. It's only in their imagination. Why do you ask? Don't tell me *you've* seen them as well!" Branwen laughed. She hadn't ridiculed Sebastian, merely made light of a situation she found unbelievable. As if Sebastian would be able to see such figures! The idea was absurd

"I just wondered." Sebastian thought about passing the question off as a joke, in order to avoid lying, but Branwen's suspicions had not been raised so he let the matter drop. "I'm going back upstairs." With that, he was gone.

Once again, weeks turned to months. Sebastian chose not to visit the garden, as he once had. The thought of seeing Lillian inconsolable, knowing anything he said to alleviate her suffering would not be heard would be unbearable. The children continued to visit him just as often, though Sebastian chose not to mention Christianity to them again. He would wait until they were a little older, and then explain the drawbacks of a slave mentality. Finally, summer turned to autumn, with all its bittersweet memories.

One day, as Sebastian sat at his piano, a distant rumble of thunder interrupted his playing. As the irregular beating of the rain upon the window panes washed over his fluid playing, he stopped. Then, *that* day came back to him, with all its haunted legions. In the decades that had passed since that fateful day, as black as night, when Lillian had sent him away, Sebastian had not had a day pass when he had not thought of her reasons for doing so. Yes, he could now see why, but shouldn't love have conquered reason? And what of the tragedy that had blighted them both? Knowing that she had wanted him but, leaving it too late, he had never known when knowing would have changed everything.

Sebastian closed the piano lid and brought himself to his. feet. Unaware of his movements, he began to pace the room. In the storm, the room had become gloomy: suffocating. Lightning cracked, irradiating everything with the blue tinge of death. For a moment, as it had flashed, he had caught his reflection in the mirror. Where the flowing locks of black hair? Where the billowing white shirt? In the mirror, only Lillian gazed back, smiling: young as he remembered her; attired in the fashions of half a century previous.

"Sebastian, death shall be yours. You've seven years."

"Lillian!" Sebastian leapt toward the mirror with outstretched arms, only to recoil, as his fingers collided with the cold glass, shattering the image so that the shards fell about his feet. "Oh Lillian, I'm sorry. I'm so, *so* sorry! Please come back … I love you." Sebastian fell to his knees amongst the broken, silvered pieces and frantically clutched at them. Blood began to drip from his hands, staining the broken remains, and the floorboards beneath. Something *was* changing as he had not bled before. Something was now binding him to the world of substance and human affairs. Uneasily, Sebastian knew exactly what that 'something' was: in the past, he had loved without motive; loved for the pleasure of loving and being loved. Initially, in seeking to hold on to the past, he had loved the possessions bequeathed him simply for their sentimental value. Now, with his finances dwindling, the hideous spectre of future poverty - and the unceasing worry that poverty brings - was making him all too human.

Months again turned to years. Sebastian's face had finally started to age as penury laid an increasingly cold and bony hand more heavily upon his shoulder. Sebastian's relationship with Branwen's children superficially strengthened. Rhiannon became the daughter he had never had yet, at times, his relationship with Ifan became strained. Ifan, being a little older than Rhiannon, remembered his father. He remembered how one day there had been Branwen, Rhiannon, his father and himself together, as a family, and living in the town; the next day, his father had gone, and those that remained had come to live at Sebastian's house. Often, he would ask himself what had happened to bring about such a collapse into the flames.

Sebastian sensed Ifan's changing attitude toward him. From the unconditional acceptance of a child, he had grown to ponder the circumstances of his family's downfall. How long could it be before both he and Rhiannon found out who had been responsible for their father's death? Maybe Branwen knew already, but what if even she had no idea? She had never apportioned blame if she had thought him guilty in some way. How could he tell her that it was he who had pushed her husband to suicide? Moreover, how long would it be before the passing years betrayed the terrible secret of his immortality? Now that he had started to age, would he slip more and more into decrepitude but still be denied the comfort of a release from the prison of flesh and bone that housed his mortal soul?

Sebastian's relationship with Branwen had found an uneasy comfort. For a long while after their brief encounter, there had been tension between them. Time had also changed it for

Denied No More

Sebastian dulling it until, like a bloom denied water, it had withered. For Branwen, however, the affection had been tended and carefully nurtured. That one moment years before when, for just a moment, their lips had touched and her eyelashes had brushed his cheek had been a seed. That seed had fallen on fertile ground. Now its root wrapped itself around her, possessing her; all the while Sebastian remained as distant as a deity. Unattainable, he had become all the more attractive.

Year piled upon year. After seven years, Sebastian wondered where was the end he had been promised as he closed the lid of Lillian's jewellery box. It had been a long time since he had last left the house. The children no longer mentioned the figures in the garden; perhaps they no longer saw them. Now, Sebastian felt safe enough to venture outside, hoping Lillian had found peace at last. He could cope with seeing Llewelyn, or any other of the sad revenants that had ever been associated with the house. What he could not cope with was seeing Lillian, bewailing her loss, nor her brother, longingly staring at the gate with haunted eyes, his chest pierced with holes. As the days turned to weeks, weeks turned to months, and months turned to years he realised that time would never heal the anguished wounds branded upon his heart.

Sebastian made his way from his room passing Lillian's, by way of a change. Unconsciously, as he passed, Sebastian checked his pocket for her bedroom key. For seven years the room had remained locked. The key was still there, safe between his fingers. He smiled and moved on. In the kitchen, Branwen and her children were having a little breakfast. Ifan, now turned fourteen years old, had the stature of a man. The look of disdain that had occasionally played around his mouth had become noticeably pronounced. Rhiannon had turned twelve. Every day she came to look a little more like her mother, seemingly losing her individuality in the process. Continuity without change. Even Branwen had matured. She had once been an insecure young mother, a little unsure of herself and her place in the world. Once, life had seemed daunting, horrible, frightening. Then she had found God and happiness.

"Good morning, Sebastian," Branwen brought the teacup from her mouth and placed it back upon the table, before nervously brushing a few non-existent crumbs from her clothes.

"Sebastian!" Rhiannon, for the moment, still appeared enthusiastic at his unexpected arrival. Ifan remained silent, staring sullenly at the floor. Sebastian smiled at the assembled group.

"I'm going for a walk."

Branwen lifted her eyes and looked at Sebastian in astonishment. In the seven years she had lived at the old house, never once had Sebastian said he was venturing any further than the garden. Sebastian noticed the look Branwen had given him but let it pass without validating himself. Making his way to the door, he opened it wide and pushed aside the honeysuckle that cascaded in. Unbeknownst to Sebastian, Branwen had followed him.

"Off to see some friends, Sebastian?" Branwen's voice assailed him like the breeze that sways the long grass of summer meadows, cool and refreshing. For a moment, Sebastian paused before the horror of life came back to haunt him.

"Friends? Friends! My best friend would be he who would take a pistol and blow out my damned wretched brains." Before Branwen could respond, Sebastian was gone.

Branwen returned to the kitchen. Her children had gone to their rooms, leaving her alone. Why had Sebastian been so hostile? She had never done anything to hurt him yet, at times, he appeared to hate her.

In the garden, Sebastian slowly moved from one flower to another. He had always sought freedom but had seldom found it. Even in the garden, every perfume, every shimmering movement, every tender touch or sound seemed heavily laden with a memory.

Sebastian took a faltering footfall upon crumbling stone steps until, finally, he came to pause in an ancient rose garden. Every flower seemed to shiver in anticipation. Upon the ground, a few roses had somehow been torn from the rosebush that had lovingly nurtured them. Now dying, Sebastian wondered what hand had so cruelly torn away their life. Crouching, he picked them up.

"Oh Sebastian, I'm so sorry." The voice wafted light upon the air, echoing, as though whispered from some distant cavern. Quickly, he turned. Lillian stood at a short distance from him, imploring him to come to her. Behind her, a white hart nuzzled close.

Denied No More

"Lillian!" Sebastian ran forward. her with arms outstretched. There was no response or reaction for nothing remained. Lillian had been no more corporeal than a shadow. "No!" In the years since Sebastian had taken tenancy of the house, he had sought to avoid just such an experience. He had never wanted to see Lillian so woebegone and desolate, and being unable to alleviate her suffering made it even worse. They had reconciled their differences upon her deathbed, but that had obviously not been enough. Was this the legacy of a lifetime of suffering? No! It was too awful. Running, Sebastian made his way back to the house, throwing open the back door, and falling through it as if the portal were a pair of huge wooden arms to love and protect him; to console him in *his* sorrow. Sebastian slammed the door shut behind him.

"Are they for me?" He had quite forgotten the dying bouquet he still held in his hand. Now? Now there was Branwen's radiant face and voice as lyrical as a child opening its first birthday presents, looking at him with undisguised joy.

"What? These? Oh yes. Yes, these are for you." Sebastian extended his arm, keeping Branwen at a distance, all the while trying to regain his composure.

"Oh, Sebastian. You *do* care!" Branwen moved toward him, lifting her arms to envelop him.

"No!" Sebastian took a step backwards. Branwen's eyes reddened and became glassy; silent tears coursed her cheeks. "I'm sorry. Please don't cry." Sebastian felt acutely the pain of rejection. Then he thought of Lillian and how she must have thought when she had sent him away.

"How can I not?"

"I truly am sorry, but I just can't talk at the moment. I must go to my room." Sebastian manoeuvred Branwen aside and walked briskly down the corridor, before mounting the stairs in a few swift bounds. Once in his garret, he slumped against its door, sitting with his back pressed against it. Breathless, he closed his eyes. Within a few seconds, a knock came upon the heavy timbers behind him.

"Yes?" Sebastian found it hard to disguise the exasperation in his voice.

"Sebastian, I have to talk to you." It was Branwen.

"No, not now," Sebastian, having opened his eyes when Branwen had knocked, closed them again. Images of Lillian flickered across his mind.

"Sebastian, I must talk now." Branwen's broken phrasing told Sebastian she was crying. Slowly he rose to his feet and opened the door.

"May I come in?" Sebastian extended a hand, gesturing Branwen into the room. She entered, gently pulling Sebastian with her. "Sebastian, I can't keep the way I feel to myself any longer. Why do you treat me the way you do? You seem to hate me, yet you must have realised the way I feel about you." Branwen moved toward him. Clutching his forearm, she brought his hand to her warm mouth before pressing her red lips against his fingers.

"It's not you, Branwen. I don't hate you, but then I don't love you either." There was a pause, as Sebastian slowly pulled his hand away and walked toward the window.

"Branwen, I love another."

"Who? Who do you love? I've never seen you with anyone!" Branwen remained fixed to her spot: this time she had not followed Sebastian.

"I am near to her, however far away. I can never forget her: never lose her. You've not seen her because she's … dead. You might ask why, then, do I still love her? I will tell you - because love knows neither life nor death. It is the one thing that survives us all."

"But I love you, and I'm here and I'm alive." Branwen moved toward Sebastian, who, by now, had turned to face her. Drawing closer, she raised her hand and with the back of it, brushed his face. The effect could not have been more dramatic had she poured molten lead upon his bare skin.

"Please listen to me." Sebastian recoiled from the woman. His eyes flashed and his brow knitted.

"Sebastian, what is my crime? What have I done?"

"Nothing! Nothing! Nothing!"

"Then why do you treat me like this when my only crime is to care about you?" Branwen made no effort to stem her flow of tears. Sebastian turned away and paced about the room.

"How can you love me? You know nothing of me! Do you want to know the real me? The *real* me is the person responsible for your family's misfortune. I came to this house one night seven years ago, met your husband ... You don't understand. I *had* to have this house! Your husband told me the house was his. I suggested a bet, waging all I had with all he had. He lost. He begged me for help. I told him to kill himself. *That's* the sort of man I am! Now, tell me you love me. I didn't give a damn that he had a family. I wanted revenge. When you came to see me, no pity flowed in my heart. It wasn't charity that made me take you in. I needed someone to take care of the house, that was all. Don't you understand? I killed your husband, and took his home *and* family from him." Sebastian had no need to go on. Branwen raised her hands to her ears. Sobbing, she ran to the door pausing only to open it with fumbling fingers.

Sebastian breathed a sigh of relief and turned to face the window. He had thought of following Branwen, but checked himself: what else could he say? To console her would have been to undo the truth. To say anything further would have been superfluous; a cruelty. Now there was nothing, save himself and his catalogue of bitter reminiscences. How could he ever feel close to Lillian again? Perhaps there was a way.

Sebastian moved to the door, checking his waistcoat pocket to see if Lillian's bedroom key was still there.

With nervous trepidation, he unlocked Lillian's bedroom door. Years of dust had robbed the room of its colour so that everything now appeared to be in shades of grey.

Sebastian made his way about the room, laying his hands upon the precious things Lillian once might have touched. In the half-light of the darkened room, he looked pitiful, as though cruel nails had plucked out his eyes, yet however sightless those sockets appeared, they brought their owner to a sharp stop upon seeing Lillian's gilded mirror. In the gloom, another face appeared, reflected and smiling. Then a shape, indistinct at first, behind him.

Sebastian turned. Ifan's white fingers enclosed the handle of a carving knife. His knuckles white.

"Romans chapter twelve, five and nineteen. 'Vengeance is mine. I will repay, saith the Lord'." There was no emotion in the young man's voice as he approached.

"Ifan?" Sebastian took a few steps backwards until he could go no further, his back now pressed against the drawn curtains and the fragile leaded glass behind.

"No, Sebastian. John chapter eleven, line fifty. 'It is expedient that one man should die for the people'. It's too late, Sebastian. My mother has spoken to me. It's too late Sebastian. Too late."

The huge knife was raised high above the young man's head and, in one deft motion, brought down until only the handle remained visible, the blade piercing Sebastian's heart.

"Thank you, Ifan! Thank you!" Sebastian reached out to Ifan, speaking in a hoarse whisper. In trying to support himself, one hand had clutched the dusty curtain behind, tearing the ancient fabric away from its rails, bringing a cascade of dust down upon an ever-increasing expanse of blood beneath, blood flowed from Sebastian's chest and out upon the floor. Sunlight made it sparkle, like a string of rubies in a lead-lined casket. Suddenly, a gentle shape stepped from the mirror. With a loving touch, Lillian took Sebastian's hand, leading him back to whence she had come. Hands entwined. With soft and tender passion, Lillian pressed her lips to Sebastian's, raising her hand to bring his face nearer her own. Sebastian responded to Lillian's kiss with a slow and passionate kiss of his own.

"I love you, Sebastian. I've *always* loved you, and *will* always love you." Lillian spoke the words that both had always known, but which had been so hard to admit.

A soft breeze entered the room. Sebastian had broken a window when he had torn the curtains from the wall. Upon the floor, the warm summer air embraced Sebastian's long black locks, blowing a few strands across his lifeless lips. The morning sun caught the colour of his unblinking eyes. Outside, happy laughter, becoming distant, filled the garden.

Mallard the Quack

Adam Nicke

Adam Nicke was born near Caerleon in Wales on the Lupercalia, just a few miles from where the Gothic author Arthur Machen was born in 1863.

In his early twenties his artistic tendencies were expressed in the designing and making of clothes, most notably for Wayne Hussey of The Mission.

In his previous novel, Temptation and Denial, he railed against the hypocrisy and misogyny of those that use religion as a tool of control; in this satirical novel his recalcitrant disposition finds fertile ground in attacking today's political ruling elite by placing their ignorance, superstition, and self-serving dishonesty in 18th century Wales. He has a degree in Literary Studies from the University of the West of England.

Adam Nicke Publishing

Do You Like My Muff, George?

"It's like this Doctor," the red-faced farmer began. Casting his eyes around the room as though he were about to betray a confidence and wanted to be doubly sure no one was eavesdropping, he drew himself forward on his seat and lowered his voice. "I'm having trouble with my *little ploughman*. I just can't get him to rise in the morning like I once could," he whispered. With that, he let out a deep sigh and slumped backwards in his chair, as though a heavy burden had been lifted from his shoulders.

"I see," replied Doctor Ivor Mallard, Surgeon, Barber and Apothecary. He, of course, was no Doctor. He had started life as a travelling quack, wandering from place to place selling his 'patented' remedies. After begging, borrowing, and stealing enough money, he had bought into a permanent practice with his long-time employer and partner-in-crime Doctor Ronald Stumpf, a charlatan of the highest rank and a firm believer in the notion that sparing the rod spoiled the child. The fact that this personal philosophy didn't adhere to just children and took in any form of malingerer, be they sick or healthy, was immaterial as all most people needed was a 'good horsewhipping'.

Over the years, both Doctors had sold their pills and potions at fayres before quickly moving on before the locals realised that *Doc Mallard's Laxative Deodorant* or *Doctor Ronald Stumpf's Holy Spirit Tanning Lotion* were not the products they'd been promised. Still, given Stumpf paid the wages, Mallard agreed the shade of orange Stumpf had turned was irrefutable evidence that the Holy Spirit was flowing through the flabby old huckster.

"Well, it's a common enough problem in men of your age," Mallard said. "Many men find they have trouble with their *little ploughman* once in a while. If you'd like to pop behind the screen and drop your britches, I'll have a look at the little fella."

"Uh, right you are Doctor," replied the farmer, looking a little nervous and beginning to frown. Nonetheless, he rose from his seat. "Are you sure this is going to help?"

Mallard the Quack

"Trust me ... I *am* a Doctor," Mallard replied, puffing up his chest and reclining in his seat, before folding his arms.

Slowly, the farmer moved to the screen and with a little reluctance, dropped his britches. Finally, naked from the waist down, his bright red buttocks quivering like apples bobbing in a barrel of water, he stood as still as he could whilst clutching his britches in front of him.

"All done, Doctor," he said, his voice cracking.

"Good, good. Now if you could just let me have a look at him," Mallard commanded, in his best Doctorly tones.

With great reluctance, the farmer moved, stepped away from the screen and walked toward the Doctor.

"Now let me see," Mallard began, moving from his side of the desk. Sitting in a chair in front of the farmer, so that his head was level with the man's groin. "Well, I can't see anything wrong. How long have you noticed there to be a problem?" asked Mallard, as he peered intently over the top of his spectacles.

"I'm not sure. I think it was when I docked his wages for coming into work drunk a few months back," the farmer replied.

Mallard unleashed his grip on the appendage so quickly one could be forgiven for thinking hot embers had been dropped into his hand.

"When you said *little ploughman*, you meant ..."

"Little ploughman. Look, there he is," said the farmer, pointing through the window at a small dishevelled-looking labourer on the far side of the road. As Mallard moved to the window and peered through the glass, the man spied the learned Doctor's attention and gave a little wave.

"Oh, so that's your little game, is it?" Ivor shouted, turning sharply on the farmer, who took a step backwards in surprise before losing his footing in the britches around his ankles and falling to the ground.

"Eh?" said the farmer, wrestling with his tangled apparel.

"Don't think I don't know what you farmers are like! Oh yes! *Let's go and see old Mallard. He's always good for a cheap fondle*! Well not me, my friend! I bet you've been scheming over this one for months, haven't you? You disgust me! Here I

Do You Like My Muff, George?

am, a qualified and caring Doctor having to put up with the likes of you! There are sick people in need of my attention and all you can think about is how you're going to get your next sordid thrill! My God, what do you take me for? Now get out of here before I stick my boot in your little ploughman's lunchbox!"

"No Doctor, it really is my little ploughman," the farmer protested.

"Unbelievable! Just because I'm devilishly handsome, *everyone* thinks they're in with a chance!" Ivor said incredulously. "I may have strong, firm Doctor's fingers but ..." before trailing off and taking the farmer by the scruff of the neck, dragging him face down to the door.

"No, Doctor, you don't understand," the farmer protested, wincing as a splintered floorboard caught him in a sensitive area.

Ivor threw the half-dressed farmer into the waiting room and brushed his hands.

"And next time you want a cheap thrill then see Doctor Stumpf!"

Meanwhile, in the consulting room next door Doctor Stumpf was busy.

"So you see, in the Gospel according to ... uh ... Neville in the Bible it states *And lo, God saw that Beelzebub had been so jealous of Doctor Stumpf's really beautiful feet he had accursed him with bone spurs and so God had a word with the Holy Spirit and they sent Doctor Stumpf some ointment and his feet were tremendous again*," Doctor Stumpf explained.

"I see," said the patient. "Have you studied the Bible, then?" the patient asked.

"*Nobody* reads the Bible more than me!" Stumpf replied.

"Yes, I can see that hermeneutics is your thing," the patient said, causing Stumpf to shift uneasily in his seat.

"Herman who?" he replied, loosening his collar.

"Hermeneutics!"

"*Nobody* reads Herman's ethics more than me! Tremendous book ... a really great guy," Stumpf replied.

"Was there anything else, Mrs Jones?" Mallard asked, unaware of what was unfolding in the surgery next door.

Mallard the Quack

Suddenly, a scream rang out from Stumpf's consulting room. "What the fu ... flip was that?" Ivor exclaimed, jumping from his chair so quickly that by the time it had fallen to the floor he had already reached his surgery door. Already he had swung it open and was halfway to Doctor Stumpf's surgery in the adjacent room.

"I was only teasing! I know you know more about hermeneutics than anyone and knew you knew it was the study of the Bible!" cried a terrified voice from far inside the room.

Quickly, Ivor opened the door. There, before him, a young man ran terrified around the small surgery, trying his best to avoid Doctor Stumpf as the flabby old charlatan snorted and sweated behind him.

"What's going on?" Ivor asked as Stumpf slumped back into his chair.

"He's crazy! He told me that there's a passage in the Bible that says his foot ointment was sent by God! Then he said I had 'softening of the brain' and that he needed to knock a hole in my head with his golf club to let out the vapours!"

"It will be really great ... tremendous! One hole in the skull and all my - uh, *your* - problems will be over!" Stumpf slurred.

With that, the patient fled.

"What was it this time, Doctor Stumpf?" Ivor inquired.

"A know-all ... far too cocky. He also looked a bit foreign," Stumpf replied, still snorting and wheezing.

"Nurse Conwy, could you please get Doctor Stumpf a pot of tea? He's not looking himself."

"Thank God for that!" muttered Nurse Conwy as she approached the open surgery door.

"What did you say?" Mallard asked, still blindly loyal to him that paid the wages.

"Oh ... uh ... God forbid," said the nurse, narrowing her eyes and looking at Mallard as Mallard narrowed his eyes and returned her gaze.

"Hmm, okay," Ivor said suspiciously as the woman left.

"How much do we pay Nurse Conwy?" asked Stumpf.

"As little as possible. Why do you ask?" Ivor replied.

Do You Like My Muff, George?

"Because she's wearing gold jewellery. Where does she get the money?" he asked. Before Ivor had a chance to respond, the two Doctors were interrupted by a quiet voice from near the door.

"I'll just be off then, Doctor."

"I'm sorry, Mrs Jones. Yes, yes of course," Ivor said, taking the woman by her arm and leading her to the front door. "And tell that husband of yours he's a lucky man," he added, thinking himself quite a charmer.

Returning to Ronald's surgery, Ivor braced himself. He had news for Ronald and had been delaying telling him. 'Strike whilst the iron is hot', Ivor thought to himself.

"Doctor Stumpf - Sir - sit down, please. I have some important news for you ... well, for *us*. I had a letter from my father today. He wrote that George - my half-brother George, remember? He's finished his studies in Edinburgh. Well, he was told to leave on account of his being a moron! Anyway, he wants to come back here and pick up some practical knowledge from a couple of old pros like us. Bloody college boys! There will be more than a few shillings in it for you …."

"Yes. He's a really great guy ... unbelievable!" came the prompt reply, interrupting Ivor's best sales patter.

"Yes? You don't want to look at his testimonials?"

"No, I certainly do not!" Ronald replied emphatically, evidently misunderstanding what was meant by the word 'testimonials'.

"Good! Then I've no reason to send word for him not to come. He'll be here on ..." Ivor said, drawing the letter from his pocket to check the date. "The fifth, which is ... tomorrow! Oh bollocks, I didn't realise he'd be here so soon."

Ronald said nothing as he took another swig of liniment rub and closed his eyes.

The rest of the day passed quietly, with Ivor making a few home remedies and Ronald 'relaxing'.

At around nine the following morning, a loud banging rang through the entire house as the knob of a cane rapped at the old back door.

Mallard the Quack

"Oh, God, another day," Ivor mumbled as the noise woke him. "Can someone answer the door?" he shouted. There was no reply.

Slowly, he climbed from his bed and made his way through the house towards the back door, stopping just before he got to it to open a door to his left.

"Nurse Conwy, someone is knocking the door. Nurse Conwy, would you open the door and let whoever's knocking it in, please?" Ivor hissed, before turning and going back to bed.

Nurse Conwy roused herself and moved towards the commotion.

"Alright! Alright! Who's banging away at this time in the morning?" she shouted, as she pulled back the bolts and swung open the door. There, she was greeted by the scrubbed and shining face of young George Uppham, half-brother to Ivor Mallard and heir to the entire Uppham estate that Mallard found himself denied, on account of his being a swine.

"Morning! Remember me? I think I'm expected. George Uppham." said George, extending his hand and taking Nurse Conwy's hand in his. He was about to kiss it until he noticed how dirty it was and thought better of it.

"Expected? I should say! You can bang away at my door any time," Nurse Conwy said, doing her best to look beguiling as she gave a smile that showed more gaps than teeth.

"May I come in?" George asked.

"Ooh, you saucy devil! I can see I'm going to have to watch you!" Nurse Conwy replied, playing with her hair.

"No, I meant ..." George felt himself redden. "May I enter?"

"Ooh, you'll be getting me into trouble!" said Nurse Conwy, giving George a push on the shoulder in mock indignation.

At the risk of saying anything further, George moved past the woman and dropped his sack and suitcase on the floor.

"I expect you're all hot and sweaty after such a long journey, what with such a full sack! I bet you can't wait to unload it," Nurse Conwy said, spying what George had just dropped.

Do You Like My Muff, George?

"No, I'm fine, honestly," George answered, as Nurse Conwy drew nearer.

"Go on! I bet you're hot and sticky all over," she continued.

"Is that George?" Ronald shouted, having heard an unfamiliar voice echo up the stairs. "I'll show you your room. Thank you, Nurse Conwy, that'll be all," Ronald said, making a motion to pick up George's things before having second thoughts and casting Nurse Conwy a withering look. "You'll have to learn to ignore Nurse Conwy," he continued, as Nurse Conwy returned to her room and slammed the door. "She's like that. I remember the time my dear friend Peregrine visited before he was thrown out of his military academy and joined a travelling ballet company in Greece. He used to weep every time she spoke to him," he added, before pausing and gazing wistfully into the distance.

"It's looking stormy out there," George said, making small talk with the old mountebank.

"What was that? I was miles away. You were saying there may be a storm tonight?"

"Yes, stormy."

"Don't say such things! I've got an aversion to *anything* stormy!" Ronald said, his face drawn into a scowl.

"Right you are," George replied, looking a little askance at Doctor Stumpf for the abrupt change of conversation.

"I'll show you your room and leave you to settle in," Ronald said. "It must be a real pleasure for you being here with me, George. By the way, you didn't forget the cheques for Doctor Mallard and me, did you?"

George patted his breast pocket and smiled, as Stumpf drew alongside George's room and entered.

"Oh damn! I wanted to have a word with the driver of your carriage before he left. Is he still there?" Stumpf asked as George moved to the window.

"He's just pulling off!" George replied.

"The filthy swine!" said Stumpf.

"Uh? Oh wait, he's finished! Now it looks like he's getting ready to leave," George said, as the crunch of wheels on cobblestones echoed up from the road.

Mallard the Quack

"Hmm," Stumpf said, drawing out the word and giving George a long look as he closed the door and left.

Storm clouds were gathering and very soon, deep rumblings came over the black hills and the gentle tapping of rain on the tiles of the town. George began to unpack his things, hoping very much for a flash of lightning. Then, all of a sudden, a quick succession of bolts darted across the sky.

Quickly, George undressed. After uncoiling a length of flex and attaching one end to a length of copper, he opened the window and clambered out onto the roof.

Ivor lit his pipe and took a swig of laudanum. With no patients today, this was his time to relax. Suddenly, there was the sound of heavy footsteps outside his door, then the handle was turned and the door kicked open.

"Have you looked out of the window?" Ronald demanded, his face dark orange with rage.

"Since we lived here, or just recently?" asked Ivor, the laudanum having already worked its wonders.

"There's a naked man just run past my window with a length of metal in his hands," Ronald shouted, becoming increasingly agitated at Ivor's lack of concern.

"Ronald, I want you to answer me truthfully - have you been drinking the liniment rub again?" Ivor asked, trying his best to sound as rational as possible.

"No! It's that halfwit brother of yours! Is it some custom around your part of the world to show everything you've got when reacquainting yourself in a district or something?" Ronald raged, not rising to Ivor's flippant retort.

"What!" Ivor said, with sudden alarm, before rushing to the window. "George, don't do it!" he shouted. Upon hearing his name, George turned but in so doing slid on the slippery wet tiles and plummeted earthwards. "Ah, well, got him off the roof, anyway," he added, turning back towards the door with a smile on his face

Ivor carried George indoors and let him rest until the following morning when he was awoken by Ivor and given a list of patients that had made appointments for the day.

Do You Like My Muff, George?

"Right George, here are the suckers you have to see today. Come on, shake a leg," Ivor said, pulling the sheets off George and poking him in the ribs.

"Yes. Sorry, Ivor. What's the time?" George said, reaching out a hand to his pocket watch on the bedside table. "Half-past eight," he mumbled to himself, shaking the sleep from his eyes and propping himself up against the headboard. Finally, he was ready to listen to what Ivor had to say about his duties for the day.

"Right, at half-past nine you have David Jones. He's had a break-up and is after something to ease his mind. At ten, you've got David Jones and he's got a problem with his feet. At half-past-ten, you have David Jones who has something horrible he's picked up at sea for us to look at. At eleven you have David Jones and he has some shot in his arse where one of the locals shot him. Last thing this morning - at half-past-eleven - you have David Jones. He fell down the stairs after taking off his belt to belt some sense into his brother and tripped over when his britches slipped down to his ankles," Ivor stated.

George looked at Ivor and burst out laughing.

"This David Jones isn't having much luck, is he!" George said, holding his bruised ribs every time he laughed.

"No, dimwit, it's not all the same man! It's just a popular name around here," Ivor sought to explain, but in so doing only making matters worse.

"These Jones' brothers sound a queer lot!" George gasped, clearly in agony yet unable to stop himself laughing.

"Oh, God, I give up," Ivor said sternly, taking a small cane that was to hand and giving George a few whacks.

After breakfast, George opened his surgery and took delivery of his first patient.

"Right ... um ... Mr Jones, what can I do for you?" George said, beckoning the man into his surgery and gesturing to a chair opposite his desk.

"It's a ewe of mine, Doctor," said Jones, breaking into tears.

"I'm sorry, there appears to have been a bit of a mix-up. I was told you'd a break-up with someone," George said, anxiously thumbing through his paperwork.

"My lovely sheep, Doctor – she's left me!" Jones sobbed. "We first met when she was still a lamb, then again a few years later. I knew then that there was a chemistry between us, and that fate would bring us together. I'll never forget that time our eyes met across that crowded field. That's why I can't believe what she's done to me," Jones said, pausing to wipe the tears from his eyes.

"What has she done?" George asked.

"She's found someone new! A wild-eyed ram," Jones sobbed.

"Well, these things happen and if it wasn't meant to be, it wasn't meant to be," George said. "Perhaps she wanted a family and lambs of her own, maybe a shed in the country. The point is, allow yourself to grieve, but move on. Then if she does come back, it will all be a bonus. No sense in bleating about it," he added.

"Yes, Doctor. I was just wondering if there was something you could give me to help me sleep?" Jones asked, lifting his head and managing a smile.

"Of course," George replied, having already spied a bottle of one of Stumpf's medicines lying in his desk drawer. "Here we are - *Doctor Ronald Stumpf's Patented Universal Panacea - Excellent as a hair restorer, furniture polish, bruise ointment, insect repellent, laxative, purgative, emetic, tooth whitener, enamel cleaner and hair dye. Protects from plague, cholera, anthrax, piles and every other disease or common ailment, including attacks by demons and liberals. Also allows those missing their sheep a good night's sleep.*" The last line, of course, was not printed on the bottle, but George had no qualms about telling a little white lie, given that Doctor Stumpf's Universal Panacea would certainly be able to help those missing their loved ones, be they sheep or otherwise.

"I don't know how to thank you, Doctor," Jones said. "And tell Doctor Stumpf my wife says he can come round on Thursday."

"I shall. Does he know why?" George asked.

"Oh yes, it's all in the Bible," Jones explained. "Doctor Stumpf told me that in the Old Testament's Book of Neville, verse two and line twenty it says *And should thy feet be playing-*

Do You Like My Muff, George?

up then thou should let Doctor Stumpf pleasure thy pretty wife whenever he feels a bit randy. It hasn't stopped my feet playing up but if it's in the scriptures ...," Jones said as he stood to leave.

"Ah, I see," said George. "I hope your sheep comes back. Don't forget to invite me to the wedding!" George joked as he watched Jones stand and move to the door.

"Doctor, how's this work then?" Jones asked as he stood at the door.

"Just give the old knob a twist," offered George.

"No Doctor!" Jones said emphatically. "I haven't done that since I was fifteen and started getting hairy palms."

George stood and strode towards the door. He gave the handle a turn, opening the door and letting Jones out.

"Now then, my beauty!" came a loud voice. As the practice door opened and Jones took his leave, a squat man with a mop of greasy hair and cheeks like a bullfrog appeared. Having pushed past the queue and Doctor Mallard, he now strode toward George's surgery door. Ivor did his best to broker an introduction.

"Uh, George, may I introduce you to Mr Eldritch? He supplies many of the better class of Doctors with medicinal materials," Ivor said.

"And bloody good at it as well," boomed Eldritch, laying a hand on George's shoulders and drawing him nearer. "Now come with me," he said, pulling George to the surgery window. "Down there you'll see my brother, behind Mrs Jones and her chickens. You'll notice how handsome he is and what fine legs he has - traits which run in the family! He's what's known as a *Fugger* - he can get you all the latest medical supplies, from dried mummy flesh to petrified frogs. You will notice too that he has a dead body with him. Now dead bodies is dead bodies to most people but to me, they're meat and potatoes. You want some stiffs? I'm your man," Eldritch boasted, then lowered his voice so that the rest of his spiel was inaudible to anyone other than George.

"Well, now that I've introduced you gentlemen to one another, I'll be off," Ivor said timidly, wringing his hands and walking backwards in a half-bowing movement.

Mallard the Quack

"Oh, Mallard, I'm going to be negotiating a little business for a while," said Eldritch. Ivor gave a forced smile that was more pain than pleasure but nodded his agreement.

An hour or so later, Eldritch had concluded his meeting with George and left. George went to his surgery door and spied the waiting room.

"Right then, next please," he said, before sitting at his desk.

"Can I come in then, Doctor?" came a voice from the doorway.

"Of course," said George, looking up to see a pale man making his way to the seat, a mass of bloody blotches under his skin. "Now then, what seems to be the problem, Mr ..."

"Jones. David Jones," said the man. "I just come back from a trip to the Indies, see, and picked up something on board ship," he explained.

George looked at the man and recollected reading something about scurvy. Unfortunately, he'd stopped reading his medical dictionary at C but was very good on Alcoholism, Anthrax, Botulism, Burns, the Common Cold, and the Colon. Unfortunately, his diagnosis tended to tail off somewhat once diseases ventured into the *Ds*. Now, what was it that was used to treat the scurvy? George smiled, frowned, looked a little confused and then, enlightened, pointed a few times before checking himself. Finally, he gave a little cough and spoke.

"I think I'd better get a second opinion on this," he said, trying his best to sound as though second opinions were what every Doctor of note was doing this season. George made his way to the door. Striding towards Ivor's room, he listened for voices within and when none came, he opened the door.

"Yes?" said Ivor, quickly turning away from David Jones, the patient with *buckshot in his arse* who now had the pleasure of Ivor gouging out every fragment with his tweezers between puffs on his pipe.

"Oh, nothing. I didn't realise you were busy. I'll go and see Doctor Stumpf," George said, closing the door and making his way to Ronald's room. Again, he paused to listen for voices within and when none came, he entered. Doctor Stumpf quickly fastened his trousers and placed a funnel, length of hose and a bottle of beer in his desk drawer.

Do You Like My Muff, George?

"Alcohol never passes my lips," he explained.

"Uh, Doctor Stumpf, I've got a patient - a sailor. I think he might have scurvy. Could you give me a second opinion?" George asked politely.

Ronald, glassy-eyed and grinning, tried to focus.

"George, I've just the thing. I'll be there in a moment," he said, a tone of relish in his voice.

"Thank you," George replied, returning to his surgery.

"Sorry to have kept you," he said to Seaman Jones. No sooner had he spoken, the door of the surgery burst open and in waddled Ronald, cracking a long whip, a look of demonic mania on his orange face.

"Scurvy, eh? I'll give you scurvy! A lick or two of the ship's cat will soon put you right, my boy," he foamed, cracking his whip at both George and Jones as they began yelping and leaping around the room. "Go on, jump!" Ronald shouted, his thrashing becoming ever more frenzied. "I'll soon lash some sense into you! Scurvy? An excuse to laze about drinking rum and fondling other sailors, more like," Ronald added, before moving away from the only door, thus affording George and Jones an exit.

They ran through the waiting room and out of the house. It was only when they were in the street that George sought to compose himself, dusting down his clothes and straightening his neckerchief.

"Right then, Mr Jones, I'm glad we've got a diagnosis," George said, his voice rising in volume as Jones continued his sprint up the street and turning a corner a hundred or so yards away. "Come again soon!"

George turned and took a tentative step back into the house. He had known Ronald to have his *funny ways*, as Ivor had warned him, but he hadn't realised they were quite so pronounced. Imagine being like that! Imagine everyone talking about your odd behaviour! George gave a little shudder and thanked his lucky stars he was so normal.

"Right then, next please," George said, as he walked through the waiting room towards his surgery door. He paused and peered through a small crack where the door had been left slightly ajar. The coast was clear! Ronald, wherever he was, was satisfied now he had thrashed some sense into another work-shy patient.

"You are?" George said, entering the surgery.

"Dai Jones, Doctor," said the man.

"Yes, I rather fancied you might be," George replied. "Now, what seems to be the problem? I'm afraid there have been a few mix-ups today and I don't have your case notes. Doctor Mallard has dealt with quite a few of my patients, as has Doctor Stumpf."

"Well, it's like this, Doctor. I'm broken-hearted, see," Dai Jones began, screwing up his face in misery.

"Go on," George encouraged.

"Well, I think I'm cheating on my wife. What's worse, it's with a male."

George widened his mouth and took an intake of breath.

"Well, if you loved your wife, don't you think you should have been more honest with her?" George asked.

"I would have been, Doctor. I knew it was doomed from the start, but it was love at first sight. It was something about those wild eyes, that dark, firm, fleecy body, that foreign bleat that spoke of far off places ...."

"Sorry, did you say *bleat*?" George interrupted, leaning back in his chair.

"Oh, sorry Doctor, didn't I mention he was a sheep? Yes, Idris has the glossiest coat! He was different from all the other rams I've met. I never thought he'd treat me like this after all I've done for him," Jones mumbled, the memories of stolen moments bringing tears to his eyes. "I'm not a prevert, mind! There was nothing sexy going on. I just found I could talk to him."

"Pervert," George said.

"There's nothing preverted about talking, Doc!" Jones said angrily.

"The word is 'pervert' not 'prevert'," George stammered.

"No! Doctor Stumpf says it's 'prevert' and he knows all the best words."

"Yes, he does. Anyway, back to business! You say Idris left you?" George asked.

Do You Like My Muff, George?

"Yes. He said he wanted lambs of his own and ... well, he couldn't ever get that with me, but it didn't bother him when we first met! Now he's run off with some doe-eyed floozy just because she flaunts a well-shaped cloven hoof his way. I always knew he'd leave me one day, but never for a blonde!" Jones sobbed.

"Oh, what a tangled web we weave," George said to himself, thinking how envious Shakespeare would have been if he could have thought of lines like that. If only these sheep had considered the trail of broken hearts they had left in their wake, would they have stopped? Would a sense of shame have called a halt to the pounding of two hearts beating as one?

"Well, you must ask yourself what you got from Idris that you didn't get from your wife," George said sympathetically. "Perhaps if you can put your finger on it, you might be able to make a go of things with her."

"I think that was the problem, Doctor," Jones said.

"What?" George asked, his brow knitting as he wrestled with the point Jones was trying to make.

"My never putting my finger on it," Jones offered.

"Yes, well I'm going to let you have some of this - *Doctor Ronald Stumpf's Patented Universal Panacea - Excellent as a hair restorer, furniture polish, bruise ointment, insect repellent, laxative, purgative, emetic, tooth whitener, enamel cleaner and hair dye. Protects from plague, cholera, anthrax, piles and every other disease or common ailment, including attacks by demons,*" George said, handing Jones a bottle of the same medicine he'd offered the other Jones. "Now you go home and drink some of this," George said, pausing and squinting at the bottle. "Sorry, my mistake! Rub this on the affected areas, and if it's not better in three weeks, perhaps you could make an appointment to see Doctor Stumpf. He's very sympathetic in matters of the heart."

"I still have terrible flatulence, mind. Last time I saw Doctor Stumpf he said my new boots were causing it. I never knew boots could do that but Doctor Stumpf quoted the Book of Colin from the Bible to me as that says 'Should thy suffer from chronic flatulence then thou should give thy new boots to Doctor Stumpf'. That was a couple of years ago and my

Mallard the Quack

flatulence is still giving me trouble but it's got to go soon if Doctor Stumpf says it's in the Bible – and he told me that *nobody* reads the Bible more than him."

At last, George had seen his final patient. After the early morning sunshine, there was now a distinct chill in the air and as soon as Jones had left, George moved towards the little coal fire in the back wall of the surgery, throwing a few sticks of wood onto the embers.

As the flames rose, he warmed his hands. Finally, he could relax. Within a minute or so, however, there came a bang at the door and Nurse Conwy entered.

"Hello Nurse Conwy, just uh ... warming my hands," George said nervously, as he rose to his feet and took a few steps backwards.

"Are your hands cold, Doctor? You with such strong Doctor's hands as well! I bet they soon get warm with your bedside manner!" Nurse Conwy said suggestively.

"Uh, no ... not really," George stammered, turning his back on Nurse Conwy and taking a book from a bookcase, a book that he had no intention of reading but which he hoped might give the impression that he was otherwise engaged.

"You could always stick them in my muff," Nurse Conwy offered.

"What! Oh sorry, I thought you meant ... oh, no matter what I thought!" George said, turning quickly to see Nurse Conwy offering a tube of material of the kind ladies of leisure tuck their hands into when the winter chill begins to bite.

"Do you like my muff, George?" Nurse Conwy asked, moving towards George as she spoke. "Slip a few fingers in and feel how warm and soft it is."

"I wanna watch!" Ronald gasped, bursting in and hopping toward them with his britches around his ankles. Both George and Nurse Conwy spun around in surprise, given that neither had known he was within earshot. "Oh, I see, I thought you two were ..." said Ronald, frowning. "I thought I heard someone firing a gun so I sprinted in to see who I could save," he explained, having noticed the small fashion accessory Nurse Conwy was offering George. Without a trace of embarrassment, he bent to pull up his britches before running

Do You Like My Muff, George?

his hand over a shelf and looked at his fingers, pretending to be looking for dust.

"I've been meaning to have a tidy up," George offered.

"Yes, that was what I came to see you about," Ronald said. "Was there anything else, Nurse Conwy?" he asked, looking in the nurse's direction and arching his eyebrow.

"My hero! You're so brave," Nurse Conwy replied. "I'm going to the market and I wanted to know if anyone wanted anything. I'm after some meat and two veg. Oh, and Doctor Stumpf has just reminded me that I need to get some mushrooms," she added, smiling at Doctor Stumpf and licking her lips before leaving the room.

George gave Ronald an embarrassed look and shrugged his shoulders, feeling self-conscious that Ronald was scrutinising him so intently.

"I've been meaning to ask you, Doctor Stumpf, I've noticed that the old cowshed isn't being used. I also noticed that it has a door straight out onto the street, so I was wondering if I could set up a little laboratory in there to do a few experiments," George inquired.

"Oh yes," Ronald smiled. "Is *that* what they're calling it these days! You must think me and Doctor Mallard to not be men of the world! A little hideaway with a quiet door that goes straight out onto the street, away from the prying eyes of the house? I know your little game!" Ronald said, laughing.

"You do?" George gulped, his eyes bulging.

"Of course. If you're anything like me then you want to entertain ladies down there, don't you?" Ronald said, giving George a playful punch to the chin.

"Oh, you're too smart for me, Doctor Stumpf!" George said smiling, his body slumping as the tension ebbed away. "We're a pair, aren't we Doctor Stumpf!"

"I'm, like, really intelligent," Ronald said. "I'm a very stable genius. You can read all about sex in my book - *The Art of The Feel*. *No one* knows more about sex than me! I do the best sex! As a medical man, I say get in there and get on with it! Don't press *anything* - it's the *Devil's Doorbell*!" he explained.

"Lock up your daughters, eh!" George said, giving Ronald a jovial slap and growling.

"Lock up foreigners!" Ronald replied.

As the two Doctors stood opposite one another, both trying to avoid eye contact and both struggling to find the words to quickly curtail the conversation, a loud rumble of thunder growled, shortly followed by a crackle of lightning and the heavy pitter-pat of rain on the tiles.

"Looks like thunder," Ronald commented making moves towards the door. "I'd better make sure Nurse Conwy has got the washing in."

"Right. Good idea," George enthused as if Ronald's plan of action were somehow exciting.

"Oh! and George," Ronald said, pausing at the door, his hand already on the knob.

"No dancing around on the roof in the nude, eh? We don't want you spoiling our good name and frightening away the patients now, do we?"

"Understood, Doctor Stumpf!" George replied.

"Are you sure?" Ronald laboured, wishing to make his point completely understood.

"No," George replied, a glazed, confused look on his face.

"Look, I don't want you on the roof at all. Not now, not ever," Ronald said.

"Oh right!" George answered, as though the new way of explaining the request had been a revelation. "Sorry, Doctor Stumpf. The wheel's turning but the hamster's dead!"

"Now don't you go trying to change the subject! We were talking about roofs, not hamsters," Ronald said sternly. "Roof, George, no! Understood?"

George raised his hands and gave a thumbs-up. At last, Ronald had made himself understood! Now he could retire for the night, safe in the knowledge that the good name of Mallard, Stumpf and Uppham would remain.

That's a Lovely Looking Leg

Ronald and Ivor gazed out of their old study, through the rain that spattered the leaded window separating them from the outside world, and out onto a lowered section of the roof. Deep rumblings of thunder growled in the distance. Suddenly, a crack of lightning lit up the whole sky for just an instant, capturing the figure of George - naked - as he leapt to and fro on the gleaming wet tiles, his arm stretched high above his head clutching a bolt of metal up to the sky whilst a length of flex trailed across the roof behind him, disappearing from view as it slid off the end of the building.

"Are you sure he's your brother?" Ronald asked.

"Half-brother, please! We have the same father - Sir Richard Uppham - but a different mother. That's why he's thirty years younger than me. If I'd known he was going to be such a ..." Ivor paused and mused carefully before making a choice, "twat, then I wouldn't have agreed to have let him come and practice here."

Suddenly, a second crack of lightning shot across the sky in an eerie blue snap, attacking the end of the rod in the young man's hand with all the ferocity of a snake seizing its prey. Poleaxed, George went rigid and fell from the roof.

There was very little visible reaction to the event from the two Doctors that were watching.

"Are you going to get him?" Ronald asked.

"I suppose I will," said Ivor, running his hands through prematurely white hair. "Little swine," he muttered, as he moved toward the door. Even by dim candlelight he still looked as miserable and unpleasant as he did in broad daylight. As he descended the stairs, the back door burst open and George naked and agitated, jumped in. Static electricity crackled all around him, his hair standing on end.

"Oh, you're alright then?" Ivor asked, not really caring either way.

"Yes, fine," George answered, his teeth chattering so that he was barely comprehensible.

Mallard the Quack

"I still can't believe that you and old Mallard are related," said Ronald, having followed Ivor down the stairs.

"Half-brothers, see!" George said, pointing to a picture on the wall. "Sir Richard Uppham!" he proudly declared. "Our father."

"So, why do you have different surnames if you have the same father?" Ronald asked.

"I can answer that!" Ivor said. "It's the name on the Doctorate I bought from that man in Builth Wells. Remember? It says my medical Doctorate is in Gastronomy. That's okay, though - if you want your gasterroids looking at. Trust my luck to choose a forger that couldn't spell Gastroenterology!"

"I don't know why you wasted your money," Stumpf said. "Just lie and if anyone asks for proof then move on!"

"You make it sound so easy, Doctor Stumpf!" George gushed, causing Stumpf to shrug his shoulders as though that fact should be a given for he was the chosen one as he could bear the curse of superiority to every other mortal in a way that no one else could, before looking back at the painting on the wall.

"People come up to me all the time and ask me how come I'm so tremendous and I tell them that's it's just the way I am … I'm just very well-endowed," Stumpf explained.

"Anyway, back to the painting. Can't you see the family resemblance?" George said, pulling Doctor Mallard near to him. "Our faces look just like Dick's," George said, pointing at the painting.

"What!" bellowed Ivor. I haven't got a face like a pen … oh, you meant a face like Sir Richard! I thought you meant … well, never mind what I thought," he added, giving a nervous smile. Ronald scowled back, whilst George simply grinned with an expression Ivor hadn't seen since he last took a group of business colleagues on a sightseeing tour around the lunatic asylum. What a day that had been! He hadn't laughed so much since he'd misdiagnosed Iron-Hoof Jones the Blacksmith's plague as hay fever!

"Don't worry Ivor, I won't need to show anyone that painting in the future. I've had a small copy made," George said proudly.

That's a Lovely Looking Leg

"Have you? Have you?" Ivor answered with savage sarcasm.

"Have you seen it?" George queried.

"Seen what?" Ivor replied, never one to follow the thread of a conversation.

"Have you seen my little Dick Uppham?" George answered.

"What!" Ivor shouted, taking a step back in disgust. "Don't be so foul! Of course, I've never seen your ... oh ... hang on ... yes, of course, you meant the painting. Sorry, I thought you meant ... oh well, no matter what I thought," he added, pretending he'd noticed a particularly interesting mark on the wall and stretching out his hand to smooth it over, thus avoiding eye contact as best he could. Ronald and George looked at one another in bewilderment.

"Anyway, did it work?" said George excitedly.

"Did what work?" Ivor snapped, seeking to overcome his embarrassment by feigning ill-temper.

"Down there," George said, lifting his arm to gesture down the corridor. Unfortunately, his arm had other ideas and flopped towards the floor a few inches up from his wrist, George now finding himself unintentionally pointing at the floor. "Oh, no, not again," he added, fainting into Ivor's outstretched and expectant arms.

When George awoke, he was in bed. Ivor sat pensively in a seat by his side, whilst Ronald stood in the doorway.

"It's a nasty sprain you've got there. Still, at least it's not broken," Ronald said, moving towards the bed and taking hold of George's arm, twisting it into a number of angles, George screaming in agony as various grating and snapping noises came from the arm. "Now tell me, does that hurt?" Ronald asked.

"Honestly?" George asked, trying to smile through the pain. Ronald nodded enthusiastically. "Well, it did smart a bit."

"Then perhaps I ought to do it to your head," Ronald muttered.

"Pardon?" George said.

"Yes, as I thought, it's a nasty sprain."

"Thank God for that," said George. "I thought it might have been broken or something."

"Honestly George! A medical man and you can't even diagnose a sprain! I despair, I really do!" Ivor said, leaning back in his chair and giving a hearty laugh, looking at Ronald in the hope he might join in. Ronald remained stony-faced, however, so Ivor quickly stopped and did his best to show concerned interest. George gave an apologetic smile.

"Sorry, Ivor. I'm just a bit thick sometimes," George admitted, as they were interrupted by a knock at the door.

"*Entrez, mon ami!*" Ivor announced, puffing himself in self-importance as he looked about him for an indication that his French had been impressive. Again, the smile quickly dropped from Ivor's face as he realised no one had paid him any attention. A second knock on the door followed, this time louder.

"Come in!" Ivor said loudly.

"Uh?" the voice from the far side of the heavy door grunted. Ivor stood up and strode purposefully towards it, pausing only to adjust his hair in the small mirror George used for shaving.

"Yes, Nurse Conwy, what is it?" Ivor asked as he pulled the door open, failing to disguise the genuine disappointment he felt when he saw who it was that stood waiting.

"Nothing for you!" she said. "It's for young George. Mr Eldritch is here to see him."

George jumped out of bed, his naked body whirling around the bedroom like a top as he sought some clothes.

"Oh! Doctor George!" said the Nurse, raising her hand to her face in a mock display of shocked virtue, but ensuring she kept her fingers splayed just wide enough to view every inch of the lithe young man in front of her.

"Great!" George enthused, just as the room was darkened by the bulky presence of the visitor. Entering the room loudly, Eldritch knocked George's mirror to the floor and Ivor into the wall, then pointed at George's exposed genitalia and let out a huge laugh that thundered around the small bedroom. All three Doctors strained to follow the direction of Eldritch's

That's a Lovely Looking Leg

outstretched finger, then laughed almost equally as heartily. Only slowly did George realise what the object of their mirth was, his smile turning to a frown.

"I've got some real bargains for you today," said Eldritch, running his fingers-fat-as-sausages through his hair.

"Brilliant!" George shouted, as though all his Christmases had come at once.

Eldritch extended a hand to shake, in a gesture of goodwill. George quickly clasped the hand in his as Eldritch took a jaunty step backwards, leaving George clutching an arm that was severed at the elbow.

"I like to have a laugh," bellowed Eldritch. "As I often say, 'if you can't have a laugh, what can you have?'" he added, looking at Ivor.

"Yes, quite. I was only saying to Ronald this morning. 'Ronald', I said ..."

"Shut up, Mallard. I hate you," shouted Eldritch. Ivor raised both hands and brought his index finger to his pursed lips. If it were silence that was asked for, then it was silence he would get!

"I got a real beauty here!" Eldritch began. "Only planted yesterday and still as stiff as a board. He's a lovely looking fella - nice legs. Then there's old Jumbo Cummings. He stinks a bit - then again, he always did! Dug 'em both up with me own fair hands last night, I did." Eldritch laughed, looking from Mallard to Stumpf. They both laughed when looked at and stopped when the gaze was lost. "I wanted to get old Prong Jones for you, as I thought you'd like something a bit unusual," he added. "Waited bloody years for him, I have, and what does he do? Gets all the way to America and drops dead the first day he's there."

"Lucky swine!" Ivor said. "I wish I could afford to die in America. I can't afford to die down the end of our road."

Ivor's aside was ignored as George and Eldritch began bargaining with one another. Vaguely inquisitive, the naturally gormless expressions of the other two Doctors focussed on Eldritch and the still nude George, as Ivor sidled nonchalantly up to Ronald

Mallard the Quack

"I don't trust that Eldritch. If I didn't know better, I'd swear he's a grave robber," Ivor whispered. Unfortunately for Ivor, his timing could not have been worse as a gap in the conversation between George and Eldritch allowed the latter to overhear every word.

"What did you say?" Eldritch said, striding towards Ivor, taking a soil-encrusted mattock from beneath his coat as he spoke.

"Ooh, you're in for it now, Ivor!" said George excitedly.

"George! Ronald, say something!" Ivor wailed, beginning to shake.

"Go on, Eldritch. I wouldn't stand for that!" Ronald said, this outburst not being what Ivor had anticipated.

"Oh, I don't intend to. You've done it this time, Mallard. I've always hated you," Eldritch said, taking a swing at Ivor with his mattock, but missing as Ivor ducked.

Ivor jumped onto the bed and dived from there to a corner of the room. Grabbing hold of George's arm, he pulled him close to use as a human shield. The constant to and fro, however, caused George to lose his balance and within a few seconds, he'd fallen face down on the bed, with Ivor on top of him. As they landed, Nurse Conwy returned, only to be greeted by the sight of Ivor on top of his naked brother, both of them sweating, grunting and panting.

"You dirty swine!" she shouted, falling to the floor in a faint. Eldritch grabbed hold of Ivor and, with one flabby left hand, wrenched him free.

"Got you, you little swine! Now, what can I do to a man that casts perspirations on my good name?"

"He could give us a song?" George volunteered.

"George! I'm sure the lovely man can think of something on his own without any help from you," Ivor said.

"No, that's good! I like that. A song is good. Get over there, Mallard," Eldritch barked, pointing to a chair and pushing Ivor toward it. "And if you move, so help me God, I'll take that head off your shoulders, see?" he added, raising his mattock threateningly.

"Uh ... any requests?" asked Ivor nervously, as he sat down.

"Just get on with it!" Ronald interjected.

That's a Lovely Looking Leg

"Alright! Here goes. Can someone count me in?"

"What a load of rubbish!" George began to chant, Eldritch and Ronald quickly picking up the refrain.

"*I am a little orphan boy, my mother she is dead, My father is a drunkard and won't give me no bread ...*" Ivor began, quickly moving to the end of the sad lament that ended when a chorus of angels came to take the starving child to heaven.

"Hooray, that was brilliant! Give us another, Ivor!" George gushed.

"George, will you shut up! Ronald, can you say something!" Ivor said in desperation.

"Certainly," Ronald replied. "Why don't you sing something we can all join in on? I'm sick of these happy songs. I don't care about starving orphans, I want a sad song about a millionaire losing some of his money."

"Not quite what I had in mind, but thanks for trying," Ivor said sarcastically.

"No! No, that was beautiful! My mother used to sing that to me when I was young," Eldritch said, dabbing his eyes and blowing his nose on the arm of his coat. "Do you know Mallard ... Ivor, in this light you even look a bit like her, save for the moustache, of course."

"I haven't got a moustache," Ivor said, shifting uneasily in his seat.

"Not you, her! I remember it well. My father was so jealous of it. A big black bush of a thing it was. We used to comb food out of it to make soup."

"Uh, I don't want to interrupt anything here, but could I please get up now ... Mr Eldritch ... Sir?" Ivor asked, looking at Eldritch with his large, watery eyes.

"Ah, go on Ivor, give us another first!" George said cajolingly.

"George, will you shut up! Ronald, can't you say something?" By now, Ivor could feel one of his panic attacks coming on, so looked to the elder Doctor for support.

"I could stay here all night," Ronald replied

"Do you know, Doctor, so could I," Eldritch said, looking to the old Quack, his voice tinged with genuine camaraderie.

"Hooray! If only we had some little nibbles or something," George exclaimed, looking around the room as though he were half-expecting to find some.

"Oh good! That's just great then. I'll just sing all night then, shall I?" Ivor said, sinking into his seat.

"I just wish Nurse Conwy were awake to enjoy all the fun," said George as he looked at the unconscious woman lying on the floor. Clearly, the form struck some deep-seated chord inside him, prompting him to rise from his seat and gently tap the woman's face. "No, it's no good, I'll see if I can hear her heart beating," he continued. As George had started his examination while kneeling behind the woman's head, as he leant over to listen for a heartbeat his backside pressed against her face just as she awoke. The unexpected sight at such close range was too much of a shock for her, and she promptly passed out again. "Ah, too bad. Maybe another time," said George, not even aware of the temporary recovery and immediate relapse, as he returned to the edge of the bed.

"Now then," Eldritch continued looking at Ivor coyly. "Mummy sing ickle Eldritch another song ...?"

By the time dawn came the next morning, all four men had fallen asleep. As the sun rose, only Nurse Conwy awoke. Rising to her feet, she gazed around the room.

"Filthy swine," she spat, striding to the door and leaving the room. As she descended the staircase, she paused a moment and flared her nostrils. It only took a moment to recognise the smell of a corpse. As she entered the kitchen, her suspicions were confirmed: two bodies lay on the kitchen table.

Taking a soup ladle down from the wall, she thrust it under the first body's midriff and levered it onto the floor, where it landed with a dull thud. Jumbo Cummins body, however, proved altogether trickier due to its bulk. Eventually, Nurse Conwy despatched him to the floor by lifting one side of the table, so that he rolled, gently at first then gathering momentum like an avalanche of blubber, hitting the floor with less of a thud and more of a splat.

With the table now free of clutter, Nurse Conwy brushed away a few flies then took a lump of meat off a hook above it and dropped it onto the dirty wooden surface, squashing the

That's a Lovely Looking Leg

few flies that remained. Taking a cleaver from a drawer, she wiped the greasy residue from its blade on her dress and proceeded to hack the flesh into lumps.

Noticing that her nails were dirtier than usual, she stopped chopping. With the corner of the cleaver, she scraped the dirt from beneath them, then carried on with her duties. All the exercise, however, caused Nurse Conwy to sweat. Streams began trickling down her face, gathering on the tip of her nose and leaving clean streaks where they had run. As more and more murky beads gathered, they began to drip onto the meat and the table beneath her.

Looking around her for something to jam open the kitchen door, the only things to hand were the bodies. Holding the door open with one hand she manoeuvred one corpse into position with the other, its lifeless head keeping the door ajar.

As the sound of the chopping echoed through the house, three of the four men stirred.

"Now then George, about my bodies ...," Eldritch began.

"I'll take the one with nice legs," George interrupted.

"Tell you what, I'll throw in old Jumbo. How's that? Buy one, get one free!" Eldritch certainly knew how to look after his customers.

Ivor opened one eye, quickly closing it again and pretending to be still asleep. Meanwhile, a sound not unlike tearing sheets erupted from the back of Ronald's britches as he rolled over with a contented look on his face.

Eldritch and George began coughing and spluttering, wiping tears from their eyes as they gasped for breath. Ivor tried his best to control his convulsions, but even after twenty years of flatulent familiarity, he couldn't help but make a series of involuntary retching motions.

"Well George, your bodies are downstairs. That'll be seven guineas for the two," said Eldritch, finally catching his breath.

George moved to his britches and pulled them on, taking a bundle of notes from his pockets.

"Here you are. You're a gentleman and scholar, Eldritch," he said, moving with Eldritch to the door, whereupon Eldritch turned.

"Say goodbye to Ivor for me. Tell him he has the voice of an angel."

"I will, I will. Maybe if you come around later, we'll have another get together."

"I'd like that," Eldritch replied then, once again, pointed at George's groin, laughed at the memory of the night before. George temporarily joined in the fun, then realised what he was laughing at, whereupon the laugh turned to a frown.

As Eldritch's heavy footsteps descending the stairs become less audible, Ivor allowed himself to open both eyes.

"Thank God for that, I thought the fugger would never go!" he growled.

"Ivor!" George shouted in salutation. "You're awake! How's about a little song to start the morni ... " Ivor's foot quickly curtailed the sentence as it connected sharply with George's groin.

"That's for last night as well, you swine!" Ivor said, leaning over George, the latter oblivious to the explanation as he jumped around the room rubbing his genitals.

Around mid-morning, Ronald came into the kitchen with a small pile of dirty underclothes.

"I'm going to boil these," he stated to Nurse Conwy, filling a saucepan with water. "I've had a little accident or two and having scraped off the worst of it, I think a good boil wash should get rid of the rest," he explained.

As Ronald's underwear began to simmer, George, now dressed, came into the room.

"Ah, Nurse Conwy," he said, seeing the nurse busy peeling vegetables. "Something smells good," he continued, before taking the ladle and dunking it deep into Ronald's saucepan, then removing it and taking a large gulp. "Mmm, soup," he said. "Unusual flavour though - very gamey."

Later that day, Ivor paid a visit to George's cowshed-cum-laboratory where the two bodies now lay motionless on planks of wood that, in turn, rested on milk churns, thus bringing the bodies to waist height. All the while, pigs, chickens and sheep wandered back and forth.

"Christ, George, it stinks in here! Why don't you get rid of the pig for a start?" Ivor gasped, burying his face in his arm.

That's a Lovely Looking Leg

"Get rid of him! I've only just brought him in here! You should have smelt it before!" George said, hardly taking his eyes from his work.

"I've been meaning to ask you, George, why do you run around the roof in the nude every time we have a thunderstorm?" Ivor asked, taking a large draw on his old clay pipe, lit in the hope of masking the odious smell.

"It's the Enlightenment, Ivor. Things are changing. Galvani and electricity and all that. I'm trying to capture power from a bolt of lightning," George answered, removing his hands from the open stomach of a cadaver and wiping them on his coat.

"One question, George - why?" Ivor asked, distinctly unimpressed by George's reason.

"It's a new age, Ivor. A new era. An era of optimism. Electricity can do anything!" George enthused, just as the surgery dog, Himbry – no one knew from where the name had come - leapt alongside the open body and dipped his head into the hole, drawing forth a considerable length of intestine and making a bolt for the door with it.

"Hey, come back! I wanted that, you little swine!" George shouted, setting off in hot pursuit. It was, however, too late as the dog was gone in a black and-white-mongrel-type flash, along with the insides of the corpse.

"Sorry about that, Ivor," George said, returning empty-handed. "Oh yes, as I was saying, electricity will be the power of the future," George continued, returning to the body to see exactly what the dog had pilfered.

"Oh really! Such as?" Ivor had suspected his brother of being stupid, but then he couldn't be that stupid, could he?

"Oh, I don't know," George answered, struggling to think of an example now he had been put on the spot. "Power a lamp so that a house might be as bright by night as it is by day. Start a heart beating again." George felt sure that would convince his older brother.

"George, George, George, George, George, you poor misguided fool! You really talk some complete balls at times. I mean, what next? Listen to Doctor Stumpf when he says that we should all go with gut instinct rather than science. You'll be telling me that ...." Ivor paused and drew the pipe away from his mouth to think of an example. "Yes, you'll be telling me next that tobacco is bad for children," he added, laughing.

"Really, Ivor! That would be stupid. Everyone knows tobacco is good for you! That's the trouble with you - you always have to exaggerate things fifty million times. I'm telling you, electricity will be the power of the future."

"Look, we all know windmills give you the cancer - we don't need science to prove it! Just go with your gut instinct, like Doctor Stumpf," Ivor added. Suddenly, a sight from the window distracted him. "Look, there's Mrs Jones! Mrs Jones!" Ivor shouted, leaning from the window and waving. "Do you know, every time I see that woman she has a cock in her hand!" he said, taking a step back into the room

"What!" George said excitedly, rushing to the window. "Oh, a chicken! I thought you meant ... oh, never mind what I thought," he added, unable to conceal his disappointment.

Suddenly, there was a knock at the door.

"Who's that? You expecting someone?" asked Ivor nervously.

"It's for you!" George replied, lifting the arm of one of the bodies and waving it in Ivor's direction.

"Will you stop messing about? It could be Ronald back from Cardiff with those tapered leeches I ordered," Ivor answered, moving to the window and trying to peer out without being seen.

"Tapered?" George asked.

"Yes, it makes them easier to insert," Ivor answered from the corner of his mouth.

George nodded as though he understood then abruptly stopped, his face registering alarm as the implication of what his brother had said dawned on him.

"It's that fugging madman Eldritch," Ivor said.

"Eldritch?" George looked confused and began rolling his eyes and biting his lip.

"Yes, George, Mr Eldritch," said Ivor, recognising the look on George's face as one of blind ignorance.

"Now I know this. Oh, don't tell me. It's coming. It's coming." There followed a long pause during which

That's a Lovely Looking Leg

George screwed up his eyes and shook his head from side to side, as though he were telling some unseen friend *no*. "No, Ivor, I give up. You're going to have to tell me."

"Eldritch! The man who gave you the stiffs last night!" Ivor said in desperation. George let out a shocked gasp and took a step backwards.

"Don't be so disgusting! No man has ever given me the stiffs! I certainly wasn't with any rough trade last night. Last night I listened to you singing." Suddenly, a look of illumination spread across his face, as though somebody had blown away the clouds inside his head, allowing the sun to shine through. "Oh, *that* Eldritch! Cuh, sometimes I'm so stupid I think I must be the stupidest man in um ... uh ... um ..."

"Wales?" Ivor offered.

"That's it! Wales. I'm useless with those long names," George confessed. A second, fiercer, bang echoed through the little room.

"That's it, I'm off. He's all yours," Ivor said, running for the door that led back to the house. George moved to the door Eldritch was loudly banging and swung it wide open on its rusting strap hinges. No sooner had he done so than Eldritch strode in, replete with corpse.

"I've another beauty for you here," Eldritch gasped, unloading the body next to the two he'd brought the night before. "Lovely legs," he continued, rolling down the corpse's stockings. "Go on, have a feel. Lovely they are and still warm, too."

George meanwhile, having moved around the corpse, had stopped at the man's face. Crouching down, he frowned as though lost in thought.

"I don't wish to be too picky, Eldritch, but this man is breathing," George said awkwardly, fearing Eldritch's reaction.

"Trick of the light. He's dead alright."

"I could have sworn I saw him breathing."

"Well, you're the Doctor. Check him over - if you don't believe me, that is."

Mallard the Quack

George hated confrontations and now embarrassed that he had doubted the word of his fugging friend, he took a deep intake of breath.

"No, that won't be necessary. If you say he's dead then I'm sure he is."

"Tell you what," Eldritch said. "If it will make you feel any better, give me five minutes alone with him and I'll make sure he's dead."

For a moment, George was taken in by the tone of Eldritch's persuasive argument and even considered thanking him for his kind offer.

"No, Eldritch, you can't kill him. Besides ..." George took another look at the man's face. "Eldritch, isn't this your brother? I'm sure he's that fugger I saw from the window."

There followed a long pause in which Eldritch looked awkward. He rubbed his fat belly then placed an index finger on the table, casually twisting it from side to side as he cast his eyes to the ground.

"Could be," he admitted. Feeling braver now that the admission was out, he added "Oh, so what if he is! He *is* dead, I promise you!"

George was now beginning to waver. He had another look at the corpse's face and placed his head against its chest.

"I promise you, fit as a fiddle he was. Just this morning he came home for a bite to eat and keeled over. No use being sentimental, I thought, not when there's rent to be paid. Besides, legs like this can fetch a good price."

"I think I'd better let my colleagues have a look if you don't mind," George said, moving to the door and calling to his fellow practitioners. Soon, Ivor came into the room, closely followed by Ronald, who had by now returned with the leeches.

"I'm having a little difficulty diagnosing death. What do you two think?" George asked.

Ivor sank his hands deep into his britches pockets and nudged Ronald, nodding at George as he did so, his wry smile seeming to say *can you believe this?* Ronald's stony grimace remained impassive. Ivor immediately lost his smile and feigned a serious and concerned look as a result.

That's a Lovely Looking Leg

"Oh yes. Clearly dead," Ronald said, whilst still a considerable distance from the body.

"He is, Doctor - drank himself to death," Eldritch offered, as Ronald moved towards the corpse.

"Oh yes, dead alright. Look, he's stiff as a ... board." Ronald lifted the body's arm, only for it to limply flop from his grasp.

"It's like this, Doctor. He died in a fire, see. Flames must have kept him warm, that's why he's not as stiff as he should be," Eldritch suggested, looking at Ivor, who nodded in agreement.

Suddenly, the corpse let out a loud snore. All three Doctors turned to face Eldritch.

"The death rattle!" Eldritch stuttered.

"Ah, yes. That explains it. Although ..." Ronald moved forward to open the corpse's eye. "Ah, damn you! Damn your eyes! Cursed! Cursed I am! It's the evil eye! The evil eye!" he screamed, as he ran from the room.

"Well, I'm glad we cleared that little problem up. If you need any more professional advice, George, please let either myself or Doctor Stumpf know," Ivor said, just as a pig in the corner of the room grunted loudly, drowning out the last of his words. Ivor turned tail and with all the professional air he could muster, strode towards the door left ajar by Ronald's hasty departure. However, the dignity of his departure was punctured by his treading in a little deposit left by the aforementioned pig and skidding through the open doorway, colliding into the wall opposite and disappearing from view.

Later that night George was hard at work and all alone in the cowshed. He had persuaded his brother to bandage up his arm and, loaded on laudanum, he whirled feverishly around the glut of bodies about him. Exposing the leg of the latest arrival, he took a step back in mute admiration. "What a work of art," he mused. With a slow method, he moved to the corner of the room to fetch his sharpest saw. He bent the blade as though he were flexing a rapier. The blade sprang from his grasp and knocked him in the face.

"I promise you, this is going to hurt you a lot more than it hurts me," George said to the corpse, wiping the blood from his nose. In the dim light, he dug his fingers into the flesh to find the exact centre of the knee and began to saw, slowly at first, then faster as the blade sank deeper and deeper into the soft tissue.

"Oh, God, my bloody leg!" came a voice from under the blanket George had used to cover the corpse.

"Who said that?" George stammered, his eyes rolling cautiously around the room. He'd read his Vathek and his Castle of Otranto and now he half expected a ghostly hand to appear suspended in the gloomy room, or some dreadful spectre to come from hell to punish him for his diabolism. There was no reply to his question, so nervously he began sawing again.

"Oh, God, that smarts," came the voice, just as George cut through the last of the leg and brought it away. Suddenly, the body beneath the sheet sat bolt upright.

"Argh!" shrieked George, dropping the leg and fleeing to the warm refuge of the house.

"Argh! Oh, God! I swear I'll never touch another drop. My head feels like death. What the fu ...?" As might have been expected, Eldritch Junior quickly realised he was minus a leg, despite the copious amounts of gin with which Eldritch senior had plied him. Sliding from the table, he hopped to the door and away into the night.

Meanwhile, the leg had not gone unnoticed. Himbry, the surgery's mongrel-cum-intestine thief, casually strolled up to it. Now, this was a new treat! Smelling the foot, he closed his eyes in ecstasy and began to lick between the sweaty toes.

"Quick, Ivor. You're not going to believe it. I've perfected the art of resurrection! I, George Uppham, have found a way to re-animate the dead!" George shouted defiantly as he burst into the surgery's living quarters, as though he had fought and won the age-old battle of life and death.

Ivor lifted himself from his comfy chair and put his hot buttered crumpets next to his tea on the tray beside him.

"George, please calm yourself. Now, what was that you said? You've found a way of re-animating the dead?" he said, pausing only to smirk. "So, you, George Uppham, have found the Philosopher's Stone - the key to immortal life?" he asked, sinking his hands into his pockets and looking at Ronald,

That's a Lovely Looking Leg

nodding towards George as he spoke. Ronald remained stony-faced; Ivor, too, quickly losing his smile and drawing his hands from his pockets. "George, I want you to answer me truthfully - have you been drinking Doctor Stumpf's liniment rub?"

"Not this time, Ivor ... cuh! Not after last time," George smiled, rolling his eyes to the back of his skull at the memory.

"I have, and the leeches," belched Ronald, lying prone on the sofa.

"What! You've been eating the leeches?" Ivor was almost speechless at the confession, looking at George to confirm the astonishment was not misplaced.

"Anyway, Ivor ..."

"Yes, sorry George, you were saying. Oh yes, might one ask how this miracle was achieved?"

"Witchcraft. Devil's work. He'll burn for it! Look for the witch's mark - give him a good pricking," Ronald mumbled, the rest of his sentence becoming incoherent as he passed out.

"A 'pricking'?" queried George.

"It's not what you think, as I used to think the same! It's what they used to do to find a witch. Prick them until they found a spot insensitive to pain. That's where the Devil was thought to have made his mark on them," Ivor explained.

"I knew all that. What did you think I thought?" asked George.

"Um ... oh look, it doesn't matter," Ivor replied, feeling his cheeks burning where he'd stood with his back too close to the fire.

"Yes, I cut off that man's leg and he came back to life just as I'd finished," George enthused.

"Oh, that's just marvellous! George, you've resurrected a corpse! Don't you think he's going to be seriously pissed off when he realises that he's one leg short of a pair? Were you hoping he wasn't going to notice? Think of the problems he's going to have!"

George looked perplexed, his face running the gamut of emotions from A to B as he wrestled with the problem.

"It's not all bad," George finally acknowledged.

Mallard the Quack

"Not all bad! I don't believe this. George, how bad do you want it to be? We've got a resurrected corpse hopping around on one bloody leg! How bad can it get?" Ivor allowed himself to slump into his chair and buried his face in his hands.

"It could be worse!" George stammered, desperate to win Ivor's enthusiasm.

"How?" Ivor leaned back in his seat and folded his arms in superior resignation. "Give me one positive aspect."

George paused, making three false starts at an answer, pointing with his finger each time an answer seemed about to arise, before checking himself.

"He'll save a fortune at the cobblers," was the best he could finally manage.

"Yes, yes he would," said Ivor reflectively. "I'd not thought of that. Yes, he would save a bit of money there."

"Mind you ..." interrupted George.

"What?" asked Ivor gravely.

"My money wouldn't be on him in an arse-kicking contest."

"George," said Ivor. "Just show me the leg."

Back in the cowshed, George and Ivor moved with trepidation across the straw-strewn floor.

"Watch out for the cowpats," George advised, as Ivor slid silently to the floor after treading in a particularly large one. Turning, and expecting to see his brother close behind him, George took a large gulp. The corpse had already taken Ivor and now it would be after him! Oh, God, he was sorry! Then cold clammy hands began wrapping themselves around his ankle.

"Argh!" he screamed.

"Argh!" screamed Ivor.

"Oh, God, it's you, Ivor! You frightened the life out of me. I thought it was ... him," George said, looking around the room. "Why are you lying on the floor? I wouldn't lie down there. Not with all those turds about."

"George! I wasn't lying. I slipped over. Now can we please take a look at this leg."

"Here it is," said George, stopping to pick up the leg. "Oh, no! The dog has only gone and had the toes. I knew I shouldn't

That's a Lovely Looking Leg

have left it on the floor," he added, handing the leg to his brother.

"Still, no matter," said Ivor, taking it into the light. "That's a lovely looking leg, I'll say that much. George, do you know what this means? It means we can bring back anyone we want just by cutting off their leg!" Already Ivor could feel his wallet bulging with the cash such a scheme could extort from the rich and famous.

"But you said ..." George began, confused by his brother's about-turn.

"George! Never mind what I said. I've changed my mind."

Like an explosion, a clap of thunder preceded the heavy patter of rain on the slate above their heads.

"Sorry Ivor," said George smiling. "I've got to ... take a pee." Ivor watched suspiciously as George skipped out of the room. Lost in fantasies of wealth, Ivor followed him, unaware that he was still clutching the leg.

George leapt around the roof in the heavy rain and crashing thunder. Nonchalantly, Ivor watched from the study window, lost in a greedy reverie. Without thinking, he scratched the back of his head with the remnants of the leg. Then, as one might take a pen, he began to tap his chin with the foot, pondering what his first acquisitions would be if he were rich. Almost before he knew it, he'd begun chewing and sucking on the foot. The taste suddenly set off some deep-seated alarm bells in his head and his conscious mind sprang to the fore.

"Oh, God!" he cried in disgust, taking a step backwards and pulling the leg far away from his face as he tried to spit out the taste. As it slowly faded, Ivor brought the leg slowly back up to his face. Had it really been as vile as he'd imagined? Flaring his nostrils, he took a little sniff - nothing. Bringing the foot a little nearer, he flared his nostrils again and took a deep snort. Vile wasn't the word! The terrible smell of strong cheese on a hot summer's day didn't so much waft up his nasal passages as take them in a strong grip and throttle them. Ivor retched as he looked through the window, just in time to see his brother plummet from the edge of the roof and disappear into the darkness.

Mallard the Quack

"Twat!" he shouted, tossing the leg to one side and drawing on his coat to mount the rescue bid that had become the expected climax to every stormy night.

Ivor carried the dazed body of his brother to his room and placed him on the bed, before retiring for the night.

When Ivor awoke next morning, the house was curiously silent. He quickly dressed and made his way to George's room, where the door was open. Inside, Nurse Conwy stood to one side whilst Ronald sat in a chair conducting a diagnosis

"Well, Doctor?" Ivor asked.

"Dead of course. I knew it! It'll soon be us, you know. It was the forces of darkness and the evil eye. Look, he's even got three nipples," Ronald said pulling back the sheets to expose a dry, flattened, piece of indiscernible food clinging to George's chest.

"What do we do then, Doctor? We don't want him smelling up the house," asked Nurse Conwy, wringing her hands. "At least, not any more than when he was alive."

Ivor looked at George in the bed, and in particular at his brother's chest as it steadily rose and fell as he breathed in and out.

"Are you sure he's dead, Ronald? It looks like he's breathing to me," Ivor said, taking a step backwards as he spoke, pre-empting Ronald's hostile reply.

"Of course he's dead! The little swine's as dead as a doornail," Ronald shouted, standing up and throwing his medical tools to the floor in a rage. "The movement you see is the humours. That'll be his phlegm."

"Phlegm? It looks like he's got a lot in there, what with his whole chest moving up and down," Nurse Conwy said.

"It's the phlegm! If I say it's the phlegm, it's the phlegm! *Nobody* knows more about phlegm than me!" Ronald shouted, stamping his foot and waving his arms, as though he were a mad Roman orator.

"Well, if it's all the same to you, Doctor, I'll just stand a bit away from him then. There must be a gallon of the stuff in there and I'm not catching it should the little swine sneeze," Nurse Conwy said, taking a few tentative steps backwards.

"What do we do now then, Ronald?" Ivor asked.

"Uh?" Ronald grunted as he turned to face Ivor.

"Well, as I see it, we have three options - we can bury him, sell him to Eldritch, or cut off his leg and bring him back from the dead," Ivor posited.

"What!" shouted Ronald.

"Bury him then?" Ivor asked, taking a second step backwards and giving a supplicating smile.

"No, sell him to Eldritch of course!" Ronald answered, barging past Ivor, evidently in pursuit of the filthy lucre that could be obtained from a fresh young corpse.

Within a few minutes, Ronald returned with Eldritch who, to everyone's astonishment, was openly weeping.

"Oh, God, no! I don't think I can go on," Eldritch began, then broke into violent sobs, throwing himself to the side of the bed and taking George in his arms.

"I must say, Eldritch, I'm touched. Here we all were thinking you nothing more than a fat, money-grabbing git willing to sell his own brother - who *did* sell his own brother, come to think of it - when all along you really do have a soft spot in that heart of stone of yours," Ivor said, dabbing a tear from his eye. "There, there, Mummy make it better," he continued, patting Eldritch's huge back as it went into paroxysms of uncontrollable grief. Eldritch temporarily stopped crying and looked up, his puffy eyes a bloodshot red.

"Do I balls! He was my best customer! I don't know what I'm going to do without his cash," Eldritch answered, turning back to George and violently shaking him. "Wake up! Wake up, you swine! You still owe me some money for that liver I sold you. Who's going to keep me in gin and filthy woodcuts now?"

"So, Eldritch, will you give us cash for the stiff?" Ronald interjected.

"What! Doctor Stumpf, please! My brother's lying dead and all you can think about is sex ... oh sorry, I thought you meant ... oh well, it doesn't matter what I thought," Ivor said, burying his red face in the arm of his coat and pretending to cry, only stopping when he thought the moment had passed and nobody was looking at him.

"Uh?" Eldritch said, standing up and doing some calculations in his head as he pondered Ronald's request.

"I guessed the thought of some easy money might change things Eldritch, you disgust me!" Ivor said with contempt.

"Two pounds and six shillings," Eldritch answered, ignoring Ivor's insults.

"Two pounds and six shillings!" Ivor shouted enthusiastically. "Fantastic!" He linked arms with Ronald and danced around the room.

"Right then, I'll just have him away. Luckily, I've brought my bag with me," Eldritch said, pulling a rough hessian sack from some deep pocket and unfurling it on the bed. With little ceremony, he scooped up his former customer and dropped him into the bag. "My, he is a big one," he added, realising George's feet protruded from the open end.

Quickly, Eldritch hoisted the sack over his shoulder and, after counting out some notes and coins, strode into the street with the bag in full view.

"Morning, Bill. What's in the sack?" asked a local, as Eldritch walked confidently down the cobbled street.

"Sack? What sack?" Eldritch asked, looking around as though he were expecting to see one on the floor or being carried by someone else.

The man took a step closer and tugged at Eldritch's sack, then took hold of the hessian bag and gave that a tug as well. The bag let out a low groan and began to move.

"Oh, *that* sack! It's a ... um ... a Mexican.".

"A what! I've never been to Mexican and if what Doctor Stumpf says is true I never will!" said the old man, beating the sack with his walking stick until he was breathless. "Thank you, Bill", he continued. "Doctor Stumpf was right! That really has made me feel so much better about myself."

"My pleasure," said Eldritch.

"By the way, Bill, where is Mexican?"

"Um ... near Aberystwyth."

"Well, I certainly I won't be going there, then!" said the local, as he sauntered off with a spring in his step.

As Eldritch reached some woodland, the sack let out a second protracted groan. Eldritch looked around, unnerved and confused as to where the noise was coming from.

That's a Lovely Looking Leg

Suddenly, the sack moved and, tearing a hole in the fabric, George pushed his head through the narrow slit.

"Hello, Eldritch!" he said, in his usual cheery manner.

Shaken, Eldritch dropped the sack and took a few steps backwards. George quickly freed himself from the bag and stood up, offering an outstretched hand to the quaking graverobber. Terrified, Eldritch clutched at his chest, went a curious colour and collapsed.

George rushed to Eldritch. After rolling the blubbery mass over, he looked furtively around then rolled Eldritch into the bag. Failing to lift the enormous weight, he began dragging the sack of limp flesh home.

Back at the house Ronald and Ivor relaxed in their living room, Ronald soundly asleep and snoring loudly whilst Ivor simply reminisced.

"You know, I'll miss young George," he said, looking at Ronald who, as if on cue, let out an enormous window-rattling snore. "Nice to know it's resting so heavily on your heart! You know, I should have cut off his leg when I had the chance. He'd be here now if I had. Then I'd have had someone to talk to! Still, if he were here, I wouldn't have you, would I, my beauties!" he added, looking to his side and patting a dozen bottles of whiskey.

Interrupting the tranquil scene came a tap at the window.

"Who ... who's there?" Call it guilt or remorse, but Ivor sensed his brother would come back to haunt him.

"Ivor, it's me - George," George said, pressing his face against the glass.

Ivor looked towards the ceiling, expecting to see some spirit hovering around the room.

"George? George, is it really you? Oh, George, I'm sorry I didn't cut off your leg when I had the chance. It was Ronald! Ronald made me do it. He said to sell you. Oh, George, please forgive me! If you want to haunt anyone, haunt him," he cried pointing at Ronald asleep on the sofa.

"Eh? I can't hear you," answered George, pressing his ear to the glass.

"I said ... oh look, it doesn't matter. Oh, George, what can I do for you so that your unquiet spirit might find some peace in its lonely wanderings?"

"You can let me in. I have a heavy weight on my shoulders."

"Alas, as you did in life, you poor, poor child," Ivor sobbed.

"You've got to let me in. I've nowhere else to go!"

"Oh, George, don't say such things! Can you find no peace anywhere? I know you were never a saint, but I didn't think they'd deny you entry to everlasting glory! Still, at least it's not ... down there," Ivor said, lowering his eyes to the floor then screwing them tightly shut and clasping his hands together as if in prayer.

"Look, can you just open the door?" By now, George was beginning to lose his patience.

"Oh, God, I'm sorry, I'm so sorry. Ronald, wake up," Ivor wailed, running over to the prone form and shaking him. "Wake up, you lazy twat!" Ivor took a step backwards and stumbled on an empty jar. Picking it up, he squinted as he read the label: Liniment Rub.

"You ..." Ivor clutched hold of Ronald's neckerchief, raising a fist in front of his face as if to punch him. "You haven't been boofing this, have you?" Suddenly, there was a shattering of glass and George entered, complete with sack, scraping to a slow stop as George released his grip on his weighty burden with a relieved sigh.

"Hello Ivor!" he said, enforcing the greeting with a cheery wave.

"Argh!" Ivor screamed, diving for safety behind the sofa. As the noise rang out, the sack let out a mighty groan and Eldritch sat bolt upright.

"Argh!" George screamed, joining Ivor behind the sofa.

"Right, you shower of swine," Eldritch shouted, as the two Doctors looked up to see his corpulent form standing over them. "Now, where's my mattock? I can feel a little sing-song coming on!"

Ahoy There, Maties!

By the time morning came, Eldritch had both George and Ivor harmonising and even singing counterpoint with one another but having become bored he'd fallen asleep.

"Here's our chance, Ivor," said George.

"Chance to do what?"

"Knock him on the head," George suggested, lowering his voice.

"Oh great! Good one, George! What do you propose we do then? We knock him on the head and then we either have a blubbery corpse to dispose of - with no buyers! - or a very irate madman with a lump on his head," Ivor said, raising his eyes to the ceiling in disgust. "No, we need to think this thing through."

"Throw him in the river?" George said excitedly, as though the perfect plan had just come into his head.

"George, just when I think you can't get any more stupid, you go and say something like that! That's brilliant!" Ivor said.

"So, will you knock him on the head, or shall I?" George queried.

"You can. I'll just stay over here and make sure nothing goes wrong," Ivor said, taking a few steps backwards.

"Right then. Wish me luck, I'm going in," George said, standing behind the sleeping Eldritch and lifting his arm high above his head. As he did so, Ivor winced and looked away. For a while, there was silence. Ivor opened his eyes, leaping backwards at the sight of George's face just a few inches away from him.

"What is it?" Ivor said, holding his chest in fright.

"I haven't got anything to hit him with," George replied, a sheepish smile spreading across his face.

"Oh look, this is ridiculous," Ivor said, pushing George out of the way. "If you want anyone killed, you've got to do it yourself," he moaned, moving behind Eldritch, taking a full bottle of whiskey from his cache as he went.

"Right, you stand there," Ivor said, pointing to an area a few feet in front of the sleeping man. "Now, when I hit him, you make sure nothing goes wrong. If he's not out cold with the first blow, we're in big trouble," Ivor said.

"Right you are," George said, bracing himself.

Ivor raised the bottle high above his head and, closing his eyes, brought it down with all the force he could muster on the top of Eldritch's head. Immediately, the sleeping man awoke and leapt from the chair.

"Quick, get him," Ivor shouted, taking a few steps backwards.

"Die, you swine!" George rasped, jumping at Eldritch and wrapping his hands around the fat throat of the dazed fugger.

"Go on, George, you've got him on the ropes! He's weakening," Ivor encouraged, as Eldritch staggered around the room with George clinging to his throat like an ineffectual scarf.

"The bottle! Use the bloody bottle!" George shouted. Ivor didn't need telling twice and tossed the bottle at George who, otherwise engaged, was in no position to catch it.

"Well, you might have made some effort to catch it!" Ivor remonstrated.

"Just kill the bugger!" George shouted, even more fearful now he realised that Eldritch had begun to notice what was going on and was now directing his attention at George.

Ivor grabbed a second bottle from his hoard and took a step forward, striking out with eyes closed. The resounding thump told him that this time he had been successful.

"That was a close one!" George said when the heaving mass of flesh lay between the two of them.

"George, *Die, you swine*? *Kill the bugger*? I must confess, such sentiments stand in stark contradiction to your status as a medical man," Ivor remarked.

"It's like this, Ivor," George said, wiping the sweat from his brow. "If a Doctor's mandate is to prolong life and ease suffering, I've just done both. The fact that the suffering we've eased and the life we've prolonged are ours and not the patient's is but a minor technicality," George observed.

"Very good, George! And that's our defence, is it?" Ivor said, folding his arms haughtily.

"That's your defence. You killed him!" George answered, collapsing in a chair.

"You conniving swine!" Ivor shouted, taking a step towards George and angrily pointing at him.

"Hang on! You forget the second part of our fiendishly clever plan. We're going to throw him in the river, remember?"

"Brilliant!" Ivor said, clapping his hands together and smiling.

"What's going on?" Ronald said, awaking and shaking his head as he sought solace from his hangover.

"It's Eldritch. He's dead and ... uh ... you killed him!" Ivor said. "Isn't that right, George?"

"I killed him? God, I really must stop boofing!" Ronald said, running his hands through his hairpiece.

"Yes, Ivor and I tried to stop you but you had bloodlust in your eyes," George said, warming to Ivor's story.

"I can't remember a thing! I remember hearing these two awful voices singing, but nothing else. Are you sure I killed him? I might have done. I never liked him. He was the first person to ever throw a leg at me," Ronald said.

"Well, there you are then! I knew there must have been a motive. A reasonable man like you doesn't go around killing just anyone," Ivor said, nodding at George to back up the story.

"Ivor and I thought it would be a good idea if you threw him in the river," George added.

"Yes, thank you, George. But of course, we didn't know he'd been killed, did we, as we've only just come into the room, remember?" Ivor hissed through gritted teeth.

"Oh, yes ... we knew nothing about it and weren't even here ... at all. In fact, we were out and the first we knew about it was when ..."

"Yes, thank you Doctor Uppham. I'm sure Doctor Stumpf doesn't want all the details, given he's still coming to terms with the terrible knowledge that he's a murderer," Ivor said, kicking George on the ankle.

"Oh, that doesn't worry me. I just sell them to Mrs Jones at the butcher's to make sausages. Trouble is, she only likes lean meat and there's too much fat on him ..." Stumpf began before Ivor interrupted.

"Mrs Jones at the butchers? Mrs Jones as in *the* Mrs Jones from Jones Street?" he asked, the colour draining from his face.

"Yes, that's the one. Do you know her?" Stumpf asked.

"Not as a patient, but I buy my sausages from her!" Ivor said, slumping into a chair. George laughed, pointed at Ivor and made a few retching motions.

"I don't know what you're laughing at, halfwit, you don't think I buy your sausages from a different butcher's do you?" Ivor remarked.

"Oh, no!" George wailed, his laughter stopping in an instant.

"Ronald, please tell me you only sell the attractive bodies to Mrs Jones. I hope that old choleric who pegged out last week didn't go," Ivor pleaded. Ronald shrugged his shoulders and closed his eyes.

"Now if it had been that young Miss Jones who stiffed when I was last here," George said, closing his eyes and smacking his lips, whilst rubbing his belly.

"I need two scoops of ice cream while I think this through," Ronald said, racing from the room.

"Give me a hand to get fatty to the river then," said Ivor, leaving the room for a few moments before returning with half a roll of sacking and a small trolley that had accidentally been left behind when they had once had a piano delivered.

The journey to the river was uneventful, but after heaving the bulk from the bridge, the two Doctors watched in dismay as instead of sinking, the body floated down the river like a dry log.

"Of course! All that fat doesn't sink, does it?" George said, slapping his forehead with the palm of his hand.

"Excuse me?" came a voice behind the duo.

"It wasn't me! He made me do it!" George gabbled, pointing at Ivor.

"I do beg your pardon but you seem to have misunderstood me. My name is Lindsey Grayson. I'm a special friend of Ronald Strumpfhosen's," said the man, dabbing his lips with a handkerchief.

Ahoy There, Maties!

"Strumpfhosen? I don't think I know him. We're Doctor Stumpf's partners, Ivor said.

"Both of you! How positively Romanesque!" Lindsey exclaimed, his lips pursing and eyes widening.

"Ronald's a one, isn't he? His mind's never off the job! He's always ready to get down to a bit of business," George gushed.

"He certainly has some special qualities," Lindsey replied, his eyes twinkling.

"We're going back to the house now so you might as well come with us," George said.

"Are you sure? I don't want to tread on anyone's toes. Jealousy is such a beastly thing, don't you think? One can hardly think of it without having to have a lie down."

"Yes, we're all a bit like that, aren't we, Ivor? If it wasn't for the patients, I think the three of us would stay in bed all day!" George laughed.

"I can see I'm going to enjoy it here," Lindsey said, drawing his fingers slowly up and down his thick ebony cane.

Back at the house, there was no sign of Ronald.

"I'll go and see if I can rouse Ronald for you," George said, mounting the stairs and making his way to Ronald's surgery. The door was slightly ajar, so George pushed it a little and entered.

"Doctor Stumpf, there's a visitor for you."

"A visitor? I'm not expecting anyone," Ronald said, frowning and trying to swallow his ice cream. "Did you get a name?"

"Lindsey Grayson," George offered.

"Doesn't ring any bells" Ronald scowled. "Is he a salesman or something?"

"At first I thought he was just a friend of yours, but I think he might be a salesman."

"Why, what is he selling?" Ronald queried.

"Toilets, I think. On the walk back to the house he mentioned to Ivor and me that he was a toilet trader," George answered.

Ronald, his mouth full of ice cream, sprayed a plume of it into the air on hearing George's words.

"Yes, I think you must have gone to an exhibition or something, as he said he met you and Father Catamite at the same time. To tell you the truth," George continued, "I don't blame Father Catamite for looking for a nice toilet - the number of times I've seen him in and out of that toilet in the town, I swear he must have the weakest bladder in Wales! Strange how he's never come to us to get some treatment for it," he pondered aloud.

"Alright, thank you, George, that will be all. If you could show my friend Lindsey up," Ronald said.

"Of course," George replied, leaving Ronald and returning to the reception room where Ivor had left Lindsey.

"I see you enjoy the finer things in life," Lindsey remarked upon George's return.

"Eh?" George replied.

"The painting, my pale Narcissus, the painting!" Lindsey said, gesturing to a canvas on the wall.

"Oh yes. There's nothing I like better than getting down to business with a few oils," George replied.

"Me too! A beautiful painting in the classical style transports me to far-off places and far-off times where a spiritual union was not a sin. Nothing gives me greater pleasure than the sight of a marble-skinned youth resting his weary head against a Doric column or two, what do you say?"

"Yes. Have you seen our books?" George replied, a little confused.

"Oh, I have, I have! Just before you returned, I had William Beckford in my hand but he became rather moist so I had to put him down," Lindsey said.

"Right. Anyway, I've spoken with Doctor Stumpf and he'd like to see you. I think he might be able to put some business your way. I don't think he'll want anything as extravagant as Father Catamite, just the usual, so long as he can afford it," George said, beckoning Lindsey to follow.

"I cater for all tastes, George. You should bear that in mind," came the reply.

Ahoy There, Maties!

"Here we are then," George said, as he and Lindsey drew near to Ronald's surgery door. George gave it a gentle tap.

"Come in," Ronald shouted.

"Ooh, that sounds familiar!" Lindsey whispered to George, as he pushed open the door.

"Lindsey," Ronald said, a short smile bolting across his lips as he gestured to the chair.

"Ronald, I hardly recognised you with your clothes on!" Lindsey replied.

"Oh, you old bugg ... scoundrel you! How's the old bare-knuckled boxing coming along?" Ronald laughed, giving Lindsey a playful slap.

"Eh?" Lindsey replied, looking at Ronald, then at George, then back to Ronald.

"Will that be all, George, or was there something else?" Ronald queried.

Later that day the gentle meditation of young George was disturbed as Ivor entered the living room and noisily sat down on a sofa opposite him.

"Where's Ronald and the dandy?" Ivor enquired.

"In his surgery," George replied.

"Still? Then it must have been those two I heard arm-wrestling," Ivor mumbled.

"Arm-wrestling?" George asked, his inquisitiveness aroused.

"Well, there's a lot of grunting and groaning going on. I hardly think he's going to have come here to help Ronald move the furniture."

"No, no! Ronald's thinking of buying a toilet from him. He's a salesman. They're probably hammering away at it like there's no tomorrow. I bet if we were flies on the wall in that room, we'd see that Ronald had him over a barrel, even as we speak!" George said, laughing.

"Maybe," Ivor muttered, lifting a newspaper in front of his face so that he no longer had to look at George.

"Anyway, you coming to the fayre tonight?" George asked.

"Fayre?" Ivor said, lowering the newspaper.

"Yes, I heard Nurse Conwy mention it. They've got some stalls and games as well as a Bearded Lady and the like," George said, his eyes widening as though he were a child excitedly speaking of an imminent birthday party. "I'm going to see if Ronald and Lindsey want to come once they've finished."

No sooner had George finished speaking than Ronald and Lindsey entered the room.

"Ah, Doctor Stumpf! We were just talking about you two," George said cheerfully.

"You were? Why? I've not been up to anything," Ronald said furtively, pulling his wig straight.

"Well, Ivor heard you two arm-wrestling and we were wondering how long you were going to be. Ivor and I are thinking of going to the fayre," he explained.

"Arm-wrestling? Oh yes, that's what we were doing," Ronald said.

"So, how do you find old Ronald? He goes hard at it when he wants his pound of flesh, doesn't he? I bet he had you over a barrel alright, eh?" Ivor said, nodding and smiling at Lindsey.

"A table, actually," Lindsay muttered.

"Tell me about this fayre, it sounds really great!" Ronald said, making sure Lindsey was cut off in mid-flow.

"They've got a German band with real Germans and an Italian organ grinder and monkey. They've some trained animals, some stalls, some people who eat real fire! Some puppet shows, alehouses, rides of all sorts, bare-knuckle boxing, as well as a whipping post and stocks," George enthused.

"How delightfully plebeian," Lindsey squealed. "Oh Ronald, do let's go!"

"This is going to be really great - unbelievable. *Nobody* knows more about fayres than me … tremendous people. Shall we go?" Ronald said, looking around the room. "But what about Nurse Conwy?"

"She's already there," George said. "She's selling something or other."

Ahoy There, Maties!

The four men made their way from the house towards the church, to where the fayre was being held.

"My masters and friend and good people draw near, And look to your purses for that I do say, And though little money in them you do bear, It cost more to get than to lose in a day," a barker at the fayre was heard to sing as the little troupe drew nearer to the fayre entrance.

"Youth, youth, thou hadst better been starved by the nurse, than live to be hanged for cutting a purse," the song continued.

"Ooh, don't talk to me about cutpurses!" George said as if he were about to impart a pearl or two of wisdom. "I remember in Edinburgh, someone tried to rip open my purse with a sharpened blade attached to his thumb. It was only by a stroke of luck that my scrotum got in the way," he confided, his voice trailing away as the bright colours and sounds began swirling around them.

"What's this then?" Ivor asked George, pausing at the first stall.

"Oh, this is brilliant!" George answered, lifting his arms so that his clenched fists were just a few inches from his chest and shaking them back and forth. "In this game, you pay the man your money and he asks you to think of a number between one and twenty. Then you tell him the number you were thinking of and if it's the same as the number he was thinking of, you get another go!"

"I see," Ivor said. "And what do I win?"

"I just told you! You get another go."

"So, all I win is the chance to think of another number to tell the stallholder, who then tells me whether it was the same as the number he was thinking, right?" Ivor said, folding his arms and looking at Lindsey and nodding in George's direction.

"It's a very popular stall, Ivor," George protested.

"All I can say is that you're easily amused, George," Ivor said sarcastically, moving on.

"Hang on, where's Ronald?" George said, looking around for the absent party.

"Oh, God, he hasn't found the ale tent already, has he?" Ivor said, his face twitching in irritated impatience.

"There won't be any boofing in there, even if he has!" said George. "Hang on, what's that commotion over there, by the whipping post?" he added, pointing at a fracas a little distance away.

"Let's have a look," Ivor said, moving toward the group. "What's going on?" he asked a stallholder as he drew near.

"It's the old man," he said, gesturing at Ronald, who by now was standing in the centre of the crowd. "I told him this wasn't a stall but the whipping post where all those convicted of offences at the fayre were beaten, and he said he didn't care and would give me two shillings if I'd let him flog a few people. I mean, if someone's going to pay me to do my job then I'm not going to be a fool about it, am I?" The man said, his face breaking into a wretched leer, revealing the blackened stumps of what once were teeth. "He even said he'd pay double if they were Mexicans! Sadly, we didn't have any Mexicans but we do have a man that wants to give women the vote! It was all I could do to stop the old fella punching *him* in the face!"

"Good! Sounds like that swine had it coming," Ivor said, turning to George. "Well, George, we can take Ronald with us but I'd rather you than me try and get him away from here! Or we can leave him to his own devices and come back for him later. You choose," Ivor said.

George looked at Ronald, who was already breathing heavily, beads of sweat dripping down his orange face.

"Such stamina!" said Lindsey.

"I think we'll leave him enjoying himself, shall we?" George suggested as the trio moved on.

"Oh look, Ivor, the oddities tent! Can we go in?" George said excitedly, pointing at one particularly drab tent.

"Who wants to see a tent full of liberals!" Ivor replied.

"Ladies and gentlemen, today we have a treat for you. All the way from another country, we have Bushy Babs, the hairiest woman in Wales. By a cruel twist of fate, this unfortunate woman has also been cursed to live a life without breasts, whilst yet another cruel blow has made her womanly parts exactly the same as a man's. Ladies and gentlemen, prepare yourself for the horror that is Bushy Babs," barked the stallholder, whipping the crowds into a state of excitement as he parted them from their cash and ushered them inside. As the lights dimmed and the curtains drew back, Bushy Babs stepped forth.

"Ooh, I say!" said Lindsey.

"That's a man!" someone heckled.

"Don't be so stupid!" Ivor said to the heckler. "You heard what the man said! Do you think these people lie for a living? We're medical men with a scientific brain! Have some sympathy for this poor specimen of womanhood!" Ivor hissed through clenched teeth, smiling as the people in front of him turned around to see who was causing the commotion.

"Next, ladies and gentlemen, we have the most unusual case yet of Siamese twins. What cruel twist of fate created this monster, we can only guess. Born with four legs, four arms, two heads, and two distinct bodies, these Siamese twins have one piece of luck on their side, in that their complete separation from one another has allowed them to lead independent lives. Ladies and gentlemen, I give you Morgan and Jones the barker said.

"This man certainly knows how to get the crowds going," George said enthusiastically.

The curtain drew back to reveal one pale and scrawny man centre stage, sitting on a stool. A minute or so later, a shorter man that looked old enough to be the first man's father ran from the wings.

"Sorry I'm late," the red-faced newcomer said.

"I suppose you'll be telling me next, George, that they're not Siamese twins at all but are just two men who aren't even related stood close to one another!" Ivor scoffed.

"You always exaggerate things, don't you? You think you're so smart! Well, let me tell you, upstairs might be for thinking but downstairs is for dancing," George answered, narrowing his eyes and bringing his face near to Ivor's.

"And what do you mean by that, young man?" Ivor said, drawing himself to the edge of his chair and turning to face his brother.

"Uh ... I don't know!" George answered with venom.

"And now, ladies and gentlemen, the climax of our performance - The Living Head! We can only imagine what it must be like to be born without feet - we can only imagine what it must be like to be born without legs or arms - but what would life be like without a body as well!"

"My dog was born with no nose," shouted a heckler, causing a few titters to ripple around the tent.

"How does he smell?" Ivor queried.

"Horrible!", said the man.

"A bit like Doctor Stumpf then", said George to Ivor.

"Please, ladies and gentlemen. If you're not going to take this very special performance seriously ..." the irritated proprietor said, gesturing for silence.

"Now this should be good!" Ivor said, craning his neck.

"Ladies and gentlemen, I give you The Living Head ..."

With that, the curtain rolled back and a large black box was wheeled out, perhaps four feet high and about two feet wide by two feet deep, atop of which was a head.

"That's incredible! In all my years as a Doctor, I've never seen anything like it!" Ivor exclaimed.

"Me neither," George answered, standing to get a better look.

"Now I suppose you're going to tell me there's a man sat inside that box with his head just poking out of a hole!" Ivor scoffed.

"That's it! I'm off to get myself a drink! Are you coming, or not?" George asked.

"Well the show's over, so I might as well," Ivor replied.

"Wait for me, Ducky," Lindsey cooed.

"Lindsey, please! It's Mallard, not Ducky. There is a difference, believe me," Ivor said, drawing Lindsey to one side.

"I hope you remembered to grease your tankard with a piece of herring before you came out," George asked.

"Come out? I haven't come out!" Ronald said, having just joined them "Oh, sorry, I see what you mean, I thought you meant ... oh never mind".

Ahoy There, Maties!

"George, why are you wittering on about greasing tankards with a herring? Are you talking in some code or slang known only to you and other halfwits?" Ivor asked.

"When you have a drink in these places it's always best to make sure you've greased your tankard first, the twisters can't give you a mug full of foam as the beer won't froth," George said, looking rather pleased with himself.

"Oh bollocks, I knew there was something I meant to do before we left. That's your fault for rushing me," Ivor said, kicking George in the backside.

"And watch out when they fill your pipe as they mix coltsfoot with the tobacco as well," George continued.

"George, how do you know so much about these scams?" Ivor enquired, only to see George smiling, keeping his lips firmly shut and nodding his head from side to side. Within a few moments, the trio arrived at the ale tent, where George managed a discreet word with Lindsey.

"I was just saying to Ivor, Lindsey. Watch they don't stuff your pipe full of coltsfoot."

"I beg your pardon!" Lindsey replied, visibly shocked.

"But if you want to grease your tankard with my herring later, don't tell Ivor," George whispered.

"Oh, dear boy, I had no idea! Of course, we can come to some arrangement. But we must be discreet about such things. I should hate to be the *fille de joie* to come between two brothers," Lindsey said, resting a limp hand on George's shoulder.

"Well, I don't want you gulping down mouthfuls of froth, do I?" George added, looking at Lindsey with some confusion.

"Oh, my alabaster Adonis! I'm sure you'd never let me suffer such disappointments," Lindsey added, pursing his lips and narrowing his eyes.

"Doctor Stumpf," George whispered, as Lindsey beckoned a serving girl.

"What is it now, George?" Ronald replied, as though it really were a chore even to speak to the young man.

"That Lindsey. Is he ... is he ... you know ... a bit funny?" George said lowering his voice for the final word.

Mallard the Quack

"What! Of course not! Ha! Funny indeed! He's no more funny than I am," Ronald replied, laughing as he mopped the beads of sweat from his temples.

"That's alright then. It wouldn't worry me - after all, this is practically the nineteenth century, so live and let live, I say - it's just that all that macho posturing of his is getting on my nerves."

"Why George, were you hoping he'd find you attractive? George, let me allay those fears at once – no one finds you attractive," Ivor said, "Especially when you're stood next to people as handsome as Doctor Stumpf and me."

"Yes, they do! Nurse Conwy fancies me," George protested.

"George, Nurse Conwy would fancy anything that could walk upright for more than two consecutive paces without dragging its knuckles on the floor Don't think of it as confirmation of your universal appeal," Ivor said, laughing.

"Right then, four gin and tonics with a dash of lemon – oh, and a length of hose and a funnel," Lindsey said, handing the drinks to his acquaintances. All four suddenly noticed the hush that had descended on the room as every eye trained upon them.

"Bottoms up, boys," Lindsey said, leaning towards George and Ivor. "And up yours, gentlemen!" he added, gesturing to the attendant throng, cheerily raising the glass to his lips as he spoke.

One drink quickly followed another, and all was well until Lindsey started loudly singing a dirty limerick about a young man from Buckley.

"Come on, I think we'd better be off," Ivor said to George.

With that, the little troop arose and left the ale tent.

"Ooh look, an organ grinder," George said, pointing to an elderly Italian cranking the handle of a hurdy-gurdy, whilst a little capuchin monkey banged a wooden bowl and eyed-up the crowd, evidently wondering how his fortunes had fallen so low.

"Isn't that Ronald?" Ivor said, pointing at an orange-faced man walking with singular determination through the crowd towards them. "I thought he was with us but he must have wandered off after we left the tent."

"All that jerking back and fore ... good job I have the best wrists," Ronald said as he approached, rubbing his wrist as he spoke.

"Oh, I gave my wrists a good workout earlier today!" Lindsey said, bursting into paroxysms of laughter and slapping Ronald on the chest.

"Oh look, Ivor, there's some bric-à-brac stalls! Can we go and see what they're selling?" George enthused, leading the gang of four towards the little clutch of stalls set slightly apart from the fun of the fayre.

"Will you look at that! There's a stall selling surgical appliances," Ivor said, his greedy eye scanning the stall for a bargain.

"And will you look at that? There's a medicine chest just like mine!" George said, picking up a mahogany case and opening it so that an array of glass jars filled with coloured powders sparkled in the light. "This is amazing, it even has my initials on it!" George said, shaking his head in disbelief.

"And that cupping set looks just like mine!" Ivor added, sharing George's astonishment at the coincidences.

"Can I help you gentlemen?" came a voice from behind the group as the stallholder returned to the stall.

"Nurse Conwy!" George said, as cheerily as ever.

"No ... I'm ... uh ... Mrs Jones," said the woman nervously.

"This is incredible!" George added. "A stall selling stuff that looks just like ours, run by a woman that looks just like Nurse Conwy."

"I wish Nurse Conwy were here, she'd be amazed!" Ivor added.

"There are more things in heaven and earth, Horatio, than are dreamt of in your philosophy," said Lindsey, froth beginning to form around the edges of his mouth.

"I don't believe this! Ivor, look! I've even found a letter from our father to a man with the same name as me who even lives at our house!" George said, shaking his head in disbelief.

Mallard the Quack

"You buying or looking, 'cause if you're looking you look with your eyes, not your hands," the woman behind the stall barked.

"We've no need to buy a thing from you, my good woman. We have all such sundries as your tawdry stall purveys in our copiously furnished surgery," Ivor said haughtily, drawing his coat around him theatrically and tossing his head, then turning and falling to the ground, having lost his footing in the overflow seeping from the gentleman's latrine.

"Come and see the genuine Blackbeard, Terror of the Seven Seas," barked a particularly unpleasant-looking hawker.

"Oh, can we, Ivor?" George said, dashing to the tent.

"Lead the way," Ivor said.

"Is it the real Blackbeard?" George asked, trying to peer inside the tent.

"The one and only," replied the man, quickly selling George a ticket.

"This is great!" George said excitedly as Ivor, Lindsay, and Ronald sat beside him.

As the bedraggled audience quieted themselves, the curtains drew back. A lithe young sailor jumped onto the stage and began dancing the Sailor's Hornpipe.

"Yoo-hoo!" Lindsey shouted, standing and waving excitedly.

"Get him back in his seat," Ivor hissed to George, who obeyed Ivor's command and pulled the back of Lindsey's coat so that he fell back into his seat.

"Ladies and gentlemen," said the sailor, having finished his merry dance. "Here he is, the saltiest seaman of them all! Blackbeard!"

With that, an overweight, sweating mound appeared from the wings.

"Thank you for coming," said Blackbeard, strapping on an accordion. "I'd like to sing you a little song. It's called *I May Be a Monocled Monoped, But I'm More of a Man Than Most* and goes like this," he said, launching into his song.

"Well, I don't think this is very frightening," Ivor said to George disappointedly.

Ahoy There, Maties!

"I do, Ivor - that's Eldritch's brother! Don't you recognise the fat fugger? I'd have never cut his leg off if I'd known he was Blackbeard!" George quaked.

"Eh?" Ivor grunted, quizzically training his eyes upon the young sailor on stage as he mimed the picking of weevils from biscuits into his routine.

"The man whose leg I cut off! The one who came back from the grave!" George stammered, clutching Ivor's coat with a look of terror on his face.

"Uh!" Ivor gasped, taking a sharp intake of breath and looking at George with the same expression of horror as George.

"And what's worse, I recognise the other one as well. He's the one Ronald took the whip to in the surgery when he came to see me about his scurvy," George said, his teeth chattering.

"Oh, God, we're done for now! This is all your fault for wanting to come into this stupid tent in the first place," Ivor said, turning his head towards George in accusation.

"Oh, that's it, shoot the messenger why don't you!" George answered, folding his arms and reclining in his seat.

"Look, George, this isn't the time to sulk. We have to use all our stealth and cunning to get out of here," Ivor said, his brow creasing and his eyes bobbing around like apples in a barrel.

"And now, Seaman Staines and I would like to sing that old family favourite – *On the Good Ship Venus*," said Blackbeard, his first song having whipped the audience into a state of apathy.

"Oh, now I like this one," George said, making himself comfortable.

"George, we've got to go! I don't think you realise how perilous our position is sitting here," Ivor hissed, bringing his head close to George's.

"Ivor, I don't like to be the one to break this to you, but it just got worse," said George.

"Eh? What are you talking about now?" Ivor asked, confusedly.

"Cast your eyes stagewards," George continued

"Oh, I don't believe this!" Ivor said, burying his face in his hands.

"He's an old hoofer though, isn't he! A real old pro!" George said as he watched Lindsey, up on stage, attempting to dance the Sailor's Hornpipe along with the tune. With his arms pressed tightly to his side and his legs lashing out at all angles, his performance only stopped when he fell from the stage and knocked himself out.

"That's just marvellous, isn't it! It means we have to sit through all of this now. We can't just leave him here, which means we've got to stay," Ivor said with unhappy resignation. "Wait! Ask Ronald if he's got his whip with him! At least then we'll have a fighting chance if things turn ugly," he added as he clutched George's arm, his face pale with desperation.

George leant over to Ronald and whispered a few things in his ear. There followed a prolonged discussion, in which George related the entire story. Finally, the discussion over, Ivor looked over to Ronald, who nodded an assured affirmation and tapped the palm of his hand against his breast pocket.

"Well?" Ivor asked, as George finished speaking and returned to his seat.

"Well, what?" George said with a look of dazed bewilderment on his face.

"Has he got his horsewhip with him?" Ivor asked, raising his hands to bring them tightly around George's throat before checking himself.

"No," George replied.

"No! Well, that's that then. We're shafted now, aren't we!" Ivor said, the colour draining from his cheeks to such a degree that he turned a shade of what can only be called *underside of trout*.

Finally, the show drew to a close and the audience left, leaving the three Doctors, Lindsey, the two sailors and the show's hawker.

"Now we're for it!" Ivor said, trying to whisper to George from the side of his mouth.

"You!" Eldritch's brother shouted from the stage.

"He's spotted you!" Ivor said.

"Erm ... sorry!" George said, shrinking into his seat as the huge figure approached.

Ahoy There, Maties!

"Sorry? No need to be sorry! You did me a real favour! I'd had enough of fuggin' around. I've never had so much money! I'm in a new career completely. I hire myself out for parties as a pirate. The women love it! I go there, sing a few shanties, dance a few jigs, tell them all that they might think I've got one-and-a- half legs but I've only got one 'cause the other's not a leg at all - know what I mean!" he leered, nudging Ivor in the ribs with his elbow.

"And I did bring you back from the dead?" George offered in his defence.

"Dead, my arse! I was drunk, that was all," Eldritch said, turning to his compadre.

"Well, we know that's a lie for a start," George said to Ivor as surreptitiously as he could manage.

"Jonesy - sorry, Seaman Staines - come and meet some friends of mine!" bellowed Blackbeard.

"Ahoy there, maties!" said Seaman Staines, bounding around with all the vitality of youth. "You!" he said, suddenly stopping and pointing at Ronald. "And you!" he continued, pointing at George.

"It was him, not me!" George said, pointing at Ronald, raising his arm in front of his face to protect himself from the expected blows.

"No! No! I want to thank you two. That beating you gave me was the best thing that ever happened to me. A damn good thrashing flayed some sense into me. Scurvy? Pah, I've had worse," he snorted.

"I remember a time when men were proud to get scurvy and lose a limb or two," said Ronald looking from Seaman Staines to Blackbeard. "It was a sign they'd become a man if they had cholera or the plague. Nowadays they have a little bit of syphilis and they're running to the Doctor as if it's the end of the world! I remember a time when I was young and so crippled with bone spurs that I could barely play a round of golf - my father cured them with his belt! And do you know what? I thanked him for it! A good thrashing is all these so-called sick need with their pre-existing health conditions! Never mind all this namby-pamby mumbo-jumbo! Get a rod to their back and beat the devils out, that's my motto," said Ronald, proudly reclining in his seat.

"Bloody liar, his father was a millionaire," Ivor whispered to George from the side of his mouth.

"Oh, but Ivor, I almost forgot! What about Lindsey?" George said suddenly remembering their unconscious friend.

"Oh, bugger! You're right. I'd forgotten about him. Sorry gentlemen, the man that got up on stage with you earlier was a friend of ours. He'd had a little too much to drink, I think, and became quite excited when he saw the sailor dancing about," Ivor explained.

"He's not looking good, Ivor," George shouted, having already moved to the front of the stage.

"No, he isn't," said Ivor, as he and Ronald drew alongside.

"Do you think we ought to call a Doctor?" George asked.

"George, we are Doctors!" Ivor said, looking at Ronald with a wry smile and nodding in George's direction, quickly losing his smile as Ronald grimaced back.

"Oh, if only Nurse Conwy were here!" George said, wringing his hands.

"Why?" Ivor asked.

"She'd be able to look at our appointments and tell us whether we're busy or not," George replied.

"I could probably fit him in Tuesday week," Ronald said.

"If he's really ill I could probably make an emergency call," Ivor added.

"Oh, this is ridiculous, let's carry him back to the surgery and have a look at the book to find out how busy we are," George said.

"George, I'm proud of you! That's the first good idea you've had all day," Ivor said, patting George on the back. "Right then Ronald, you grab his legs and I'll grab his arms," he added, pointing Ronald towards Lindsey's feet, lest he'd forgotten where they were.

"See you, fellas," Ivor said to the two sailors as he staggered to the tent exit. "Loved the act! Very professional! Break a leg now!" he added, as Blackbeard saw the joke and playfully pretended to shoot them.

Ahoy There, Maties!

"Oh Ivor, look! They've some children fighting! Can I have a bet please?" George wailed, rushing towards the roped ring where a rum-looking villain was taking a few bets on the next bout.

"Well, we're going to take Lindsey back to the house. Don't be long, you hear," Ivor said, allowing George his last frisson.

Back at the house, Ivor and Ronald dropped Lindsey onto the couch.

"Phew! He was a weight, wasn't he!" Ronald said, taking a handkerchief from his pocket and mopping his brow.

"Perhaps you should have had him on your back instead," Ivor suggested.

"What! What are you insinuating? I've never had a man on my back in my life. Oh sorry, I thought you meant ... oh, it doesn't matter what I thought. Look, here's George! Hello George!" Ronald said, rushing to take him by the hand.

"Eh?" George grunted, looking at Ronald and then at Ivor, who shrugged his shoulders indicating he didn't understand either.

"Did you win?" Ivor asked cheerily.

"No, it was fixed!" George moaned, flopping into a chair. "I thought I had a dead cert until Tiny Tom started using his crutches. From there on in, the game was over."

"Oh well, never mind," Ivor replied.

"How's Lindsey?" George inquired.

"That's right, I knew there was something we had to do! Nurse Conwy! Nurse Conwy!" Ivor shouted.

"Yes," Nurse Conwy said flatly, opening the door to her door and standing silhouetted against the red glow of her room, the wind billowing through the open window going some way to mask her breathlessness.

"Have you been running?" Ivor asked.

"No! Was that all you wanted?" Nurse Conwy hissed.

"No. Can we see Lindsey? Do you know?" Ivor asked.

"What? There he is, on the sofa," Nurse Conwy replied pointing at the prone figure of Lindsey curled up on the sofa.

"Yes, I know where he is, but can we see him?" Ivor explained.

"What Ivor's trying to say is, do you know whether we're busy or not?" Ronald added.

"Are you going to perform another miracle Doctor Stumpf? You remind me more of Jesus every day!" Nurse Conwy said.

"You're not the first person to have said that, Nurse Conwy, but I'm actually *better* than Jesus as I'm British! I also charge for my miracles whereas Jesus did it for nothing! Think of the profit he could have made feeding the four-hundred thousand! Yes, *nobody* reads the Bible more than me!" Doctor Stumpf explained.

"Nelly, this is costing me money what with you charging by the hour," came a voice from within Nurse Conwy's room.

"Uh, sorry, I have to go," Nurse Conwy said hurriedly.

"What was that? Have you got a man in there? I don't pay you good money to have men in your room!" Ivor said, trying to follow Nurse Conwy.

"Are you surveilling me?" she asked. "First it was the oven and now it's you!" she added as she slammed the door in his face.

"Incredible!" Ivor said, turning back. "And what are you looking so glum about?" he asked George.

"I thought she fancied me," he answered miserably.

"George, I've said it once and I'll say it again! No one fancies you."

"I've had enough of this. I need a drink," George said, quickly standing up and moving towards the drinks cabinet.

"Our faces might very well be like Dick's, George, but you'll never be as attractive as me! Didn't you see those Romanies there tonight with their swarthy good looks? I could tell they were wondering whether I was one of them," Ivor said smugly.

"You're not wrong there. Most people think you're one of them," Ronald slurred.

I'll Have a Kiss Behind the Cowshed

George opened the drinks cabinet and perused the array of drinks inside, making a mental note of which drinks he could use for his favourite cocktails.

"Right then, who's for a *Quickie*?"

"No, George! I absolutely forbid it!" Ivor said sternly.

"A *Quickie*?" Ronald asked, his curiosity aroused.

"Yes, it's one of my cocktails," George said, making growling noises and shaking his head from side to side.

"Oh, it's a drink, is it? Boring!" Ronald said, despairing at the anti-climax.

"George, you're not to make one. I forbid it," Ivor said sternly as George took a pair of pint pots from the drinks cabinets and reached for a bottle of whiskey.

"Oh, shush!" said George.

"George, put that whiskey down! I don't want you touching that!" Ivor said, trying to enforce his threats with a pointed finger. George, ignoring Ivor's disapproval, continued unabated.

"George, you're not to pick up that liniment rub. I won't allow it!" Ivor said.

"How do you like your lemons?" George asked Ronald.

"What are you implying?" Ronald said furtively.

"George, you're not to put that in that drink," Ivor demanded.

"Here you are, then," George said, as he picked up the drinks and walked toward Ronald.

"George, I don't want you drinking that drink! Remember what happened last time?" Ivor said.

"Down the hatch!" George said, clinking glasses with Ronald.

"A cheeky little number," George commented, turning red and breaking into a sweat. "But with a really earthy nutty, flavour that lingers long after the drink has gone, reminding one of those long summer days!" he added, his eyes rolling back so far into his skull that only the whites remained visible.

"I don't have my funnel with me," Ronald said.

Mallard the Quack

"Oh, okay," George said, loosening his clothing.

"Unbelievable! Of all the stupid things to do! I can't believe it! My own brother! And Ronald – don't even think about it! You ought to have more sense, a man of your age," Ivor said, throwing himself into the back of his chair and drawing the corners of his mouth down, looking around the room in disgust.

"Don't you preach to me! I may be having a little company later and I want to be relaxed. I want to make sure I'm at my most charming!" Ronald said.

"I thought everybody loved you!" Ivor said, laughing, but the barb was ignored as Doctor Stumpf retired to his room, pulling a length of hose from his pocket as he left.

"Do you fancy another one, Doctor Stumpf?" George shouted, struggling to stand.

A few minutes later, Doctor Stumpf returned taking tiny steps and clenching his buttocks. He opened his mouth only to find that, for a moment, he'd forgotten how to speak.

"I said, do you fancy another one, Doctor Stumpf?" George asked.

"Covfefe. Get me a covfefe," Ronald slurred.

"Has Ronald been boofing, Ivor? No wonder he can say that alcohol never passes his lips! He can't even say coffee," George whispered to Ivor.

"That's Doctor Stumpf to you! He pays the wages, don't forget," Ivor admonished.

"Okay, party-pooper! Would you like a cocktail … to drink!" George countered.

"No, I would … well, maybe just a small one! You know what I'm like when I've had too much to drink!" Ivor said, shaking his head as though he were letting long tresses fall free.

"Right then, three *Quickies* it is," George said, staggering back towards the drink cabinet.

"I'm a fool to myself! I just know I'm going to regret this in the morning," Ivor said excitedly.

"Ivor, have we got any soap?" George said, turning to Ivor and squinting as he tried to focus.

I'll Have a Kiss Behind the Cowshed

"Oh, don't tell me we've no clean glasses!" Ivor said in annoyed disappointment.

"No! No! Plenty of clean glasses. I just wanted to froth up the drinks a bit, you know? Give them a bit of a head," George slurred.

"Oh, don't worry about that. I'm sure they'll be fine," Ivor added.

"Well, if you say so. I don't want you to think I've sacrificed quality in my haste," George added, turning back to the cabinet and mixing the drinks with aplomb. "Here we are then," George said, returning with a tray of drinks.

"It's been a long time since I had one of ..." Ivor said, bringing the glass to his mouth and taking a long slurp.

"I feel warm all over. It's as if I'm wrapped up in warm feathers," Ronald said, suddenly opening his eyes. "Did I just say that out loud?"

"Ivor, you alright?" George asked, looking at Ivor, who was sitting completely immobile staring ahead with unblinking eyes and a frozen expression.

"I never remember it being like this!" Ivor confessed. "The last time I felt like this was that time I accidentally injected myself when practising involuntary euthanasia on Dangleberry Jones."

"Is he still around?" Ronald asked.

"Not any more!" Ivor smirked. "He'll rue the day he ever tried not paying Doctor Ivor Mallard!"

"Do you know, Ivor? You're my best mate, you are!" George said, resting a hand on Ivor's shoulder.

"Thanks, George. I'm very fond of you too," Ivor said, looking a little embarrassed.

"No, but you're my *best* mate!" George emphasised.

"I know, George, you just said," Ivor replied, frowning and laughing at the same time.

"Eh, you know me! Is my name George or what?" George asked.

"Yes, it is George. That's why I call you George," Ivor said slowly, emphasising each word.

"Are you making fun of me?" George slurred. "Don't try and make me look stupid, 'cause I'll do you any day of the week,"

George said, trying to stand and beckoning Ivor towards him with both hands.

"I really don't think you need me to make you look stupid!" Ivor said sarcastically. George looked to Ronald and then back to Ivor in strange, jerky movements.

"Don't get funny with me, pal! I could have you any time! You say the time and the place and I'll be there," George said, rolling up his shirt sleeves.

"Leave it, George, he's not worth it," Ronald slurred.

"George, sit down," Ivor insisted

"Oh, that's it! Soon back down when you see a bit of muscle, don't you?" George scoffed.

"George, I don't want to fight with you. You started it!" Ivor said.

"I started it? Me!" said George, drawing back his arm and closing one eye to aim, as if he were about to fire an arrow. "I'm gonna get you for that."

George lunged forward with all his force, missing Ivor completely and sending himself into a spin, culminating in his falling to the floor in a tangle of limbs.

"There, feel better now?" Ivor asked, moving towards the drinks cabinet for another *Quickie*.

"I'm sorry Ivor!" George sobbed. "I really, really love you! You're my best mate, you are. I know women find me attractive but that's because I'm young. You're just handsome you are, Ivor," George said as he crawled across the floor on all fours, crying.

"If you can't beat 'em, join 'em," Ivor mumbled and took a large swig of his drink. No sooner had the last drop been quaffed than his knees buckled and he fell to the floor in a sweating heap.

"I love you, George," Ivor said, trying to stop the room spinning above his glazed eyes. "You've always been like a brother to me."

George and Ivor burst out laughing and hugged each other, each using the other to try and get themselves upright.

I'll Have a Kiss Behind the Cowshed

"If only Lindsey weren't unconscious," said George, as he flopped into a seat next to the comatose dandy. "He'd teach us a thing or two, wouldn't he!"

"You're not joking there," Ivor added

"Hey Ivor, is he a bit of a hard case? He's pretty keen on all that machismo stuff, isn't he?" George asked.

"Well, he gave me twenty per cent off that toilet I ordered when I told him you were a bare-knuckle champion and wanted to give him a leathering," Ivor laughed, stuffing his pipe with something 'medicinal'.

"You what?" George said, temporarily sobering.

"I told him you'd give him a good seeing to unless I got the toilet I ordered cheaper," Ivor confessed.

"You swine! How dare you!" George said, trying to shake some sobriety into his befuddled head.

"Oh, grow up! You wanted an inside toilet, didn't you? You were the one always moaning about your arse sticking to the rim on the outside one in winter. Well, now we've got a nice indoor one! All you have to do is say that you're in training if he asks," Ivor advised dismissively.

"I can't believe you said that about me! Me? Your own brother! Wouldn't it have been easier for you to ask him for a fight, or an arm wrestle, for a discount?" George queried.

"Oh, I tried that first, believe me!" Ivor said earnestly.

"And?" George demanded.

"The bugger beat me!" Ivor said quietly.

"He beat you!" George exclaimed as Ronald began laughing.

"He's stronger than he looks!" Ivor remonstrated.

Suddenly, there was a quiet tap at the door.

"That'll be my lady friend," Ronald said, his face glowing like an orange ember. He made his way to the door and after some difficulty in remembering how doors worked, managed to swing it open. There, in the light from the room, stood Bushy Babs, the bearded lady who they'd seen at the fayre.

Remembering their manners, Ivor and George managed to stand as the woman entered the room.

Mallard the Quack

"I'm George, you must be Bushy Babs," George said, extending a hand of greeting that was already shaking from the effects of the alcohol.

"No, that's my stage name. My real name is Clive ... uh ... Clivella, I mean," came the gravelly reply.

"Clivella, that's a pretty name," said Ivor. "Is it French?"

"*Oui, Monsieur,*" Clivella replied.

"That's really great – unbelievable. *Nobody* knows more about bearded ladies than me ... tremendous people. Please, my dear, take a seat. Your little poppet shan't be a moment," Ronald said, skipping as lightly as clenched buttocks and his bulky frame could manage, across the room, and over to George.

"Get us a drink, and make it one that doesn't burn! I couldn't sit down for days last time!" said Ronald, squirming at the memory.

"Well Clivella, we're all having a little drink. Would you care to join us?" George asked.

"Please," said Clivella, nervously toying with her Adam's apple. George finished mixing the drink and turned to walk towards Ronald and Clivella, who were now sitting next to one another on the sofa. Ronald nibbled at Clivella's ear, winding his tongue around a particularly coarse tuft of beard. Almost before he knew it, the hairs had wound tightly around his dentures and as Clivella reached forward to take her drink, Ronald's dentures were torn from his mouth and plopped into Clivella's lap.

"You seem to have ... uh ... dropped something," Clivella said, picking up the teeth as large trails of saliva sought freedom now that they had the opportunity to escape.

"Oh, God, sorry!" Ronald said, his face looking as if a workforce of tiny miners who'd been excavating the inside of his head had just experienced a major cave-in.

"I say, old Ronald is going for it," George said, returning to his seat and almost sitting on Ivor."Look at him now!" George exclaimed.

As the two Quacks looked over, Ronald was unbuttoning his shirt, revealing a flabby pair of pectorals and a stomach that resembled last week's balloons, if balloons came in the colour of burnt tangerines.

"So, gentlemen, did you see the show tonight?" Clivella asked George and Ivor, as Ronald continued his attempts at foreplay.

"We did! And very good it was too," Ivor slurred.

"We couldn't believe The Living Head could we, Ivor? As scientific medical men, we know a thing or two about the human body ...," said George.

"I should say!" Ivor interrupted

"But we've never seen anything like that. I mean, where's his arse?" George asked.

"Oh really, George! Not in front of a lady!" said Ivor disapprovingly. "You'll have to excuse my brother. He's the uncouth one in the family. Actually, we're both a pair of nobs! Show Clivella your little Dick Uppham, George," Ivor encouraged.

Clivella looked surprised but managed a smile as she took a sip of her drink.

"Not now, Ivor, I'm too drunk," George said. "I hope you don't mind us prying," he continued.

"No, that's quite alright. People often ask questions. A lot of people don't believe I'm a woman and ask if I'm a man," Clivella said, laughing.

"Now that's ridiculous!" George scoffed.

"Ooh!" came a groan from the far side of the sofa as Lindsey stirred.

"Lindsey's back in the land of the living!" George said.

"Thanks to us!" Ivor added. "If it hadn't been for our medical care, who knows what could have happened!"

"Oh, my head hurts. Where am I?" Lindsey said, sitting upright and rubbing his temple.

"You fell off the stage when you were dancing with that sailor, remember?" Ivor offered.

"What!" Lindsey said, standing upright and walking towards Ivor with a swagger.

"I don't know about you, Ivor, and I can't put my finger on it but he seems a bit different. Do you think that bang on the

Mallard the Quack

head has done something to him?" George said quietly, looking at the floor as he did so.

"Oh, I say, I love the frock!" Lindsey said, his attention having been drawn from Ivor towards Clivella.

"Would you like a drink, Lindsey?" George offered, standing as he spoke.

"Bloody right I would. Got any snuff as well? I reckon I could snort a lungful!" Lindsey said, jumping towards George, shadowboxing as he moved.

George handed Lindsey his drink and returned to where he had been sitting, next to Ivor.

"I've got it!" George whispered.

"Have you? Well, don't come and sit next to me! It might be catching!" Ivor said, shifting uneasily in his seat.

"No, about Lindsey. The difference, remember?" George explained.

"Oh yes! What? I must confess, he seems a little different to me as well," Ivor said thoughtfully.

"Maybe. I think it's the snuff," George said.

"You're right! Oh, God, why do these things always happen to us? Everywhere I go I seem to be surrounded by sick people!" Ivor said, wringing his hands in despair.

"Hey! What are you pair of turds whispering about?" Lindsey shouted, watching - with a mixture of amusement and disgust - Ronald's flabby torso wobbling and shuddering in lust.

A huge bang suddenly came from Nurse Conwy's room, as the door was flung open to reveal who her customer had been: Eldritch!

"You! I want a word with you!" Eldritch said, grabbing hold of George by the throat.

"Eldritch, I thought you were dead!" George gasped.

"Hoped, you mean! No, I've been pleasuring the lovely Nelly with my company. A Ploughman's Lunch and every 'orrible thing you fancy for tuppence," Eldritch said, his fat fingers digging into George's neck.

"Tuppence? That's very reasonable"! George gasped.

"Go on, George! I can tell by the look in his eyes that he's running scared," Ivor enthused from a safe distance.

I'll Have a Kiss Behind the Cowshed

"Leave the boy alone!" came a voice implacable and chilling.

"Eh?" grunted Eldritch, loosening his grip on George who fell to the floor gasping for breath.

"You heard me, fatty. I said leave the boy alone!" Lindsey said, his eyes narrowing, a cheroot smouldering between his lips.

"Why, do you fancy some?" Eldritch said, lunging towards Lindsey with his arms outstretched.

As he did so, Lindsey brought both arms up swiftly in a praying motion, parting Eldritch's arms in one deft move. Then, knocking Eldritch's right forearm with his left, he launched a powerful right hook into his face.

Before Eldritch had time to respond, Lindsey grabbed a hold of Eldritch's left arm and, using his massive weight, spun him like a top towards a window. It was all too unexpected for Eldritch and he could do nothing to save himself from plummeting from the window and onto the road below.

"Well, that's just marvellous, isn't it?" said Ivor, running to the window and peering into the street below. "For the second time in twelve hours, we've got Eldritch's dead body to get rid of. This man has more bloody lives than a cat!" He added, running his hands through his white hair.

"Ah well! All that throttling has put me in a party mood," said George, rubbing his hands together. "Lindsey, do you fancy a *Quickie*?"

"What sort of man do you think I am?" said Lindsey, giving George a slap with the back of his hand.

"What was that for? I was only offering you a drink," George protested.

"He was, you know. I distinctly heard him," Ivor added. "A *Quickie* is a drink. Same as a *Kiss Behind the Cowshed*, only with laudanum instead of gin to give it that bit of ...."

"*Je ne sais quoi*," George offered.

"Exactly! I knew the Germans would have a phrase for it," Ivor said.

"It's all that Sangria they drink," George added, making his way to the drinks cabinet where he began making a large punch bowl of drink. Ivor alternated between looking at the large splat made by Eldritch underneath the window and frowning. Lindsey swaggered around the room, belching and scratching. whilst Ronald's seduction continued unabated.

"I love your hairs," Ronald whispered, running his fingers along Clivella's forearm. "They're so soft!"

"Oh, Ronald," said Clivella, playfully grabbing Ronald's nose and giving it such a hard tweak that Ronald's eyes watered.

"Please don't change! I always want to remember you as you are now, here with me," Ronald said. "Here, together, the moonbeams catching the flecks in your bush," he continued, hoping his words were hypnotising Clivella into a trance.

"I won't!" said Clivella. "I want to remember you too, as you are now, the soft glow of the candlelight on your tangerine cheeks, the gentle twinkling of the candelabra upon your toupee, the moonlight shimmering on your dentures ..." Clivella said, closing her eyes and taking a large swig of her drink.

"Right, here we are!" George said, returning with a full punchbowl. "Who's up for a *Quickie*?" he asked, snorting like a naughty schoolboy.

"Ronald's hoping," Ivor mumbled.

"Lindsey, do you want a *Kiss Behind the Cowshed* or would you rather have a *Quickie*?"

Lindsey took a step back in astonishment, looking around the room as though he could hardly believe what he was hearing.

"You what?" Lindsey began, his lip curling in astonishment for a moment, just before leaping toward George and chasing him maniacally around the room.

"I can give you a *Knee Trembler* if you'd prefer?" George offered, as he ran in frantic circles around the last piece of furniture they possessed, but the attempt at placating Lindsey fell on deaf ears.

"Come on, Ronald, do something!" Ivor said helplessly.

"Stand aside," Ronald said, pushing Ivor out of the way and standing in the place he had vacated.

"What are you going to do?" Ivor asked.

"It's an old trick my father showed me," Ronald said, taking his teeth from his mouth and swinging them in his arm as though he were bowling in a game of cricket. Suddenly, without warning, the teeth spun from his hand and hit Lindsey straight between the eyes, knocking him out cold.

"Hooray!" George applauded. "That was just like David and Goliath! Only Lindsey's smaller than you ... and you used your teeth and not a rock."

"And Goliath hadn't just been asked if he fancied a *Knee Trembler*," Ivor observed.

"Good point," George conceded. "Anyway, I hardly like to ask, but who would like a drink?"

Drink followed drink followed drink.

"Are you alright, sweetest?" asked Ronald, concerned that Clivella didn't seem to be enjoying herself. "I was hoping a few drinks might loosen your draw ... tongue, sorry, and we might talk until our little hearts beat as one."

"I *am* drinking. I'm just a girl who can hold her liquor," Clivella said coyly, causing both George and Ivor to snigger, both of them now crawling around on the floor.

"Have some of this, man," Ivor said, handing George a clay pipe full of sweet-smelling herbs from Lebanon. "It'll blow your stockings off!"

"Hey, Lindsey! Lindsey!" George said, poking Lindsey in the ribs.

"Leave it, George, he's not worth it," Ivor mumbled.

"No! Lindsey," George said, dismissing Ivor's suggestion and continuing to poke Lindsey as hard as he could. "Lindsey, man, have a suck on this."

"As the actress said to the bishop!" Ivor said, bursting into high-pitched laughter.

Slowly Lindsey came to and took a large toke on Ivor's clay pipe.

"I've gone numb all over," he said, blinking and trying to focus.

"I know. Great, isn't it!" George said. "Do you want some Doctor Stumpf?"

"No! The Devil's Lettuce isn't for me!" Ronald shouted.

"George, go and get us some biscuits, will you? I'm starving!" Ivor slurred.

"God, Ivor, I could murder some food!" George dribbled.

"I'll go!" Clivella said, jumping from her seat. "Where is the kitchen?"

"Over there somewhere," Ivor said, drawing himself up onto his elbow, his eyes a fearful blood red.

"Now, won't you have a *cocktail*, Lindsey?" George asked, emphasising the fact that he had changed the offending term.

"Yes, go on then," Lindsey said, picking up the dentures that had knocked him out and looking at them with some confusion before realising what they were.

"She's been gone a long time, hasn't she?" Ivor asked, referring to Clivella.

"Are you drunk?" came a voice Ivor hadn't expected to hear, causing him to open puffy red eyes and focus.

"Oh, it's you, Nurse Conwy. I thought it was a woman come in here for a moment," Ivor slurred.

"Answer me! Are you drunk?" Nurse Conwy repeated.

"I should bloody well hope so! I've drunk enough," Ivor answered in irritation, causing George and Lindsey to let out a few giggles and Ronald to let out a snore. "Doesn't look like Ronald will be getting any tonight then!" Ivor said, turning his head jerkily, closing and opening his eyes with exaggerated movements as he spoke.

"No, but I know a very, very naughty boy who will," Nurse Conwy said seductively, taking Ivor by the hand and leading him to her room.

God, My Head Hurts!

"Oh, God, my head hurts!" George said, lifting his head from the floor for an instant, then letting it return and screwing up his eyes. "My eyes feel as though there's somebody behind them trying to lever them out with a spoon."

"My God, what was in that drink last night?" Lindsey said, raising his hands to his temples and pressing them so hard his knuckles went white.

George sought to move himself, but the effort was too much for him and he collapsed in a heap, pressing his eyes in a vain attempt to make them feel they were in back their correct orbits.

"I only wanted a few drinks at the fayre," he explained. "Where did it all go wrong?"

"Oh, don't mention drinks! I think I'm going to be sick!" Lindsey said, rolling from the sofa and crawling to the window from which Eldritch had hurtled the night before.

George managed to sit upright and began rubbing the back of his neck, carefully opening his eyes.

"Doctor Stumpf, wake up!" George said, spying the old Doctor, saliva dripping from his toothless mouth in huge drools, his flabby breasts visible through his open shirt, resting like two slices of squashed orange tripe upon one another.

"Where's Bushy Babs gone?" Lindsey said, taking a huge gulp of fresh air from the open window before turning back into the room to confront the odours of chemicals, alcohol, sweat and flatulence.

"Never mind the lovely Clivella, where's the furniture gone!" George said, opening his eyes wide as he suddenly realised that all that was left in the room were the two sofas upon which Ronald and Lindsey had lain.

"And our clothes!" Lindsey said, looking down at himself clad in nothing but his drawers.

"And where's Ivor? He's can't have been stolen as well?" George said, looking under the sofas.

"Help!" came a whimpering voice from Nurse Conwy's room.

"Did you just hear something?" George said nervously.

Mallard the Quack

"Leave me alone. I'm trying to stop myself feeling sick!" Lindsey answered dismissively, placing his head on the windowsill and letting out an agonised groan.

"Help!"

"There it was again!" George said. clambering to his feet. Nervously, he made his way to Nurse Conwy's door and pressed the side of his head against its dark panelling.

"Help!" came the voice, soft and desperate.

George gave the handle a careful twist and peered through the gap. There, in front of him, was Ivor, shackled and chained to Nurse Conwy's bed.

"Well, well, well, what have we here?" George said, letting the door swing open.

"Look, George, it's not what you think!" Ivor said, struggling against his bondage.

"Who's been a naughty boy, then?" George said, walking into the room.

"I can't remember what happened, George. It's your fault! If you hadn't been giving everyone a *Quickie* this would never have happened."

"Oh, so it's my fault, is it?" George asked, bemusedly.

"Of course! If you hadn't been so busy having a *Quickie*, you'd have been able to have kept an eye on me. You know what I'm like when I'm drunk. I can't believe I had that drink at the fayre in the first place! That was the start of this whole debacle," Ivor said, retching as he thought of the gin he had quaffed at the fayre the previous night and how it had precipitated the mess in which he now found himself.

"Ivor, why are these sheets so wet?" George asked, patting the sheets on which Ivor lay. Ivor smiled back sheepishly.

"And where did that donkey come from!" George continued, suddenly spying the animal resting in the corner of the room after the rigours of the night.

"Oh look, George, can you just untie me!" Ivor barked

"I don't know about that now!" George said, shaking his head as if he really wanted to untie Ivor but to do so would be more than his job was worth. "Doctor Stumpf, Lindsey! Come and look at this! Ivor's been a naughty boy!"

"George, you swine! I'll get you for this," Ivor helplessly hissed as Lindsey staggered to the open door, quickly followed by Ronald.

"So, where's the lovely Nelly?" Lindsey asked.

"Ivor kissed her and she turned into an ass," George said, pointing to the corner of the room and the indignant-looking donkey.

"Look, we're not at some sordid peep show you know! Why don't you just wheel me down to the fayre and charge the punters a penny each to come and have a gawp? You obviously think the spectacle is good entertainment!" Ivor hissed, again straining at the chains that bound him, but to no avail.

"I know one thing," Ronald observed. "He'll never be nicknamed *Ivor Whopper*!"

"Alright, so I slept with Nurse Conwy! Are you happy now? Yes, I was drunk and yes, she charged me fourpence ... and I didn't even get a Ploughman's Lunch thrown in!" Ivor said wistfully. "Now, the joke's over, can you please untie me?"

With the distraction quickly losing its appeal, George's head began to thump again in the same discordant manner as the German oompah band that had tyrannised the fayre the previous evening. Now, the thought of all those huge bearded Germans in their tight leather shorts made his stomach turn and he too began to feel sick.

"Anyway Ivor, just to start the day with a smile, I thought I'd tell you that Nurse Conwy's disappeared," George said, struggling with Ivor's shackles.

"Well, that's one bit of good news!" Ivor squirmed.

"Trouble is, so has all the furniture and Clivella," George said, looking at Ronald.

"Oh, balls!" Ronald shouted, stamping his foot and returning to his seat, whereupon he folded his arms and sank into a moody sulk, evidently only just realising Clivella had gone.

"All the furniture?" Ivor asked.

"Well, not all the furniture! We've two sofas left," George joked.

"Where's it all gone? Who's taken it, for Christ's sake?" Ivor asked.

"I don't know. That's what's puzzling me," George answered. "Look, Ivor, this is no good. It's padlocked! I need a key. Hang on, what's this?" George said, reaching out for a letter beneath Ivor's pillow.

"What is it?" Ivor asked

"It says 'Mallard, I left the keys where I usually leave your change - Nelly," George read aloud. "Right then, Ivor, where's that? On the mantelpiece?"

"Er, not quite, George," Ivor said blushing. "In fact, I think it would be better if you got some bolt cutters."

"Don't be daft, just tell me where the keys are and I'll have you out in a jiffy," George said, scanning the room.

"George, just get some bolt cutters please," Ivor implored.

"But the keys ...."

"George! If you go to my room, you'll find some bolt cutters I stashed away just in case something like this ever came up. They're under the squeaky floorboard.

George shrugged his shoulders and did as he was bid, **returning** a minute or so later with the bolt cutters.

"There you go!" George said as the last of the chains were cut.

"Thank God for that!" Ivor said, jumping to his feet. A large bunch of keys fell to the floor as he did so.

"Look, they were here all the time!" George said, stooping to pick them up as Ivor quickly kicked them to one side.

"We don't need them now, do we?" Ivor reasoned, taking a sheet from the bed, wringing it out and wrapping it around himself so that he looked like a stained Nero.

"Yes, here they are," George said, wrinkling his nose. "They smell of cheese!"

"Of course they do! I've had them in my drawers – what do you expect!" Ivor said.

"Why didn't you tell me? George asked.

"I didn't want you rummaging around in my undies!" Ivor said indignantly.

"Yes, you're right – we don't need them," said George, dropping them on the floor and wiping his hand on his shirt. "You look just like Socrates!" he added.

"I always fancied myself as a philosopher actually," Ivor added. "You know, I had the brains and didn't use them. Still, it's part of my giving nature to help mankind, so medicine has always been a calling. I just thank God for making me such a tremendous person."

"Unbelievable," chimed Doctor Stumpf.

"Thank you, Ronald!" said Mallard

"Right then," George said, slapping his hands together and rubbing them in anticipation.

"Right then, what?" Ivor asked, looking at George blankly.

"I don't know! You're the philosopher!" George bleated.

"First, let's go and sit down on our sofa," Ivor suggested, wandering into the living room and sitting himself down. "God, my head hurts as well!" he mumbled.

"As well as what!" George asked.

"Uh, as well as ... um, Oh, God, as well as ... yours, of course!" Ivor finally said with relief.

"So, what do you think, Ivor?" George said, sitting on the sofa opposite.

"Well, I think all the furniture's gone missing," he reasoned.

"And my lovely Clivella!" Ronald added, screwing his face in grief.

"And the not-so-lovely Nurse Conwy," George said, causing Ivor to give an involuntary shudder.

"I think, and let me run this idea by you, that the furniture has been stolen," Ivor said cleverly.

"And, therefore, whoever stole the furniture must have stolen Nurse Conwy and Clivella as well," George posited.

"Brilliant!" Ivor replied, slapping his hands together then extending the right hand to shake with George to congratulate him on his incisive perception.

"You don't think that woman who was selling stuff at the fayre had anything to do with it, do you? I didn't like the look of her at all" George said.

"Could be, could be. One thing's for sure, we can't get the justice involved in any of this," Ivor said, squeezing the bridge of his nose between two fingers.

"Why not?" George asked.

"Because, dimwit, they're going to ask why we didn't witness it and why we didn't stop them. What are we going to say? 'I'm sorry, Sir, I was manacled to a bed, my friend was trying to shag a bearded lady in a dress whilst my two other compatriots were comparing the subtle qualities of some ridiculously named cocktails."

"We can't afford to jeopardise our good name," Ronald concurred.

"Oh, God, why did this happen to me! I never asked to be born," Ivor wailed, standing up and wringing his hands.

"Oh, cheer up, Ivor, it's not all bad. At least you had a night of passion! Think of poor Ronald. He's had all his things stolen and he didn't even get the memory of a night of love as a bit of a sweetener," said Lindsey.

"I don't call my encounter a 'night of passion', I assure you! It was more akin to being beaten up, only slightly less pleasurable ... hang on a minute!" Ivor blurted, suddenly interrupting himself. "We've still got that other little problem as well, haven't we!"

There were vacant faces all around, even though Ivor was pointing at the window.

"Eldritch, remember?" Ivor said in exasperation.

"Oh, no!" George said, running to the window with Ivor.

"He's gone!" Ivor exclaimed, looking at the dent in the cobbles where once had lain Eldritch's mortal remains.

"Maybe old Jones from the glue factory has taken him to melt him down," Ronald suggested, still staring at the floor in regret.

"We can but hope, Doctor Stumpf, although with my luck he's probably up on the roof as we speak, stripping the lead," Ivor said.

"What was that?" George asked, leaning back out of the window.

"What was it?" asked Ivor.

"I don't know," George answered, thrusting his head out of the open window just in time for a large strip of lead to catch him in the back of the neck and pull him into the street.

"You get back in here this instant, young man!" Ivor demanded. "Running around the streets in your drawers! It was bad enough having you on the roof in the buff, without you spoiling our good name by doing it in the street!"

George clambered to his feet and ran to the front door. In a few seconds, he was back in the house.

"God, that was a close thing! Mrs Jones almost saw me!" George said, pretending to fling sweat from his brow.

"Anyway, back to more pressing things. Who's stolen the furniture, and where have Nelly ... uh, I mean Nurse Conwy ... and Clivella gone?" Ivor said thoughtfully.

"So, what have we got? We have an empty house and two missing people. From this, we can deduce that either a lot of people stole our furniture *and* the two women, or that the two women worked very hard and stole it all themselves," Ivor reasoned.

"Or both," Lindsey added.

"Or both, as you say, Lindsey," Ivor accepted.

"It's demons! They drove us to drink and fornicate. Now they've taken everything we own!" Ronald howled, falling to his knees and pretending to pray.

"Then again," Ivor reasoned, "we have Ronald's idea."

"I didn't like to mention it before, Ivor, but even though I was drunk last night, and in an unconscious state, I vaguely remember hearing some very funny noises. Lots of grunts and snorts, a bit of screaming and howling as well," George added, looking at Ronald who now had his eyes screwed tightly shut, silently mouthing prayers for his sinful soul, his hands clasped together in front of him.

"Yes, well ... uh ... I really don't think *that's* too important," Ivor said, turning red.

"Hang on, what's that? Look, Ivor, it's another letter," George said, spying a soiled piece of paper that peeped out from under Ronald's cushion and was only visible now that Ronald had fallen to his knees in prayer.

Mallard the Quack

"Well, come on then! Read it!" Ivor said impatiently.

"Dear All, I have been robbing you for months but you were too stupid to realise. Do you really think I enjoyed being your Nurse or pretending I liked that halfwit George? I just wanted to get one of you in a compromising position so that I could blackmail you. Then I met Clive at the fayre the other night when selling all your medical equipment and we decided that we'd clean you out at our first opportunity. I knew last night would be the night, as Clive had seen you all drinking at the fayre and I know Ivor can't handle his drink and that the evening would end with you losers passing out. Eldritch was in on it too. PS, Clive says to tell Ronald that he's a crap kisser," George read, folding the letter in two as he finished.

"Can you believe it!" Ivor said. "Me not handle my drink? I've never heard such rubbish."

"I'm the best kisser! *Nobody* kisses better than me!" Ronald added.

"Hmm, it's all a bit of a mystery, if you ask me," George pondered. "What I'm wondering is who wrote this letter. If we knew that, we'd have our man. My money is still on that woman we saw at the fayre. I didn't like the look of her."

"George, it was Nurse Conwy," Ivor answered.

"I'm not so sure. I think you're jumping to conclusions," George said, thinking himself jolly wily for being more thorough in his conclusions than his brother. "Why do you say that?"

"Because the writer of the letter says she hated being our Nurse and having to pretend she fancied you!" Ivor said in astonishment. "Surely that should narrow it down! If it said that she hated pretending to fancy you, we could narrow it down to one person given no one else does, but given she's our Nurse and the person that pretended to fancy you then I think it's pretty obvious who it is. That said, there's still something I don't get - we didn't see anyone selling medical equipment other than the woman that looked like Nurse Conwy.

"And Clive says Doctor Stumpf is a crap kisser!" George shouted mockingly, looking at Ronald as he pulled a variety of faces, all of them variants on the theme of sucking lemons.

"Let me see that letter," Ivor said, snatching the paper from George's hands. "What's this 'PTO' at the bottom?"

"I didn't see that," said George, slumping to the floor as Ronald's dentures caught him squarely on the temple.

"Oh, no! Oh, no, please!" Ivor said, collapsing onto the sofa, the open letter falling from his hand to the floor. "What is it?" George asked, picking himself up and rubbing his head. "Our father and your mother are coming to visit us. They want to make sure that the money they're investing in you is being wisely spent. Well, that's really shagged it!"

"Mummy and daddy coming here? Oh, wonderful! How exciting! I can't wait to show them all the things I've bought and all the medical equipment I've amassed," George said excitedly.

"Well, unless you know where it all is, halfwit, you're not going to be able to, are you!" Ivor said angrily

"Tis but a trifle, Ivor. Doctor Stumpf has the house and all its contents insured. I know this, as I've sent him the money myself every month," George replied nonchalantly.

"Oh, you do, do you? Care to explain, Doctor Stumpf?" Ivor said, arching an eyebrow.

"I spent it all on filthy woodcuts from Scandinavia. Eldritch has contacts over there," Ronald answered flatly.

"Oh, God!" Ivor said, burying his face in his hands.

"When are they coming?" George asked, excitedly. Ivor picked up the letter and scrutinised it for a date.

"Oh, God, they're coming tomorrow!" he wailed. "George, I can't even remember the name of that mother of yours. I've always known her as 'that dreadful woman who deprived me of what was rightfully mine'."

"It's Francesca - Lady Francesca - although everyone in the family tends to call her Franny for short," George answered.

"Fanny?" Doctor Stumpf asked, the word having roused him for his reverie.

"No, *Franny*! We must try and remember that as I don't want any more embarrassing cock-ups. Still, none of this helps us out of our current dilemma. Namely, we have virtually no clothes, hardly any furniture and no medical supplies," Ivor said woefully.

Mallard the Quack

"What excuse can we give? Two were drunk, Doctor Stumpf was busy kissing a man in a dress and you too tied up to stop everything we own being stolen from under our flippin' noses!" George pondered.

"I didn't know it was a bloke!" Ronald ranted.

"Neither did I, but how many women have you seen that hairy - and with an Adam's apple!" Ivor commented.

"My sister! My mother! Anyway, I liked her for the person she was," Ronald explained.

"He's *so* dreamy!" Lindsey said, looking at Stumpf, his eyes twinkling in admiration.

"That's not strictly true, is it! You only liked *her* because she was the first person to give you a snog since old Jones' Jack Russell was bitten by that adder and you said you thought the snake had bitten its tongue so you had to suck out the poison!" Ivor remonstrated.

"No, that's where you're wrong! It was a wasp and not a snake. Now who's looking stupid!" Ronald said smugly.

"Look, this is getting us nowhere. Ronald, can you get the house insurance paperwork? As soon as we get that cashed, we can get some new furniture and things," said George.

"Doctor Stumpf to you!" Ivor sighed. "Try and understand, George, Ronald was lying when he took your money. There is no insurance and he spent all your money on himself."

George looked at Ivor for a moment, then at Ronald, who narrowed his eyes and looked back in the hope that such an expression made him look focussed and determined.

"Oh, right. What are we going to do then?" George said cheerily.

"George, you're not really like other men, are you?" Ivor commented.

"That's what they used to say to me at boarding school. 'George', they used to say, 'you're not like all the other boys'. I knew then I was special and that little something extra I had could really open things up for me," George effused.

"That's what Ronald's girlfriend must have thought," Ivor said, bursting out laughing and elbowing Ronald in the ribs. "Look, as stupid as George is, we do need a contingency plan.

God, My Head Hurts

We've got until tomorrow morning to think of something, otherwise it's going to look pretty bad when Sir Richard and Fanny ...,"

"Franny," George said, interrupting his brother.

"Alright, Franny, arrives. Now, any suggestions?" Ivor asked, looking around the room optimistically.

"I have a suggestion!" said George.

"Excellent, this is more like it, now we're really getting somewhere! Yes, George, what's your suggestion?" Ivor asked.

"Only joking," George said sheepishly.

"I have an idea," Ronald said. "Why don't we invite a lot of other men to come here and we can all sit around talking about what it really feels like to be a man in our underwear. It will be a bonding experience."

"I couldn't agree more!" exclaimed Lindsey.

"I can't see it catching on," Ivor said diplomatically. "After all, I know two of you and don't really like seeing you in your undies, so God knows how horrific the experience would be for a stranger."

"We could get a lodger in!" suggested George.

"Brilliant," Ivor said. "George, you've done it again. It's not hard to see we're from the same stock. Naturally intelligent, you know."

"Hang on, you've had all your clothes stolen, all your medical equipment was stolen and all the furniture stolen. You have one day to replace it all. How much were you thinking of charging this lodger for one night's accommodation in a bare room?" Lindsey asked.

"Damn! I knew there'd be a drawback somewhere," said Ivor in annoyance.

"Let's hire out Doctor Stumpf as a hitman!" George suggested.

"No good. How long are those teeth going to last him, the way he's been chucking them around? No, the way I see it now is that we've got no other choice other than to be honest about this," said Ivor. Ronald shuddered at the word 'honest'.

"But what if they stop my allowance? I'll have to actually start working for a living!" said George, curling himself up in disgust.

"And if they do that I'll never get my hands on your cash ... er ... I mean ... oh crap ... you'll never get your hands on your cash," Ivor said, blushing a deep red.

"But I can't see a way out," George mumbled. "If only we hadn't had those gins at the fayre."

"It was you giving us all a *Knee Trembler* that did it," said Ivor.

"Oh right, blame me, why don't you! It was you that sacrificed yourself on the altar of decadence!"

"How dare you! I've got a good mind to take my belt off to you!" Ivor said affronted.

"You can't do that," Lindsey advised.

"Don't you tell me what I can and can't do. I won't be spoken to like that in my own home," Ivor said, standing up as if to make his gesture all the more defiant.

"You can't because you don't have a belt, nor britches, boots or a waistcoat. In fact, you've no clothes at all, remember?" said Lindsey.

"Then I'll ... take off *his* belt to you," Ivor said, moving to the window and pointing at a man walking past in the street below.

"Go on then!" George encouraged.

"I will! Just see if I don't," Ivor said, beginning to lose his nerve.

"You haven't got the guts!" Ronald added, beginning to make clucking noises.

"Right, that is it!" Ivor shouted. "Excuse me! Up here. Yes, hello. Might I borrow your belt, please? I wish to chastise my brother for saying it was my fault all our clothes were stolen because I'm a pervert," Ivor explained. "Well, that's charming! And the same to you, you old git!" he added, quickly drawing his head back into the room and wrapping the sheet tightly around him

"Well, what did he say?" chortled Lindsey.

"He said, uh ... that he was a little busy at the moment but would try and call around later, seeing as how it was me."

"Anyway, this still leaves us the problem of what we're going to do," whined George.

"I know what I'm going to do," Ivor said in annoyed resignation. "I'm going to just say balls to it!"

"Oh right," George said, a little taken aback.

"Well, what can we do? There's no way we can raise the cash and it's not as if we can make one or two rooms look full by taking furniture from some of the others, is there?" Ivor said in resignation.

"Couldn't we use Lindsey's house, saying that it's our new surgery?" George said, directing the remark more as a question to Lindsey than a reply to Ivor.

"No can do. I live in a garret, and you're not going to convince anyone that three Doctors are practising from one room," Lindsey replied.

"Does anyone have any idea of the time? Since I don't have a watch either, I don't even know what day it is," Ivor confessed.

"No, my watch has gone as well," Lindsey said.

"And mine," said George.

"Mine too," Ronald added.

"I tell you what would be really funny though, Ivor!" George said, suddenly laughing.

"I'm glad you can find something amusing, George but pray, do tell me what would be *really* funny?"

"If you really didn't know what day it was and that Sir Richard and Lady Francesca were coming today," he giggled.

"Oh yes. That's about as funny as a Shakespeare comedy. Don't even joke about such things ..." Ivor began, before being interrupted by a loud and officious bang at the door.

"Oh, no! That would be just too cruel a coincidence," he continued, moving to a side window that afforded a view of the steps that led to the front door.

"Well?" George asked.

"Balls! It's them. What's her name?" Ivor said, his eyes beginning to bulge and a large vein in his temple to throb.

"Who?" asked George vacantly.

"Your flippin' mother!" Ivor said, grabbing George by the throat and shaking him back and forth.

"Oh, is it mummy? It's Francesca. Franny, you know, Fanny with an 'r'." George replied, as his tongue began lolling from his mouth and his face turning as strange a colour as Doctor Stumpf's.

"Fanny with an 'r'. Fanny with an 'r', Fanny with an 'r'," Ivor muttered to himself, desperately trying to remember the name so that the first meeting in years with George's mother might be a success and that he might be able to ingratiate himself into the family and, most importantly, move him a step closer to the Uppham millions. "George, answer the door," Ivor barked, all the while still muttering the name: "Fanny with an 'r', Fanny with an 'r'."

"Mummy! Daddy!" George said pulling open the heavy door and greeting his parents with affectionate hugs, despite wearing nothing but his underwear.

"George," nodded Sir Richard.

"Hello darling, aren't you a little cold?" asked Lady Francesca, kissing George on the cheek.

"Father," Ivor oiled in sycophantic salutation, extending towards his father a hand which was dutifully received and a firm shake exchanged. Ivor smiled at Lady Francesca and took her hand, bowing as he did so, not noticing that Doctor Stumpf had arisen from his torpor and taken Sir Richard by the arm.

"Your Fanny is *so* beautiful," Ronald whispered to Sir Richard.

I Love Your Money!

"I beg your pardon!" said Sir Richard.

"Fanny - I know words. I have the best words," Ronald said. "What are the oranges of that really beautiful name?"

"Oranges?" said Sir Richard, moving closer to his wife.

"He means origins," Ivor explained, looking nervously around the foyer as every other face looked back at him blankly. "My colleague must be thinking of Princess Fanny of Nambia. Do you know her? I shouldn't really boast that she's a patient of Doctor Stumpf's, but she is. I suppose your rare beauty must have reminded him of her for just a moment," Ivor said, his eyes narrowing.

"Phew, well done, Ivor," said George.

"And this is Doctor Ronald Stumpf, the senior Doctor in the practice," Ivor said, making a few introductions. "And this is Lindsey Grayson, a toilet trader who seems to have become fond of the place!" he laughed.

"Well, George, I now see this is how you've been spending your allowance!" Sir Richard said, looking around the room at the bare boards, three grown men in their underwear and one in a stained sheet.

"Well, we've had a bit of trouble with the locals," George began.

"Yes, we were all called out to a fight that broke out at the Undertakers and Gravediggers Annual Gala. Apparently, someone stole the spade that was to have been the first prize in the raffle. God, it was like the French Revolution in there," Ivor explained.

"Yes, there were all these aristocrats' heads on spikes and they were guillotining people," George added enthusiastically, exploring the theme.

"Alright, don't overdo it," Ivor hissed, as discreetly as possible. "But that was in the real revolution, of course," he laughed, one more directing his comments to the assembled group.

"And there was need of a toilet salesman at this dreadful event?" asked Lady Francesca.

"Well ... uh, I almost shat myself," George said, helpfully.

"And? I take it this story goes some way to explaining your current circumstances?" Sir Richard said, looking Ivor up and down and ignoring George's comment as best he could.

"Of course! Of course! I'm just thinking," laughed Ivor, screwing up his face and looking at the ceiling in the hope of divine intervention.

"We were there so long that when we got home, all our furniture had been stolen by some callous rapscallions who knew we were out caring for the injured," George suggested.

"Brilliant, George! Yes, that was it! In serving humanity in our humble status as carers for the needy, we were burgled," Ivor said, shaking hands with George and giving him a pat on the back.

"You lot might have been, but I certainly wasn't. I've not been burgled in years," Lindsey said indignantly.

"That's burgled, Lindsey! B-u-r-g-l-e-d," Ivor spelt out the word. "As when one has all their possessions stolen from them."

"Ah right, I thought you meant ... no matter," Lindsey added, embarrassed at the misunderstanding.

"I see, I see," said Sir Richard, pondering the story.

"Then what happened to your clothes?" asked Lady Francesca.

"Oh crap!" Ivor said through gritted teeth. "Yes, George, what did happen to our clothes?"

"Um ... uh ... we were beaten and robbed and left by the roadside to die and if it hadn't been for the Samaritan on his way from Damascus to Jerusalem, we'd have all died," George blurted out, evidently caught on the hop.

"Ha! Ha! Ha! No, no, because that's a Biblical story, George!" Ivor said, resting his hand on George's shoulder and pinching his neck.

"Oh yes, sorry!" George said, drawing down the corners of his mouth and blushing.

"No, I've got it! The fight was so nasty and brutal that all our clothes were either torn from us or covered in blood," Ivor said.

I Love Your Money!

"So, what you're saying is, you now have no clothes or furniture?" said Sir Richard.

"That's about the size of it," Ivor answered.

"As the actress said to the bishop!" George began before being stopped by Ivor with a well-aimed elbow to the side of the head.

"And your medical equipment?" Sir Richard asked, taking a handkerchief from the pocket of his britches and mopping his brow.

"All gone, I'm afraid," Ivor confirmed.

"So, none of you were drunk then?" Lady Francesca asked, half laughing and half-serious.

"Mumsie, I'm shocked!" George said. "Do you really think that all along I've been telling you a lie? It's exactly as it happened. We were called out to the … uh … Navvies and Drunkards monthly bash and a fight broke out when someone stole a pickaxe," George said indignantly. "That was the story you gave them, wasn't it?" he whispered to Ivor as an aside.

"This really isn't good news at all," said Sir Richard. "Firstly, let's get you some clothes. I never liked the sight of naked men at the best of times, especially when they look like him," he added, gesturing to Doctor Stumpf who, wearing nothing but his drawers, now resembled a week-old party balloon with a head.

"Obviously none of you is really in a position to come with us, so I suppose we shall have to go on our own and come back with a selection for you," Lady Francesca suggested.

"Well, that went pretty smoothly," Ivor said as Lady Francesca and Sir Richard left and he closed the door behind them.

"Sweet as some nuts. We're home and dry!" added George.

"She's a lovely looking woman, your mother," Ronald said to George as he made squeezing gestures with his fingers.

"There you are, George, you could have Ronald as a stepfather!" Ivor laughed, watching George's nose wrinkle up as if an offensive smell had just passed underneath it.

"I'd rather not," George said.

"One thing does bother me, though," Ivor said, his forehead creasing as he tapped his chin with his index finger.

"Eh?" George grunted as he made himself comfortable on the sofa.

"Why have they come here? Come on, how often do we see them! Sir Richard couldn't wait to pay off my mother when your mother fell pregnant and as soon as I was old enough, he kicked me out. If it hadn't been for the good fortune of meeting the amazing Doctor Stumpf and his snake oil business then who knows what might have become of me!" Ivor pondered.

"Hang on a moment! My life hasn't been all plain sailing you know! If I hadn't used my wit to con those that believe I'm a Doctor then who knows what could have become of me!" George argued.

"Yes, you could be sitting around in a house with no furniture, clothes or money. Imagine!" scoffed Lindsey.

"So, why are they here now?" Ivor pondered.

George put his elbow on his knee, clenched his fist and rested it against his forehead.

"Don't try and ponder as well, George, it doesn't become you. Remember those wise words you said to me at the fayre? 'Upstairs for thinking, downstairs for dancing'," Ivor said, spying George's attempts at mimicry that simply resembled a small child copying their parent without any knowledge or understanding of why.

"Yes, it is odd," George said wistfully.

"What?" Ivor asked, slightly annoyed that his train of thought had been interrupted.

"Why you never see a swallow in a tree. I reckon it's because they've got no feet. And what about mice, eh? I saw one crawl under a door once and the gap was no wider than the width of my pinkie fingernail! Now you try and tell me that a mouse has bones! Never!" George said. Ronald and Lindsey looked at George and then at one another in complete confusion.

"Yes, George. It's good to see that you're looking at this mystery from all possible angles. Might I be so bold, however, as to suggest that you're thinking a little *too* laterally?" Ivor said, smiling smugly, looking at Ronald and Lindsey as he spoke, whilst gesturing to George with his head. The pair of stony faces that greeted him, however, quickly turned Ivor's expression to one of thoughtful contemplation.

"Perhaps they're finally going to accept you as part of the family," Ronald suggested.

"Yes, maybe," Ivor said indifferently. "Perhaps they're going to give me some cash!" he added, and a greedy smile crossed his face as the thought suddenly came to him.

"Well, it looks like you might find out sooner than you think," Lindsey said, rising from his seat. "Here they come!"

"Lindsey, it's rude to stare!" Ivor said.

"Oh crap, they've seen me!" Lindsey said, trying to quickly duck from view, only to smash his head on the windowsill.

"Oh dear, that sounded painful!" said George, pursing his lips and taking a sharp intake of breath as the hollow ringing sound from Lindsey's head echoed about the room and his unconscious form slumped to a heap on the bare boards.

"Oh, that's just marvellous, isn't it!" Ivor said jutting out his bottom jaw and drawing his hands into upturned claws.

"Well, at least he might be his old self again when he wakes up. That bang on the head at the fayre turned him into a right one," George said.

As anticipated, there was a loud knock on the door and, once again, George opened it wide, clad only in his drawers.

"George, please! You'll be getting the company a bad name opening the door in such a way!" Lady Francesca protested.

"Well, here you are," Sir Richard said, draping a pile of new clothes over the back of the sofa. "Having you all dressed will be a start, at least."

"Bags I the green frock coat," George said, as Ivor made a snatch for it.

"Ha! Ha! I had my eye on that! Finders keepers, losers' weepers!" Ivor said, trying his best to squeeze himself into a coat that was obviously too small for him

"Dad, tell Ivor! He stole my coat," wailed George.

Mallard the Quack

"There! A perfect fit," Ivor said, straining to pull the coat around him, even though the arms remained three or four inches above his wrists.

"No, it's mine!" George said, his mood suddenly turning from tears to anger as he jumped behind Ivor and tried to tear the coat from his back.

"No! You have the grey one. Grey suits you better - you're a grey sort of person!" Ivor hissed, writhing around under George's grip.

"No, you swine! You knew I wanted that coat! That's the only reason you wanted it."

"Rubbish! It's to bring out the beautifully understated green flecks in my eyes. I shall bestride the next Surgeon and Barber convention like a colossus with the flecks of my balls twinkling."

"Ooh, you don't need a coat to do that, Ducky," said Lindsey, rubbing his head and drawing himself up onto his haunches.

"It's Mallard! How many times have I got to tell you?" Ivor shouted, finally freeing himself from George's grip.

"Lindsey, you're back!" said George, pleased to see his new friend's old personality re-emerge.

"Why, have I been somewhere?" Lindsey asked, rubbing his temple and looking a little bemused. Only then did he realise he was almost naked, save for his drawers. "Oh, good heavens, where are my clothes? I say, we have been naughty boys, haven't we!"

"No. We were robbed and beaten, remember?" Ivor said emphatically.

"Were we? Oh, how dreadfully disappointing!" Lindsey replied, looking crestfallen.

"What's all this then? Why doesn't he remember?" Sir Richard said, beginning to smell a rat.

"Oh, you know. It's what we in medical circles call a 'softening of the brain'. I'm afraid he caught one fist too many last night and can't remember a thing," Ivor explained.

"Ooh, sounds like I missed a real ding-dong!" Lindsey said, with a twinkle in his eye.

I Love Your Money!

"Well, come on, children! Get dressed. Sir Richard and I have some news for you," Lady Francesca said, ushering the group toward the neatly piled heap of attire.

"I can't take off my underwear in front of a lady," Ronald said.

"You feel like that as well do you, Ronald?" Lindsey asked, resting a hand on Ronald's shoulder.

"Then I'd better wait for you in that room, over there," Lady Francesca said, moving towards Nurse Conwy's room before Ivor had a chance to intercede. As Lady Francesca opened the door, a loud braying echoed around the empty room as the donkey, previously the soul of discretion, saw its chance of freedom and bolted into the living room.

"Excuse my noisy ass," said Ivor.

"I've heard worse!" Lindsey added.

"What the devil!" Sir Richard shouted in disbelief as the donkey came to halt and relaxed, now that it found itself in such an urbane soiree.

"Those burglars! They must think of this as some sort of sick joke!" protested Ivor furtively, scanning the room from the corner of his eyes.

"Perhaps it's a calling card! You know, some burglars, when they burgle a place leave a card behind. Maybe ours left a donkey," George suggested helpfully.

"Oh yes, I can just see that, can't you? A swag bag under one arm and a donkey under the other," Ivor said sarcastically.

"Maybe they stopped to rehearse A Midsummer Night's Dream and left their Bottom behind," Ronald suggested.

"Oh, no! Believe me, I know a good Bottom when I see one," said Lindsey, "and that isn't a good one even by the most degraded of standards!"

"Look, none of you is making this very easy for me," Ivor said, leaning over to his friends and hissing the words harshly through clenched teeth.

"It's alright. No need to clench your teeth with us," Ronald said.

"Definitely! Just relax, I always say," Lindsey added.

"This bed is soaking!" Lady Francesca shouted from behind the closed door.

"Those depraved animals!" Ivor shouted in disgust, emphasising the abomination with his arms.

"That was Ivor," George said.

"What!" exclaimed Sir Richard, becoming ever more suspicious.

"No, George, it wasn't, now was it!" said Ivor, kicking George in the small of the back, given George was now sitting on the floor pulling on his stockings.

"Yes, it was, don't you remember, Ivor?"

"Uh, no!" said Ivor, going red and shifting uneasily.

"Yes, you do. Last night ..." George continued, as Ivor winced. "All those tears you shed when you realised that all our worldly goods had been stolen and that we had nothing to show for our endeavours other than a place in heaven, and how the few pennies we'd saved for the orphans would now have to go on a few sticks of furniture instead."

"Brilliant! Yes, I remember it all now. That's exactly how it was! Funny the things you forget when you're tired from helping the needy," Ivor said, leaning over George and giving him a congratulatory pat on the shoulder.

"My boys! I am standing proud," Sir Richard began, bringing his index finger to his lips as he saw Lindsey about to speak. "As soon as you are dressed, I want to sit down with you both and get something off my chest, something I meant to tell you when first you began working together," he added, pacing up and down. Ivor and George looked at one another with some concern and quickly finished dressing. "I should like, if you don't mind, to speak to my sons in private," Sir Richard said to Ronald and Lindsey. "Could give us just a little privacy for a moment or two?"

"Of course. I know how important a little privacy can be when men get together," Lindsey added.

"Thank you, chaps. I'm sure George and Ivor will tell you in due course, but for their sake, I think they should be able to choose the time," Sir Richard said with sincerity, as Ronald and Lindsey left the room, leaving the fully attired George and Ivor standing awkwardly in front of him, neither knowing what fate awaited them.

I Love Your Money!

"I'll just go and get Lady Francesca," said Sir Richard, returning a moment later with his wife.

"Shall I begin?" Sir Richard asked his wife, who nodded her acquiescence. "I know this involves you both, but it will probably come as a bigger shock to Ivor. Ivor, you've always known I was your real father. What you haven't known is that Lady Francesca is also your real mother." The colour drained from Ivor's face as he looked from Sir Richard to Lady Francesca, then blankly back at Sir Richard.

"I don't understand," he murmured. "Was I given away or something?"

"Yes," Sir Richard said honestly.

"Why?"

"Well, we just didn't like the look of you very much. We thought about keeping you and fattening you up for Christmas, but the turkey worked out cheaper," Sir Richard confessed.

"Well, thanks for dressing it up for me!" Ivor said indignantly. "You might have softened the blow by saying you were too young or you were too poor or that I'd been unplanned. Now I find out I lost by a short neck to Reggie the Rooster!"

"If it's any consolation, he was very tasty," Sir Richard added.

"And we did drink a toast to you," said Lady Francesca.

"Well, on the first Christmas anyway," Sir Richard clarified.

"This is bloody marvellous, isn't it?" stormed Ivor. "Hang on a minute ... if I'm legally your child that means, as the oldest, I'm entitled to the estates and that George is no longer the heir to the Uppham millions!"

"Yes, I suppose it does. We'd not thought of that," Sir Richard said, looking at his wife.

"I'm rich! Wa-hey! I'm rich! I always knew destiny had me marked out as special. Cock-a-bloody-doodle-do!" Ivor bellowed, running around the room making flapping motions with his arms.

"I must say, Ivor, you're taking this a lot better than I'd anticipated," Lady Francesca remarked.

Mallard the Quack

"Lindsey, Ronald, come in, quickly!" Ivor laughed, running to the door and calling up the passage.

"What is it?" Ronald asked as he entered the room, followed by Lindsey a moment or two later.

"I'm rich! I'm on the gravy train at last! Can you believe it?" Ivor said, running on the spot and flapping his arms wildly.

"How come?" Lindsey asked.

"I'm the eldest son. George isn't the heir to the Uppham millions at all - I am! For the first time in my life, I really feel as if I'm getting somewhere," Ivor said excitedly.

"Hang on a minute," Ronald said. "You're not rich yet, are you?"

"What do you mean?" said Ivor, suddenly stopping his frantic movements and taking on a serious disposition.

"Well, you might be rich on paper, but you don't have a penny at the moment. Neither of them has left you anything - yet - on account of their still being alive," Ronald pointed out.

"Oh, bollocks!" Ivor shouted, staring at the floor. "Why does every silver lining have to have a cloud?" he muttered, moodily slouching into a chair.

"Well, I'm sorry if our still being alive is a disappointment to you," Sir Richard said, haughtily.

"S'alright, I suppose," said Ivor, sulking.

"Come on Ivor, it's not all bad. After all, what's the average age people live to these days? Forty? Fifty? Well, we can count our lucky stars that we haven't got very long to wait, have we?" George said, giving his brother's leg a shake. "I mean, look at him!" he said, pointing to his father. "He's seventy if he's a day, overweight, with a blood pressure problem and unless a complexion that shade of red is in fashion this season ... whilst her ..." George said tutting. "Well, what does she know about money? We can settle her down into a little gatehouse somewhere once the big cheese pops his clogs! Give her a few pounds a month and all the sherry she can drink and she won't grumble about a thing."

"Thanks, George. I know you're trying to be nice to me and that's very sweet of you, but it really is awful being so near to

I Love Your Money!

all that cash and yet so far," Ivor said, wiping a tear from his eyes.

"Well! How sharper than a serpent's tooth it is to have an ungrateful child," said Sir Richard.

"Ooh, listen to her!" said Lindsey.

"I'm sorry, Father," said Ivor. "And an apology to you as well ... Mother," he added humbly.

"After all, you haven't given us any cash to buy some new equipment yet," George added.

"Yes, thank you, George! I was coming to that!" Ivor said, kicking George on the ankle.

"Is that all you want from us?" Lady Francesca said in exasperation, looking to her husband to see if he shared her indignation.

"Well, I like that! You were the one that gave me up me in favour of a chicken," Ivor fumed.

"It was a turkey, actually," Sir Richard said pedantically.

"Oh Ivor, I'd have never passed you up for a turkey!" Lindsey said sympathetically. "A goose maybe ..."

"Alright, thank you, everybody! I think we've established that in God's great scheme of things I'm vying neck and neck with an assortment of poultry, but if anyone's trying to make me feel better here it isn't working," stormed Ivor.

"He's very good, isn't he!" Ronald whispered to Lindsey.

"Excuse me! Excuse me! Do you think this is some sort of an act? I come *this* close to inheriting a fortune and I can now see it drifting away from me by ... oh, I don't know ... words fail me," Ivor said slumping into a chair. "George, put the kettle on and make some tea, can you?"

"I can't, Ivor," George replied.

"Oh, don't tell me! You've broken your leg trying to get up again?"

"No, it's not that this time."

"A hernia?" Ivor asked, his curiosity aroused.

"No, not that either."

"Elephantiasis of the scrotum?" Ivor asked, closing his eyes in defeat.

"No. Do you want me to tell you? We haven't got any tea. It was stolen, remember?" George said, pleased that he had been able to impart some information of which his brother had been ignorant.

"And the cups, kettle, milk, sugar and tea strainer," Ronald added.

"Not forgetting the stove," Lindsey pointed out.

"I've seen quite enough of this circus," Sir Richard said, taking his wife by the hand. "I'm not going to give either of you a penny! You're a pair of lunatics and as soon as I get home, I'm disinheriting the pair of you. If this is what education does for you, God help us!"

"We're the new elite, getting the country back on its feet," said George proudly.

"And where do you two think you're going?" Ivor said, jumping from his seat and hurdling a sofa, blocking the door as Lady Francesca and Sir Richard made advances to leave. "So long as there's a penny in that fat wallet of yours, you're not going anywhere," he added, waving his index finger menacingly.

"Well, it's nice to know all you want us for is our money! What about love?" asked Lady Francesca.

"I love your money!" Ivor said greedily. "Besides, if you never gave us any love, how can you expect us to start giving *you* love now? You bought your freedom from us! Well, now it's time to pay! Lindsey, grab his fat wad ... and no smutty remarks! Ronald, you make sure they have a carriage to get them away from here. George, you just stare vacantly into space - I shouldn't want you to break the habit of a lifetime!"

"This is scandalous! What about the bonds between parents and children?" stammered Sir Richard as he was relieved of his wallet.

"Scandalous? Do you really think so? Don't give me that! You only bought these clothes to ease your guilty conscience and the money you ploughed into this business wasn't so much philanthropy as you seeing an opportunity to make a quick buck out of poor stupid George. Well not me, I'm too smart for that and rumbled your little game, didn't I?" Ivor said, thumbing through the banknotes.

"Shall I tie them up?" asked Lindsey.

"Yes, you better had," Ivor said, now fancying himself as a swashbuckling highwayman.

"I shan't be a moment then," Lindsey said, leaving the room for a minute or so. "All done," he said on his return.

"Eh? I thought you said you were going to tie them up?" Ivor asked.

"I have," Lindsey said.

"I meant these two," Ivor said raising his eyes to the ceiling and pointing at his parents. "God, I shudder to think what you've been tying up."

"Oh! Them as well? Sorry, I'll just go and get some rope," Lindsey said, walking bow-legged from the room, leaving Ivor and Ronald sharing confused looks with one another and George staring from the window in his usual manner.

"Right, now tie *them* up," Ivor commanded as Lindsey returned with the rope.

"All done," Lindsey said, having quickly accomplished his task.

"Thought you could outfox us, did you? Thought you were smarter than us, did you? Get in there, you mercenary pair, and I don't want to hear a peep out of you whilst you think about the way you've treated poor George and me," Ivor said, pulling a door open and pushing Lady Francesca and Sir Richard through it.

"Ha-ha! Job done," Ivor said as he closed the door and dusted his hands.

"Ivor," said Lindsey

"Not now Lindsey. Let me savour the moment. It's not often I've had any power in my life. Now I have money and revenge, and it tastes pretty damn good," Ivor said, slapping his lips.

"It is quite important," Lindsey insisted.

"Oh Lindsey, what is it, for God's sake?" Ivor snapped.

"You do know that the door you just opened was the front door and that you bundled them both out into the street, don't you?" Lindsey said, wincing as he spoke.

"What! Oh, bollocks!" Ivor shouted as he opened the door, only to see Sir Richard and Lady Francesca hot-footing it down the road.

"Bollocks! Bollocks! Bollocks! It's your fault," he said, reaching out a hand and slapping George around the side of the head.

How Much for a Shag?

"What was that for?" asked George, rubbing his head.

"It's for driving our parents away," Ivor said.

"How did I do that then?"

"Oh, cheer up, Ivor. Things could be worse. At least you have some clothes on your back and a wallet full of money," Lindsey reasoned.

"You're right!" Ivor snapped, walking backwards and forwards whilst tapping his chin with his index finger. "For the moment I'm rich, but it does present us with a problem. Namely, no more allowances."

"What?" George wailed, rising to his feet. "No more allowances! That means I'll have to work for a living! Oh, God, what a thought! What else will I be expected to do? Have a few starving children? Drink pints of beer? No! I won't do it."

"But hang on a minute! You and Ronald have been Quacks for years. You must have a bob or two stashed away in a bank somewhere," Lindsey said.

"How dare you! You wander in here with your cheap-jack latrines and then have the nerve to call me a Quack!" Ivor said, his face glistening with contempt.

"Banks are for swine," Ronald added.

"And as Doctor Stumpf's well-observed argument points out, banks aren't the place for wages earned in caring for the sick. It is too holy a calling to be sullied amongst the rank and file of foul businessmen and those dreadful working classes," Ivor said, angrily.

"So, neither of you have any money at all?" Lindsey asked in amazement.

"Not a penny," Ivor said haughtily.

"The beauty of me is that I'm very rich ... people love me! And you know what? I've been very successful. Everybody loves me!" Ronald added, taking his teeth out and wiping them on the arm of his coat.

"Still, I can see one pertinent thing you've pointed out, Lindsey," Ivor said smiling.

"What's that?"

"I have money now. Therefore, let us eat and drink, for tomorrow we shall die!" Ivor shouted, jumping onto the sofa with one foot resting on its arm and his arm raised aloft in proud defiance.

"It's always great when someone else is paying! We can spend, spend, spend!" Ronald said, rubbing his greedy hands together.

"Hang on! What's all this 'we' business? This money is mine!" Ivor said, clutching the wallet close to his chest.

"And mine!" reasoned George.

"Well ... oh ... oh balls ... I suppose so. I'll split it with you seventy thirty," Ivor said, pouting and looking exasperated.

"That's not fair! It's eighty twenty or nothing," George argued.

"Alright then - nothing!" Ivor said, jumping from the sofa and holding the wallet as high as he could, out of George's reach.

"You know what I meant!" George said, jumping up and down and trying to snatch the wallet from Ivor's hand.

"Well George, you drive a hard bargain, but eighty twenty it is then," Ivor conceded.

"Ha-ha! See? I can be ruthless when I want to be," George scoffed.

"Oh, I see that all too clearly now, George," Ivor answered, sitting on the floor and opening the wallet. "My God, there's over fifty pounds in here!"

"So that's ..." George said, screwing up his face and looking aloft in concentration.

"That's ten pounds for you and forty for me, which leaves us with thirty-pound left over," Ivor said.

"And that's mine," Ronald said quickly.

"Is it? Well, you'd better have it then," Ivor answered, looking at Ronald, recognising something wasn't quite right but not knowing what.

"Right then, Ivor, what are you going to spend the money on?" George asked.

"Well, I suppose we'd better think about furnishing this place," Ivor said, looking around him at the bare walls and floors. "We certainly need some tables, chairs, desks and things. Anyone got any suggestions?"

"I vaguely remember reading about a furniture sale going on in the indoor market in town today. I didn't pay much attention but I'm sure it was today," Lindsey said.

"Then I think that should be our first port of call," Ivor said decisively. "We do, however, need to set ourselves a budget. What shall we say to furnish the entire place? Fifty pounds? Split that three ways and that leaves us having to pay ..." Ivor put the palm of his hand over his eyes and stuck out his tongue in concentration.

"Here's my money," Ronald said, throwing a few coins into Ivor's lap.

"Oh right, so if I put in my money, that just leaves George to put in his ..." Ivor grimaced.

"Seventy pounds," said Ronald.

"Yes!" Ivor said, suddenly illuminated.

"Is that right?" George asked, looking suspiciously at Ivor and Ronald.

"Of course, it is," barked Ronald.

"No, I'm not having that," George said dismissively. "Three seventy pounds does not make fifty pounds".

"You know, you're right, George! You should be giving us eighty, not seventy. Good job you noticed, George. You're too sharp for Ronald and me," Ivor said.

"You'd have to get up pretty early in the morning to catch me out," George said triumphantly.

"I can see that, George. We're obviously going to have to be very careful around you, aren't we Ronald?" Ivor said, winking and grinning inanely at Ronald who looked back stony-faced. Ivor immediately lost his look of glee and took on a stern, serious countenance.

"We might as well be off then!" Lindsey said, rising to his feet.

"Do you want to take the lead?" Ivor replied.

"Well, it's not my usual role, but what the hell! I can throw caution to the wind just this once," Lindsey replied.

Mallard the Quack

"I hate this indoor market," George said, as the group walked down the street. "It always smells like strong cheese and rotting fish on a hot summer's day."

"Is that what it is, is it? I'd wondered what it was. I'd always thought it was Mrs Jones who run that little knocking shop up Pit Street," Ivor replied.

"It is her as well," Ronald added. "She's usually there stocking up on those little nibbles I like before I ..." his voice trailing off as he realised how large a hole he was digging himself.

"Please, can we change the subject? My constitution isn't all it should be today, and talk of food is making my stomach churn. My God, this is Wales, not the last days of Rome!" Lindsey said, holding his stomach as he spoke.

Very soon, the cold and imposing facade of the indoor market came into view. As they ascended its steps the sudden chill of the place made a startling contrast to the warmth of the sunny day outside.

"Ah, this is just the thing," said Ivor, looking around at all the various stalls laid out in front of him, each selling a variety of bric-à-brac that ranged from the smallest of ornaments to the largest of wardrobes and desks.

"Look, Ivor! There's that woman who was at the fayre. Remember? The one that looked like Nurse Conwy," said George excitedly.

"So it is. Let's go and see if she has any medical supplies. We could certainly do with a few now that all ours have gone," Ivor said, leading the group of three to the stall, Ronald having already absconded.

"Look at that! If I didn't know better, I'd say that was my wardrobe," said George, pointing to a large Dutch mahogany and marquetry affair, decorated in flowers, birds and ornate vases. "Look, it even has clothes in it that look just like mine," George said, opening the door and shaking his head in disbelief at such a coincidence.

"And to think the very same woman had stuff on her stall yesterday that was monogrammed with your initials," Ivor added, equally bemused.

How Much for a Shag?

"I don't like it at all, Ivor. It makes me think I've got a double somewhere and that he's going to come up and touch me and I'll explode or something," George said fearfully.

"That's science talking again!" said Ivor, looking around the stall.

"I don't believe it! I don't think there's anything on this stall that we didn't have one just like," he said, stroking his chin and shaking his head in astonishment.

"Are you sure you're not Nurse Conwy?" asked George.

"Get stuffed, halfwit," the woman said, taking a letter opener and pointing it threateningly at George's abdomen.

"You even talk like her! You really should have met our nurse," Ivor continued. "The similarity between you and her is uncanny."

"Yes, but she was stolen along with all our furniture when we got drunk last night," George confided.

"Yes, we all had a *Quickie* after a *Kiss Behind the Cowshed* from my brother," Ivor explained.

"Did we? God, I must have been drunk! I haven't been to a party like that since I was an undergraduate and Oscar Beckford and I joined the all-male acting club, just so we could attend their nymphs and satyrs' ball. Oh, to be the golden-haired Apollo I once was!" Lindsey said wistfully.

"Oh look, Ivor," George said, pointing at a pair of old paintings of a Cormorant. "Isn't that a Shag?" he tittered.

"Ah, yes," said Ivor, spying the object of George's fascination. "Excuse me, Miss ... Miss? How much for a Shag?" Ivor asked, leaning across the table.

"Same as it was last night ... uh," replied the woman, taking a sharp gasp as she realised she'd betrayed her cunning disguise.

"So, you *are* the real Nurse Conwy! What happened to the woman who had the stall at the fayre?" Ivor stammered, standing upright and pointing at Nurse Conwy as he spoke. "And perhaps you can tell us what the people who stole you have done with all our furniture? We're not Doctors for nothing, you know! We know how many beans make five and so does our friend, the toilet salesman," he added.

Mallard the Quack

"Clive took it all, along with all your furniture," Nurse Conwy said contemptuously, looking Ivor up and down as she spoke.

"So, where is it all now then?" George asked, thinking himself a particularly hard interrogator.

Nurse Conwy looked at the array of goods on her table and then at the unenlightened faces of the three men in front of her.

"It was all stolen from us ... uh, him," Nurse Conwy said.

"Ha, I thought as ... much," George said, his sentence trailing to a whisper as it dawned on him that Nurse Conwy hadn't given the answer he'd anticipated.

"So, do you want to buy anything or not?" Nurse Conwy said, throwing her arms wide open and gesturing to all her wares.

"Not from you," Ivor said snobbishly. "I wouldn't be seen with rubbish like this in my house. I have standards to be maintained! Come, Lindsey, George! Let us away from this foul harridan."

"G'day gentleman," said one particularly scabrous individual maintaining a stall a few rows down from Nurse Conwy's. George couldn't help but stop and look at the array of exotic goods of Moorish and Middle Eastern origin.

"Hello!" said George cheerily. "This looks interesting," he said picking up a jug made from a human skull. "What's it made of?"

"Ah, I see that you are something of a dilettante," said the stallholder.

"Well, I'm not one to boast but I'm certainly glad that it shows," Ivor said, smiling broadly.

"What you have there, young Sir, is a jug that was once owned by John Dee, Magician and Alchemist to Elizabeth the First," said the stallholder, his walnut features looking as though they were about to crack at the exertion of speaking.

"Oh, go on!" said George.

"And here, Sir, we have a haunted wardrobe," the stallholder said, pulling a sheet off a particularly drab but large wardrobe.

How Much for a Shag?

"Ooh!" uttered George in childlike awe. "How much is it?"

"It's ten pounds, given it's a very special wardrobe."

"Ooh, I don't know. Will you take twelve?" George bartered.

"I don't know," the man answered, thanking his lucky stars. "Alright, you drive a hard bargain, but as I need the money, it's yours."

"Hooray!" said George, quickly parting with the last of his money, then giving the man his address and making delivery arrangements.

"Ivor! Lindsey! I've just bought a wardrobe!" George gushed, running up to his friends who had continued meandering from stall to stall when they had seen George waylaid in conversation.

"Which one?" Ivor asked excitedly.

"That little beauty there," George said, pointing.

"That's a bit ... crap, George. It's even got a crack in it! How much did you pay for it? I hope you haggled," Ivor said.

"Well, he wanted ten, but I haggled a bit and got it for twelve," George replied.

"You've not really grasped this haggling business, have you, George? You're supposed to haggle *down,* not up. It's to save you money. I still think twelve is very expensive, George. You should have offered him eleven," Ivor said paternally.

"Eleven? Are you crazy?" George said, a look of incredulity on his face. "You don't understand, Ivor. It's a haunted wardrobe," George explained, hoping the fact might justify the expenditure.

"So, you've spent all that money on an old wardrobe?" Ivor said, crossing his arms and looking down his nose as George visibly shrunk under the scrutiny.

"I'm a bit of a twat, aren't I!" George offered in defence.

"Yes. Still, if you want to spend the money I stole on rubbish, that's up to you. I'm still intrigued as to why you should want a haunted wardrobe in the first place," Ivor added.

"Oh, it'll be exciting! Imagine - a foul and unholy presence might come and haunt my britches ..."

Mallard the Quack

"Nothing new there, then!" Ivor remarked.

"No, I think George might be onto something," Lindsey added. "Just last Wednesday I walked through that dark old graveyard in the centre of town and felt these rough hands all over me. Unfortunately, it was too dark to see who, or what, it was. I went back the following night but even though I waited around for hours I didn't get so much as a sniff!"

"Well, all I can say is *don't tell Ronald*. You know how he feels about ghosts and the supernatural," Ivor said. "And children come to think of it… and old people … and people his age!"

"And men!" George added.

"And women, come to think of it," Ivor added nodding in agreement. "And exercise, windmills, foreigners, salads, dogs, sharks, vegetarians, cauliflower hidden in his mashed potatoes, single scoops of ice cream, umbrellas, chocolate cake that isn't beautiful, anyone from the borders - anyone who doesn't live in the same town as us, come to think of it! In fact, he probably doesn't like people that make wardrobes either, so it's not going to make much difference whether you tell him it's haunted or not!"

"Does he like anyone?" Lindsey asked in astonishment.

"His daughter. Money, obviously. Wait! There was one person a long time ago who lived a couple of streets away who he was simply indifferent to. I suppose that counts," Ivor recollected.

"And why did he like him?" Lindsey asked.

"He used to make cat o' nine tails for seamen, only his had bits of metal embedded in the lashes so that they were more painful," answered Ivor. "I think he thought they made better sailors once they'd had a good horsewhipping."

"And that's why sailors have rough backs!" added George.

"Oh fancy! I'd often wondered," Lindsey retorted.

"Talk of the devil!" George said. "Here's Doctor Stumpf. Hello Doctor Stumpf, have you bought anything?"

"Only this old whip," Ronald answered grimly, giving it a flick at some passing migrants.

"Did you haggle with him?" Ivor asked.

How Much for a Shag?

"Well, I did beat him down, in a manner of speaking," Ronald answered, a sinister smile flickering across his face for an instant before his usual expression returned and the moment passed. "Did you buy anything?"

"A few bits and pieces whilst George busied himself buying a wardrobe. I've bought a job lot of furniture, just to get the house full, rather than look around. We could spend weeks doing this and we now have the more pressing matter of actually working for a living and not simply living off the Uppham allowance that George was getting," Ivor said, noting the pain in the faces of George and Ronald as he mentioned the word 'work'.

"I've been meaning to ask you, Lindsey, how come you don't have to work?" said George.

"I do work, dear boy. Thing is, I'm a very good salesman who really likes to get close to his customers and the product he sells. In fact, the closer the better. I'll tell you this in confidence, there's big money in toilets for the right man," he whispered.

"Is there? I've never noticed. They certainly didn't teach us that in medical school!" George said in astonishment. Did either of you know that?" he asked Ronald and Ivor, both of who looked equally astounded.

"Are you sure about that, Lindsey? Money from waste?" Ivor asked.

"Ivor, perhaps you could get some more of those sausages that gave us all food poisoning! We'd be laughing all the way to the bank!" George said.

"Banks are for swine," Ronald said, evidently standing firm on the opinion he'd voiced earlier that day.

"Yes, a slight misunderstanding. Still, no matter. Shall we carry on or have we all seen enough?" Lindsey said, indicating he wished to continue browsing even if the others had seen enough.

"Well, I suppose we could have a little look around before we leave, now that we're here," Ivor said.

"I was hoping you'd say that! I'm looking for some soft furnishings for my boudoir," Lindsey said.

Mallard the Quack

"Well, there's a stall," George said pointing and skipping off towards it.

"Anything particular in mind, Lindsey?" asked Ivor.

"Not really. So long as it's beautiful and a feast for the eye."

"Look at this pouffe, Lindsey," George said.

"Oh, you dear boy! You don't know how long I've been looking for one of these! Here, let me try it out," he said, taking the pouffe from George's grasp and placing it on the floor, whereupon he squatted down until fully recumbent on it. "I have very refined tastes when it comes to matters such as these," he said. "Too hard is wonderful to begin with but one quickly becomes sore - too soft and one simply slips out of the saddle, so to speak. One has to have a pouffe that is neither too hard nor too soft for one to be able to lie back and relax completely."

"How is it?" George asked.

"Far too hard, I'm afraid," Lindsey said, handing back the pouffe with a look of melancholy. "I used to believe that the harder the pouffe, the better. Age, however, has softened the recklessness of youth. Now I prefer comfort to the fleeting thrills of yore."

"Well, if we've all quite finished, we might as well go back to the house and await our deliveries," Ivor said, leading the little troupe from the building and back out into the warm sunshine of the day.

As the group made its way back to the house, Lindsey, George and Ivor walked a little way in front of Ronald, as he wanted to threaten children with his new whip and tell them that now they were seven years old it was time to set aside childish pleasures and get a job down the coal mine in which he had shares and *dig beautiful, clean coal*.

"Remember what I said about that wardrobe, George. Don't go mentioning the fact that it's haunted in front of Ronald. You know how these things upset him. He might only be looking for an excuse to become upset, but there's no sense in giving him something to go berserk about," Ivor said, making sure that Ronald was out of earshot.

"Do you know, boys, I've had the most splendid idea! Now that you're all having to work for a living, a moneymaking sideline might be to open your house to the public as a haunted house," Lindsey said excitedly.

"Yes, come and see the haunted wardrobe! Ooh," George said, without any hint of sarcasm and doing a feeble impression of a ghost as he spoke.

"Do you know, that's not a bad idea," Ivor said, giving the matter serious consideration. "Of course, in order to capitalise on the wardrobe, we'd have to tell Ronald about it and that would scupper the plan before it even got off the ground."

"You could always lie," Lindsey suggested. "Tell him it's an ordinary wardrobe and that you're working a sting on the plebs."

"Yes! He'd certainly go for that. He's made it his life's work to be a charlatan of the first rank, so if he thinks we're simply pulling a fast one and telling the public we have a possessed wardrobe when we don't, it should work a treat. Do you know, I think we may be on to something here!" Ivor said excitedly.

Rather surprisingly, once back at the house, neither Ivor nor George had long to wait for the first of their deliveries.

"Ah, my furniture," Ivor said, as the first of the delivery men mounted the steps to the door. "If you could take that to my room," he added. "Lindsey, could you show this man where to discharge his load, please?"

"It'll be a pleasure, Ivor," Lindsey said, looking the man up and down.

"Ronald, this looks like some of your stuff," Ivor said, as a bed was brought from the wagon.

"It *is* my bed!" Ronald said.

"How can it be? Your bed was stolen, remember? I've just bought these!" Ivor said, shaking his head dismissively.

"I've been meaning to ask you, Ivor, why didn't we report all our things stolen again?" asked George.

"George, we've been through this. How would it have made us look? 'I'm sorry officer, all our things were stolen whilst we were unconscious on a drugs and cocktails binge'. Yes, that would have been good, wouldn't it?" Ivor answered sarcastically. "If I've said it once, I'll say it again. We have our good name to think of in this town."

Mallard the Quack

"Oh look, here's my wardrobe," George said, pointing from the window and jumping up and down.

"Right, don't mention it to Ronald. Just make some light small talk!" Ivor said.

"Trust me, Ivor. They don't call me Small-Talking George for nothing!"

"Well, weave some magic, as here he is," Ivor said, quickly turning to the window and whistling as Ronald returned from his bedroom.

"What do you think of that then, Doctor Stumpf?" George asked. "We're taking delivery of a haunted wardrobe and we all know what a nutcase you are about demons and witchcraft and all that."

"What?" Ronald raged, already reaching inside his coat for some hitherto secret weapon.

"George!" Ivor shouted, his face flushing. "What are you talking about?"

"I thought I'd try the old double bluff," George said, leaning over to Ivor so that Ronald wouldn't hear.

"Well double bluff your way out of this!" Ivor said as George felt a light breeze and a *whoosh* sound by his ear. Turning quickly, only to see Ronald wielding a heavy cudgel which he had evidently used to take a swipe at George's head.

"Sorry, Ronald, I was lying. Wardrobe? What's a wardrobe? I don't even know what a wardrobe is! What is a wardrobe, Ivor?" George pleaded as he ran around the room, quickly followed by the self-appointed Witchfinder General.

"Quick, George, the window!" Ivor shouted.

"Yes, Ronald, I meant window, not wardrobe," George shouted. Ronald's swipes continuing unabated.

"It's no good, Ivor. He doesn't seem to like the thought of those either," shrieked George hysterically.

"No, I meant stand in front of the window!" Ivor explained, flinching and flexing as though he was avoiding Ronald's wrath and not George.

"Right you are," said George, coming to an abrupt stop. "He's coming, Ivor, I hope you know what you're doing."

"Trust me," Ivor said.

How Much for a Shag?

"He's very fast for a man of his age, you know, Ivor. If you've got a plan, can you get it going please?" George squealed, his voice rising in pitch as the sentence progressed.

"Right and ... move," Ivor said, pushing George just as the wild beast that was Ronald was about to bear down on him. Like an unstoppable force, Ronald could do nothing more than twist his face in a moment's panic before he smashed through the window and landed with a thud in the street below.

"Thank God for that! I thought I was a goner," George said, holding his chest and gasping for breath. "What about Ronald, though? We can't leave him in the street!"

"Oh, balls to him! We'll pick him up later. We'll just tell him he fell from the window whilst looking for patients with pre-existing health problems to flog. He won't be any the wiser. Trust me, I *am* a Doctor," Ivor said, puffing up his chest with pride.

"But what about our good name?" asked George.

"I don't care about his good name. It's only my good name I care about," Ivor said as he pointed in various directions to various workmen.

"Do you know, if I didn't know better, I'd swear we'd bought back all our own furniture," George said.

"Oh, not you as well!" Ivor hissed, acknowledging Lindsey as he arrived back in the front room, his face flushed and sweating.

"That was a big one! We could hardly squeeze it in," he said.

"I'm glad you're back. That gentleman over there with the bulging sack - can you show him where he can empty it?" Ivor asked.

"Oh, I am a busy boy, aren't I," Lindsey said, tripping off to do Ivor's bidding.

"And you needn't think you're getting out of it either, you idle twat. Get over there and show your man where he's to take your wardrobe," Ivor said, pulling George by the ear, then pushing him in the general direction of a large delivery man, groaning under the weight of what didn't look like an especially heavy wardrobe.

Mallard the Quack

"You're going to have to give me a hand with this," the man said. "Either I'm getting old or these things are getting heavier," he added.

"What's in this drawer?" George asked, pointing to a large drawer at the base of the haunted wardrobe. It was a rhetorical question, as he didn't expect the man to know, and even as he asked, he'd begun pulling the handle to find out the answer himself.

"Locked, is it?" asked the man.

"Seems to be. I'd guess that's where the problem is. Who knows what foul, dank things lurk inside," George added, looking at the man as he spoke to see if his words had struck a chord of fear.

"Dirty laundry, you mean? Could be! My underwear tends to get like that in the summer as well," the man said.

It wasn't quite the reply George had anticipated.

"Something disgusting and unholy from ... the other side. Something neither dead nor alive yet having life."

"Steady on! I don't know what you've heard, but I change my drawers every month whether I need to or not," the man replied indignantly.

If they were going to advertise the house as a haunted house, George thought, then it probably wouldn't be best if he were in charge of marketing and advertising.

I've Just Rolled onto Something Hot and Fleshy

"Right then, get that eyesore out of here," Ivor barked.

"But he's helping me move the wardrobe," George protested.

"I meant the wardrobe, dimwit!" Ivor replied, clapping his hands in an attempt to gee everyone up even though no one was paying him any attention.

"I found these French letters in that sack," Lindsey said, coming back into the room, leafing through a few tattered sheets of paper in his hand.

"So? What do they say?" Ivor asked, only half-interested and not even bothering to look, preferring to keep his attention on the constant stream of furniture entering the house.

"Well, they're all addressed to you," Lindsey said.

"Are they?" Ivor said, his interest piqued.

"Not all from the same person, but definitely all addressed to you."

"Now that is a strange coincidence. Furniture that looks exactly like mine containing letters addressed to me. I'm beginning to think it's not just George's wardrobe that's haunted," Ivor said.

"Ivor, I've been meaning to ask - and please tell me to mind my own business if you think it's nothing to do with me - but why did your father have so much money on him?" Lindsey asked.

"Yes, I was wondering that. He comes to visit for the first time in years then, when I mugged him, he had enough cash on him to buy the town. I can't help thinking it's curious as well. It's almost as if he wanted me to have it," Ivor said, guiding two workmen through the door, although neither paid him the slightest attention.

"Well, to have that much money, he was obviously going to buy something or, at least, pay someone for something," Lindsey added.

"That's the last then," said a ruddy-faced delivery man in the broadest Welsh accent Ivor had ever heard.

"Oh right. Right, you are then," Ivor said, bidding the sorry party goodbye and closing the door. "Where is that useless brother of mine?" he said aloud, directing the question to himself as much as to Lindsey.

Ivor walked briskly to the foot of the stairs and shouted his brother's name. There was no response. Quickly, he mounted the stairs and made his way to George's room, opening the door with a little trepidation.

"George? Oh, you are here. Why didn't you answer me?"

"Sorry Ivor, I was just looking at my new wardrobe. It's great, isn't it? George said, sitting against the wall opposite his new purchase.

"Well it's a pity you've no money left to buy any clothes to go in it," Ivor said, moving around the item and giving it his first proper look.

"Isn't she a beauty?" George said.

"No. To be honest, George, it's the ugliest wardrobe I've ever seen, but as Lindsey suggested, it may make us some money, so I'll let the matter drop for the time being. Start thinking about what you want to say in an advert. If we can get it in the newspaper office before midday tomorrow, it should make the following day's edition. You'd better leave the explaining of it to Ronald to me," Ivor said.

"Righty-ho," George replied, taking a pencil and a sheet of paper from the dressing table Ivor had purchased in his job lot. *Do you enjoy a bang in the middle of the night?* he wrote. *Do your underpants fill when you hear strange noises coming from big cracks? Ever been poked roughly from behind, only to turn and find no one there? Ever awoken, only to find hot breath gasping against your cheek? Then visit Mallard, Stumpf, and Uppham!*, he scrawled, underlining the work as he finished. "There, if that doesn't get them flocking in droves, nothing will!" he said to himself, smiling as he perused his handiwork.

Dashing downstairs, George flung open the door.

"That was quick, George! Still, it's probably good to get this thing perfect before we rouse Ronald. Right then, take it line by line and we'll see what we think," Ivor said, with Lindsey nodding in agreement.

I've Just Rolled onto Something Hot and Fleshy

"Right you are. God, this is exciting!" George said. "*Do you enjoy a bang in the middle of the night?*" he began.

"Hmm, I'm not sure *enjoy* is the right word. We're trying to frighten them, remember? How about *Have you ever been awoken in the middle of the night by someone banging away at you?*" Ivor suggested.

"Brilliant," George said, crossing out the original sentence and putting in the amended version.

"Right, next line," Ivor demanded.

"*Do your pants fill up when you hear strange noises coming from big cracks?*" George read.

"It depends where the crack is. After all, we have to expect these things as we get a little older," Lindsey said.

"No. How about *Do big cracks keep you up all night?*" Ivor suggested.

"God, that's good," George said, jotting Ivor's sentence down. "*Ever been poked roughly from behind, only to turn to find no one there?*" he continued.

"Oh, God! More times than I care to remember!" Lindsey said, flopping back in his seat as if the memory were too much for him.

"Alright, but let's hit them hard with this, George. Let them think that there's a real chance the ghost might get them. How about *Do you want to get poked roughly from behind?*" Ivor suggested.

"You know, you should have written this, Ivor. Your ideas will bring us in a fortune," George said.

"Next," Ivor asked.

"*Ever awoken, only to find hot breath gasping against your cheek?*" George read.

"Oh, you dear boy! Which cheeks do you mean?" Lindsey queried.

"Not so good, George. I'm thinking *ectoplasm* - how about *Ever had something hot and sticky shoot all over you? Do you fancy some?* Remember, this is the hard sell we're going for," Ivor said. "How's about *Then come and work up a real lather looking at our big box?* Now then, read the whole lot back to me."

"Right, here goes - *Have you ever been awoken in the middle of the night by someone banging away at you? Do big cracks keep you* up all night? Do you want to get poked roughly from behind? Ever had something hot and sticky shoot all over you? Do you fancy some? Then come and work up a real lather looking at our big box!"

"That is brilliant!" Ivor said, jumping to his feet and linking arms with George, the two of them dancing around the room to the imagined sounds of coins chinking in their pockets.

"If that doesn't get them in, nothing will," Lindsey added, also using the occasion as an opportunity to dance, even though he wasn't a part of the money-making scam.

As the dancing stopped and Lindsey could see the two were in an exceptionally good mood, he broached a delicate subject about which he had been biding his time to mention.

"Now that Ronald is out of the way and I have the two of you on your own, there is a certain delicate matter I want to speak to you about."

"Lindsey?" said Ivor, looking confused and furrowing his brow.

"Things haven't been as wonderful for me at my home as I might have had you believe. I've been the victim of a smear campaign. Some blackguard has put it about that my mannerisms are affected."

"That's ridiculous," Ivor said.

"Crazy," echoed George.

"You're both very sweet. Alas, however, I feel I'll have to find somewhere else to live and was wondering - seeing as how this house is so large and you'll now need every penny - whether you'd consider me as a lodger?"

"You can move in as soon as you like. I'm sure your reputation will rise to its former glory once people see you living amongst such educated professionals," Ivor said.

"That's great news. Can I move in tonight?" Lindsey asked eagerly.

"We might need your help in getting Ronald in first. He is still lying in the road, isn't he?" Ivor said, moving to the window. "Ah, look at him there! Sleeping like a baby!"

"Right, shall we do it?" said George.

"We better had," Ivor replied, moving to the front door.

Within a moment or two, all three men were standing over Ronald's prone body.

I've Just Rolled onto Something Hot and Fleshy

"Remember, mind! Don't mention the wardrobe!" Ivor said, leaning over Ronald and giving him a few slaps across the face.

"He's not looking too good, Ivor," George said.

"No, but then he never did. Only two things will wake him – hearing someone say his name and the mention of money! Stand back, I'm going to see if this works," Ivor said. "Doctor Stumpf, your son-in-law, Gerald, is here. He has the money you stole from your charity for you but has said that given you're unconscious he'll spend it on himself."

Suddenly, Ronald went into convulsions and began coughing, his eyes beginning to roll.

"Hey, it's worked!" George said as Ronald sat bolt upright as though in shock.

"Now don't worry, Ronald, you've had a little accident, that's all," Ivor said in his best bedside manner.

"Oh, no, these are the only pair of drawers I've got," Ronald said, shaking his head as though trying to free himself from a daze.

"No, not that sort of accident this time. No, you were leaning from the window looking for some children to whip when you slipped and fell. You've been out cold for a while, so we'd better get you inside," Ivor said, nodding to George and Lindsey that it was now safe to approach. "It's like I said to you before, Ronald - go for the sick and injured ones first!"

"They can't get away so fast," George advised.

"Well, if you don't need me, I'll just be off," Lindsey said. Unfortunately, turning his back on Ronald and moving quickly away proved a mistake, as Stumpf sprang into action, unleashing his bullwhip and catching Lindsey on the back of his legs.

"Ooh, there's a man who knows what he likes!" said Lindsey, dusting himself down as Ivor and George did their best to restrain the old huckster.

"Quick! Go now!" Ivor said. "We'll deal with Ronald."

Within a few brief moments, Ronald had been taken back into the house and lain on a sofa to recuperate.

Mallard the Quack

"Now Ronald, you know we've been put in a situation where we have to try and get some money. We've been having a bit of a think around the problem and have come up with the idea of doing some guided tours around the place, advertising it as a haunted house. We all know it isn't - God forbid that we should be messing around with the dark side, us all being devout Christians - but it seems like a pretty good way of getting the plebs to part with their money. What do you think?" Ivor said.

Ronald pulled a face that he imagined made him look implacably determined.

"It's just another scam, Ronald, just like the good old days. Money for old rope!" Ivor enforced.

"I don't know. He who sups with the Devil should have a long spoon," Ronald said.

"Ronald, it's not like that. We're *pretending* the house is haunted for hard cash. That's the end of it. You must be able to see that that's easy money?" Ivor coerced.

"You might even get to flog a few stragglers!" George said as an aside, unaware of how strong a selling point money and cruelty would be to the old mountebank.

"Tremendous! I think this sounds like an unbelievable business idea!" Ronald said, stroking his chin. "And *nobody* knows more about business than me!"

"I'd also like your opinion on our getting a lodger as it will be easy money," Ivor asked.

"Easy money? That's tremendous! Really beautiful! Unbelievable!" Ronald replied.

"Phew, that's settled then," Ivor said, rubbing his hands in glee.

"Shall I read Ronald our advert?" George asked.

"Now that would be a good idea. I think it's important that Ronald understands the sort of customers we're targeting."

"Right, here goes! *Have you ever been awoken in the middle of the night by someone banging away at you? Do big cracks keep you up all night? Do you want to get poked roughly from behind? Ever had something hot and sticky shoot all over you? Do you fancy some? Then come and work up a real lather looking at our big box,"* George read excitedly.

"Well, what do you think?" Ivor asked, looking at Ronald, who seemed to be thinking about what he'd just heard.

"Unbelievable! Really great! This is going to be tremendous! *Nobody* knows more about haunted houses than me!" he said, giving a thumbs-up gesture.

"Anything you'd like to change?" Ivor asked.

"My drawers," Stumpf replied.

"No, about the advert," Ivor said, now used to Stumpf not following conversations unless they were about himself.

"More sex!"

"Well, we hadn't thought of putting any on. Maybe we could get George in a dress but it wasn't top of the agenda. Do you think we need to sell that angle to make it a success?" Ivor asked.

"Definitely! *Nobody* knows more about sex than me!"

"Right, George, you can show the people round in a dress!" Ivor said.

"Right you are!" George replied, confusing 'in a dress' with 'the address', and feeling rather important that he had suddenly been promoted to the chief tour guide.

Sometime later, there came a noise from the street.

"That sounds like Lindsey," Ivor said, as a voice from the street shouted a cheery 'Yoo-hoo' and a few taps rapped out on the door.

"That was quick," remarked George as he swung open the door, only to see Lindsey on the top step with an array of furniture removers behind him.

"Yes, I like my men to be fast," said Lindsey, ushering his entourage inside. "Be careful with my Saint Sebastian as it's very precious to me," he said to one burly youth manhandling a picture of the tortured martyr.

"Very nice," said George, nodding at the painting.

"Right, if I can have all the Gothic on this side of the room and all the Neo-Classicism on this side," Lindsey said, clapping his hands to capture the workmen's attention, then watching as they milled about in abject confusion.

"Perhaps you ought to let me handle this, Lindsey," Ivor said. "I know how the peasantry thinks," he began before one of the delivery men interrupted.

"Right, if you could all look at the artefact you're holding and appraise it for dominance of form over content, technical precision over an expressiveness torn from one's soul, artistic restraint, clarity of style over the free play of one's imagination and the ambiguous extravagance that some seem to think the latest thing," he explained, as Mallard, Stumpf, and Uppham gazed at each other in mute confusion. "I can see that you're obviously making a critical assessment," the delivery man continued, now addressing his remarks to the three Doctors.

"Will you rotten shower get it upstairs!" Ronald shouted.

"Ivor! I hadn't realised you'd employed such an aesthete," Lindsey said joyously, clasping his hands together and broadly smiling.

"Well, yes. I've always been a keen sportsman you know. I used to do a fair bit of boxing and rowing when I was younger so wanted someone fit enough to lift things," Ivor said, shuffling uneasily.

"God, Ivor, and I thought I was thick! You're thinking of *athlete*. Lindsey meant one of those little white parrot things, didn't you Lindsey?" George said. Lindsey, however, had already lost interest and was busy ensuring none of his precious artefacts had been broken under Ronald's onslaught.

Surprisingly, once all Lindsey's possessions had been taken to his room, he managed to get them arranged quite quickly into a style with which he could live.

As night drew on, George became ever more excited about what might be unleashed from his wardrobe. It was only after everyone had retired for the night, exhausted by the frantic pace of the day, that George was finally able to set his mind to nothing else.

After he had been lying in repose for thirty or so minutes a gentle knock came at his door startling him as he sought to locate the sound, thinking it may have come from his new acquisition.

I've Just Rolled onto Something Hot and Fleshy

"George, I've found this old dress amongst some of the things delivered today. I know it's not your colour and it won't do you justice, but I know how difficult it can be to get used to the fabric against your skin," Ivor said, tossing the dress George's way as he turned to inspect the wardrobe.

"Eh? Nobody said I'd have to wear a dress! Why have I got to wear a dress?" George said, rubbing his eyes, half hoping he had been imagining his brother's request.

"We did, downstairs, don't you remember? You agreed to it after Ronald said the public wants sex," Ivor said.

"Eh?" George grunted, beginning to feel more and more alarmed.

"Just put the dress on and tell me how it feels," Ivor said sharply.

As George slid into the dress, his initial hesitation left him and he began to walk up and down the room, enjoying the flow of the fabric. Suddenly, however, there came a loud tearing noise and an awful smell permeated the room.

"Don't look at me like that! It wasn't me," Ivor said, holding his nose.

"Well, it wasn't me either. Ladies don't do that sort of thing!" George replied.

Then came a terrible groaning and a slow rhythmic tapping that gradually got faster then suddenly stopped.

"Ronald reading *Fanny Hill*, again?" George suggested.

"No, the groaning wasn't loud enough," Ivor said dismissively, craning his neck to locate the sound's origin.

"Ivor, look!" George said, staring fearfully at the wardrobe, which had begun shaking from side to side.

"Oh, God!" Ivor shouted, running from the room as quickly as he could, back to his room and sanctuary. Shutting the door behind him, he leapt for his bed before pulling the sheets back and diving under the covers, quickly pulling them up and over his head. No sooner had he done so, than they were torn forcibly from his grip.

"Go away! It's not me you want! It's George! It was his idea to sell you as a cheap sideshow. It was him that bought you," Ivor said, his eyes screwed up in terror.

"Ivor, it's me! I'm coming in! I'm frightened," George said shaking, clambering into the bed before he'd even had an answer.

"Shh, be quiet! I think I can hear something," Ivor said as the two of them lay panting as quietly as they could, straining to hear the slightest creak.

"God! There it was again!" George said.

"Oh, God! This is all your fault! If you hadn't bought that damn thing in the first place, none of this would have happened. Ronald was right! We are messing with the forces of darkness. Oh, God! Oh, God!" Ivor whimpered. Suddenly there was a loud bang as if the wardrobe had fallen over.

"I'm off to Ronald's room. He'll know what to do," Ivor said, running desperately to the door and flinging it open.

"Well if you're going, so am I. You're not leaving me here on my own, you swine! That's what you want, isn't it? To come back in the morning and find the shrivelled husk of your brother with all his juices having been sucked out," George said, leaping from the bed and grabbing hold of Ivor's arm.

Ivor sprinted across the hall and pushed open Ronald's door, pulling George into the room behind him before slamming it shut.

"I'm coming in with you, Doctor Stumpf," George explained, tearing back Ronald's sheets and diving under cover

"So am I! Something is going on out there," Ivor said, following his brother's lead.

"I heard something as well. I thought it was one of you two!"

"Ronald, I think it's a ghost!" said Ivor.

"Shut up, will you?" George said, pulling the sheet above his head.

"Don't tell me to shut up," Ivor said, reaching over to slap his brother.

"Don't or I'll ... uh ... oh, God! I've just rolled onto something hot and fleshy," George said.

"Oh, God, don't say that! It's him, he's got his hand in the bed," Ivor said, flailing his arms wildly.

"No, it's mine!" Ronald said.

I've Just Rolled onto Something Hot and Fleshy

"Well can you keep your hands to yourself, please!" George said indignantly. "I didn't come into this bed to get groped!"

"It's not my hand, dimwit!" Ronald replied.

"Oh, God, that's even worse! Ivor, can you tell him!" George said in disgust.

"Look!" Ronald said, pulling back the sheets. "It's the last of my sausages. I felt hungry, so I made myself a late snack. I was eating them when you two burst in," he explained. "Oh, God, pull your nightshirt back down, can you?" Ronald said, turning to Ivor and noting that his wild thrashing had caused his nightshirt to ride up above his waist.

"Shh! What's that?" George said, freezing in terror.

As he spoke, footsteps could be heard on the landing outside. Moving from bedroom to bedroom, something was opening each door in turn.

"He's looking for us! It knows where we are and is looking for us! This is all your fault!" Ivor said, reaching across Ronald and grabbing his brother by the throat.

"Oh, God, look!" said Ronald, pointing with his sausage.

As the three Doctors looked, even in the dim orange glow of Ronald's oil lamp, the handle of the door could be seen twisting, its various bumps and dents throwing off reflections that made it scintillate.

The door swung open and there, silhouetted against the landing light, was Lindsey.

"Oh, my boys! My beautiful, beautiful boys!" said Lindsey, gazing rapturously at the scene before him. There, in the small bed, lay George, his lithe body clad in a flimsy dress stained with squashed sausage; Ivor, his nightshirt high above his waist, exposing all his lower half, his hands wrapped tightly around George's throat; and Ronald, pointing at the door with the firmest sausage Lindsey had ever seen.

"I had no idea. I'd never have interrupted, had I known," Lindsey."

"Lindsey, this is not what it looks like," Ivor began.

"No! After Ivor got me into a dress, the groaning and banging got too loud in my room so we sneaked into his. From there, we came to Ronald's room, hoping he'd give us the benefit of his experience, not realising he was busy with his sausage. Then, when we heard you coming, we didn't know what to do," George added.

"Don't worry, George. We're all men of the world. I'm sure you weren't up to anything I haven't seen many times before," Lindsey said, his eyes twinkling.

"Yes, George, you're not helping," Ivor said, pulling his nightshirt down as Ronald took a bite of his sausage.

"No, I heard a knocking and a deep, heavy groaning. I thought I'd better investigate, but I think the mystery's been solved," Lindsey said, bowing courteously as he bade farewell.

"No, wait, Lindsey," Ivor said.

"Yes, Ivor?" Lindsey replied, eagerly jumping back into the room.

"We heard the banging and groaning too."

"Well, I hope you don't think it was me!" Lindsey said indignantly.

"No! We know what the noise is and where it came from, that's the problem. It's from that wretched wardrobe that George bought," Ivor explained.

"The haunt ... the hau ... the war ... the walnut one?" Lindsey stammered, remembering halfway through that the word 'haunted' was never to be used in earnest in Doctor Stumpf's company.

"That's the one," confirmed Ivor. "Well, now that we're all together, perhaps we ought to go and take a look at this wardrobe. You know, safety in numbers and all that."

"I'm game," said Lindsey.

"I suppose," George said uneasily.

"Ronald?" Ivor asked.

"Let me just finish my sausage and I'll be with you."

Queenie Will Turn a Few Tricks for You

"Right you are. Let's be off," Ronald said, swallowing the last of his sausage.

"I'm nervous," George said, grabbing hold of Ivor's arm when he wasn't looking, causing him to leap in the air.

"Will you stop that! If it hadn't been for you in the first place, none of this would have happened," Ivor hissed.

"Shh!" Ronald sounded, as he drew near the door. "Well, I can't hear a thing," he said as he twisted the handle and entered the room.

The other three followed, all the while gearing themselves up to flee at a moment's notice.

"It looks the same," George said, moving about the room, then towards the wardrobe, sniffing carefully in the thought that it was somehow the safest means of contact.

"What's in the drawer?" Ronald said, bending down and pulling the drawer handle until his face went a burnt orange. "Ah, it must be a fake one," he concluded.

"Well, that's that then, isn't it?" Ivor said, brushing his hands and trying to regain control. "It was all in George's imagination! It's a good thing I was here to put his mind at rest."

"And yours! You imagined it too!" George bleated.

"Now, perhaps we can all get some sleep?" Ivor suggested, brushing George's comments to one side. "I'm hoping for a busy day tomorrow. Our advert should be out and I'm expecting quite a crowd."

Ivor, Ronald and Lindsey slowly filed out of the room, leaving George alone. George walked around the wardrobe and nervously touched it a few times. He hadn't imagined anything, he knew that. Now, the whole room felt as though an awful presence was in it. George slowly pulled the dress up to his shoulders then, as quickly as he could, pulled it over his head, lest the ghost, beast, or whatever it was, struck him in that brief second when he wasn't looking. It might have been the Age of Reason, but it didn't cost anything to take such things for granted!

He climbed into bed, a difficult task given he was loathe to take his eyes off the wardrobe for even an instant. As soon as he was in bed, he pulled the sheets over his head. No! That was worse. Now *it* knew he couldn't see what things it was up to and had come out into the bedroom and was waiting for him to pull back the sheets! Then it would strike! What cruelties! Why wouldn't it just finish him off now, when he couldn't see? Why wait until he had torn back the sheets, only to stare into its demonic eyes? Because it thrived on his fear, that's why!

This was unbearable! He couldn't spend all night cowering under the covers whilst the thing filled the room about him with its huge slimy presence, waiting in cold satisfaction! No, he would tear back the sheets and fight! That was the thing to do! George pulled back the sheets and flailed his arms about him, his eyes screwed up in abject terror - for these things had a tendency to go for the eyes - that much he knew!

When George opened his eyes, he was surprised to find the room as quiet as it had been when first he had gone to bed. It must have read his mind, and knowing he was about to pull the sheets back, leapt back into the wardrobe! That was worse! Now it could read his mind, so there could be no escape, for it knew what he was about to do before he did it!

George propped himself up against the headboard with his pillows and, being undecided as to whether one was safer from such things with one's head under or over the sheets, concluding that the safest course of action would be to pull the sheets up to a level just below the eyes. Now he could see what was going on in the room and feel halfway protected by the sheets.

It wasn't until the first rays of the morning sun began to enter the room that George allowed himself a little sleep, what with monsters being nocturnal beasts. Now he had the safety of daylight on his side, no monster could get him!

By the time Lindsey knocked on his door at around nine that morning, George had had just a few hours' sleep.

Queenie Will Turn a Few Tricks for You

"Hello George," Lindsey said. "I've brought you a cup of tea after your fright last night. My heart went out to you, it really did! I haven't seen anyone shudder so much since I was an undergraduate at Oxford and the young Montague Ryley-Gould had a touch of the vapours when performing in Apuleius' *Golden Ass*."

"Thank you, Lindsey," George said, rubbing his tired eyes and taking the tea.

"I think this might be a busy day," Lindsey continued, as he pulled back George's curtains. "Ivor's already gone to the shops to get you a few new frocks. We need to have you looking your best, don't we? As much as I like scarlet, I don't think it shows off those eyes of yours. A nice emerald green or a bright blue is what you want."

"Good. I can't wear the dress I wore last night again until it's clean," George said, yawning and stretching

"Is it dirty?" Lindsey asked, sitting himself down on the edge of George's bed.

"Yes, I got this dreadful mark down the back of it from Ronald."

"I *knew* something was going on last night! I must say, he's a game old bird, isn't he?" Lindsey laughed.

"No, you don't understand. It's stained with juice from Ronald's sausage," George explained.

"You don't need to explain to me," Lindsey said. "It's us against them in this world, George."

"Anyway, the advert goes out today," George said, taking a sip of tea and trying to change the subject.

"Oh, I'd forgotten that," Lindsey replied, then paused for a moment or two. "Oh, don't say there's some dreadfully boring reason Ivor's buying those dresses," he said in disappointment.

"That's the only reason!" George answered, half choking on his tea.

"Oh, how dreary. I hadn't realised business came before pleasure," Lindsey replied wistfully.

"And what's your role in this new venture?" George asked.

Mallard the Quack

"I don't think I've been accorded anything yet. Ivor said he's going to slip me in wherever he can."

"I suppose I'd better be getting up," George said. "Uh ... out of bed, I mean."

"Then I'll leave you to it," Lindsey said, leaving George to prepare for the trials of the day.

George dressed quickly. As he descended the stairs, Ivor opened a door.

"Ah, George! I'm glad you're up. I've some frocks for you to put on."

"Do I have to?" George answered, pulling a face.

"It's money in the bank, George," Ivor replied.

With some reluctance, George removed his masculine apparel and pulled over his head the first dress from the pile - a bright blue muslin number with a double-breasted bodice and the skirt cut away at the front to reveal a full muslin petticoat.

"Don't forget this!" Ivor said, gathering a long muslin scarf around George's shoulders, crossing it over his chest and securing it in his waist ribbon. "There, how do you feel?"

"Like a princess!" George said. "I could dance my life away."

"I'll dance with you," Lindsey said, leaping to his feet and taking George in his arms. "Oh, the Waltz! Queen of all the Dances! What was it Goethe said? *Never have I moved so lightly. I was no longer a human being. To hold the most adorable creature in one's arms and fly around with her like the wind, so that everything around us fades away*," he said, closing his eyes as he whirled George around the room.

"So ... uh ... you think you'll be able to get used to wearing a dress then, George?" Ivor asked nervously. "Right, I'll tell the dressmaker we'll take that one, shall I?" he added when his first sentence was ignored, only to find his second was also ignored.

"Sorry Ivor, you were saying something?" George asked.

"Yes, I was asking if that's the one," Ivor said.

"Oh yes. I've never danced with anyone so light on their feet," George said, smiling at Lindsey, who bowed and blushed.

Queenie Will Turn a Few Tricks for You

"No, the dress, you dimwit! You're supposed to be a sexy vamp, not some queen of the ball swanning around the place. Remember what Ronald's sister used to say? 'Sex sells!'"

While Ivor went back to the dress shop to take back the other dresses and pay for the one George had chosen, George changed back into his frock coat and britches.

"Do you know if Ivor's thought of any itinerary, or are we going to play it by ear?" George asked, sitting down to breakfast and directing his question at Lindsey who sat on a sofa at the other end of the room.

"He did say something about writing something down, but I don't think he's got around to it. I know he's had a poster printed up to advertise though. He's putting it in a few shop windows," Lindsey replied.

"So, what is Ivor's role in all of this?" George asked with concerned curiosity.

"He says he's coordinating."

"I see. Sitting on his backside doing nothing and getting paid for doing it, in other words," George replied.

Within a few minutes, Ivor was back, looking flushed and excited.

"It's happening! I can't believe the interest my leaflet has created. George, get your dress on. You're giving your first guided tour at ten this morning," Ivor said, running around like a dervish.

"Hang on a minute! What do I say? Who's coming?" George asked, almost choking on his toast.

"Does it matter? I think about half a dozen people are coming. Just make it up as you go along. For God's sake, just use some imagination, it can't be that difficult," Ivor said abruptly.

As George finished the last of his breakfast and pulled on his dress, there was a knock at the door. Ivor answered.

"We've come about the advert," said a gaunt, elderly man, a little out of date in that he still wore a wig, albeit unpowdered and tied at the back with a black ribbon.

"Yes. If you could just purchase some tickets from our ticket vendor," Ivor said, ushering the group towards Lindsey, who looked around the room for the newly appointed vendor until he realised Ivor had been pointing at him.

"Right, if you could all bear with me. I'm quite new to this game - God, it's been years since I last said anything like that! - but I'm afraid I don't have any tickets at the moment. I can gladly take your money and Queenie over there will turn a few tricks for you, although I can also put my hand to anything if the price is right," Lindsey said, taking the cash and pointing at George.

"Yes, thank you, Mr Grayson," George said. "As my colleague mentioned, my name is Queenie," he said, casting a long, dirty look in Lindsey's direction. "Queenie Uppham and I'm your tour guide this morning. If you'd all like to follow me."

With that, the little troupe walked from the main room to a dining room that had once doubled as a surgery.

"In here, strange and terrible things are said to have happened," George began, once the group had drawn around him. "Even now, if you listen very carefully, you may hear a terrible groaning," he added, anticipating that Ronald's snoring would be resonating through the house. As if by clockwork, the snore came, causing a little hubbub amongst the group. "It is a known fact that in this room many people have met painful deaths," George said, remembering the time he and Ivor had tried to cure baldness by offering head transplants.

"Right, please follow me," George continued, ushering the group from the room and catching the eyes of an old lecher, who brought up the rear of the group, for the first time.

George made his way down a passage, towards the door that led to his cowshed-cum-laboratory.

"Here, we have a cowshed," he began. "You will notice the strange, unholy smell in this room," he began, pointing out the cowpats and human viscera as he spoke.

"Dear God, what a smell!" said a voice from the back.

"Yes, perhaps we won't linger in this room too long," George said gesturing, right and left, at nothing in particular as he wafted from the room. "Right, if we mount these stairs,

Queenie Will Turn a Few Tricks for You

we shall now see some more rooms in which many a terrifying presence has been felt."

George came to Ivor's surgery and gave the doorknob a turn. As he opened the door, Ivor was revealed there naked, rubbing his body with the money they had just taken.

"Uh, perhaps we won't go in there," George said, quickly slamming the door as he saw the scene and the look of horror shooting across Ivor's face.

"I want you, you honey-hipped strumpet," said the elderly man quietly, and out of earshot of the others, pressing himself up against George.

"Let's move on," George said, grinding his heel into the man's little toe, whilst glancing back in the hope that he had stolen one of Ronald's sausages and that it had been that that had been pressed so firmly against him. "Here, we come to one of the most evil rooms in the house. Even I have had a terrible experience in this room. Why, just last night I rolled over and felt something hot and fleshy pressing against my back," he confessed, catching the old man's eye as he spoke, only to see him lecherously flicking his tongue and winking.

George opened the door to Ronald's room and waited a moment to allow the unforgiving stench to seep out, watching as it coiled its way up the legs of the visitors like ghostly vines.

"Here you will see the late Doctor Ronald Stumpf," George said, pointing at Ronald asleep in the bed.

"But he's breathing," said a voice.

"And snoring!" came a second.

"And flatulating!" came a third as a terrible sound echoed around the room, giving the distinct impression that Ronald had somehow torn the sheets in two without moving a muscle.

"Yes, many people have remarked on his near lifelike appearance. Not only that, but his body also refuses to decay ..."

"Well, it doesn't smell like it!" said the elderly man, holding his nose.

"But his flesh remains incorruptible. Many have said that dark forces are at work and, should his body ever arise again, he will wreak havoc and destruction on those who have disturbed his eternal repose," George said, warming to his task at last.

As the group made to leave, George lingered back, knowing full well the old man would follow suit.

"Look," George said, pushing the old man toward Ronald's bed, tripping him up as he did so, and slamming the door loudly enough to wake the sleeping Doctor. From the cries and desperate scrapings on the other side of the door, George knew the old lecher had been dealt with in no uncertain terms.

"Where's my father?" said one of the all-male group as George re-joined them.

"Oh, he found that last room so fascinating he asked if he could stay on and be given a real going-over ... sorry, give it a real going-over," George replied, stammering so much he almost gave the game away. He quickly pushed his way to the front of the group, avoiding eye contact with the three remaining men, all of whom were either arching eyebrows, preening sideburns, or running their fingers through their hair. Ivor had been right! Sex was selling!

"And now we come to the climax of this morning's entertainment," George said, opening the door to his room. "Gentlemen, I give you the haunted wardrobe!"

There was not the merest hint of a response as the attendant faces looked back expressionless.

"The haunted wardrobe!" George said again, trying to give his act a little pizzazz by gesturing to the wardrobe with both arms and a big smile on his face.

"And?" asked one of the men, as if there should be something else.

"What do you mean *and*? What do you want it to do? It's a wardrobe and it's haunted. It can't, therefore, be anything other than a haunted wardrobe, can it?" George said indignantly.

"So, does the man come out of there?" asked the second tourist.

"Ah, we don't know it's a man. It could be a woman!" George said, taking a step back as the word 'woman' raised a cheer amongst the group. "Or even a beast!" he added, again taking a step backwards in surprise as an even louder cheer erupted.

"So, what time does the show start?" said one of the men, sitting on the edge of George's bed.

"What time does the show start? It's finished! The show is over!" George said, shaking his head in confusion.

"Have we missed it then?" said the second man.

"Missed it? You just had it!" George replied.

"Look, let's not beat about the bush. We've come to see a sex show and we want to know what time it starts," the man on the edge of the bed explained.

"A sex show! No, I'm afraid this is a haunted house. There's never been any sex here," George blushed.

"Look, your advert asked if we wanted to see someone getting *poked from behind* and then get *something hot and sticky shot all over them*," the third man said aggressively.

"And it also said you had someone here with a *big box*!" said the man on the bed.

"No, you've misunderstood! We were trying to make the advert sound sexy. That's why I'm in a dress. You'd never usually find me in a dress," said George

"I say, it's pretty liberated!" said the first man, arching his eyebrow and gazing at George in mistaken longing as the other two cheered.

"We've paid for a sex show!" said the second man.

"And that is what we'll get," the third man said, pulling a small pistol from his boot.

"Oh, *the* sex show! Right, I'll just go and see if they're ready," George said uneasily, making his way to the door.

Quickly, George plunged down the stairs and burst in on Ivor, who by now had dressed and had begun counting the money instead of rubbing himself with it.

"They want a sex show!" George said breathlessly.

"What! Not in my house! Wait ... how much did they offer you?" Ivor asked.

"Not with me! They want to watch one. They think we're going to put on a performance!" George explained.

"What! My God, George, what have you been saying to these people? I said 'sex sells', but I didn't expect you to say we'd throw in an erotic floorshow," Ivor shouted.

"No, it was the advert. They say they were misled and that they didn't come here to see a haunted house at all. When I said that there wasn't a sex show one of them pulled a gun out on me and threatened to kill me unless they had their show," he stammered.

"And is his shooter loaded?" Ivor asked.

"Yes, it's in his hand as we speak!"

"And the gun?"

"Yes, that as well," answered George.

"We need to think fast," Ivor said, pacing the room and looking at the floor. "I have it," he snapped. "I'll go into town and buy three false beards."

"Ivor, we're in trouble! This is no time for a fancy-dress party!"

"No, dimwit. We'll give them some crap story about having to wear beards before they can see the show. Then, when they've got the beards on, we give Ronald a *Knee Trembler* and tell him Clivella has returned with her sisters and that they all want a piece of his wrinkled old arse."

"I don't get it," said George.

"Well, he's going to go in there in a frenzy, isn't he? Can you imagine the scene when all three spurn his advances? God, it'll be like The French Revolution!" Ivor reasoned.

"Ivor, that is the work of a genius! No wonder you've scaled the heights with such a cunning mind," George replied, slapping his brother across the back.

"Right, you get Ronald, I'll get the beards and we'll see if Lindsey can give us a *Kiss Behind the Cowshed*," Ivor said, dashing from the room.

George followed as quickly as he could, then made his way to Ronald's room, instead of downstairs after Ivor.

"No, I meant the drink, you idiot," Ivor's voice bellowed up the stairs before the back door slammed shut.

"Doctor Stumpf?" George said quietly, tapping at Ronald's door as lightly as he could. He braced himself as he heard heavy footsteps approaching from the other side and the noise of the knob turning.

"Yes?" Ronald said.

"I think Ivor wants to tell you something. I believe it's rather urgent," George said.

"Of course! No problem," Ronald said cheerily.

"You seem in good spirits this morning, Doctor Stumpf," George ventured.

"Yes. I just met someone that was in my year in school. There was no laughing at 'Stumpf's stump' today, that's for sure! Not so brave without Donkey Davis or Plums Price to back him up!" Ronald said wistfully.

"Then I think this is your lucky day. If I'm not mistaken, Ivor's got some very good news for you."

As they descended the stairs together, the front door burst open with a fearful noise.

"Excuse me, Doctor Stumpf," George said. "I'm a bit nervous," he added, just as Ivor returned with the false beards, beckoning George to one side.

"Here you are. Get them upstairs and onto the faces of those parasites as quickly as possible," he said.

"Blonde? Clivella's hair was as black as it coal," George said.

"Look, it was the best I could do at short notice, alright? Anyway, Ronald likes blondes and after Lindsey gives him a *Knee Trembler*, I don't think he'll care what colour it is so long as it's warm and hairy."

As fast as he could, George ascended the stairs and ran straight to his room.

"Uh, gentlemen. I have a somewhat strange request. You are, indeed, about to encounter an experience you will never forget. Our show, however, is an interactive experience in which you - our audience - will be called upon to join in the fun! In order, therefore, to protect your anonymity - and to give you something with which to tickle our performers! - we're supplying you with these beards. If you could keep them on at all times, the management would be very grateful," George said.

Mallard the Quack

Then, as if on cue, an enormous drunken bellow came thundering up the stairs and the door to George's room burst open.

"Quick, George, get out while you can!" Ivor shouted, tugging George by the sleeve of his dress and pulling him from the room just a second before Doctor Stumpf entered, slamming the door firmly behind him.

"Old Ronald will give them a sex show they won't forget, won't he!" George laughed

"Well, they'll certainly get some sex, and it will certainly be a show, but I don't think the experience will be a completely erotic one!" Ivor said, as the door burst open and three men in beards sped past, fleeing for their lives.

"Thank you. Come again!" George shouted after them, laughing with hysterical relief.

"Hello boys," came a loud voice, unexpectedly interrupting the premature celebration.

"I know that voice," Ivor said, squinting into the room.

"So do I. Now don't tell me!" George said. "It's Eldritch!"

"Fancy a song, lads? I've got my mattock - or tuning fork if you prefer! This is a particular favourite of mine and is in the key of B flat," he said, taking a well-aimed swipe at Ivor and George. "What do you know? Two birds with one stone," he said, congratulating himself, as the two Doctors tumbled to the floor. "Be flat. Get it? Oh well. Please yourselves."

Fancy a Quickie?

"Oh, God, my head hurts," Ivor said, rubbing the back of his neck and moving his head around in the vain hope that one position might be more comfortable than another.

"Mine too," said George, pushing his closed eyes around in their sockets.

"What were we drinking, for God's sake?" Ivor asked.

"I don't think we were, were we? I think I'd know if I'd had a *Quickie* after a *Kiss Behind the Cowshed* and I don't feel as though I've had either," George replied, opening his eyes. "Oh, God, now I remember," he added, nudging Ivor with his elbow.

"What is it? Can't you leave me alone? You can see that I'm ill and you're still keeping on!" Ivor moaned.

"No, it's not that. I remember why we feel so bad, and it's nothing to do with the drink. It's Eldritch!" said George, looking at Eldritch lying on George's bed, as he watched them regain consciousness on the floor opposite.

"Oh please, George! Don't even mention that fat fugger's name, even in jest. The thought of him coming back sends a shiver down my back," Ivor replied, giving an involuntary shudder.

"Oh, it does, does it?" Eldritch said indignantly.

"Stop it, George! I know you're good at impressions, but I don't want you doing him. God, for a moment there I thought he was actually in the room with us," Ivor said, finally opening his eyes. "Ah, Eldritch. How strange that you should be here just as George and I were talking about another Eldritch we know. Do you know him? He's an awful man!" Ivor stammered nervously.

"Don't give me that balls, Mallard! I know you were talking about me," Eldritch scowled.

"Nonsense! We like you, don't we, George?"

"Yes. In fact, I think I'm falling in love with him," said George, straightening his dress.

"Eh?" said Eldritch, a look of shock on his face.

"Don't overdo it, halfwit," Ivor hissed. "No, what George meant is that he loves you like a brother. You're almost family to him," Ivor explained.

"Yes, that's what I meant. Sorry," George said, abashed.

"It's alright boys. I know I'm not a well-liked man," Eldritch admitted.

"That's rubbish! I don't know anyone who's as popular as you!" Ivor said. "Alright, so a few people in the town might have objected to you digging up their relatives and selling them, but what they don't understand is that a man has to make a living," he added.

"Exactly!" Eldritch agreed, moving to the edge of the bed, beginning to involve himself in the conversation

"I mean to say, how else are you going to pay for gin and filthy woodcuts?" George ventured.

Before Eldritch could answer, there came a groaning from the wardrobe.

"See, it's the ghost! It's back again!" George said nervously.

"Ghost? No, that's that old Doctor friend of yours. I locked him in the wardrobe after he tried to kiss me. I couldn't believe it! Running his fingers through my beard, he was, and telling me I was the most beautiful woman he'd ever seen and how he liked his women carrying a bit of baggage as it gave him something to hold on to when the action started," Eldritch said in disbelief.

"Yes, that sounds like Stumpf alright. He must have mistaken you for his last girlfriend," explained Ivor.

"Anyway, I hit him with the mattock and put him in that drawer I was in before," said Eldritch.

"Oh, so it was you! God, that's a relief. I thought it was a ghost!" laughed George.

"No! Listen, boys, I do have a bit of a confession to make. You're probably wondering why I was in your wardrobe drawer, to begin with, eh?" he said.

"If you want to climb into our drawers, Mr Eldritch, then I can't begin to tell you how happy I am about it," Ivor grovelled.

"My drawers are always open to you ... uh, in a manner of speaking," George stammered.

Fancy a Quickie?

"Well, anyway. I went into a little business venture with a few people. They wanted you lot out of this house. I thought to myself I could come around here and throw you out, but that would have caused too many arguments and I don't like upset. The other idea was to come around and slit your throats, but then I'd have all those bodies to get rid of and seeing as how you lot are my best customers, it'd be like slitting my own throat, so to speak - or biting the hand that feeds you if, you prefer. So, anyway, Nelly suggested to me that we wait until you had a drink one night and we'd be able to clean you out, seeing as how Ivor would be the first to pass out and the others would quickly follow. With you all unconscious, we could take away all your things and then, given you'd have no means of making a living, you'd not be able to stay living in the house and would move out of your own accord. I'd get the job done with no mess, a few bob from the furniture and a few bob from that Uppham bloke for getting him the house," Eldritch said.

"I won't stand for that! Where did this vicious rumour start that it's always me that's the first to pass out? What about George? One good ... hang on a minute! Did you say that a man named Uppham was paying you to get rid of us?" Ivor asked.

"Yes. He should have been here a few days ago with the cash. I know why as well! He was intending to buy up all the houses in the street as there's an underground stream running beneath these houses and it's got a rich vein of gold in it."

"Swine! His own children! He was quite prepared to have seen you kill us both, just to get his hands on some gold in a stream?" Ivor ranted.

"Don't take it so personally. Worse things happen at sea," Eldritch said sympathetically.

Once again, a loud groaning came from the wardrobe.

"Shut up, you old git," Eldritch shouted, banging the wardrobe with his mattock.

"So how did you come to be in the wardrobe?" George asked.

"That's where it all went wrong. You remember I'd been enjoying the company of Nelly," Eldritch began. "Well, when

Mallard the Quack

I came out and met that friend of yours we got into a little tussle, during which he threw me from that window, and I'll admit I was dazed for a while and didn't know what to do. Then, Nelly comes out and says the coast was all clear, as you'd all been drinking and we could now clean you out. That took us a good few hours. Then, as I was waiting outside loading up the last wagon, that hairy boyfriend of Doctor Stumpf's knocks me on the head. Next thing I knew, I was waking up in the wardrobe. I suppose you must have bought it by then, as once I managed to get the thing open, I was here."

"God, it's amazing isn't it?" George remarked.

"What?" said Eldritch, wondering which part of his story George had found so astonishing.

"How God made the world in six days. God, it takes me that long just to get my clothes clean after a night out!" George remarked, looking vacantly into the distance. "God, he's great, isn't he!"

"Who?" asked Ivor, confused as to where George was taking his new strand of conversation.

"God, of course! Imagine being God! 'You've been a bad boy, Mr Jones'," George said in a deep voice that was the best impression of God he could manage. "'Therefore, I'm going to give you piles. That'll take the spring out of your step!' And what about those angels eh? What a great bunch of fellas they are! God, it must be just like being a member of the Masons up there. I hope I don't get blackballed when it's my turn!"

"I'm sorry Mr Eldritch. Please ignore my brother. He's got this disease called Idiocy. He's had it since birth, but it seems to be getting worse," Ivor said with irritation.

"This is why people don't like me," Eldritch said, his voice quaking with emotion. "Even when I try to be nice, people find me boring. I can't win. They're either frightened of me or I bore them to death."

"You ought to have a chat with Doctor Stumpf," Ivor suggested. "He's particularly good when it comes to matters of the heart."

Fancy a Quickie?

"Well, let's let him out then!" Eldritch said, jumping from the bed and pulling open the wardrobe drawer, exposing the semi-clad body of Doctor Stumpf filling the drawer so completely it looked as if he'd been poured in.

"And this time, no tongues," Eldritch warned, as Ronald sat up in the drawer with a suggestive look on his face.

"Ronald, you remember Mr Eldritch," Ivor said.

Ronald squinted at Eldritch.

"Eldritch my arse!" Ronald replied.

"God, his eyesight must be going. It's all that reading he's doing. I bet his palms will be hairy next," Ivor said to George. "Well, we'll be off then," Ivor continued, rising to his feet.

"You sit down there or, so help me God, I'll take that head off your shoulders," Eldritch snarled, jumping to his feet with his mattock at the ready.

"Alright! You were saying?" Ivor asked, quickly sitting back down.

"Yes - why I'm unpopular - it's not that I don't want to be liked, 'cause I do. It's just that I find it hard to let people get close to me."

"Nonsense! We're all in the same room as you now! How much closer do you want to be?" George asked.

"No, I meant emotionally close," Eldritch said, his eyes filling up.

"I used to know a man down the docks like that," Ronald interjected.

"I suppose it's come as bit of a shock to me to realise how unpopular I am," Eldritch said, ignoring Ronald's remark. "I don't know where it all went wrong. I wasn't like this when I was younger. Alright, so I had the odd scrape - like when I loosened that bell in the church tower and killed the congregation - but what child doesn't get up to the odd bit of mischief? There was no real devilment in me, even when I blew up that vicarage."

"You mustn't be so hard on yourself," George said. "You know, we only get one life and if we're always looking backwards, then we're not living for today."

"That's very good, George. Did you think of that all by yourself?" Ivor asked, looking at George in astonishment.

Mallard the Quack

"Well, no. Old Jones said it to me. He kept looking backwards and kept walking into things. It was only when he looked in front of him that it stopped."

"The things you see when you haven't got your gun with you," Ivor said in disgust, turning back to Eldritch with a real look of fake concern on his face.

"Have you always had this trouble with letting people see the real you?" Ivor asked.

"Definitely. I often go out in a mask," Eldritch said affirmatively.

"We all wear different masks, Mr Eldritch, depending on who we're with," Ivor said sympathetically.

"Oh, are you wanted by the law as well then?" Eldritch replied with surprise. "Yes, sometimes I go out in my Cyrano de Bergerac mask. That's very popular with the ladies as they like the nose," he added. "Know what I mean!" he said, laughing lecherously. "Then again, sometimes I go out in my Shakespeare mask. But I'm not so keen on that. After all, no one likes a slaphead, do they? I also get sick of all these kids coming up and kicking me, then saying things like 'we liked English until we had to sit through your crap, you abstruse swine'."

"Yes. Perhaps we ought to leave the idea of masks behind," Ivor said. "Tell me about your parents instead."

"Oh, don't mention them! I think I told you about my mother. A big fat thing with a moustache like a bush," Eldritch began, Ronald sitting up and taking notice at the first mention of hairy women. "Then there was the old man! He was a skinny little runt with a drink problem."

"Yes, but did you ever feel real affection from them? How many times can you remember one of them taking you in their arms and telling you that they loved you? Did you ever feel wanted?" Ivor delved.

"Balls! My parents never told me they loved me! The only affection I got was when my father hit me with an unbroken bottle instead of a broken one," Ronald interrupted. "He didn't need to say a thing on those days for me to see the love in his eyes. And as for feeling wanted? Of course, I was wanted! There was even a reward out for me when I was younger!"

"Bottles? Sounds like luxury to me!" Ronald said, folding his arms in superiority. "Mine hated me and I tell you another thing! It's never done me any harm! They were really great - unbelievable. *Nobody* knows more about parents than me ... tremendous people. And look at how really great I've turned out!" he added, looking around the room for admiring glances. "People come up to me all the time and ask me 'How did you turn out so great?' and I tell them it's just the way I am ... tremendous!"

"Lying git, his father was a millionaire and he was a spoilt brat," Ivor whispered to George. "Well, I think it depends on how sensitive the child is," Ivor said to Ronald. "Ronald, you were a well-adjusted and robust child and, therefore, have become a well-adjusted and robust adult. Maybe Mr Eldritch had sensitive leanings."

"I told you. Just like that bloke down the docks. He used to lean sensitively for a penny a go ... uh, so I'm told," Ronald said, looking around the room furtively.

"No, to tell you the truth, Mallard, I never really felt wanted. The only time I was held as a child was when they were checking how heavy I was, to see if it were me or the turkey that was going to be the next Christmas dinner!" Eldritch said, casting Stumpf a sidelong glance.

"Ahh, now that's good! If you can cry at something like that, it shows you can feel something inside. How do you feel when you see a couple in love? Does it make you cry for the little boy inside you that wishes he were in love as well?" Ivor probed.

"Little boy inside you? You're not pregnant, are you?" Ronald asked.

"Ronald! Haven't you ever felt as if there were someone inside you for whom you grieve?" asked Ivor

"Nope. I ate those sausages you bought a few weeks ago and grieved that I'd sold Crusty Jones to the Butcher. By that time there were bits of him inside me and giving me bloody food poisoning! I suppose I do hear these voices now and again, telling me to persecute someone. So, I do, and that's the end of it. I don't like it when I hear them laughing at me and telling me I'm a terrible Doctor."

"No, I can't say as I cry. If I see a couple in love I usually just go and give the bloke a few slaps, tell the woman she could have had me, and that's the end of it," said Eldritch.

"I think we're getting away from the point here," Ivor said, shifting uncomfortably on the bare boards upon which Eldritch had made him sit. "I'd like to know why you think violence is a means to an end."

"Now you really are talking balls!" Ronald protested. "Violence is not a means to an end, indeed! It doesn't have to be! It's enjoyable for its own sake, so long as the person you're hitting can't hit you back! Why hate yourself when you can hate someone else! There's always someone worse off than you so hate them!"

"I know what they say about violence being a form of expression used by the inarticulate man when he feels threatened, but I think that's cobblers! I just like a good punch-up," Eldritch said, nodding in agreement with Ronald, the two of them looking at Ivor for his side of the argument.

"But wouldn't it be better if we could all get along? Why is it so bad to love one's brother?" asked Ivor

"You *sure* you never met that bloke down the docks?" Ronald asked.

"Hang on! We're brothers," George piped. "I'm not loving you, you dirty sod. Anyway, it's illegal, isn't it?"

"Not that sort of loving! I meant just embracing a fellow man and saying 'I love you'," Ivor said with some annoyance.

"Really!" Ronald smirked. Suddenly, there was a knock at the door.

"Who's that?" Eldritch mouthed.

"I'm guessing it's Lindsey ... the new lodger," Ivor replied.

Eldritch clambered from the bed and moved stealthily to the door. As fast as he could, he snatched the door open and grabbed hold of Lindsey, pulling him into the room and sending him crashing to the floor.

"You! I know you. You're that bloke I met the other night. You're a bit handy with your fists, aren't you?" Eldritch said, pointing at Lindsey from behind the safety of his mattock.

Fancy a Quickie?

"Well, I don't like to boast, but it has been commented that I have quite a deft touch. It's only come after years of practice, I assure you. Still, I can't say I recognise your face. Then again, I don't suppose I would, would I?" Lindsey said, dusting himself down before squeezing in between Ivor and George.

"We were just asking whether it's wrong to embrace a fellow man and say 'I love you', Lindsey. What's your opinion?" Ivor asked.

"What is this? Truth or Dare? Of course, I'm all for it, but that's my biggest downfall - I give too much too quickly then, before I know it, I'm nursing a broken heart and they're off," Lindsey said wistfully.

"Right, there you are then. Can we go now?" George asked.

"You stay there! I'm just getting into this! I love the control I have over you all," Eldritch said, his face breaking into a sinister smile as his fingers ran up and down his mattock.

"Yes, you have a problem with power and control, don't you?" asked Ivor. "Was it because you felt powerless as a child, unable to control your environment or the circumstances in which you found yourself? Do you think that's why you seek to control everything around you now?"

"Nah, I just like being horrible and watching you maggots squirm," Eldritch said. "You trying to say to me Genghis Khan ruled his empire with ruthless cruelty, from the Black Sea to the Pacific, just because his mother didn't tuck him in at nights? No! Don't you like looking at the tear-stained face of an old friend as you wrench their teeth out to sell to some backstreet dentist?"

"I do!" Ronald said. "Do you know, gorgeous, I didn't realise you and I had so much in common. I have all this fun causing misery, but you try and tell this pair about it and all they want to do is hug you! Do you know, just yesterday, I was lucky enough to bump into an old friend. As I showed him just how big I am in the britches department these days I could have been right there, back in my old classroom!"

"The happiest days of your life, aren't they!" Eldritch said, going misty-eyed.

"Certainly were. That was the grounding that made me the unbelievable man I am today!"

"Hard but fair," Eldritch said.

"You've hit the nail on the head!" Ronald agreed

"So why are we all up here?" Lindsey asked.

"Because Mr Eldritch is holding us hostage," Ivor explained. "He was in the wardrobe all the time. All that grunting and groaning you heard last night was him."

"Boys! I'm not holding you hostage. I just don't want you to go anywhere so am making you stay here with the threat of violence should you try to leave," Eldritch said.

"Why, though? I don't understand," George asked. "What do you want from us?"

"Well, I must admit, I've enjoyed the probing I've had from the three of you," Eldritch said.

"Ooh, have I missed out on all the fun again!" wailed Lindsey.

"But I'm also waiting for this Uppham character to come with my wad," Eldritch continued, looking at Lindsey suspiciously.

"What do you want from him?" Ivor gulped. Had it all been a trick? Had he, Doctor Ivor Mallard, been duped? Was Sir Richard about to return, having conspired all along with the evil Eldritch? What then?

"Well, I promised to get rid of you lot for him. Good job I didn't, if he had no intention of paying me. Should he turn up today, though, I'll just mug him and let you boys off, seeing as how we're now all friends," Eldritch said, moving to the window and peering down the street, in the hope of seeing Sir Richard.

"Sir Richard? Oh, he's been and gone," said George

"What! When?" Eldritch said, taking George by the scruff of his neck.

"No, he hasn't. Have you been drinking again, George?" Ivor said, panicking.

"No, you remember, Ivor. God, I thought it was me that was thick! A few days ago. That's how we got all the new furniture so quickly, remember? You mugged him of that ten pounds that he had on him ... oops ... sorry, Ivor!" George said, realising too late he'd let the proverbial cat out of the bag.

Fancy a Quickie?

"Where's the money, Mallard? God help me, I'm not a materialistic man, but I'll kill every one of you if I don't get my hands on that cash!" Eldritch spat.

"It's all gone. We spent it. Like George just said, we bought new furniture and clothes."

"We had all our clothes bought for ... ouch!" George began before Ivor curtailed the latest admission with an elbow to his ribs.

"Hang on a minute! Ronald has got all his left! He only gave us his share for the furniture and I know he's only bought a bullwhip. That man is worth thousands," Ivor said, getting to his feet and pointing an accusatory finger at Stumpf.

"Right then, you old huckster! Business is business and I want some cash!" Eldritch shouted, lifting Ronald over his shoulder and striding to the door with him. "And just in case any of you tossers get the bright idea of trying to escape, I'm locking the door and taking the key with me. If I hear so much as a peep out of any of you, I'll be in here as fast as my fat legs can carry me, ready to kick your arses out of that window."

"Well, I don't think much of him! What a dreadful philistine. Please tell me he's not a friend of yours, Ivor. I simply couldn't bear to go on living here if I thought you fraternised with such people," Lindsey said, as Eldritch closed the door and turned the key in the lock.

"Look, Lindsey, we might not go on living at all. The man is mad! For God's sake, he sold his own brother to a Doctor-cum-resurrectionist!"

"No, he didn't! He sold him to me, actually!" George said proudly.

"Yes, George, I know it was you but I was trying to save you embarrassment."

"But how on earth do you know him? Was he a patient of yours?" Lindsey asked.

"I think I knew his brother first," Ivor said, screwing up his face as he tried to remember.

"Oh, the fat fugger?" George volunteered.

"Yes, the fat fugger. You remember, Lindsey? At the fayre? He was the chap playing Blackbeard whilst his friend danced the hornpipe," Ivor said.

"Oh yes! Do I ever," Lindsey said, a smile on his face as the memory came back to him.

"Yes, well his brother used to get all my medicinal supplies. This was when I was still travelling around from place to place. I think I bought some mummified flesh from Egypt off him and it turned out to be bogus. We took it back and got a refund but the funny thing was that the bogus stuff worked better! When we asked him where he'd got it from, he said his brother made it by painting new bodies in asphalt and leaving them for a few months so that they looked old. He then put us in contact with his brother - Eldritch - and Bob's your uncle," Ivor said.

"And Fanny's your auntie!" George quipped as a shrill scream penetrated the house.

"Oh, God, poor Ronald! What foul perversions is Eldritch exacting on him, just to get him to talk?" Ivor said aloud.

"Perhaps he's showing him some erotic woodcuts of Nurse Conwy," George said.

"Poor Ronald!" Lindsey remarked, wrinkling his nose.

"Yes, alright! Our dear partner is down there now, possibly sacrificing his life so that we might live. I don't think it's right we should be getting some sort of thrill from trying to imagine the most painful death we can think of for him, do you?" Ivor asked.

"Perhaps he's boiling his head in oil!" George said excitedly,

"God, that would be a good one, wouldn't it?" Ivor said, his eyes lighting up. "Or maybe nailing his scrotum to a tree, all the while beating his bare buttocks with a burning log just to make him dance ... and dance until he's danced a confession out of him! No, this is not right!" he said, crossing his hands in front of him and throwing them wide apart as though he were banishing such thoughts from his mind.

"We need to do something to take our minds off things!" pondered George.

"I don't think talking about what might be happening to Ronald is going to ease our minds. After all, he might get a taste for torture and wish to refine his craft on us," Lindsey said.

"Oh bollocks! I'd never thought of that," said George, starting to shake, his bottom lip beginning to quiver.

Fancy a Quickie?

"Look, we must stay calm," Ivor advised, just as a second scream echoed through the house.

"I recognise that scream," George said. "That was the sound old Jones made when I spilt that peppermint oil on his haemorrhoids."

"What a charming story!" Lindsey remarked.

Before any more observations could be made, the sound of a series of banging doors caused the small group to all to hold their breath in terrified expectation. As they listened in mute silence, the sound of heavy footsteps drew nearer and nearer the door.

"Oh, God, we're done for," George said, gripping Ivor's arm and burying his head in his shoulder.

"Ronald!" Ivor shouted, jumping to his feet and knocking George into the wall. How did you get out of that? We all thought you were done for!"

"Ivor said he wanted Eldritch to beat your bare buttocks with a burning log and make you dance for him," George said to Ronald as he pointed at Ivor.

"Shut up, George. Don't be silly! Ronald knows I'd never come out with anything as ridiculous as that," Ivor snapped, blushing to the roots of his hair.

"Nobody messed with the Stumpf," Ronald said proudly

"Well? What happened?" Ivor gushed.

"She carried me down to my room and threw me on the bed. She then made a few threats, so I showed her the money and said if she'd like a *Quickie*, the money was all hers," Ronald explained

"Ronald, why are you calling Eldritch 'she'? He's a fat git with a full beard! Anyway, I'm not surprised he didn't fancy a *Quickie*! Those drinks are for *real* men," Ivor laughed.

"Who's talking about the drink?" Ronald slavered.

"You mean ... uh!" George gasped.

"Well, she wasn't having any of it, so when she grabbed the cash there was a bit of unpleasantness," Ronald continued.

"What, you hit her ... I mean *him*?" Ivor asked, his eyes bulging from his head.

"No. I broke wind and she passed out. I dragged her down the stairs and left her on the doorstep," Ronald concluded.

"Ronald, *he* is not a *she*. Put your specs on!" Ivor said in exasperation

"Ivor, I *am* a medical man. I flatter myself I know the difference between a man and a woman. If these chunky babes want to grow a bit of bush on their faces, it's not going to fool me! It just gives us proper men more to hang on to when the real action starts," he drooled.

"Well, at least we're out of that pickle. Hooray for Ronald!" Ivor said, loosening his neckerchief and breathing a sigh of relief.

"Hadn't we better get rid of him off that front doorstep, Ivor?" George asked. "You know, it really isn't good for business to have an unconscious grave-robber on your doorstep."

"Good point. I'm loathe to go and look, but I suppose we're going to have to," Ivor conceded.

As the four descended the stairs, Ivor moved stealthily to the window.

"No, he's gone!" said George cheerily, opening the front door.

"George, I was going to look through the window first," Ivor said. "Supposing he had been there and had jumped on you?"

"Yes, but he wasn't, was he?"

"No, but you didn't know that!" Ivor replied.

"No, but I do now, so what's your point?"

"The point is, be a bit more careful next time and don't be a smart ass. No one likes a smart ass, least of all me," Ivor said, poking George in the eye.

"Is this your dog?" came a shrill agitated voice.

"I'm sorry, did you say something?" Ivor said, looking around the room.

"It was me and I asked you if this is your dog," said a woman, holding Himbry the surgery dog. He panted heavily, little disguising the fact that underneath that bluff demeanour he was looking very pleased with himself.

"Madam," Ivor said haughtily, "You know full well the dog is mine. May I take it that you have some other reason for asking, other than the general enquiry of ownership?"

Fancy a Quickie?

"He's gone and got my Molly pregnant, that's all," the woman shouted, raising her finger and thrusting it to within an inch of Ivor's face.

"It would seem then, that your daughter should pick her boyfriend's more carefully. Might I suggest a man next time? He's a beautiful dog but he's no ... um ... Doctor Stumpf," Ivor said, getting a thumb's up and a wink from Ronald.

"Don't come that with me! My Molly's my little dog. And your bloody dog has taken her innocence!"

Ivor gasped and took a step backwards.

"Thank you, Mrs Jones. I'll deal with this now," he said, taking Himbry from the woman and closing the door behind him.

The Way the Buggers Bounce

"Oh, God, I don't believe this," Ivor said, flopping into a chair. "Why couldn't you have been more careful? For twelve years I've given you everything! Tried to show you right from wrong, given you a good set of values by which to live and then what happens? You turn around and do something like this! Why, when we were happy as we were, did you have to go and do this? I don't know what your mother would say if she were still alive."

"Now you know why I don't like dogs," Ronald muttered. "No morals. You've brought shame on the house," he added, emphasising his disapproval with a wagging finger. "He's not even taking this seriously! This dog of yours is winking at me!"

"He's not winking at you, Ronald, he's walking away from you," Ivor said in exasperation. "Put on your specs, you vain old fool!"

"I don't need specs! I have the best eyesight. *Nobody* has better eyesight than me!" Ronald said indignantly.

"And what's all this 'my dog' business? He's always 'our' dog until he does something wrong then, all of a sudden, he's 'my dog'. That's just so typical of you!" Ivor retorted, ignoring Doctor Stumpf's boast. "My mother warned me this is what you'd be like, but would I listen? No! I thought I knew better. 'He's not like all the other Quacks I've met', I said. 'I really think I can trust him', I said. God, I must have been blind to think you were any different from the others! Well, all I can say is that it's not hard to see where this dog has picked up his bad habits, is it?"

"You should write for the fake news! And as for your mother! Don't you start bringing her into this! I was warned at the time that if you want to know what your business partner's going to be like in twenty years all you need to do is look at his mother," Ronald said, waving his arms in despair.

Mallard the Quack

"And what's that supposed to mean?" Ivor said, standing up and moving over to Ronald who had now folded his arms in affected superiority.

"Do I really have to explain?" said Ronald. "I'd have thought that your father would have been the one to tell you - that is if he's still allowed to have an opinion that doesn't differ from your mothers!"

"That's a horrible thing to say! That woman spent hours – literally, *hours* - on my education, turning me into the caring person I am today. I don't think your mother ever did the same, did she?"

"You leave my mother out of this," Ronald said, Ivor's barbs suddenly penetrating Ronald's paper-thin armour.

"Oh, now we've found a weak spot, haven't we?" Ivor said smugly. "The truth hurts, doesn't it!"

"Well, at least my mother was my real mother! My mother didn't give me away because I came a poor second to the Christmas turkey!" Ronald said vehemently.

"How dare you! Get out of my house," Ivor said, taking Ronald by the arm.

"But I've only got my drawers on!" Ronald protested.

"Well, you should have thought of that first, shouldn't you?" Ivor hissed.

"Besides, it's my house," Ronald said, playing his trump card.

"Then get out of *your* house!" Ivor shouted.

"Hold on a minute. Aren't we getting away from what this argument's all about?" Ronald asked.

"Yes. Yes, we are," Ivor agreed. "You see the trouble you've caused?" he added, turning roundly on Himbry, who now hung his head in shame. "We never used to be like this! We were happy until you dragged our good name through the gutter!"

"I don't know what you were thinking," Ronald added solemnly. "Didn't you stop to think of the consequences for just one second, before following such impulses? Weren't you capable of any self-control?"

"Now I see how it really is! You've never cared for us at all, have you?" Ivor said, looking at Himbry who, by now, was lying on the floor with his paws over his face, looking thoroughly ashamed of himself. "We were just a convenience for you. Somewhere to lay your head and fill your stomach while, all along, you led a life of depravity - a life you knew would be the ruin of us! Is that how you repay us? Is it? You don't even seem like the same dog I nursed as a little puppy. You were such a beautiful little puppy," he added, wiping a tear from his eyes. "I was so proud of you that first time you brought your stick back to me. So proud that first time you sat when I asked. I can't help asking myself 'where did it all go wrong?' Was it my fault? Was it something I said or did?"

"I knew naming him Hombre was a mistake! He's a Mexican!" said Ronald, waving a finger at Ivor.

"Come on, you two," George said, in his most sympathetic tones. "You only did what you felt was right, all along. There's no sense in pointing the finger now, trying to find someone to blame. All we can say is that it's happened, so let's deal with it."

"Yes, you're right, George. I know that. It's just come like a bolt from the blue. I'm too young to be a grandfather!" Ivor said, dabbing his eyes. "And I'm too old to hear the scamper of tiny paws about the place. Getting up in the middle of the night, making sure they're clean and fed, worrying myself sick when they're ill. I can't take it! I'm not a young man anymore."

"Are you happy, eh? Happy now that you've caused so much trouble?" Ivor said tearfully, leaning over Himbry, who shuffled uneasily and slapped his lips in self-consciousness, before lying on his side and trying to dig a hole in the carpet in which to bury his shame and humiliation.

As the tension in the room became so heavy it threatened to suffocate the group, there came a defiant knock at the door.

"Oh, balls! If it's that Jones' woman she'll get a piece of my mind, just see if she doesn't," Ivor said, angrily getting to his feet and marching to the window.

"And mine!" added George, helpfully.

"Who is it?" asked Ronald, watching the colour drain from Ivor's face.

Mallard the Quack

"It's Sir Richard. I thought we'd seen the last of him. I knew he wouldn't go to the law on us because they'd ask too many questions but I didn't think he'd have the balls to come back here, especially given that plan of his that Eldritch told us about," Ivor said, suddenly turning into the room and pacing up and down in a frantic, scheming manner.

"Daddy! Ivor said it was you. He saw you through the window," said George who, unseen by Ivor and the others, had opened the door and beckoned his father to enter.

Ivor stared incredulously at George, wishing a huge weight would suddenly fall from the sky and smash him into the ground.

"George. I suppose I don't need to ask if your brother is here as well, given you've already said that he is. May I come in? There's something I feel you both ought to know," Sir Richard said flatly.

"Sir Richard! I hope you didn't take offence at my little joke last time you visited? I'm afraid my humour can be a little black at times," Ivor said, bowing and smiling as broadly as he could manage.

"Joke? Well, I didn't see the funny side," he muttered, making himself comfortable on a sofa. "I hope you don't mind, gentlemen, but the matter is rather delicate," he added, looking at Ronald and Lindsey, neither of whom took the hint to leave the room.

"Well, it's nice to see that you've got all your furniture back. That must have been some joke, moving all that just to kid your mother and I that you'd been burgled," Sir Richard said suspiciously.

"Oh, no, we had been burgled. All this furniture is new," George said. "And do you know, the funny thing is that that desk over there," he added gesturing, to a Dutch oak bombé fronted bureau in the corner of the room, "had letters from you to a man who lived in this house at the same time as me with the same name! Can you believe that? Talk about strange coincidences!" George added, shaking his head in amazement.

Sir Richard looked astonished, then a little confused, before finishing in a state of agitation.

"And that's what you firmly believe, is it?" he asked.

"No. I'm afraid George is entirely mistaken in the matter," Ivor interrupted.

"Well, thank God one of you has a little sense," said Sir Richard, breathing a sigh of relief.

"You idiot, George!" Ivor continued, giving George a slap around the head. "Sometimes you can be such an embarrassment! Those letters weren't in that bureau at all - they were in the desk upstairs! Yes, you wouldn't believe that for a coincidence, would you? When George first showed me, I could hardly believe it myself. I mean, someone with the same name, getting a letter from you, living here and keeping it in a desk just like the one we used to have. I mean, what are the chances of that! I don't know about you but I find the whole thing a bit spooky."

Sir Richard looked from Ivor to George and back again, trying to find some nervous twitch, tick, or trace of a smile that would betray the two as having another joke at his expense. e didn't believe the first one to be a joke and the expressionless faces that now greeted him indicated this was no joke either.

"Well, perhaps I was bit impetuous last time, disinheriting you both," Sir Richard began. "You're my sons, and even if I don't like either of you, I feel duty-bound to let you know where you stand financially. As you might know," he added, before moving to the window and clasping his hands, self-assuredly, behind his back, "I sowed a few wild oats when I was younger. For years, Ivor was under the impression he was a bastard, but I felt he should know he was not."

"Yes, he is!" interrupted Ronald.

"What have I done now?" Ivor asked, his bottom lip beginning to quake.

"Anyway, as I was saying …," Sir Richard said.

"Yep, and I'm rich, baby!" Ivor said, pretending to shoot George with a make-believe pistol.

"That's what I wanted to talk to you about. You *were* rich," Sir Richard began.

"Hold on a minute! What's all this 'were' business? George was the heir until my handsome face popped out of the woodwork. I'm still the oldest, so what's changed?" Ivor asked, his face dropping to the floor.

"Well, I was married before I met your mother. I was always led to believe that my first wife was tragically clubbed to death by a gang of crazed Eskimos who mistook her for a walrus as she took the sea air at Weston. This, I've come to find out, was a mistake. She was not bludgeoned at all but simply left me for a sailor she'd met on a day trip to Frinton. I've recently received communication that she had been with child when she left and that her new man brought the children - I say *children* as I'm told they were a *pair* of strapping boys - up as his own, giving them his name. I've also found out they moved back to this area sometime later, both children going on to be upright pillars of the community."

"Who are they? Do we know these people?" asked Ivor, his mouth going dry as he felt the money slipping through his fingers like grains of sand in an egg timer.

"Not Mrs Jones down at the brothel? I just knew it would be him! I could tell by the way his eyes were too close together, just like Ivor's," George said, shaking his head at yet another coincidence.

"No, George, not a brothel keeper. I'm afraid I don't know the children's given names, only the surname - Eldritch," said Sir Richard.

To Ivor, the words seemed to echo around the room for centuries.

"Oh, no! Please tell me this can't be happening!" Ivor said, resting his head in his hands.

"Yes, well you're not the only fertile one around here!" George taunted Sir Richard, the penny having finally dropped.

"You mean ...?" Sir Richard said, turning from the window.

"Yes! Himbry's going to be a father as well," George said smugly.

"My God, what's that?" Ivor said, suddenly looking up and pointing through the window.

Sir Richard quickly turned, and as he did, Ivor propelled himself from his chair at high speed, pushing Sir Richard from the window so that amidst the shattering of glass and the splintering of timber, he tumbled to the road below.

"Oh, I get it! The old push-your-father-from-the-window-and-into-the-street routine, eh? Very clever," said George, trying another tactic he thought might give the impression of intelligence or foresight.

"No, George, you have no idea why I did that, so don't pretend you do. I was thinking of asking if he'd excuse us, but I knew he'd be too suspicious after what we did to him last time," Ivor explained.

"Oh, that practical joke you played! That was very funny," George laughed.

"No, George, it wasn't a joke. I was lying to make him believe it was a joke," Ivor said with increasing irritation.

"Well, you certainly had me fooled, you cunning old dog you!"

"Look, George, just shut up a minute, for God's sake! I pushed him from the window to buy us some time," Ivor said.

"Oh, has he got some more money on him then?"

"Eh? No, *buy us some time* is a figure of speech, halfwit! God, if I could buy time then I'd buy the last ten minutes back and push you out of the window instead," Ivor said, grabbing hold of George by the scruff of the neck.

"Oh right!" George said, as if the way Ivor had now explained it had fully clarified his misunderstanding.

"Yes, so listen. Sir Richard is lying out in the street unconscious, right? He hasn't changed his will yet, as he's only just found out that Eldritch is his legal heir, follow? Therefore, if we can stop him changing the will, all the money will still come to me ... uh, I mean us. Understand?" Ivor asked.

"Ooh, I don't know about that! If Eldritch is his legal heir, then it should be him that gets the money," George said, pursing his lips, sucking in air and frowning.

"George, you don't understand. It also makes Eldritch our half-brother! It's bad enough that I'm related to you, without having to be related to him and that ridiculous fake pirate brother of his as well," Ivor reasoned.

"Still the law's the law ... ouch!" George began, doubling up in agony as Ivor kneed him in the groin.

Mallard the Quack

"I would explain further, George, but we just don't have the time."

"I thought you said violence was never a means to an end?" George gasped breathlessly.

"It is for everyone else. I'm different," Ivor said, lifting George to his feet.

"Right, this is what we'll do. We'll bring him in. You or Lindsey can give him a *Knee Trembler* - which reminds me, I'll need to get some liniment rub. Make sure Ronald is kept in another room but slip him a couple as well."

"Er, I am still here," Ronald said, his attention having wandered as no one had been talking about him but reanimated at hearing someone mention his name.

"Meanwhile, I'll nip down the shop and get a false beard, stick it on Sir Richard and let the mighty Ronald weave some magic. If those witch-prickers could get those women to recant their witchcraft, it shouldn't be hard to get old Sir Dick to recant the fact that he's Eldritch's father."

"We'll knock some sense into him!" George said.

"That's the spirit!" Ivor smiled, giving George a pat on the back.

"Remember what I've always said, George - cash ..."

"Cash ...?" George queried, frowning and rolling his eyes.

"Yes, George, *cash* ... where does cash come, George?"

"Oh sorry, *cash comes first*!" George shouted, his face breaking into a beaming smile.

"Right then, let's go and get him inside," Ivor said, rubbing his hands.

"Said the spider to the fly," George said, seeing Ivor rub his hands and copying him.

"Eh? Can't you keep your mind on the job? Why are you talking about flies and spiders?" Ivor asked, curling up his top lip and frowning. George nodded a *no*, indicating an explanation wouldn't be worth the effort, so Ivor pressed on, moved to the door and, checking that no one was in the street tip-toed down the steps, closely followed by George.

"Bollocks! He's gone!" Ivor shouted in disbelief, staring at a dent in the road.

"Hey! Keep that language down! It's not hard to see where that dog of yours gets it from," shouted Mrs Jones from next door, slamming the upstairs window from which she was leaning before Ivor had a chance to respond.

"And not hard to see why that dog of yours had to go elsewhere for some affection, is it!" Ivor shouted.

"Doctor! Doctor! Thank God I've caught you!" a local muttered, hobbling up the road and holding his side as blood seeped through his fingers, dripping down his soiled clothing and onto the floor.

"Yes, what is it?" asked George.

"Hang on a minute, I think you'll find he was talking to me," Ivor said, pulling George's arm so that he turned to face him.

"What! I didn't hear him say *Doctor Mallard*, did you?" George asked.

"Well, I'm the more senior Doctor, so he's obviously going to be calling for me, isn't he?" Ivor said, looking George up and down with contempt.

"By 'senior', I suppose you mean old?"

"How dare you! Experience counts for everything in matters like this."

"Maybe. Of course, some would argue that those keeping abreast of the latest developments in medicine are the ones at the forefront of patient treatment."

"Please," said the man. "I don't care which one of you treats me."

"Well that's charming, isn't it?" Ivor said. "I could just be a lump of meat to you, couldn't I, just so long as I satisfy your selfish demands! What do you think I am? Some sort of a surgical slut? You're just the type of man who gets a wife simply to cook and clean for him, never sparing a second thought for her feelings! No wonder she never wants to sleep with you! She could be just *anyone*, couldn't she! You come home after an easy day's begging, expecting your food on the table, then its drawers down for a quick knee-trembler, isn't it! There's no love there! She could be anyone, just so long as she'll let you get on with your filthy business! She's just someone on whom to slake your vile lust! Well, let me tell you, buster, you're not going to use me like that! I'm no medical moll! If I wasn't good enough to begin with, then I'm not good enough now! There now. I've had my say. I don't think there's anything further to discuss between us."

"Actually, Ivor, I think he's stopped listening," George said.

"Typical! These people come along, expect you to drop everything just to treat a gaping wound in their stomach, and what thanks do you get? I'll tell you what thanks you get! None. No bloody thanks whatsoever. Then they can't even be bothered to listen to you!"

"No, I think he intended to listen, it's just that he's slipped into unconsciousness," George said.

"Typical! Just because they can't get their own way, they slip into unconsciousness! Don't fall for it, George. It's only a step up from crying and stamping their feet. Well, I'm not treating him! If he wants to play the martyr then that's entirely up to him. I'm sticking to my principles on this one. My God, whatever next!"

"Hang on, let me check his pockets," George said, bending over the man and rattling a pocket full of coins.

"Money?" said Ronald, his beady eyes ceasing to swivel for a moment. "This is going to be really great – unbelievable. *Nobody* knows more about gore wounds than me ... tremendous," Ronald said, having left the house to listen a little better when the commotion started and now trying his best to appear concerned.

"He won't thank you for it. He'll wake up and it'll be 'oh thank you, Doctor,' and he'll trundle off back to his hovel without even asking your name."

"Still, if he's got money then it's the right thing to do," Doctor Stumpf said, dragging the man by his collar to his surgery.

"Ooh, that's a nasty one," George said, having helped place the man on the surgery table and lifting his shirt. "Looks like he's been gored by a bull. Now ..." George continued, looking around the room blankly, evidently debating his next move.

"Cauterise the wound?" Ivor suggested.

"I know," said George wiping his finger on his coat before dipping it in the bloody hole. "Well, it's deeper than my finger, anyway," he added.

"Shall I stick a poker in the fire?" Ivor asked, lighting his clay pipe from a taper he'd lit from the surgery fire.

"Ivor! I'm trying to treat a sick man!" Ronald said.

"I meant a poker to cauterise the wounds not to poke the fire!" Ivor retorted

Ronald nodded a *yes* as he lowered his face to the bleeding hole and peered inside.

"Here, let me have a look," Ivor said, taking the pipe from his mouth and blowing a plume of smoke across the man's stomach, before placing his eye to the hole.

"You always try and take over, don't you?" Ronald protested.

"Just stick your poker in his hole and let's have a think about where Dick's gone," Ivor said, brushing all protestations aside.

"Ooh, I hate doing this," George said, taking the glowing poker from the fire and walking toward the man.

"Then let Ronald do it! He loves doing them! Trouble is, he likes doing them even if there's nothing wrong with the patient."

"Right, here goes," George said, plunging the poker downwards, looking the other way at the last moment.

"George, I hate to tell you this, but you've missed. That's his navel you've just cauterised! Good job the cut wasn't on his buttocks, eh? We'd have another Edward the Second on our hands!" Ivor laughed.

"Oh, it's no good! You'll have to do it," George said, handing Ronald the poker.

"Alright. Let's get this thing hot," Ronald said, walking to the fire and plunging the metal into the hot embers. "I should have been a blacksmith, you know. I'd have been a great blacksmith! *Nobody* knows more about being a blacksmith than me!" he added. Gesturing to the unconscious man with a flippant nod, he took the poker from the fire and walked back to the table. "Right then, here we go," he said, plunging it into the gaping wound. A loud hissing noise erupted as the skin

Mallard the Quack

blackened and burned, then curled up like overcooked meat. Skeins of smoke billowed from the burning flesh.

"Oh, God, that smell!" George said, turning away and retching.

"It's lovely! Reminds me of Christmas," Ronald said, sniffing even more than usual.

"Burnt food does not smell like that!" George remonstrated.

"Not the food, you halfwit! When my father came home, realised the food was burnt, and set fire to the cook. The whole family knew he was just being sarcastic," Ronald added.

"Right, we'll leave him here till he comes round," George said.

"Get the money first. You know what these people are like. They see the job done and they run out on you. What can you do then? You can't undo what you've done, can you?"

"You could always stab them," offered George.

"Don't start listening to Ronald about these things. That's the sort of thing he'd do, but no brother of mine is going in the stocks for stabbing his patients. We have the good name of Mallard, Stumpf and Uppham to think of, remember?

"Speaking of Upphams ..." reminded George.

"Yes. I wonder where that little toerag's gone. It comes to something when you can't even throw your own father from a window without him running off. I don't know what's happening to this country. In my younger days, you could throw someone from the roof and you knew by the time you got down they'd have the decency to still be lying there."

"And they say it's all the young people's fault," George said.

"I know! What can you expect when so-called pillars of the community like Sir Richard Uppham are up and away?"

"He hasn't stopped for one minute to think about the example he's setting to us," George said in disgust.

"No, you're quite right. It's alright for him and his generation though. It's us youngsters who'll suffer when we get to their age and find the country ...."

"Like Mexican!" Ronald interrupted.

The Way the Buggers Bounce

"Isn't it Mexico?" Ivor queried.

"I know words. I have the best words! Nobody knows words like me," Stumpf blustered.

"Ah, well - imagine that, eh! Anyway, we need to think about this. Already I can feel that huge estate of his slipping through my ... uh, *our* fingers," Ivor said, staring anxiously at the floor as he curled and uncurled his fingers into a clenched fist.

"Well, my money's on Eldritch turning up. Remember when Eldritch was here? He said Sir Richard had promised him money to get rid of us. That means Sir Richard must know who he is," George posited.

"Yes, you're right! I should have known they were related by the way the buggers bounce when you throw them through windows," Ivor said angrily. "So, you reckon he's gone in search of Eldritch, eh?"

"Oh, yes! But who's to say he's hasn't told Eldritch the same story he's told us? Maybe he's playing us off against one another - maybe he's kept Eldritch for all these years with a promise that the estate is going to be his, only to now tell him you're a long-lost son, so all the estate is yours."

"God, that would annoy him, wouldn't it? Still, you might be right. Eldritch was a lot friendlier than usual the other night, wasn't he? And he wanted to talk about family and things ... hang on a minute! Eldritch would never believe I'd been unmasked as his elder brother! I look years younger than he does," Ivor protested.

"I look younger than both of you!" Stumpf said, shrugging his shoulder and closing his eyes as if to indicate that was just the way of things and he had long ago learned to accept that he was far more well-endowed than other men.

"Oh yes, I, uh ... hadn't thought of that," George said, pandering to his brother's vanity. "But what I don't understand is why Sir Richard wants us all out of the way. After all, he helped with an allowance. Now all of a sudden he wants us out of the way."

"That's something I can't answer, George. But I bet I know what's at the heart of it – money! He must have some money-making scheme that we're spoiling. God, it makes me sick that people can put money before their flesh and blood!" Ivor said, shaking his head in disgust.

"But why doesn't he just give us some money to go elsewhere, if all he wants is the house?" George persisted.

"I don't know! I'm not a flippin' philosopher! Why don't you ask him when you see him?" Ivor snapped. "But you could be right about him playing us off against Eldritch. If that's the case, we can certainly expect him to come along sooner or later, just to put a grotesque end to my life of quiet contemplation and healing.

"That said, we know how thick Eldritch is - he might just think 'older than me - oh, it couldn't *possibly* be Ivor, it must be Ronald'. Which gives me a great idea! Obviously, Eldritch is going to be back, right? Well, we know he's not going to turf us out as he said he wasn't going to the other night, right? If what you think is true, he's going to be told today that I'm not only his brother but the heir to the estate as well, so he's going to come looking for *me*. If we can persuade him the person he wants is Ronald, we're home and dry," Ivor said, breaking into a wide smile and throwing his arms around George.

"Hang on a minute! Supposing he's come here to kill the heir to the estate and we persuade him it's Ronald, doesn't that mean he's going to kill Ronald?" George said with slow suspicion.

"Uh ... no," Ivor said emphatically, not daring to confirm George's insight and realising that Ronald was still in the room.

George's eyes began to roll as he screwed up his face in contemplation, looking towards the ceiling for divine inspiration.

"Oh, yes it does!" he said, after lengthy deliberation.

"Oh, who cares about that old twat! He's had a good innings anyway. He can't grumble, can he? Besides, which would you prefer? Ronald up and about or me ... uh ... us with our hands on that cash? Remember what I said now?" Ivor asked in expectation.

"Cash comes first!" George said proudly.

"Good boy!" Ivor replied, patting him on the head and giving him a sweet from his pocket.

"Listen! What's that noise?" George asked, craning his neck and straining to listen.

"It's someone trying to break in! Oh, God, it must be one of them," Ivor said, beginning to shake.

"Wait here! I'll have a look," said George, moving to the window of his surgery and peering out into the road. "You're right! It's Eldritch. No sign of Sir Richard though. Only Eldritch and that dog of his.

I am Don Juan

"Right then, here's the plan," Ivor said, drawing alongside and leaving Ronald out of earshot. "You go and finish off Eldritch, while I hide."

"Alright. What then?" George said, nodding his head in affirmation.

"That's it. That's the plan," Ivor said.

"But what about the plan we had to give Ronald enough alcohol to boof and let nature take its course?"

"Good! I like that idea. Yes, I'll go and give Ronald a few cocktails and tell him his lady friend has turned up and she can't wait to see him," Ivor said rubbing his hands and congratulating himself on his cunning.

"Right, let's do it!" George said enthusiastically.

As quietly as they could manage, George and Ivor crept from the surgery and back to the living room.

"God, I can hear him! He's out there being unstable, I just know it," Ivor said fearfully.

"It's alright for you! All you have to do is give Ronald a *Knee Trembler*. It's me that has to face *him*," George replied, his teeth beginning to chatter.

Congratulating himself on his plan, Ivor mixed two large jugs of drink, stopping every time he heard a twig snap or a leaf rustled outside.

"Oh, no! I forgot we're out of liniment rub!" Ivor said to himself, looking at the two empty bottles in the drinks cabinet.

"Oh, just use some of that anaesthetic instead," George suggested.

"Yes, he'll like that! Hot and sweet, just like his ladies!" Ivor replied, pouring some diethyl ether into the jugs.

"There should be some morphine over there as well. Give him a good slug of that. That should loosen him up!" George continued.

"By the way, George, have you got anything with which to hit Eldritch?" Ivor asked George who, by now, had moved to the window that afforded a view of the front porch.

"Only these," George said admirably, raising two clenched fists and adopting a sparring stance.

"As I thought! Nothing. Well, just in case Ronald doesn't want to play ball, you'd better come with me," Ivor gestured, nodding to Nurse Conwy's former room.

"Why, what's in there?" George asked.

"Here you are," Ivor said, lifting a floorboard. "Here are some chains, some manacles, shackles, a whip, a mask, some all-purpose restraints. Take your pick," he added, handing them all to George.

"But what's all this doing here?" George asked in astonishment.

"Oh, I ... uh ... advised Nurse Conwy to get it in, just in case an emergency like this ever arose. Lucky, eh?" Ivor replied furtively.

"I should say!" said George, taking them from him. "And what a piece of luck all this leather gear is so sticky! Someone could have a nasty accident if it were all shiny and slippery."

"We *want* someone to have a nasty accident, halfwit! We want someone dead, remember? He's not going to die without meeting a *very* nasty accident, is he?" Ivor asked.

"Oh, right! Leave it to me, Ivor! When have I ever let you down?"

"Oh, God, this just isn't going to work, is it? Why don't I just kill myself and get you to hand me to him on a plate?" Ivor sighed.

"Oh, come on, Ivor! Never despair," George said cheerfully as the noise of a dog yelp came from outside. "God, even his dog sounds murderous."

"Yes, thank you for trying to allay my fears, George! I'm off to see Ronald and give him a *Quickie*," Ivor replied, turning on his heels and running as fast as his jugs would allow. Scaling the stairs two at a time, Ivor quickly arrived at Ronald's room. By now, it was late afternoon, so Ivor knew Ronald would be 'relaxing'.

"Ronald! Ronald! It's me, Ivor. Can I come in?" Ivor asked, only to be greeted by absolute silence. "Oh, God, please let him be in!" Ivor said to himself, putting his jugs on the floor and twisting Ronald's knob.

I am Don Juan

As Ivor opened the door, Ronald turned around in his chair to face him, the pipe from an enormous hookah trailing from his mouth.

"Peace, man," Ronald mumbled as he slid back into his chair, a look of absolute bliss spreading across his orange face.

"What do you mean 'peace'? Since when have you ever been into peace, you swine! With Devil's Lettuce as well!" Ivor shouted, putting his jugs on Ronald's desk.

"Hey man, don't spoil my scene. I've got a real good groove going on here!" Ronald muttered.

"No. You don't understand! That big woman who was here a few days ago. The one you left on the doorstep, remember? She's back, and I think she's got love on her mind," Ivor said desperately. "I've brought you a few drinks to get you in the mood."

"No, man, I'm just chillin'. Tell her to come back some other time."

"No, you swine! It's now or never," Ivor said, taking hold of Ronald's head and attempting to empty one of the jugs down his throat. Only then did he spot *Doctor Ronald Stumpf's Patented Enema Kit* lying nearby. "I'm sorry Ronald. I would explain, but you're not really in a position to listen," Ivor added, grabbing hold of the kit and pouring the drink into the bag that was still half-full of soapy water. Taking the pipe, he thrust it down Ronald's throat, giving the bag as hard a squeeze as possible.

Ronald's eyes bulged for a moment before he slid to the floor and underneath the desk. Ivor took a step back fearing the worst. The effect could not have been more dramatic. Suddenly the table rattled violently then, as if propelled from the floor by springs, Ronald jumped to a standing position, foam and slaver drooling from his mouth.

"Ronald?" Ivor asked nervously

"No, I am Don Juan. The greatest lover in all of Mexican!" Ronald answered in a fake Spanish accent.

"Mexico," Ivor said, waving a finger.

"Mexican! I have the best words," Ronald said, clicking his fingers above his head as though they were castanets.

"Don Juan? Well, Donald, there's a chunky babe downstairs with a bushier beard than Sancho Panza. Go to it, tiger!" Ivor said, breathing a sigh of relief as Ronald waddled to the surgery window, only becoming concerned when Ronald stepped from the window and shimmied down the drainpipe, dropping into the garden below. Ivor watched in amazement as Ronald then plucked a rose and placed it between his upper and lower dentures, before unbuttoning his shirt and moving off like a flamenco-dancing Don Juan in search of his Elvire - the unsuspecting Eldritch!

"What's going on? I heard someone gagging and had to come and investigate," said Lindsey.

"It's Eldritch. He's back and he means to kill me. I've just talked Ronald into dealing with it," Ivor explained.

"Oh, how gallant of him! It's just like a chivalric romance," Lindsey said, clasping his hands together and smiling broadly. "We must go and see how he fares," he added, leading Ivor to the door.

"I'm not sure. I really think I ought to keep a low profile on this one," Ivor said.

As if circumstances weren't bad enough, at that moment an almighty crash of thunder exploded in the heavens, followed by the gentle patter of rain.

"Oh, no, that's all I need," Ivor said, curling himself up into a ball and rocking back and forth, burying his face in his hands.

"Oh, go on! You're not frightened of a bang or two, are you? A big strapping Doctor like you?" teased Lindsey.

"No, it's not that. This is the first thunderstorm we've had since you lived here, isn't it?" Ivor said, looking up at Lindsey.

"Yes, but I don't get your point."

"Well, George thinks electricity is going to be the power of the future and every time there's a storm, he runs around on the roof in the nude trying to capture power from a bolt of lightning."

"Does he now! Fancy that!"

"The problem is, I've asked him to help me deal with Eldritch as well, but I know full well he's going to be up on

I am Don Juan

that roof parading around with no thought for anyone but himself," Ivor said helplessly.

"Then we must go and look," Lindsey said, creeping along to George's room. Even before they arrived, Ivor knew his worst fears had been confirmed. George's door was open, as was his window. A powerful wind gusted in, blowing the curtains around and giving the room an eerie and abandoned look.

"Yoo-hoo!" Lindsey shouted, leaning from the window and waving. "No, it's hopeless. He can't hear me. What a shame he's in profile. I've always thought his profile his poorest angle," he added.

"Lindsey, please tell me this isn't happening! I've got a madman trying to kill me and who, even as I speak, is trying to break in. My brother's on the roof in the nude, without a care in the world, and Don Juan down there is flamenco-dancing his way around the garden, trying not to get thorns caught in his false teeth! Could things get any worse?"

"Well, it's not looking great for you, is it?" Lindsey said with resignation. "I still think we should go and have a look for this Eldritch ourselves."

"Wait! I have it. If I give you a *Knee Trembler*, you could lay out old Eldritch for me, just like you did the other night," Ivor said excitedly.

"I beg your pardon? You're taking a few liberties, aren't you? I've heard about landlords like you. Isn't it called *payment in kind*? Well, you can forget it, you sordid little man," Lindsey said.

"No! No! I want you to drink it, and then put those hands of yours to some good use!"

"Right, that is it!" Lindsey said, rising to his feet and storming from the room.

"Oh, God! So, it's just me and old Eldritch! Where is Ronald! Oh, God, if only I wasn't so nice then none of this would have happened! Still, if I am to die, it'll prove the saying that only the good die young," Ivor said to himself.

Suddenly there was a loud crash downstairs, along with the sound of splintering wood. Ivor braced himself and walked slowly to the top of the stairs, descending them one at a time until, finally, he had the barest of vantage points from which to see but not be seen.

As he looked down the passageway, the paunchy figure of Eldritch strode into view.

"Ivor, I need to speak to you. I'm very upset by what you just said to me," Lindsey said curtly, descending the stairs behind him.

"Well ... um ... uh ... Lindsey, this really isn't a good time, you know," Ivor said as quietly as possible.

"When *would* be a good time? I won't be fobbed off you know! I don't know why you think you can take such liberties with me!"

"Lindsey, be quiet! Eldritch is down there with bloody murder on his mind, with the bloody murder victim being me!" Ivor hissed, making frantic motions with his hands.

"No, I won't! There are some things about which you just can't keep quiet, and this is one of them," Lindsey said, dabbing his eyes.

"Where am I? What's going on?" came a strange voice. Ivor turned and squinted. It was the local Ronald had cauterised earlier that day. Now wandering around in a daze, he supported himself by resting his hands against the walls, in so doing leaving a trail of bloody smears behind him.

Ivor watched as Eldritch stopped and listened, given he had heard the same voice as Ivor. His nostrils flared as he moved his head, trying his best to find out from where the sound originated.

As the storm howled and raged outside, a huge gust of wind rattled every window in the house, banging the roof tiles and whistling through the cracks, then blowing open the door that led to the cellar, exposing precipitous stone steps that led down into the darkness.

Ivor screwed up his face and closed his eyes, bringing his hands up and wishing he was somewhere else. Alas, if wishes were horses then beggars would ride, for when he opened them again, yet another character had entered the scene.

Himbry, evidently buoyed by his earlier conquest, had now become a canine Don Juan, striding cockily into the hall, evidently acting upon the glad eye he had for Eldritch's dog.

I am Don Juan

"Come by, girl," Eldritch said hoarsely, slapping his thigh as his dog moved off. It was too late! Cupid's arrows had been fired and, in an instant, Himbry had begun that at which he had lately proven so adept.

"Hey!" Eldritch shouted, striding over to his dog and trying to part the two of them. As the wind continued blowing ruthlessly through his hair, he and the dogs stood atop the cellar steps.

"Where am I? What's going on?" came a voice in the distance.

Eldritch struggled to pull his dog from the throes of passion but to no avail. Only then, like an avenging angel, did Ivor notice the rapid-fire clicking of castanets and the stamp of a Cuban heel as Ronald came racing up the passageway as fast as his bone spurs would allow.

"I see you are waiting for me, my dear!" Ronald leered in fake Andalusian, the seductive effect considerably diminished by the toilet paper stuck to the sole of his shoe.

For a moment Ivor caught the surprise on Eldritch's face, just before Ronald's thrusting hips caught Eldritch roughly from behind sending him crashing, head first, down the stone steps of the cellar.

"Ah, you little tease!" Ronald shouted, quickly following.

"Where am I? What's going on?" came a voice in the distance.

"Oh, God! Thank you! Thank you!" Ivor shouted, blowing kisses towards the sky then running down the stairs and across the passageway, towards the splintered door.

"George, you selfish swine!" Ivor shouted as soon as he got outside, spying his brother on the roof.

"Where am I? What's going on?" came a voice in the distance, the cauterised local now hopelessly lost in the large old house.

"Eh?" George shouted, cupping his hand to his ear and leaning from the roof.

"And put on some clothes! What'll our patients think!" Ivor shouted.

Mallard the Quack

"I'll tell you what they'll think - they'll think you're all as bad as that dog of yours!" Mrs Jones from next door said, poking Ivor hard in the back.

"Listen, you old bag, why don't you bugger off!" Ivor said, spinning on his heels. "Don't you think I've got enough to worry about! I've got a hairy madman trying to kill me, my senior Doctor thinks he's Don Juan and is trying to seduce a hirsute lunatic in the mistaken belief he's a bearded lady, and my brother's on the roof in the nude! As if that wasn't enough, my lodger's crying because I've unwittingly offended him, a gored patient is getting his filthy hands all over my walls and a stack of cash is slipping through my grasp even as I speak - and all because my father bounced when I threw him from the window!" Ivor shouted, his eyes becoming wild and glazed.

Mrs Jones took a step backwards, picked up her dog and ran back to her house.

"What was that?" George shouted, the rain still beating heavily on the roof tiles and his naked body.

"I said I'm going to wring your scrawny neck when I get hold of you!" Ivor shouted.

"Eh?" George replied. "I can't hear you. Anyway, I don't want to worry you, but ..." he added, pointing a little way up the road.

"Oh my God!" Ivor said, turning quickly, only to see Blackbeard Eldritch walking towards him, his face clouded with murderous intent.

Ivor ran back into the house and desperately began piling furniture against the splintered remains of the door. From the few cracks left unfilled, the one-legged buccaneer could be seen drawing nearer and nearer, like a forest fire in its unstoppable fury.

"Well, that's it. I've had it! One of them was bad enough, but there's no way I'm going to get rid of two," Ivor said aloud, resigning himself to his fate. "Oh, God, I'm not a bad person! Why do so many bad things get sent my way!" he cursed, raising his fist to the sky and shaking it defiantly.

Just when Ivor had given up hope and could swear the *clump-tick, clump-tick* of Eldritch's walk was ringing in his ears, there came a terrible crashing of roof tiles followed by a sickening thud as if a ton of clay had been dropped onto a marble plinth. Cautiously, Ivor opened one eye and pressed it to a crack in the door to look outside.

"Look out, George! He's behind you!" Ivor shouted, now that he could see George had tumbled from the roof and landed slap-bang on top of the approaching villain. "George, watch where he's putting that peg-leg of his! Ooh!" Ivor winced, closing his eyes and looking away. "George, quick! Take it out and hit him with it! Hooray, you did it! You bloody well did it!" he added, tearing the furniture away and running into the road.

"I wouldn't let you down, would I, Ivor?" George said, stepping over the ocean of flesh that separated them.

"That's two down, one to go," Ivor said, taking the naked George by the hand and waltzing with him down the street, despite the rain and the sight of Mrs Jones and her pooch watching from her window.

"Mummy!" George said, abruptly breaking from Ivor's embrace and running up the street to a carriage that had just drawn near.

"Is your father here, George?" Lady Francesca asked, stepping down into the street.

"Not yet, but we are expecting him," George answered tentatively.

"Then would you mind if I came in and waited for him?" she asked, beginning to sob.

The rain continued to cut into the three figures as they quickly made their way back to the house.

"Oh darling, you really should cover yourself up," Lady Francesca said to George, just before her attention was caught by the mountain of flab laid out a few feet from the door.

"Oh, not again!" Ivor said, looking at the body. "I don't know who keeps leaving these here!" He looked up and down the street as though he were expecting to see a small army making a hasty retreat. "After all, we're only Doctors, not miracle workers," he added, looking at Lady Francesca from the corner of his eye. George helped his mother step over the body and held her hand as she took a few steps towards what was left of the front door.

"Oh, no! Don't tell me we've been burgled again!" Ivor said, wringing his hands, as the three of them stared aghast at the remains of the door.

"No, it looks like everything's here," George said, glancing up the empty corridor.

"Where am I? What's going on?" came a voice close by, a moment before the local rounded a far-off corner and entered the passageway. Spying the open door behind George, Ivor and Lady Francesca the local ran, as best he could, past all three before falling headfirst into Blackbeard Eldritch, disappearing from view as the rolls of flab folded around him like soft blankets.

An agitated bark came from the top of the cellar steps as Himbry and his beloved struggled to be free of one another, presaging the entry of the practice's senior Doctor.

"She's not the woman I loved!" Ronald cried as he mounted the cellar steps, and came face to face with Ivor, George and Lady Francesca.

"Who's?" Lady Francesca asked, taking Ronald by the arm, and looking helplessly at Ivor and George.

"The only woman that I, *El Burlador De Sevilla*, ever loved," Ronald said, raising one hand in proud defiance as he stretched the vowels of his words to breaking point, whilst slipping his free hand around Lady Francesca's waist.

"George, go and get some clothes on. I'll try and deal with this," Ivor whispered, pulling George to one side.

"Right," George said, giving Ivor a thumbs-up.

"Lady Francesca ... Mother, this is Ronald," Ivor began. "You'll recognise him from your last visit. Unfortunately, he seems to have ..." Ivor's words trailed off as Ronald took Lady Francesca's hand in his and smothered it in mad kisses. Lady Francesca pulled a face, as though a large slug were sliding over it.

"Psst, Ivor!" George said, calling from the same vantage point on the stairs that Ivor had occupied earlier.

"What is it?" Ivor asked, half-running towards George whilst trying to keep an uneasy eye on Ronald.

I am Don Juan

"Lindsey's very upset. He just said to me that you don't show him any respect and that you wouldn't have spoken to him like that if he'd been a woman!" George said.

"I didn't mean anything by what I said. He's too sensitive. Now, will you get some clothes on!" Ivor shouted through gritted teeth.

"But if Lindsey was a woman, he wouldn't have a pair of these!" George sniggered, adopting a bow-legged stance and pointing at his wedding tackle.

"Neither will you if you don't get your backside in that bedroom and get dressed," Ivor said.

"Oh! That reminds me! The second thing I meant to tell you!" George said, slapping his forehead with the palm of his hand.

"Oh, no! What have you forgotten now?"

"I went to put on some clothes and who do you think I saw from my window? Yes, it was Sir Richard! I have to say, he didn't look at all happy ...."

"You saw Sir Richard? Was he coming here? Why didn't you tell me straight away? I think it's a bit more important than Lindsey's prima donna routine," Ivor shouted.

"No, but Lindsey as a woman!" George giggled.

"Look, George, on your head be it but when Sir Richard finds out you've killed his two eldest sons, I wouldn't like to be in your shoes," Ivor reasoned, trying a different line of attack.

"Both of them? It was only the one and that was a mistake!"

"You swine! You had me believe you did it just for me! You didn't do anything of the sort! It was just luck that you fell on him, and then you only hit him because he started hitting you," Ivor said, trying to grab George by the lapels but, given that George was naked, grabbing a handful of chest hair instead.

"Oh, so you want to fight dirty, do you?" George said, pinching Ivor's nipples.

"Look, this isn't getting us anywhere," Ivor winced.

"You're only saying that 'cause you're losing," George said, giving his hands a half turn, back and forth.

Mallard the Quack

"Swine!" Ivor said, releasing his grip on George's chest hair before taking aim with his finger and releasing one well-aimed flick that caught George in that sensitive spot that only men know about, felling him like an axed tree.

"Ooh," George gasped, releasing his grip as he fell into a quivering mass on the floor.

"Play with fire, sonny, you get your fingers burned," Ivor said, blowing the end of his finger as though it were a pistol.

A door slammed across the landing and Lindsey strode past, carrying a suitcase and weeping.

"You don't think he's off out for a drink, do you? I could so do with one," George said breathlessly.

"No, I don't think The Pig and Ferret will be beckoning tonight, somehow. I wonder where he is going?" Ivor said thoughtfully, walking to the top of the stairs and craning his neck to try and see where Lindsey had disappeared.

"Excuse me, have there been any visitors here over the last few hours?" someone asked. As Ivor squinted, he could see it was Sir Richard, who'd waylaid Lindsey at the front door.

"Well, no one's visited me," Lindsey said. "But then they wouldn't, would they!" he shouted, turning and dropping his suitcase. "After all, I'm just a freak, aren't I? Just a convenience! Who'd visit me because they like me when they can visit me and exploit me?" he wept.

"Yes, the swine! I feel the same way. I paid a couple of friends of mine to come around and throw them out," Sir Richard said to Lindsey, looking around the hall for signs that the deed had been done.

"A-ha! Thought you'd got one over on us, did you? Though we'd believe those Eldritch brothers were our brothers as well? Well, you were wrong! We're just too smart for you! We knew your plan even before you did. Then - to the very last detail! - we knew how to outwit you," Ivor said, swaggering down the stairs, full of bravado, followed by George, who had now dressed.

"I've spent a fortune on you useless pair over the years. As soon as I realised that I'd never get the money back, what else was I to do but get this house off you and sell it?" Sir Richard stormed.

"What! That's just what I'd have expected from you! Putting money before your own flesh and blood! You'd see us homeless just to recoup some money! You disgust me!" Ivor said with contempt.

"I've something to announce!" Lady Francesca said as Ronald carried her from the living room into the hall. "Ronald has asked me to marry him and I've accepted," she giggled. "Just as soon as my husband gives me my divorce."

"Ronald?" Ivor said in astonishment, sitting himself down on the stairs as his knees buckled.

"She could not resist the charms of her Sevilla sweetheart," Ronald explained, kissing the end of Lady Francesca's nose.

"Fran! How could you do this to me?" Sir Richard bleated. "I blame you two for this!" Sir Richard said, pointing a stubby finger at Ivor and George. "The best day's work I ever did was getting rid of you and keeping that turkey! Well, if we're on the subject of confessions, here's one! I've disinherited the pair of you!" he added, turning as fast as he could and punching Ronald squarely in the face. In the commotion that followed, George laid a hand on Ivor's shoulder as the two of them watched the fight's progress.

"Well, look at it like this, Ivor," George laughed. "You aren't any poorer, as it was money you never had. And you haven't so much lost a father, as gained a stable genius!"

"Could everyone listen," Stumpf shouted, bringing his tiny orange finger to his lips. "I've lost the only loves of my life twice today so I'm emigrating to America. There's big money to be made over there for a man like me! It's going to be *unbelievable!*"

Immortal Seduction

Adam Nicke

Adam Nicke was born near Caerleon in Wales on the Lupercalia, just a few miles from where the Gothic author Arthur Machen was born in 1863.

In his early twenties his artistic tendencies were expressed in the designing and making of clothes, most notably for Wayne Hussey of The Mission.

In 2015, after being plagued by years of depression and being told that nothing but counselling would help, he collapsed and underwent neurosurgery for the removal of a previously undiagnosed tennis ball-sized brain tumour.

He has a Bachelor of Arts degree in Literary Studies from the University of the West of England. His thesis was written on The Metamorphosis of the Devil in Legend and Literature.

Adam Nicke Publishing

Chapter One

Cassandra Wyvern hadn't been at her friend, Anna Harris', house for very long before the floodgates of frustration opened.

"Why should I feel embarrassed to say that I'm a woman who enjoys sex?" said Cassandra.

"You shouldn't, babe," said her friend, Anna.

"Thank you! Simeon makes me feel like a slut if I suggest something new. I don't even enjoy sex with him as his idea of foreplay is me giving him a blowjob! He won't even try a sixty-nine with me as he says – and I quote – 'I'm not licking a drain'," Cassandra said, rolling her eyes and shaking her fists at the heavens in exasperation.

"The cheeky bastard," Anna said, widening her eyes in shock. "Let's have a glass of wine and go into the garden - and we can set the world right."

"Only the one? After the sex I'm getting, I need a bottle! Haven't you got any gin?"

"A drop of mother's ruin? Why not!" Anna laughed, opening a bottle of gin before going to her fridge for a bottle of tonic water.

"He also tells me he can do better than me," Cassandra said.

"I've never met this guy, Cass, but he'd have to be pretty special to get someone better than you."

"Thank you," Cassandra replied. "He tells me I'm ugly."

"What a crock of crap!" Anna said. "You look like Shannyn Sossamon – and she's beautiful."

"Thank you, that's very kind of you – but doesn't she have short hair?"

"She has long hair in a few movies but I was talking about her face. God, the things I'd like to do to her!" said Anna.

The two women made their way from Anna's kitchen, through her dining room and out onto her patio.

"I don't want to brag but my sex life is great!" Anna said, sitting down on a bench attached to her picnic table.

"Sex life? If it wasn't for my vibrator, I don't think I'd have a sex life! Sex with Simeon leaves me feeling frustrated as it's just a few minutes of him grunting away, pulling a face like he's drunk a glass of vinegar, rolling off, then telling me it was great. Well, no, it was crap. I want to be seduced, kissed, touched. I want every part of me to want sex. I want to know I'm the only one he's thinking of when we're doing it and that the look he has on his face is because he's doing it with me. He makes me feel like anyone would do, he's just doing it with me as I happen to be there and it's easier than spending a night down the pub on a Saturday night trying to pull."

"Except he can't even do that because of the lockdown," Anna interjected.

"Exactly! This lockdown has made it even worse as we're stuck with each other. The only time we go out is when we go to the supermarket. I swear, much more of this and I'll be passing a note to that old fella on the checkout asking him if he fancies giving me a seeing to on his conveyor belt!"

Both women laughed at the thought of Cassandra's libido driving her to such a desperate measure.

"Was it always crap between the two of you?" Anna asked. Lockdown had now been in place for a year and while Cassandra had been with her partner for a little while longer than that they had only been in a relationship for a few months before the pandemic lockdown began.

"Honestly?" Cassandra asked, brushing her dark hair from her face, and looking at her friend.

"Yes," Anna replied, knowing that Cassandra would tell her sooner or later, whatever her response. Cassandra and Anna had met at university and had, at one time, enjoyed a few lesbian trysts with one another. Anna enjoyed Cassandra's company as she was always honest with her.

"Yes. I knew internet dating wasn't a good move. Jo was saying that if they're such a great catch then why are they having to advertise themselves? What's more, you don't know their history or why the women in their town are giving them the cold shoulder. He was the best of the lot. God, remember

Chapter One

the one with no teeth? And the one with dirty fingernails that spent the date rolling his own cigarettes and spitting tobacco at me!"

"Yes, and the one you thought had trodden in something, only it was him!"

"Oh God, I'd forgotten about him!" laughed Cassandra.

"But just because the one you're with now is the best of a bad lot, it doesn't mean he's the one for you," said Anna, returning the conversation to Cassandra's current partner and giving her friend's hand a caring squeeze.

"I know, but it now feels like we're stuck with one another. I gave up my flat because I believed him when he promised me the earth. He's made it more and more difficult to see my friends. The lockdown was a gift to him," Cassandra said, pausing to collect her thoughts and taking a large gulp of gin and tonic. "The sex was never great but I thought it would get better once we loved one another and got used to what we like and don't like but, if anything, it's worse," she said, pausing to think. "It's not fulfilling - sometimes I feel like I'm just letting him do it as any sex is better than no sex. I now feel trapped as I don't have money, a job, or even a place of my own. I'm stuck with it," she added, then sighing and brushing her hair from her face.

Anna took a large sip of her gin and tonic and made herself comfortable on the wooden bench.

"I know it's no consolation but I'm having the best sex ever," Anna said.

"Ever?" Cassandra asked.

"Well, the best sex I've ever had with a man!"

"That's better!" Cassandra said, both women giggling as they remembered the nights that they had spent with one another.

"Remember the idiots we slept with at university? A few drinks, a grope and a fondle with some twerp that was too drunk to even undo a bra!" Anna said, slapping her thigh and laughing.

"Remember? I'm still having sex like that! Just last night he got so drunk he couldn't manage it," Cassandra replied.

"Like playing pool with a length of rope instead of a cue? Yes, been there – and bought the t-shirt!"

The sun had gone behind clouds as the women had entered the garden but now that those clouds had moved the two women were suddenly bathed in a warming amber caress. Cassandra reached for her bag and, after a moment's rummaging, removed her sunglasses.

"I wish I'd never moved to Wales," she said. "I think leaving Bristol and crossing that Severn Bridge was one of the worst decisions I've ever made," she added, as she put on her shades.

"Aw, don't say that. I'm here. Get out in the pretty valleys, the mountains, and the forests - it's a place of myth and magic!"

"Yes, but you're one of the few people I know, other than Simeon and his moron friends," Cassandra sighed. "Speaking of myth and magic, did you know that Wales and Wallachia have something in common? Both their names come from the old word *walhaz* – the strangers."

"There you go, you always said you wanted to meet someone mysterious," Anna said, giving her friend's shoulder a playful push.

"You do make me laugh, Anna! Why can't I find a man like you?"

"Well, who needs men?" Anna replied.

"Well, it would be nice to be kissed now and again."

"Then give me a kiss," Anna said, her jollity turning serious.

Cassandra leaned forward and gave her friend a peck on the cheek.

"No, a proper one," Anna said moving forward and pressing her lips to those of her friend.

"Oh, that feels so nice," Cassandra said. "Your lips are so soft - kiss me again."

Anna leaned forward and kissed her friend, running her fingers through her friend's long, dark hair as she did it.

Brushing her fingers across Cassandra's face and neck, she took her hand in hers and brought it to her lips, gently kissing

Chapter One

her fingers as she ran her hand up and down Cassandra's bare arms.

"You're such a tease," Cassandra said.

"Who says I'm teasing, babe?" Anna said, reaching forward and running her fingers down the soft skin beneath the open neck of Cassandra's unbuttoned shirt, the top few buttons of which were unfastened. "You like that?" she asked.

"You know I do," Cassandra sighed. Her body starting to shiver with excitement.

"Are you cold, babe?" Anna asked, noticing her friend trembling.

"No, just a little excited," Cassandra confessed, taking another drink from her glass of gin and tonic,

With all the buttons now undone, Anna leaned forward to give her friend a lingering kiss. Once again, Anna stroked Cassandra's bare arms, rising to her shoulders and neck and pulling her toward her so she could kiss her again. Gently, Anna moved her hands around Cassandra's neck and slid them down her back, pausing to teasingly twang the elastic strap of her bra.

"Oh, Mrs Waters, you certainly have a gentle touch," Cassandra breathlessly sighed.

"Thank you, Miss Wyvern," she replied.

Anna moved from her chair and knelt between Cassandra's legs. Once again, she kissed her friend's full and passionate lips while gently trailing the back of her fingernails from Cassandra's neck, down her torso and onto her bare stomach. Then, back up, before pausing to gently caress her friend's breasts.

"Oh God, that feels so nice," Cassandra said, as Anna kissed her neck, then moved down to her breasts.

"You like that, beautiful lady?" she asked.

"Very much."

"How about this?" Anna said, flicking her tongue across Cassandra's erect nipples before taking one in her mouth and tenderly sucking it.

"Don't stop, please don't stop," Cassandra quietly gasped, running her fingers through Anna's hair before pulling off Anna's t-shirt and tossing it aside. "Kiss me again," Cassandra said, standing. Anna also rose and pressed her soft body against the body of her friend.

Cassandra put her arm around Anna's waist and tickled the small of her back before bringing them up Anna's back and, with one deft motion, unhooked her bra. That, too, fell to the floor.

"I think we'd better go inside," Anna said, suggestively widening her eyes. "There are things I want to do to you that we can't do out here."

Taking Cassandra by the hand, she led her into the house. As soon as they were inside, Anna fell to her knees and undid her friend's jeans. As they fell to the floor, Cassandra stepped out of them. Drawing Cassandra close, Anna pressed her lips to the thin fabric of Cassandra's underwear and breathed in deeply then exhaling and letting the warmth of her breath penetrate the white cotton to the soft skin beneath.

Anna stroked Cassandra's legs, running her hand up and down them, pulling her close with her free hand.

"I think we'd better get you out of these," she said, sliding down Cassandra's underwear.

Again, Anna ran her hands up and down the outside of Cassandra's legs, relishing how soft the skin felt beneath her fingers. Then, moving her hands to the inside of Cassandra's legs, she slid them up her inner thighs before pausing to gently part Cassandra's lips.

"Oh God," said Cassandra. "That feels amazing."

Anna moved forward and flicked her tongue across her friend's lips, parting them with her slim fingers and giving her clitoris a lick.

"You'll smear your lipstick," Cassandra sighed.

"You're worth it, babe," Anna replied, her tongue darting back and forth as she began stroking Cassandra with practised fingers.

"My knees are trembling it feels so nice," Cassandra said. "Shall we lie down?"

"Whatever you want, babe," Anna said.

As Anna lay down, Cassandra knelt next to Anna and undid her friend's slacks before pulling them down.

Chapter One

"Ooh, no underwear," Cassandra said with delight. "And so wet, too," she said, running her hand up her friend's leg, pausing to lightly touch Anna's swollen lips.

As the two naked women lay next to one another, they kissed and caressed one another's warm bodies that, now that the sun was bathing them in warm rays, began to glisten in the heat. With each woman gently teasing one another with a delicate, feminine touch it wasn't long before Anna's back began to arch, and her eyes close with pleasure.

"Oh God, I'm going to cum," she gasped. "Don't stop."

"I won't stop, I promise," Cassandra breathlessly whispered, as she also began to reach a peak of sexual ecstasy.

"I'm cumming," Anna said, said, her face showing unmistakable signs of pleasure.

"Me too," Cassandra gasped, French-kissing her friend.

"That was amazing," Anna said, as the two lovers held each other, stroking each one another's soft skin, each trying to catch their breath as the waves of pleasure that had swept over them began to subside.

"I needed that," Cassandra said, tears filling her eyes. "There's more to life than sex, I know, but I don't even like him very much," Cassandra said, her mind wandering back to her problems at home. "He's not very bright, he's ill-mannered, and the things he likes bore me to tears. Why do grown men enjoy running around a wood pretending to shoot each other? They call it Airsoft but I call it pathetic! I want to have walks in the country, have long talks about books, art, music, and our future together. I want a knight in shining armour, not a tosser in tinfoil!" she laughed.

"So, what are you going to do about it?" Anna asked, stroking her friend's side and gently kissing her.

"I don't know. The chance of meeting someone else while this lockdown is in place seem remote – and would I even want him, if I did? I'm getting pissed off being made to feel like a whore because I want more than two minutes of missionary position sex a couple of times a week. I swear he'd rather stuff his face than have sex with me. I want a man who when he sees me in the kitchen bends me over the kitchen table and tears my knickers off with his teeth before giving me a good seeing to, French-kissing me as he's cumming! I don't want a man who, when he sees me in the kitchen, clicks his fingers and tells me to hurry up with his dinner as he's meeting one of his dickhead friends to buy a new toy gun!"

"Sex in the kitchen can be great fun," laughed Anna. "Just last night Andy had me on the kitchen table, rubbing ice cubes on my nipples and licking my clitoris after cleaning his teeth. There must have been spearmint still in his mouth as it was … wow!" she enthused, her eyes glazing over at the memory.

"I have a very vivid imagination. For the right man, I'd be the woman he'd been looking for all his life," said Cassandra. "He seems to think it's alright for men to want filthy sex but if a woman is like that then they must be a slut as his 'Mother was never like that'."

"Oh my God, he never said that did he?"

"Yes, he bloody did! Despite lockdown, she still visits and I can see her looking around to see whether the cleaning has been done and the clothes put away. I even caught her running her fingers over the windowsill and then looking at them to see if they were dirty."

"Yikes", Anna said, drawing the corners of her mouth down in dismay.

"Now his father has got into genealogy and thinks the family may own some land in the Wye Valley."

"Ooh, nice," Anna replied.

"Yes, dickhead wants to go and look at it and wants me to go with him."

"That's good, no?" Anna said, stroking her friend's bare back.

"No. He only wants me there so that he can make sure I can't see you. I swear he wants me on a short leash so that he can keep an eye on me," Cassandra said, leaning forward to kiss her friend on the mouth.

"See, I told you I wasn't worried about you smearing my lipstick," Anna laughed, as Cassandra leaned back on her elbow with her lips now smeared in Anna's lipstick. "Come here," Anna said, wiping the lipstick off Cassandra's face with her thumb.

"Thank you," Cassandra said.

Chapter One

"My pleasure, babe," Anna replied. "So, are you going to go with him tomorrow?"

"Well, it's a day out but I know it will end in an argument with him and him saying something nasty or comparing me to someone he'd seen online."

"I hate that," said Anna said in agreement. "We can't all be Kim Kardashian but then even Kim Kardashian isn't Kim Kardashian, the amount of work she's had done."

"God, I hate the twenty-first century. It's all pandemics, lockdowns, Facebook, and bullshit," Cassandra said, looking around for her drink and then remembering she'd left it in the garden.

"Yes, it seems geared to make people feel crap about their lives – hey, spend a little more money on crap you don't need and you, too, can lead the life of a millionaire z-lister!" Anna said, mocking the way adverts are geared to make what's being sold seem a necessity.

"I want to go back a hundred years and meet a real man. I want to be loved, cherished, and seduced. I want to know that when he looks at me that he feels lucky to have me and not thinking 'Oh, she'll do until something better comes along'."

"So, let's think what we can do to get you out of this rut, Cass. I was watching *The Witches of Eastwick* the other night, and they manifested their ideal man."

"Hang on, I don't want Jack Nicholson. Wasn't he supposed to be the Devil in it? That said, I would love someone mystical and mysterious," Cassandra said, lost in thought as she looked through Anna's open patio doors and at the trees at the bottom of Anna's garden.

"Then try manifesting him," suggested Anna, stroking her friend's bare back.

"What do you mean?" asked Cassandra, Anna's suggestion rousing her from her reverie.

"Be clear about what you want and ask the universe to send it to you."

"That sounds like mumbo-jumbo to me," laughed Cassandra.

"What have you got to lose? If it doesn't work then you'll be no worse off than you are now. If it does work then you may have to buy yourself a more comfortable kitchen table!"

Both women laughed and fell silent before Cassandra sat up and looked around the room for her clothes.

"Write it down," Anna said, moving her hand as though she were writing before she also began to dress.

"Yes, I do know what the word means," laughed Cassandra. "Funnily enough, though, it was just what I was thinking. Have you got some paper and a pen?"

"Sure," Anna said, rising to her feet and walking back to her kitchen. Cassandra could hear her rummaging through a kitchen drawer before, a few moments later, returning with a pen and notepad. "Make it succinct, that way you can repeat it to the universe as often as you remember."

"I want to be seduced," Cassandra said, saying the words as she wrote them down.

"That should do it," laughed Anna, blowing her friend a kiss. "So, are you going to go tomorrow?"

"Yes - it beats staring at four walls," Cassandra replied.

Now that they were both dressed, they finished their drinks.

"Well, I suppose I'd better get going," Cassandra said. "Thanks for the sex!"

"You're more than welcome, babe. I'd half-forgotten how good it feels to have a woman in my arms," Anna replied, kissing her index finger, then pressing her finger against Cassandra's lips. "You've still got a bit of my lipstick on your face," she added.

"Will you wipe it off for me?" Cassandra asked. "I don't want dickhead thinking I've been enjoying myself!"

With the evidence of their latest tryst removed, the two women said their goodbyes and Cassandra left, as Anna stood in her doorway for a moment to wave goodbye before closing the door once she had seen Cassandra had closed the front gate and stepped out onto the pavement that ran alongside the road of the quiet cul-de-sac.

With dread, Cassandra began the walk home.

Chapter One

"I want to be seduced," she repeated to herself, repeating the phrase all the way home. "I want to be seduced, I want to be seduced," she murmured, as though it were a mantra. "I want to be seduced."

Chapter Two

The sun rose early next morning and with no cloud in the sky to mask its warming rays, those rays fell on the small Welsh town as its inhabitants awoke to the new day.

"Are you coming, or what?" Cassandra's partner, Simeon, asked.

"Yes. I'm sick of sitting here looking at these four walls," Cassandra replied.

Simeon let out a sigh and rolled his eyes before moving to a map his father had printed off for him the night before.

"Well, if you're not ready in ten minutes, then I'm going without you," he said.

"I'm ready now," Cassandra replied, biting her lip. Any argument now would cause Simeon to leave her at home for the day and a day out would be a welcome break, even it was only to enjoy the change of scenery.

Simeon sighed a second time and checked his pockets for his car keys.

"I need to concentrate today, so no whinging - please," he demanded, drawing out the final word so that it sounded sarcastic.

Soon, the pair were in his car and driving toward their destination in the Wye Valley.

"It's beautiful here," Cassandra said, admiring the old houses and ancient ruins that sat amongst the verdant landscape. "Why haven't we come here before?"

"I have," Simeon replied.

"Yes, but I haven't."

"Ah well, you have now," Simeon said, making no attempt to hide the irritation in his voice.

He indicated right and drove his car across the small bridge that left Wales behind and entered England. Lost in thought, Cassandra was surprised when he parked and quickly turned off the car's engine.

"Is this it?" she asked.

"Is this what?"

"The place you said your father wanted you to visit."

"No, that will involve a bit of walking. Are you ready, fatty?" he asked as he leaned into the car, slamming the door without waiting for a reply.

The pair walked alongside the beautiful Wye, Cassandra admiring the view and Simeon texting his friends.

"I feel like I've been here before," Cassandra said, mistakenly saying the words aloud.

"Yes, of course you do," Simeon replied, frowning as the words Cassandra had spoken jolted him from his messages.

"It can't be up here," Cassandra said, as Simeon pushed aside some brambles and began walking up an overgrown path, past stones and trees that were damp with moss.

"Do you want to read it!" Simon barked, pushing the map into Cassandra's chest.

"I was just saying," she responded.

"Well don't," came the brusque reply.

"It says it's a nature reserve."

"Did I not warn you not to start?" Simeon replied.

As the pair ascended the broken path, treading carefully and occasionally slipping on a knotted root or taking a small jump as their route crossed a small woodland stream, Simeon slipped.

"Oh, bollocks," he said, brushing the dirt from his jeans.

"Is that a house?" Cassandra asked, pointing at what appeared to be a chimney amongst the leaves and branches.

"I wouldn't have thought so," came the terse response. "There are no lanes to it and the only path is the one that we've just walked. I'm knackered," he added.

The two of them walked a little nearer to what appeared to Cassandra to be a cottage. A dry-stone wall, common in the depths of even the densest of woodlands in the area, prevented a direct route. Simeon spied a gap, and what remained of an old wooden gate. Attempting to open it, it fell off its hinges and broke in two.

"It is a house," he conceded.

"See, you never believe me," Cassandra replied.

"Don't start," he remarked, giving her a look of contempt.

Chapter Two

"Just saying."

"Well don't," he responded, drawing down the corners of his mouth in disgust before making his way to what appeared to be a curtain of ivy. "Hey, here's a door," he said, sounding the first note of enthusiasm he had sounded that day. "Let's see if there's anything worth nicking," he said aloud, laughing at the thought of such easy pickings.

"Open!" Cassandra said with surprise, pointing at what appeared to be a shop sign behind the glass of the door.

"Don't know what that is," Simeon said as he turned the door's handle, the idea too challenging to think about as he pushed the door open. As soon as the door was wide enough, he entered; Cassandra followed him.

"It looks like some sort of shop," he said as he spied the counter, dusty shelves, and an ornate cash register. As the sunshine barely penetrated the dense foliage outside, he squinted into the gloom of the ancient room.

"Is it some sort of apothecary shop?" Cassandra asked. "There seem to be a lot of bottles and potions on those shelves."

"A what?" Simeon asked, betraying his ignorance and making Cassandra wince.

"An apothecary – like a chemist or herbalist, but maybe with a few spells," she enthused.

"Let's see if there's anything worth taking," came the response.

Cassandra squinted about the darkened room before letting out a startled gasp as her gaze fell upon someone sitting in the darkest corner, looking back at her.

"There's someone in here," she whispered to Simeon, taking a few steps backwards.

"Yes, of course there is," Simeon scoffed, filling his pocket with something he'd taken off a shelf.

"No, really – over there," she replied, looking at Simeon and gesturing with her thumb in the manner of a hitchhiker. She had only looked away for a second but when she looked back the figure had gone. Next to where it had sat, a heavy velvet curtain billowed, as though moved by a breeze.

"I warned you not to start," Simeon said, adding an impatient tut.

"No, really. He was there - gaunt, with wispy white hair and dressed in black."

"Are you sure it wasn't the butler from *The Rocky Horror Picture Show*?" Simeon asked facetiously, once again laughing at Cassandra.

"Actually, he looked very similar to him," Cassandra responded, not rising to Simeon's barb.

"Come on, let's go," Simeon said, stuffing the last of what he'd found that was worth stealing into his pockets. "I'll have to come back when I've got a torch. We'll be stumbling around like a pair of idiots if we look around the rest of the place, what with all that ivy over the windows."

"I don't need a light, I'm sure I've been here before," Cassandra replied.

"When was that then? An hour ago you were saying you'd never been to the Wye Valley! Then you said something about the river and now you've been here!"

"What did I ever see in you?" Cassandra said, her patience having finally snapped.

"I was wondering what I ever saw in you," he countered. "We have nothing common - except for sex."

"And that's crap," she hissed.

"What? The sex or that being all we have in common."

"Both," Cassandra hissed, her eyes flaming so brightly that even in the little light afforded by the open door, Simeon could tell her emotions were running high.

"Let's go," he said, taking a few short steps to the door, opening it wide before slamming it behind him, leaving Cassandra alone inside the room and having to prise the door open for herself.

The walk back to the car was a silent one, as was their journey home.

"I'm sick of this," Cassandra thought to herself. "I want to be seduced – and seduced by someone that values me."

Chapter Three

The journey back home remained a silent one right back to the street in which they lived. When they pulled up outside their house, Simeon almost leapt from the car the moment the engine had stopped running; he then briskly walked to the house and after opening its door he entered and slammed it shut behind him, leaving Cassandra to search in her purse for her keys in order to open it.

"Well, that went well," Cassandra said to Simeon, as she entered the house and closed the door behind her.

"Pretty much as I expected," came the reply.

"So, what's the problem? If you hate being with me then why did you ask me to give up my place to move in with you?" she asked, taking off her jacket and tossing her long hair over her shoulders.

Simeon ran his fingers through his thinning hair, puffed out his cheeks, and pulled up his jogging bottoms.

"I figured you'd do until something better came along. I wasn't expecting a pandemic to scuttle that fucking plan and leave me stuck with you," he said.

"So, you had me give up my place and move in with you knowing you were going to end it when you got bored? You asshole!" Cassandra said, shouting, and pointing her finger at Simeon in rage.

"Yes - it was just sex and I figured as soon as I got bored with shagging you, I'd move on to something better," Simeon said, his face breaking into a grin as he folded his arms and waited for her reply.

"So, you just wanted me for sex?"

"Yes. I hadn't realised that even that would be crap. I need a woman that likes sex, not someone frigid – like you."

"Frigid? You have no idea! I am a very passionate woman. Ever thought that given you're such a selfish asshole out of bed that you're also a selfish asshole in bed?" Cassandra said, moving to the kitchen to put away some dishes she had left on the draining board. Shaking with rage, she dropped a plate and it shattered on the hard kitchen floor.

"I'm great in bed – if I find the woman I'm screwing attractive. No man wants to spend half an hour on foreplay just to have someone whinge that they didn't have an orgasm. You don't understand men if you think any of them will put up with that," he said, kicking the broken fragments of china across the floor.

"So, you don't even find me attractive? You're hardly Johnny Depp yourself! Do you think any woman is dying to have you sweating away on top of her for two minutes a few times a week?" Cassandra said, pointing at Simeon's stomach.

"You saying I'm fat? It didn't seem to bother you when we got together. I thought you'd be grateful of finding anyone, the way you act," he shouted, unfolding his arms before slapping away her hand, taking a step forward and pointing a finger into her face.

"Don't try and intimidate me, you bastard – I'll stick a knife in you," she said, picking up a knife from the draining board and pointing it at her aggressor, the wild look in her eye causing Simeon to take a step backwards.

"Look, we got together without even knowing each other," he began, taking a second step backwards, then pacing the room and trying to add emphasis to his words with flailing hand gestures.

"And now I know it was just so you could drain your balls a few times a week," Cassandra hissed.

Simeon stopped pacing up and down in front of Cassandra before smiling and nodding in agreement.

Cassandra pursed her lips, closed her eyes, and shook her head in disgust.

"You don't understand women at all, do you? I'm uninhibited but I need to feel needed, wanted, attractive, and desired – and loved."

"Yeah, well good luck with that," he scoffed. "And uninhibited! You freaked when I tried to stick it in your ass the other night."

"You don't do something like that without even asking! Everyone has their likes and dislikes and to just assume you can do what you want when you want is taking the piss," she

Chapter Three

seethed, running her hand through her hair and tying it into a ponytail. "So, where do we go from here?"

"I don't know. Tinder? Plenty of Fish?" said Simeon, smirking.

"You seem to forget that there's a pandemic," Cassandra replied, causing the smirk to drop from his face.

"No, I didn't - it's the only reason you're still here," he said, reminding Cassandra that she had been little more than a stop-gap for him.

"Well, make the most of it as I won't be here much longer," Cassandra said with confident resignation. "You're a slob and I deserve better."

"And you're a frigid nutcase that doesn't know a good thing when she sees it," came the hostile rebuke. "I'm off on the Xbox," he added, leaving the kitchen, and walking a few paces to the living room.

Cassandra put the rest of the dishes away, then went to their bedroom. A few hours later she heard Simeon's footsteps on the stairs.

"Fancy a shag?" he asked, as though the events of just a few hours earlier had never happened.

"Yes, I'd love one," Cassandra said, as Simeon smiled and began sliding down his sweatpants.

"Great," he said.

"Just not with you," she added.

"You bitch," he hissed through gritted teeth, leaving the room, and returning to his Xbox in the living room downstairs.

Cassandra walked to the airing cupboard in the spare room and removed a duvet.

"Ah, I knew you were joking," Simeon said, having suddenly appeared in the doorway behind her. "I'm the bomb."

"Yes - but with a three-inch fuse," Cassandra replied, pointing at his groin before brushing past him and descending the stairs for a night on the sofa.

Chapter Four

The next morning, Cassandra awoke from a fitful night's sleep. Making her way to the bathroom, she took a shower. Knowing what Simeon really felt about her and how he must have felt when he'd had sex with her made her feel so dirty that she tried her best to wash every trace of him off her. All night long she had dreamt of the figure she had seen in the apothecary shop the previous day. She had felt a strange sense of déjà vu as Simeon had driven through the Wye Valley. Then, when they had crossed the little bridge leaving Wales behind and entering England, it seemed as though imagination and memory had merged; like seeing the face of an old friend who, while still being someone she recognised, had suffered much by the march of time.

"I want to be seduced," she told herself as she dried herself, remembering the imprecation to the universe that her friend Anna had suggested she repeat.

After breakfast, she washed her bowl and picked up her car keys. Something seemed to be pulling her back to the place she had visited the previous day.

Cassandra closed the front door behind her and made her way to her car. What was the force compelling her to make the return journey alone, she wondered?

As she passed the nearby racecourse and entered the snaking lanes in front of her she began to feel unburdened, as though the recent memories of life with Simeon were falling from her grasp like the loose pages of an old book.

As she crossed the bridge from Wales into England what felt like memories, but which she told herself must be her imagination, blew away the cobwebs of her despair and frustration.

She drove past the old pub and parked on the hill that led out of the village.

"My God, this is such a beautiful place," she said to herself as she parked. After locking her car, she walked back down the hill and then onto the path that ran alongside the silently flowing river that she had walked alongside the previous day. To her right, a few old houses and cottages were embracing the morning sun; to her left, the river and, beyond that, old woodland that stretched away from her with such beauty it left her spellbound.

A cold chill ran through her as she passed the old stone boathouse, as though the pleasant memories she had felt a little while before had been replaced by something terrifying.

Silently, she made her way to the overgrown path, pushing aside brambles and nettles and then on into the woodland. Above her, a verdant canopy; below her, knotted tree roots and broken stones; rising in front of her, the woodland seemed to welcome her with outstretched arms.

"Ah, no people," she whispered, as sunbeams penetrated the leaves and kissed her pretty, smiling face. Only the sound of birdsong and the gentle breeze through those leaves gave a voice to nature.

Had it really been such a steep climb the day before? Narrow and, at times, slippery she continued her climb. Thoughts of Tolkien's tales flashed across her mind. Just when she thought that she must have taken a wrong path and that no house could be in such an inaccessible place, let alone a shop, she saw its chimney and the dry-stone wall that surrounded what must once have been a garden.

She stepped over the remains of the gate that Simeon had broken in two the day before and entered. If there hadn't been a chimney breaking free from the clutches of ivy that sought to hold it in its grasp, ivy that hung in a thick cascade around the property, one might be forgiven for not even realising that a house lay beneath the jade blanket.

Taking a few steps forward she found the door through which Simeon and she had entered the previous day.

The room was just as dark as the day before, lit only by the narrowest shafts of sunlight that pierced the ivy hanging about the windows.

"I've been expecting you," came a voice, causing Cassandra to jump.

Chapter Four

"I'm sorry - the sign on the door said that you were open," Cassandra said, apologetically, pointing at the sign that hung on the door.

"Indeed, I am - it's just been a very long time since I had a customer," the voice replied, again causing Cassandra to start as this time its owner had silently moved behind her. Then, an unseen hand closed the door.

"It's very dark in here," Cassandra said, as she began feeling that her return to the shop had not been such a good idea.

"I shall light a lamp for you," said the apothecary, lighting an old oil lamp that resided on the edge of one of the shop counters.

The light was soft and just bright enough to show Cassandra the same gaunt and withered features she had seen the day before. His frock coat and trousers, at one time, must have been black but now decades of dust had turned them grey.

"Why were you expecting me?" Cassandra asked, her heart fluttering like a bird in a gilded cage.

"You don't remember?"

"Remember? Yesterday? Yesterday was my first visit," Cassandra replied, her forehead creasing into a perplexed frown.

"Then you don't remember," the man observed, letting out a sigh.

"No - anyway, I'm Cassandra Wyvern. You are?" she asked.

"Lucius - Lucius d'Orléans," Lucius offered, extending a hand.

"French? I thought you had an accent," Cassandra responded, trying to sound upbeat even though she now felt a little panic-stricken.

"Yes, I am French - despite the centuries I've been here, I still have an accent," Lucius replied. "I think it's because I haven't fraternised very much with the locals – I'm not the most sociable of people. When you spend fifty years without talking to a soul you forget the local vernacular."

"Centuries?" Cassandra queried, but not wishing to press the matter when she didn't receive a reply.

Cassandra gazed around the dusty, darkened room and tried to imagine how it must have once looked. Antique bottles full of powder and potions sat on shelves whilst a large wooden counter sat in front of three of the walls; the back counter had a large and ornate till on it.

"That was a very inciteful description that you gave of an apothecary yesterday," Lucius said. "Not all of us cast spells, of course - or practise the art of divination."

Cassandra looked at Lucius and even in the twilight world in which they stood, she noticed the sapphire blue of his eyes shining bright on his lined and aged face.

"Divination? I'd love to know my future," Cassandra said with excitement.

"Then step this way," Lucius replied, walking toward the back wall, and sweeping aside the heavy velvet curtain that Cassandra had seen moving the day before. "Please, sit down," Lucius said, pulling an old chair away from a large, dark table that formed the centrepiece of the room, for his guest.

"I'm a bit nervous," Cassandra said, trying to make herself comfortable, as Lucius walked to a bureau and took from it a deck of tarot cards.

"These are rather special," he said. "They were produced by my friend Jean Noblet in Marseille in the year sixteen-fifty."

Returning to the table, he placed the cards down and dragged a chair across well-worn floorboards before sitting in it, opposite Cassandra.

"What happens now?" Cassandra asked as Lucius moved the oil lamp that he had brought with them from the room in which they had met. Cassandra felt a little shocked to see Lucius leaning toward her.

"What are you doing?" she asked, letting out a fearful gasp.

"Shuffle the pack and then give them to me," he said, tapping the cards with his index finger.

Cassandra picked up the pack and gave them a shuffle but because nerves were now getting the better of her, she dropped them.

"It's alright, don't be nervous. Please, try again," Lucius said.

Cassandra shuffled the cards a second time and then handed them to Lucius who proceeded to spread them face down on the table.

"Pick three," he said, his piercing eyes staring at Cassandra as she looked at the cards. Picking three, she pulled them away from the rest of the pack.

Chapter Four

"Right," said Lucius, turning over the first card. "Ah, *Le Pendu*," he said. "Sorry, the Hanged Man."

"Not good?" Cassandra asked, thinking the card must be a bad omen.

"Maybe, maybe not. It would suggest that you're feeling trapped, and stuck in a situation that is making you unhappy. But," he continued, "do you notice the halo around his head? That suggests that with thoughtful actions you can change things."

"I think I know what that means," Cassandra enthused. "It's very accurate."

"Please, turn over the next card," Lucius said.

A second after he had spoken the words Cassandra turned over the cards and let out a fearful sigh.

"Ah, *La Mort*. Sorry, Death," Lucius said, scratching the side of his face and looking at Cassandra for a reaction.

"Oh no, not more misery - I've had just about as much as I can take," Cassandra said, her voice beginning to quake with emotion.

"No, it can be a very positive card," Lucius said, reaching across the table and giving Cassandra's hand a gentle squeeze. "It means the death of an old chapter in your life, and the beginning of a new one - major changes may be coming your way."

"Thank God for that," Cassandra said, wiping a tear from her cheek. It wasn't what the cards had predicted that brought forth a tear but the fact that it had been such a long time since anyone had held her hand and that simple act of kindness had touched her.

"Would you like to turn over the last card?" Lucius said, smiling at Cassandra.

"Yes," she whispered, turning over the last card.

"Ah, *L'Amoureux*," Lucius said. "The Lover."

"What does that card mean?" Cassandra asked.

"Well," Lucius began. "If you're in a relationship, it could mean that there will be a rekindling of love and romance."

"I can't see that happening," Cassandra laughed, running her free hand through her hair.

"It signifies a very intense bond between two people that goes beyond infatuation. This card represents a deep and intense attraction," Lucius said, pausing for breath. "Passion, romance, and understanding."

"Really? That sounds perfect – amazing," Cassandra enthused.

"I'm glad that they were all so positive for you," Lucius said.

"The sooner the better," Cassandra replied. "I don't want any more flings. All my friends have found someone - what's wrong with me!"

Cassandra had meant it as a rhetorical question so was not expecting an answer.

"Nothing - you're beautiful," Lucius replied.

"No one has ever said that to me," Cassandra said, feeling both embarrassed and tearful.

"Yes, they have – I said it to you. I said it just then, and I said it to you a century or two ago," Lucius replied

"I need to think about all this," Cassandra said, feeling so confused that her mind began to spin. "I don't know what you mean when you say you said it to me a century or two ago."

"You don't remember?" Lucius asked.

"I remember something but I don't know what," Cassandra replied. "They feel like fragments of a dream."

"I'm sure it will all come back to you – in time," Lucius said, reaching out for the cards and putting them in a neat pile.

"I'm confused," Cassandra said, biting her lip as though she were puzzling over something. "You know when you visit somewhere new or meet someone for the first time and it feels like you've either been there before or met them before?"

"Yes, I know that feeling very well," Lucius said, giving Cassandra a smile.

"Well, that's how I feel – and I can't believe I'm telling you that, given we've only just met."

"No, we've not just met. We've known each other over a few lifetimes," Lucius said.

"Yes, that's what it also feels like to me. It's not a feeling I've ever had before."

"Is it a nice feeling?" Lucius asked.

"It was terrifying down by the boathouse but now that I'm here, it feels like nothing I've ever felt."

"As though dust and dirt are turning to gold?" Lucius asked.

Chapter Four

"Yes, I suppose so," Cassandra replied, feeling a little uncertain.

Lucius swept his hand across a dusty shelf on a wall to his left. Pouring the dust he had gathered from his left hand into his right hand, he threw the dust in the air. Cassandra sat in awe as the tiny particles turned to gold and lightly fell on the table in front of her, shimmering in the light of the lamp.

"That's amazing!" she said. "I really need time to think about this - but I will say this, Lucius," she added.

"What's that?" Lucius asked, his curiosity piqued.

"You're amazing!"

"Thank you, Cassandra. I was hoping you'd still feel the same way about me as I feel about you."

"Lucius, I need time to think," Cassandra said, looking up at the ceiling, as though seeking divine inspiration.

"Of course - please, do whatever makes you happy," Lucius said, again reaching across the table to tenderly touch Cassandra's hand.

"I must go," Cassandra said, reluctantly removing her hand from the warm-hearted embrace with which Lucius held it.

"Well, you know where I am," he said, walking with Cassandra to the shop's door.

"Yes, you've been very kind," she replied. "I shan't forget it."

Cassandra made her way back down the narrow woodland path, pushing aside the brambles and nettles that blocked her way. Then, once again, she found herself on the banks of the beautiful river. Lost in a reverie of what had just happened at the cottage, what her fortune had told her, and the kindness Lucius had shown her, the half an hour it took her to walk back to her car seemed to pass by in just a few minutes.

Back at the house that she shared with Simeon, she expected an argument and an interrogation over where she had been. Instead, she found a note.

"Gone to Paul's for a few days. Hope you're gone by the time I get back. Stick your keys through the letterbox. Hatefully yours, Simeon," Cassandra read, whispering the words to herself.

Cassandra screwed up the note before having second thoughts and unfurling it. Walking to her oven she switched on a gas ring and set it alight.

"Screw you, asshole," she muttered, as it turned to ashes.

Chapter Five

That night, Cassandra spent a second night on the sofa, despite Simeon not being home and the bed they had once shared lying empty. All night she thought of what her cards had said – and the man that had interpreted them. What was it about him that felt so familiar? She had never had a feeling of déjà vu about a person but when he had held her hand it felt as though it had reawakened a long-forgotten memory, yet try as she might she could not remember where or when they had ever met. Then there were those eyes! The white hair might have been thin and wispy, his skin that of an old man, yet his eyes seemed to be a doorway to her past.

She arose early that morning, showered, made herself breakfast and made up her mind to return to the shop deep within the woodland of the Wye Valley. The wretched lockdown was still in place, so she knew that any unnecessary travel was forbidden but this journey felt to be a journey that she needed to take if only to speak to Lucius and to ask him how she might know him and where before they had met. He may not have the answers but the alternative was to stay within the four walls that were no longer those of a home but those of a house, all the while waiting for the sound of a key in the front door that would tell her that her ex, Simeon, had returned. Then she paused: in thinking of such things, she had said the word 'ex', rather than sully her mind or lips with his name.

The drive into the Wye Valley felt strangely familiar but not the familiarity one might have of a recent memory but the memory one has of a first embrace, kiss, or homecoming. She sighed with pleasure as she realised that it felt safe and softly secure, something she had missed.

As she arrived at what should have been the turning to the village she had visited the day before, its bridge had gone. Strange, she thought, as she parked her car on the Welsh side of the valley. Within a few minutes, she had found and descended some steps and walked to the water's edge. There, a small craft was ferrying a few passengers across the small expanse of water. Patiently, she waited her turn, feeling uncomfortable that the locals not only appeared to be dressed in clothes of a bygone age but that her clothes seemed to be a cause of concern and alarm to them.

As she reached England, she couldn't help but notice that the tarmac road with double-yellow lines that she had seen the day before had gone and been replaced by one made of cobblestones. A horse and cart passed her, then another.

"Well, it is a rural village. Maybe it's a quaint tradition," she told herself, remembering her days at university and reading of the May Day traditions in Gloucestershire and the Forest of Dean that often involved Morris Dancers.

Hadn't the old pub been named something different when she had passed it the day before? As she began walking alongside the river, two women walked towards her, both dressed in garb that to Cassandra looked more than a century out-of-date. Both women looked at Cassandra in mute astonishment. She glanced back to her car on the far banks and spied a small group of people standing beside it, pointing at it as if it had been an Italian Supercar.

"Haven't they ever seen a car before!" she said to herself.

Walking alongside the river, again the old boathouse made her shudder as she passed it. Then she looked at it again – old? It now appeared considerably less old than it had the day before.

Cassandra looked for the overgrown entrance to the path but it appeared as if someone had removed the brambles, nettles, and ferns since the previous day and she now had no trouble finding the route that led to the old steps.

The path was as broken and precipitous as she remembered, with every footfall a gamble as to whether the damp moss that covered the stones would send her tumbling. Onwards she walked, again thinking about how the journey from the river to the shop seemed longer and steeper than she remembered. With eyes downcast to ensure each step was a safe one, she came to a sudden stop. When she raised her eyes in anticipation of seeing the thick curtain of ivy that had yesterday covered the house, today all the ivy had gone.

Chapter Five

Cassandra pressed on, now feeling a little unsure as to whether she had somehow taken the wrong path. Had the path forked and she, watching where she carefully trod, taken a wrong turn and somehow lost her way?

The young woman came to an abrupt stop when she saw the little gate that had, just a few days before, fallen off its hinges and broken in two as Simeon had touched it. Now it appeared new.

"What's going on!" she said aloud, deciding that the only way to find an answer to such a question was to enter the apothecary shop and see if its proprietor was Lucius d'Orléans, the man that had such an effect on her the previous day.

"There's the 'open' sign, so it's definitely a shop of some sort," she told herself.

With some trepidation, she opened the door and was astonished to see every counter, cabinet, jar, and bottle gleaming.

"Hello," came a voice to her right. Quickly, Cassandra turned and saw a man she guessed to be around the same age as her. Perhaps Lucius had a son, she thought, given his eyes were the same colour of brilliant blue; but gone were the wrinkles and white wisps of hair, replaced by taut skin and black hair.

"I'm sorry, I was looking for Lucius d'Orléans," Cassandra said.

"I am he," the man said, smiling and extending a hand.

"I'm confused. I don't understand what's going on – it's as if I've stepped back in time. What year is this? When I left it was twenty twenty-one," Cassandra said in bewilderment.

"This is eighteen ninety-one," Lucius replied.

"Eighteen ninety-one! Is this for real?" Cassandra stammered, rubbing her face with her hand, and looking around the shop for something familiar.

"Yes, this is eighteen ninety-one. What year was it when you visited yesterday?" Lucius asked.

"That was also twenty twenty-one. Are all those people I saw half an hour ago living one hundred and thirty years ago?"

"No, they're living now. Every moment in time is happening right now. Ghosts aren't the spirits of the dead but a moment, or two, in time that has somehow availed itself to us. Of course, people die ..."

"So, why aren't those people dead?" Cassandra interrupted.

"They are in twenty twenty-one but you're in eighteen ninety-one. You've somehow stepped from what we think of as the future into what we think of as the past," Lucius said. "Our concept of time is an illusion and is nothing more than our memories - everything that has ever been and ever will be is happening right now. The only reason we feel like we have a past is because our brain contains memories."

"And you? I spoke to you yesterday when you were old and yet today you are young. That means you must have been one hundred and sixty when I saw you yesterday!"

"Far older than that," Lucius said.

"Older? So why are you young-looking today if you're even older than one hundred and sixty?"

"Because yesterday I had nothing to live for and today I have you," Lucius said, closing the door. "Even now – in eighteen ninety-one – I have been waiting almost a hundred years for you to return to me. When we met yesterday, it was almost two-hundred and fifty years since we first met - and my loneliness had become unbearable."

"Hold on, you're going to have to explain a few things as that seems crazy. I do feel something strange about this place – about you, but I don't know what. It feels like déjà vu."

"I am French. I came over here with the Normans in the eleventh century. I was a member of the *Rose-Croix*. People think that Brotherhood only began in the seventeenth century but it was built on the esoteric truths of an ancient past. We discovered the secret of everlasting life."

"The *Rose-Croix*?" queried Cassandra,

"Yes - they're more often known as the Rosicrucians," Lucius said, looking intently at Cassandra for a reaction. "You're looking as if you've not heard of them."

"No, I haven't. Who are they?" Cassandra replied, the wheels of her mind turning as she sought to remember where she had heard the name.

"Lord Lytton wrote of us in *Zanoni* and Shelley in *St. Irvyne the Rosicrucian*," Lucius said. "Legend has it that we've been in existence since the sixteenth century and a popular theory is that our name was derived from our supposed founder, Christian Rosenkreuze, but I don't believe that such a man ever existed.

Chapter Five

"In the popular imagination, it is believed that we originated in Germany, in the early seventeenth century, in the town of Cassell. An anonymous pamphlet was published that was supposed to be a message to professors of magic and mysticism that urged all men of science to band together as the writer was concerned about the moral welfare of the world and thought that a synthesis of all the arts and science could return mankind to a state of perfection. This, the writer imagined, could only be achieved with the assistance of the illuminated Brotherhood – the children of light who had been initiated into the mysteries of the Grand Orient.

"The writer stated that the head of our movement was someone known as C.R.C, a magician of the highest rank. At the age of fifteen, it was written that he undertook an arduous journey to Damascus, arriving at an unknown Arabian city named Damcar where he obtained arcane knowledge from a secret circle of theosophists who were all experts in the magical arts. There, the magi informed him that they had long been expecting him and related to him passages of his past life. After three years of instruction in the occult arts, he travelled to Egypt and onto the city of Fez. It was there that other masters taught him how to invoke the elemental spirits. After a few more years of study, he travelled to Spain, to both learn and to speak to the professors of that county. Scholars from that country derided him and told him that the principles and practice he had learned must have been taught to him by Satan. Other countries treated him in the same manner, and so he returned to Germany where he became a hermit."

"Is that why you're also a hermit?" Cassandra asked, causing Lucius to smile. "Sorry, I wasn't being facetious," she added.

"Back in Germany, he perfected the transmutation of base metals into gold and the elixir of life. The assistants that he had gathered about him became the basis of the Rosicrucian fraternity. In time, C.R.C died, and for over a century his burial place was a secret. It was only a later generation of adepts that found his tomb while rebuilding one of his secret dwellings. His body was found in a state of perfect preservation, and many marvels were found buried alongside him, marvels that convinced the Brotherhood that they had a duty to make their secrets known to the world.

"Another year passed, and the *Confession of the Rosicrucian Fraternity* was published, addressed to the learned of Europe. Applications to join the Brotherhood, however, were ignored and by sixteen-twenty the Brotherhood had all but disappeared.

"The published pamphlets leave the reader in no doubt that the Rosicrucians believed in the same alchemy, astrology, and occult forces of nature as Paracelsus. It is also stated that we believe that man contains the potentialities of the whole universe," Lucius said, all the while remaining motionless and silhouetted, his back against the shop door.

"But you said that none of that history goes back beyond the sixteenth century," Cassandra said. "Yet you also said you first came to this country in the eleventh century."

"Yes, I did - all those histories allude to an ancient Brotherhood that was far older than the Brotherhood of the sixteenth century," Lucius said, giving Cassandra an inscrutable smile.

"So, where and when did we first meet?" Cassandra asked.

"Six hundred years later was the first time we met and became lovers," Lucius said, smiling at the memory. "You meant everything to me, and a day with you meant more to me than the six-hundred years that had preceded them, years I had spent alone. Sadly, the French Revolution parted us as we had cause to visit the country in seventeen eighty-nine. We were viewed with suspicion by the *Montagnards*, revolutionaries led by Robespierre, Danton, and Marat, and were shot trying to flee the county in seventeen ninety-two - before I could impart to you the *Rose-Croix* secret of eternal life."

"So, where did we meet? Here, or France?" Cassandra asked.

"In the eighteenth century?" queried Lucius.

"Yes."

"Oh, we met in Paris."

"How did we meet?" asked Cassandra.

"You were a courtesan. I wasn't a client of yours but I used to see you in the gin palaces of Montmartre and thought you were the most beautiful woman I had ever seen."

Chapter Five

"I was a prostitute!" Cassandra said in astonishment, looking for a seat but finding none and leaning against one of the shop's counters.

"Yes, and it broke my heart to see you being used and abused by those unworthy of you. One night we chatted and took a walk by the banks of the Seine - it was there that I first kissed you."

"That sounds incredibly romantic," Cassandra said.

"Yes, ours was a passion that I had never known, nor ever imagined. I suppose the intervening years took their toll on me but just a few years ago you returned to me. Again, we became lovers, despite you being married. Ours was a passion like no other and threatened to consume us both. Then, just a few months ago your husband found out and killed you."

"What! Where?" Cassandra asked, hardly able to believe what she had heard, or that she had once been murdered.

"He hit you with a rock and threw you in the river, by the boathouse, down there," Lucius said, gesturing with an outstretched arm and pointed finger at where he imagined the boathouse might be, near the river Cassandra had walked past several times over the past few days.

Lucius looked at Cassandra, awaiting her reaction.

"And did she look like me?" she asked.

"Yes," Lucius replied.

"That explains why those women were staring at me," Cassandra said, the moment of elucidation causing her to raise her voice.

"They must have thought you were a ghost," Lucius said.

"This is very strange and difficult for me," Cassandra said, looking around the room to distract herself, before walking to the glass jars that lined the walls.

"Yes, I'm sure it's very difficult to be here, but you've found your home. You've returned to me." Lucius said, pausing a moment. "Your immortal spirit has found me."

Cassandra felt a warm glow on hearing the words but feared turning, lest her expression betrayed her thoughts.

"You're a very seductive man, Lucius," she said.

"Thank you – and you're a very seductive woman."

"Bergamot, lemon oil, lavender oil," she said, running her hand across the mysterious bottles and reading their labels, labels which the day before had looked like faded parchment but which now looked new.

"Yes, do you like perfumes? Here, I have a perfume for you – a bottle of *Hammam Bouquet* by *Penhaligon*. It has lavender, bergamot, Bulgarian rose, orris root, jasmine, cedar, sandalwood, amber and musk. It was made for men but is too feminine for a twenty-first-century taste. What with the scent of old books, powdered resins, and ancient rooms I thought of you," Lucius said, lifting a small bottle from beneath the shop counter.

"That's so kind of you, thank you. How did you know I'd return?" Cassandra asked, looking at Lucius over her shoulder and feeling a little embarrassed and unworthy that he had bought her a gift.

"You forgot the tarot?" he asked. "I know the future as well as the past for, as I said, every moment in time is happening right now."

"Jasmine, orange blossom, rose, violet," Cassandra continued, the magic of the bottles having cast their spell over her.

"Here, let me put a little on you," Lucius said. Cassandra hadn't heard his approach so was a little startled to hear him speak the words while standing so close to her. "May I?" he asked.

"Of course," Cassandra said, in joyful abandon.

Standing behind Cassandra, Lucius swept aside Cassandra's hair, exposing her delicate neck. Dabbing the stopper of the bottle on her bare skin, he closed his eyes in ecstasy as both the perfume and scent of Cassandra left him feeling intoxicated.

"But why do you make such beautiful perfumes if you never have a customer?" Cassandra asked.

"I want to give the world beautiful things," he said. "Just because no one buys them, it doesn't devalue them. I must do something with my time and rather than destroy, I create – and what better things are there to create than something that is beautiful? Think of the author writing beautiful books that no one will read – his words are no less beautiful because they're unread."

"Kiss me," Cassandra said, turning so that her eyelashes brushed his face. Looking up, her lips met with his. Lucius'

Chapter Five

fingers entwined with those of Cassandra. Then, letting go, he reached an arm around her waist and drew her close to him.

"I won't let you get away so easily this time," he said.

"I have a lot to think about but I will be back – I promise," Cassandra said. "I must go, but I shall return."

With that, Cassandra left the shop and made her way back to her car. How long had she been in that embrace, she wondered, as it was now getting dark; a twilight sun already penetrated the verdant canopy above her.

Cassandra made her way back to the ferry and again felt uneasy at the silent trepidation with which the ferryman spied her. Shades of a setting sun were now caressing the village. Stepping back into Wales, she was relieved to find that her car was no longer eliciting the same curiosity that it had earlier that day. Driving away from the little town, she glanced in her rear-view mirror not quite believing that she was leaving a village - and time - a century before she'd been born.

The drive back to the house she shared with Simeon, and the thought of seeing him again wasn't something that caused her anxiety as she assumed the house would be empty; it was only when she drove into the street in which the house sat that she noticed that there was a light on in its living room, the tell-tale flickering suggesting it was either a TV or computer game. Only then did her anxiety cause her stomach to tie itself into twisted knots: Simeon had returned.

Chapter Six

Cassandra placed her key inside the front door's lock and turned it. Breathing heavily with anxious fear, she pushed the door open and entered before closing it quietly behind her

"What are you doing back?" Simeon asked. He had heard the key in the lock over the sound of his computer games and now stood leaning against the door frame of the door that entered the living room.

"I won't be staying," Cassandra replied.

"Eh? But you've got nowhere else to go."

"You said in that note that you wanted me to leave, so I'm leaving."

"What note? I didn't write any note." This wasn't the first time Simeon had done something and then denied having done it in the hope of having Cassandra doubt her sanity.

"Don't try and gaslight me, Sunshine! I burnt it," she responded.

"And what am I supposed to have said in this note?" Simeon asked, trying his best to sound both incredulous and exasperated.

"That you wanted me to leave - so I'm leaving,"

"But you've nowhere to go," Simeon replied, his voice betraying his fear that his attempt at gaslighting Cassandra had this time failed.

"That's what you wanted, wasn't it! Separate me from my friends and family, have me give up my home and job, then I'm utterly dependent on you," Cassandra said, pushing past Simeon and making her way to the kitchen. Simeon having now moved from the doorway, attempted to hinder Cassandra's access to the kitchen.

"Friends? Those slags! Why do you want to hang around with them? If the pubs were still open they'd be dragging you out, telling you that you can do better than me - and getting you to act like them." Simeon said, raising his hand and pointing at Cassandra to enforce his point.

"No, they wouldn't - and even if I did meet up with them do you really think that I'm so easily led that I'd do what they said? That's you and your insecurities - if you felt better about yourself then you wouldn't feel so paranoid and imagine that I'm dreaming up ways of leaving you! Well, this time I am."

"To go where? You've met someone else, haven't you? I knew it! Fucking women, I'm pissed off with all of them – they're all unfaithful, looking for someone with more money or a bigger car."

"I have not cheated on you, you ended it! Remember? It hasn't been working for months and knowing you were only waiting for something better was the final straw. I'm not a fucking doormat – I deserve to be more than someone's fuck buddy! I deserve to be loved and cherished and even if you changed, I don't want to be loved and cherished by you," Cassandra shouted, her eyes blazing in fury.

"Who is he?" Simeon asked, taking a step forward and trying to look threatening.

"You ended it! I've been back to the shop we visited and the spoken to the man there …" Cassandra began, before being interrupted by Simeon.

"That old bastard behind the counter?" Simeon scoffed.

"I thought you hadn't seen him?"

"I didn't see him - I just remember you saying he looked like the butler from that crap film you like."

"I thought you never believed anything I said," Cassandra said, pushing past Simeon and making her way to the bottom of the stairs.

"I don't, but you must have met someone. Women like you can't ever go it alone and always have to have a bloke in tow to pay their bills."

"Bullshit! I don't need a man for *anything*. I want to feel loved and cherished – everyone needs someone to make them feel special. You just made me feel like a stop-gap, someone to be used, abused, and tossed aside," Cassandra shouted, pointing her finger at Simeon who took it as his cue to again try and intimidate Cassandra by taking a step closer and puffing up his chest.

Chapter Six

"You can't leave me," he said.

"Why? Because you're so kind? Because you make me feel so special? You didn't treat me nicely when you had the chance and now that I'm going, you're acting like a child that's had his toys taken off him."

"You bitch," he shouted.

"Come on, Si," came a man's voice from the living room. "I thought we were playing a game."

"Who's that?" Cassandra asked, shocked to realise that they were not alone.

"Just a few of the lads," Simeon replied. "I'll be there now," he shouted, turning his head toward the living room.

"I'm going to get a few things and then I'll be gone," Cassandra said. "I've had enough of twenty twenty-one and this pandemic – and had enough of you. I'm going back to a different time and place."

"What the fuck are you talking about?" Simeon asked, drawing the corners of his mouth down, into a disgusted sneer.

"Today, I visited eighteen ninety-one, and that's where I'm going," Cassandra said, hissing the words with contempt before Simeon burst out laughing.

"You're a nutcase! Any man that wants you must be crazy."

"Well, that's my problem, isn't it!" Cassandra said as she ascended the stairs.

"What have I done that's so wrong? This is how men are," Simeon said, following her.

"No, they're not. You and your cretinous friends might be like it but there are men out there that love the things I love - and know that they have to treat a person they love with kindness as the thought of losing them is unbearable."

"You don't know men if that's what you think!" Simeon said with derision. "All we want is food on the table, a roof over our head, and a whore in the bedroom."

"Well, good luck finding the woman of your dreams. I'm sure you'll be very happy together," Cassandra said, turning her back on Simeon.

Suddenly, Simeon grabbed her hair and tried to pull her back down the stairs. Somehow, Cassandra freed herself and quickly turned.

"Don't hit me, you bastard," she said, taking a step backwards.

"How else are you going to learn?" Simeon said. Only now could Cassandra smell the smell of alcohol on his breath.

"I'm not a child. Who the hell are you to teach me anything? I have a master's degree and you're an unqualified clown. I'm sick of hearing you tell me how you're the best in the world at everything, or telling me how intelligent you are."

"Nobody knows more about the Nazis than me," Simeon remonstrated.

"Yes, they do – and even they didn't, who is that going to impress? It just makes you sound like a right-wing dickhead."

"No, it doesn't," Simeon said. "We have to learn from history."

"And what have you learned? That everyone in the world speaks English if you only shout the words loudly enough at them? You seem to always take an opposing view from the consensus and I've realised that you do it in the hope that people will say 'Wow, that Simeon Danton is so smart!'"

"I think you'll find all the educated people agree with me," Simeon said, pulling up his jogging bottoms and tightening its drawstring.

"Yes - all those lucky ladies you've romanced with your anecdotes about the Nazis."

"Look, you're nothing special," he said. "Other than me, who's going to want you?"

"And that's the way to make someone feel special, is it?"

"Oh, shut it," Simeon said, gesturing to Cassandra to close her mouth by snapping his fingers against his thumb.

"What's more, I've been to see Anna."

"You what!"

"I don't need your permission to go and see her, either."

"You wouldn't like it if I was going to see some old tart I'd slept with, would you?" Simeon asked.

"No one understands a woman's needs like another woman," Cassandra said. "Why does everything have to be about sex with you? Now I know a bit more about you, I'm surprised you didn't turn up on our first date with your jeans round your ankles to save time!"

"You bitch," again Simeon lunged at Cassandra, lifting his leg as though he were about to kick her. Cassandra pushed him away

Chapter Six

but the combination of alcohol and being caught off-balance, caused him to topple backwards down the stairs.

Quickly, Cassandra grabbed a few clothes and tossed them into a holdall, all the while trying to block out the fearful groaning assailing her from the bottom of the stairs.

"We need to ring an ambulance," said one of Simeon's friends.

Only then did Cassandra realise that the fall Simeon had taken down the stairs had been serious and that it had resulted in him lying motionless, a wound on his head staining the carpet beneath him.

"Oh, shit," Cassandra said as she descended the stairs, her voice shaking with fear.

"What happened?" said a second of Simeon's friends.

"He lost his balance on the stairs," Cassandra said.

"Did I bollocks! You pushed me," Simeon said. By now, he had rolled onto his back and was trying to sit upright.

"I'm going - I won't be back," Cassandra said, relieved that Simeon wasn't gravely injured but pleased that he was in no state to prevent her from leaving.

Quickly, she moved to her car, throwing her belongings into the passenger seat, and slamming the driver's-side door shut.

She turned the key to start the engine and heard nothing but a click.

"Don't do this now, you bastard," she said, banging the steering wheel with the palms of her hand. She turned the key again just as the house door opened and Simeon stood in its portal, a towel wrapped around his head. Cassandra turned the key a third time and the car's engine started. Cassandra slammed the car into reverse, then through the gears, grinding the clutch in her haste. Within seconds, Cassandra had left the street and breathed a sigh of relief. Not long after that, she was on the road back to the Wye Valley, the nineteenth century, and Lucius.

Chapter Seven

After the attention Cassandra's car had caused on her previous visit, she decided to park it outside the nineteenth century and walk the rest of the way on foot. Again, the village seemed quiet. How different it must have been in eighteen thirty-one when a doctor at the larger village nearby wrote to a minister in Bristol stating his concern about the spiritual state of the villagers and their predilection for drinking, gambling, and fighting.

At first, Cassandra's presence caused no attention as there was no one from the nineteenth century to see her.

A different ferryman to the one that had ferried her across the river the previous day was working today and although he looked askance at her, Cassandra didn't feel too alarmed at his interest.

As she walked along the banks of the river, she spotted a figure in the distance, walking toward her. When they got within such a distance that their mutual features rendered them recognisable to one another she could see the alarm on the woman's face. It couldn't be the clothes she was wearing, Cassandra thought, as there was such a look of terror on her face one might be forgiven for thinking she had, as Lucius had suggested about the reaction Cassandra's appearance had elicited in the other villagers, seen a ghost. As if that wasn't enough, the woman began screaming and crying before running from the field in a state of terror.

Cassandra finally came to the entrance of the ascending path that led through the ancient wood and began to make her way to the old shop that lay deep within.

"I'm back," she said, pushing open the shop door.

"I've missed you," Lucius said, rising from his seat and coming to greet her. Taking her hands in his, he kissed them; then, taking a step forward, he kissed her lips.

"I know this will sound strange," Cassandra began, "but even though we only met a few days ago, I can't now imagine how life would be without you – or even remember how lonely I was until I met you," she confided, tears filling her eyes.

"I know, I feel the same way about you - you feel as if you're a part of me," Lucius said, kissing her again.

"I don't ever want to return to the twenty-first century," Cassandra said. "It was horrible. I don't have any place to call home," she added, before pausing. "May I stay here – with you?"

"I'd be heartbroken if you didn't," Lucius replied. "Let me get your bag," he added, picking up Cassandra's bag and walking to the room in which he had read Cassandra's fortune.

"Where can I stay?" Cassandra asked.

There was a pause for a moment before Lucius turned and spoke.

"I was hoping you would stay with me," he replied.

"Yes, I was also hoping for that," Cassandra said, smiling a broad smile as Lucius led them to the bottom of a short and narrow staircase.

"This way," he nodded, gesturing to the stairs that led to his bedroom with his free arm, as he bade Cassandra walk in front of him.

A few seconds later the pair were on the cottage landing.

"This is it," Lucius said, allowing Cassandra to enter first.

"What a beautiful room!" she exclaimed, walking to the room's open window, and wallowing in the sunlight and sound of birdsong as she looked down the sylvan valley.

Lucius let go of the bag and walked toward Cassandra, wrapping an arm around her waist, and standing alongside her. As she had not heard his silent approach, his touch surprised her. Turning to face him, in the sunshine his eyes sparkled. Lucius also turned and raised his hand to her face, tenderly touching her cheek before drawing her toward him and kissing her again.

As much as Cassandra wanted to satisfy her frustrated desires, she held those desires in check knowing that the anticipation of such delights would make those delights all the more exquisite when the wellspring of her passion could no longer be held in check.

Chapter Seven

"I had such a strange experience as I was coming here," she said.

"A woman in the field seemed terrified of me."

"Like she'd seen a ghost?" Lucius asked.

"Yes! How did you know I was going to say that?"

"You're not of their time," he explained. Have you ever seen a ghost?" he asked.

"Yes, I have," Cassandra replied, feeling a little coy at the admission.

"Those are people from what we think of as the past that have strayed into what we think of as the present. You, on the other hand, are a visitor from what we think of as the present into what we think of as the past," he explained. "Not only that," he began, before walking to a dressing table. "There's this," he said, removing a sepia photograph and giving it to Cassandra.

"It's me!" she exclaimed.

"Remember that I said we were lovers at the time of the French Revolution? And again in the nineteenth century? Well, this is the nineteenth century and we were lovers until last year when your husband found out about our clandestine affair and killed you. That's you in that photograph," Lucius said, pointing at the photograph in Cassandra's hand.

"Whoa, I was murdered? What happened in the eighteenth century?" she asked, forgetting that Lucius had already told her.

"We were lovers," he began. "And what a lover! I had never known such passion. It still breaks my heart to remember but we were caught up in the French Revolution and you were killed."

"I was killed twice?" Cassandra said, slumping into a chair and looking at Lucius with bewilderment. "How come you weren't able to predict those murders and save me?"

"I didn't dare to look at what future you and I had together, lest I found out that we would be parted. I waited over a century for you to return to me, and return you did," he said, pausing for breath. "Sometimes, knowing what fate awaits us isn't a good thing."

"I suppose," Cassandra said.

"This is a lawless area that had – and still has - criminals and the unwanted from both Wales and the Forest of Dean coming here to make a living on the dock. You arrived here last year from

Wales, the wife of such a criminal. We met in the village and our souls recognised one another," he said, pausing again to regroup his thoughts. "You know how you can meet someone and instantly dislike them?"

"You disliked me!"

"No, no – quite the opposite," Lucius replied.

"That's alright then – please, go on," said Cassandra, still unsure of where the conversation was leading.

"Well, you know how you can meet someone and instantly dislike them - and then meet someone else and instantly feel that you like them?"

"Yes,' said Cassandra, moving from her seat and sitting on the edge of the bed.

"Well, if you're lucky, once in a lifetime you'll meet someone and know that somewhere, somehow, you were destined to be together – forever."

"But the photo?" Cassandra asked, looking down at the photo in her lap.

"Yes, you were killed and I spent a century desolate and inconsolable at losing you. You saw my home when first you visited and how it looked? I had given up on life – then you came back to me and gave me a reason to live again. Somehow, you slipped back in time so even though I waited over a century for you, you have returned to a time little more than a year after your death – or, I should say, the death of the woman in the photo – and a century before you, the beautiful woman sat on the edge of my bed, was born."

"That's very kind of you but you seem very taken with her," Cassandra said, feeling a pang of jealousy.

"Not her, you - it was always you. I'm more than taken with you," he paused, before kneeling in front of Cassandra and taking her hands in his. "I love you," he said, looking at Cassandra to gauge her reaction.

"It makes crazy sense in some ways as I can look at you and feel like I've known you forever. You feel like the missing part of me that makes me feel complete," Cassandra said, whispering the words and looking at Lucius for his reaction.

Lucius stood and moved toward Cassandra and, once again, held her hands in his, lifting them so that Cassandra rose to her

Chapter Seven

feet. Gently, he touched her neck, brushing aside her hair. Leaning forward, he kissed her neck before looking up at her face and kissing her lips.

"You don't know how good that feels," Cassandra said. "I want you."

Slowly, Lucius unbuttoned her top, sliding a hand underneath it and then running his hand down the length of the soft skin of her back.

"Oh God, that feels so nice," she whispered.

"As nice as this?" Lucius asked, kissing her neck where it joined her chest, slowly working his way down until he came to her exposed breast.

"Don't stop, please don't stop," Cassandra gasped, clutching Lucius by the hair in order to draw him even closer to her. His warm breath on her nipple caused it to harden beneath his lips, as Lucius flicked his tongue over it and gently sucked.

"Oh God, I want you inside me," Cassandra whispered.

Lucius unbuttoned Cassandra's jeans and slid them down, and helped her step out of them. Then, standing, he ran his hand down the sides of her bare torso. Cassandra tore at his shirt, baring his chest and pressing herself against him.

Lucius again ran his hand down Cassandra's back until he reached her hips, pausing a second before slowly easing down her underwear. Pressing himself against her, Cassandra touched him through the thin fabric of his trousers. Easing the buttons open, she gasped as she felt him stiffen at her delicate touch.

Cassandra sank to her knees and took his erection into her mouth, before flicking her tongue over it and running her lips along the shaft until it glistened.

"I want to taste you, too," he said, lifting her to her feet and laying her down on the bed. Slowly, he eased her thighs apart and gave her clitoris a gentle caress before bringing the fingers he'd used to his mouth and licking them; then he tenderly trailed those same fingers down her body, letting one wet finger slip inside her.

Starting with her face, he moved his lips down her quivering body, savouring the taste on her skin as it glistened in the heat of the room.

Tenderly, he parted her lips and, once again, brought the fingers he'd used on her to his mouth and licked them. By now, Cassandra could feel the stubble on his face on her stomach and moving down. Lucius savoured the taste and again slipped a finger inside his lover as he began licking her, running his tongue across her clitoris until she quivered beneath each lingual caress.

"Straddle me," he whispered a few minutes later, before lying down, his back on the bed. "Maybe you can suck me as I lick you."

"Ooh, a sixty-nine," Cassandra said.

"*Oui, un soixante-neuf,*" Lucius replied.

"Oh God, how could I refuse," Cassandra replied.

Now that he was lying flat on the bed, Cassandra straddled his face, then bent forward. Taking his erection in her mouth, she began to suck.

In turn, Lucius grabbed a hold of her bare buttocks and buried his face between her pouting lips.

Gasping with delight, Cassandra returned to her duties and again took Lucius in her mouth, sliding her mouth up and down his rigid erection.

After months of frustration, the intimate pleasure of bare skin on bare skin was too much for them.

"Oh God, I'm cumming," Cassandra gushed, just a few minutes later, taking her mouth away from Lucius' erection and masturbating him as her whole body shuddered with an orgasm.

"I'm about to cum as well," Lucius said. "Don't worry, I won't cum in your mouth," he gasped.

"You can if you want - I came in yours!" she giggled.

"Only if you kiss me with it still on your lips," Lucius teased.

"Yes, with pleasure," Cassandra said excitedly, frantically pulling at him until he ejaculated, a little landing on her cheek and lips and the rest into her warm mouth.

Lucius groaned, his back arched, and he closed his eyes.

"Kiss me," he said.

Swiftly, Cassandra turned and kissed Lucius deeply, passionately.

"I could taste myself on your lips," she giggled.

"And I could taste myself on yours," he laughed. "It's been too long," he added. "My God, I've missed you."

Chapter Eight

The next few hours were spent in one another's arms, lost in a post-orgasmic torpor.

"I need you again," Cassandra murmured, taking hold of Lucius' member and giggling as it stiffened in her hand, each caress causing Lucius to groan with pleasure. "I can hear your heartbeat," she said, resting her head on his bare chest.

"I want you to fuck me," Lucius said, his voice almost inaudible. "Get on top."

"Ooh, my favourite position," Cassandra said, as she straddled Lucius. Parting her lips, she rubbed Lucius' erection between them until it glistened; then, slowly lowered herself onto it until it was completely inside her.

"Oh God, that feels so good," she gasped, grinding her pelvis against him.

Lucius opened his eyes and reached up to caress Cassandra's breasts, pinching her nipples.

"Pinch them harder!" she panted.

"*Oui, mademoiselle*," he replied.

"Harder – it makes me want to cum,"

"This hard?" Lucius said, squeezing a little harder, and harder still.

"Oh God, that feels amazing," Cassandra gasped, grinding her pelvis into the pelvis of her lover.

"It feels wonderful," he gasped.

The two lovers' ground against one another until the heat of the room made them glisten.

"Don't you cum mind," she said. "Not until I've had my orgasm."

"Anything for you, dear lady," Lucius replied.

"Oh God, you make me feel so full - I'm cumming," Cassandra moaned, leaning forward to French kiss Lucius, her breath hot on his lips, her breasts pressed against his chest.

"Turn over," Lucius said. "Now, I'm going to fuck you – hard!"

"On all fours?" Cassandra asked, her eyes brightening at the thought.

"Yes," Lucius said, lifting Cassandra off his swollen, rigid member and moving behind her. Moving his erection between her wet lips, he pushed himself deep inside.

"Oh God, you're so deep. You're hitting my G-spot – I can feel your balls banging against me," she gasped, taking her hand, and cupping her lover's genitals, urging him to thrust even more deeply than before.

Lucius leaned over Cassandra and reached around to massage her breasts, all the while thrusting himself in and out of her. Steadying himself, he removed a hand and ran it up and down the soft skin of Cassandra's back.

"Cum inside me," she begged. "I want to feel your cum deep inside me and then oozing out," she gasped.

Taking both hands and parting her buttocks, Lucius thrust again, thrusting as deep as he could and causing Cassandra to let out a squeal of delight.

"I'm going to cum," Lucius said, looking down at his erection as it slid in and out of his lover.

"Yes, give it to me," Cassandra gasped.

Lucius grunted and leaned over Cassandra, turning her head so he could French kiss her as he ejaculated deep inside her.

"I'm cumming," he gasped into her open mouth.

"I can feel it! I can feel it pulsing," Cassandra gasped, reaching between her lips, and touching herself.

Slowly, Lucius withdrew and Cassandra slumped to her side in ecstatic exhaustion.

"I'm a very oral person," she said, slipping a finger inside herself before bringing it to her mouth and licking it with eager delight.

"And me," Lucius said, leaning forward and kissing his lover, tasting the taste of their union with the same pleasure as before.

"That was amazing," Cassandra whispered. "I want to do *everything* with you."

"And I want to do everything with you – use my body like you would your own. No need to ask if it's alright, just do it," he

Chapter Eight

replied, breathing so heavily that he had to rest his head on the pillow of his bed.

"The same goes for me – do anything you want. I want to do everything with you," Cassandra replied, leaning forward to kiss him.

The morning sun of the new day now penetrated the window and fell upon the two naked forms that lay entwined, before Cassandra moved.

"I suppose we'd better get up," she said. "What shall we do today? I'm in a new century and would love to see what it's like."

"Of course. Shall we go for a picnic? I can show you the area," Lucius suggested.

"That sounds nice," Cassandra replied, climbing from the bed, and walking to a dressing table where stood a jug of water and a large china basin. "Just let me have a quick wash and I can make us some food," she added.

Lucius got dressed and as he buttoned his shirt he walked toward Cassandra; moving aside her hair, he kissed her cheek.

"I've missed you so much," he said, his eyes glistening as tears of happiness began to fill them.

"You're the one I've waited a lifetime to meet," Cassandra said, wrapping her arm around him before pulling him toward her and kissing his lips.

"What should I wear?" she asked, remembering the attention her modern-day clothes had caused the day before.

"I have a wardrobe full of clothes that I bought for you before you were taken from me last year," Lucius said. "They've never been worn," he added.

"Ooh, let me see!" Cassandra said with excitement.

"The dresses are simple as I didn't like the bustle that was popular a few years ago," Lucius said, opening a wardrobe door. "I think you'll like the undergarments! They're muslin and decorated with bands of lace. Suspenders replaced garters a few years ago and can be buttoned to your corset. Drawers – or should I say knickerbockers – are in that drawer there," he said, pointing at a drawer on the dressing table. "The shirt is like mine - with a high collar - but it's definitely a woman's shirt, I promise! There's also a double-breasted waistcoat or two. I think you may need a jacket in case the weather changes so there's one or two of those, too. They have those 'leg of mutton' sleeves that seem very popular at the moment," he said, pausing. "There are also some nice black stockings in those drawers over there," he said, pointing to a chest of drawers. "Oh, and boots over there," he added, pointing to a few pairs of high buttoned boots that sat alongside laced-up shoes that had large buckles decorating the front of them.

Lucius smiled at Cassandra, moved to the door and descended the stairs.

Within an hour, Cassandra had both dressed and finished packing a small hamper, before moving from the kitchen to the shop, where Lucius sat behind a counter.

"Ready when you are," Cassandra said, as Lucius rose to his feet.

"You look lovely!" he said, moving toward Cassandra. Looking her up and down, he leaned in to kiss her on the cheek.

"I found a few dresses that look like they might have been worn by a Can-can girl at the *Folies Bergère* so I decided to wear one of those," Cassandra said.

"And you look very beautiful in it, I must say," Lucius said. "Here, let me carry that," he added, taking the hamper from Cassandra.

The two then walked hand in hand to the door, their footsteps sounding on the shop's old floorboards.

"I'd better lock the door," Lucius said, as he opened the door for Cassandra to exit.

"What a lovely day," Cassandra said, squinting into the sunshine that oozed over the valley like warm honey.

The two made their way down the steep steps and narrow path, over ancient stones, and knotted roots thick with damp moss and lichen.

"Here we are," Lucius said, taking Cassandra's fragile hand in his as the two began their walk alongside the beautiful river.

"Where are you going to take me?" Cassandra asked.

"Let's just stroll a while, shall we? On a day like this who needs a plan?"

Within an hour, the two had reached the village; Cassandra gazed up.

"No wires," she said. "I really *am* in the nineteenth century."

Chapter Nine

As the two entered the village, Cassandra's attention was first drawn to the road. Gone was the tarmac of the twenty-first century; here was a road little changed since the Middle Ages.

"There's the weird guy that was looking at me on the ferry," said Cassandra, leaning towards Lucius in order to whisper the words into his ear.

"Which one?" he asked, turning his back on the three labourers that were looking at them, their soiled, tattered clothing and dirty faces giving them an unsettling appearance.

"The one in the middle," Cassandra replied.

"That's John Wintour - he's a cousin of the husband you had that murdered you last year."

"No wonder he's looking at me – he must think he's seen a ghost," said Cassandra, feeling uneasy as she thought about how he might react.

"And what happened to my husband?" asked Cassandra.

"He was hung," Lucius said. "He had quite a criminal record," he added, after seeing the look of shock on Cassandra's face.

"Oh great!" Cassandra said disconsolately. "I always seemed to pick such idiots before I meet you."

"Thank you, sweetheart. Don't worry, he's not that bright. He seems to recognise you but it doesn't look like he can remember where from," Lucius said, holding Cassandra's hand a little tighter as they passed the dock workers who, by now, had sat down near the banks of the river. All three fell silent as the lovers approached.

"See, he didn't say a thing," said Lucius.

Passing the old pub and taking a right turn as they came to the medieval Monks' Hall, the two continued to hold hands and as they walked up a small lane and into a darkened wood.

"Ooh, I like it here," Cassandra said, sunlight filtering through the leaves and falling on her pretty face, still a little flushed from the sexual rigours she had enjoyed earlier that morning.

"There's an interesting viewpoint up here," Lucius said. "It's named The Devil's Pulpit."

"Oh, I've heard of that! Isn't that where the Devil is supposed to have appeared and preached his gospel to the monks tending the abbey gardens in the Middle Ages?" asked Cassandra.

"Yes, that's the one. This is a land of myth and magic - and why I chose to live here," he said, as they climbed the steep path through the sylvan glade.

"I think it must have also been the place where Wordsworth sat when he wrote his poem about the abbey," Cassandra said.

"William Wordsworth? Yes, I remember him coming here. In fact, he visited the place twice – once in seventeen ninety-three and then again five years later. The first time he had written a poem about a child that lived in a cottage in a churchyard at Goodrich – about seventeen miles from here," Lucius said.

"You met Wordsworth! That's incredible," said Cassandra.

"I also met Percy and Mary Shelley when they visited the area in eighteen fifteen. They'd come to look at a house but it was too small for their needs and wasn't even half-built and so they moved on to Europe to see Byron."

"Ah, and there they had their *haunted summer*," Cassandra replied.

"Their what?" Lucius asked.

"Their haunted summer. They spent it at the Villa Diodati on the shores of Lake Geneva but it did nothing but rain and so Byron suggested that they all write a ghost story. Byron's physician – Doctor Polidori – wrote *The Vampyre* and Mary Shelley wrote *Frankenstein*," Cassandra said, remembering her studies on the subject at university.

"I liked Percy Shelley. Did you know that he was also a vegetarian? I also liked his liberal politics," Lucius said.

"This is so weird," Cassandra said. "Who's ever going to believe me if I tell them that I know a man that knew Shelley!"

"Such a tragic death, too," Lucius said.

"Didn't he drown?"

Chapter Nine

"Yes, and being an atheist, they buried his body on the beach. A few days later they had second thoughts and went to find the body but none of them could remember where on the beach he was buried. So, they all began digging and one of them hit the front of his head with a mattock, removing a portion of his skull," Lucius said, gesturing with his hand how the mattock must have opened wide the front of the poet's head.

"Oh my God, is that true?" Cassandra said.

"Absolutely," Lucius replied. "His heart was also cut from his chest to give to Mary, who kept it with her for the rest of her life."

"How macabre," Cassandra replied, as Lucius stopped to catch his breath, before continuing the steep climb uphill.

"They had built a funeral pyre to cremate his body but as the flames grew higher," he continued, "the heat caused the flap of bone at the front of his head to pop open, whereupon his brains were seen to bubble, like 'stew in a cauldron'."

Cassandra, sensitive to the idea of skulls being opened and brains exposed, given her personal experience in such matters, made no mention of what Lucius had said.

"Mary Shelley's mother is something of a hero of mine," said Cassandra.

"Mary Wollstonecraft?" queried Lucius.

"Yes - a great advocate for women's rights."

"Here we are," Lucius said, stopping at a promontory of rock that jutted out over the trees below it, thus allowing visitors a view of the abbey far below.

"So, we're in England and that's Wales?" asked Cassandra.

"Yes, that's right."

"I love it here! It can't have changed much in centuries," Cassandra said, turning with arms outstretched.

"No, it hasn't - the docks have all but gone, as have the pubs, the whores, and the 'rustic pursuits' that they once enjoyed."

"Rustic pursuits?" queried Cassandra.

"Fighting, gambling, dancing, whoring," he paused. "And cockfighting,"

"Bastards," Cassandra said, her smile turning to a scowl.

"I agree - at one time I hoped to change them but it was like casting pearls before swine."

"I'm a vegan," said Cassandra.

"I know – so am I. We've known each other for centuries, remember?"

"Why is it that you don't eat meat?" Cassandra asked.

"I don't feast on corpses," Lucius replied, causing Cassandra to throw her arms around him and kiss him.

"That's exactly how I feel," Cassandra said.

"I've missed you so much," Lucius said, looking at Cassandra and wondering how he had survived a century without her. Taking Cassandra by the hand, he led her back down the path from whence they had come.

"Let's find somewhere where we can rest awhile, enjoy the view, and have a bite to eat," said Lucius.

"I can't wait to feel the sun on my face – I've spent too long in lockdown," Cassandra said, squeezing Lucius' hand. "A field would be nice."

Silently, the two walked, each knowing that the feelings they had for one another could stay unspoken, knowing that such feelings aren't easily expressed with words.

Pausing for a moment, Lucius pointed at a yew tree.

"See that tree?" he asked.

"Yes, what about it?"

"That was growing here when I first came to this place in the eleventh century," he said, smiling at the tree as though he had seen the face of an old friend.

"That's amazing," Cassandra said. "I've read about yews and why there are so many in churchyards but can't quite remember as it was a long time ago," she added.

"Would you like me to tell you?" Lucius said.

"Yes, please."

"The yew has been associated with death - and the journey of the soul from this life to the next - for thousands of years. As such, it was sacred to Hecate, the Ancient Greek Goddess of Death, Witchcraft and Necromancy. It was also thought that yews purified the dead as they entered the underworld of Hades. The druids in Celtic Wales also saw yews as sacred, planting them close to their temples as they used yews in their death rituals. Because it is such a long-lived tree, it came to represent eternal life.

Chapter Nine

"Many churches were built on the sites of what were once Celtic temples. As we might expect, Christianity borrowed a lot of pagan imagery and beliefs when trying to convert those pagans. In fact, in the year six-hundred and one Pope Gregory suggested that places of pagan worship could simply be converted into Christian churches."

"I love things like this," Cassandra said. "Visiting old churches and seeing yews in the cemetery puts us so close to ancient history."

"Very near, given every moment in time – past, present, and future – is happening right now," Lucius replied.

"And I'm proof that the people we once loved are never more than a fingertip away," Cassandra said, touching Lucius' hand.

Lucius stopped and smiled.

"There was another reason why Christians viewed yews as holy, and that was because the heart of the tree is red, while its sap is white - and as every Catholic knows, these colours symbolise the blood and body of Christ. It's also a very hardy tree that can thrive on apparently infertile soil so it also suggested rebirth and resurrection," he added, stopping, and looking about him.

"What is it?" Cassandra asked.

"This is Offa's Dyke," Lucius said.

"Now I've also heard of this but can't remember the details. What is it?"

"A large earthwork border that's named after Offa, the Anglo-Saxon king of Mercia from seven sixty-seven until seven ninety-six who, legend has it, ordered its construction. It was the old border between Anglian Mercia and the Welsh kingdom of Powys."

"Wow, that's so old," said Cassandra.

"Older than that," Lucius said, "as it was started in the fifth century. It had a ditch on the Welsh side with the soil from that piled into a bank on the Mercian side. Throughout its entire length, the Dyke provides an uninterrupted view from Mercia into Wales. It is to Wales, what Hadrian's Wall is to the Scottish," he said, pausing for a moment. "Thirty years ago, the writer George Borrow wrote that it was customary for the English to cut off the ears of every Welshman who was found to the east of the dyke, and for the Welsh to hang every Englishman that they found to the west of it."

"Crazy!" said Cassandra. "And what about the French?" she added, giving Lucius a wink.

"Ah, that he didn't say," Lucius said, kissing Cassandra's cheek. "This would be a nice spot," he added, setting himself down at the top of a steep pasture that afforded them panoramic views of the village and the valley.

"I've found a place I can call home," Cassandra said, sitting down and gazing into the distance.

"Are you sure?" Lucius asked.

"Why do you ask?" Cassandra said, a little hurt to think that he did not feel the same way about her as she did about him.

"Because you've strayed from your moment in time into this one. Many people go missing every year and some are never heard from again. It's not always the case that they've gone some *place* else, but some *time* else. These gateways to the past – or the future – don't stay open for long. I would be heartbroken to lose you again but you had your life in the twenty-first century. What if the doorway in time closes and leaves you stuck here?"

"I don't care! I hated my life in the twenty-first century. I was an only child and both my parents are now dead. All I had was an oaf that was using me whereas here, here I have you," she said, then paused for a moment. "And this," she gestured with a sweeping wave of her hand at the lush green of the verdurous valley that lay before them.

"I couldn't be happier - each day apart from you is a day to be endured," Lucius replied, taking Cassandra's hand and kissing the backs of her fingers.

The lovers paused a while and ate their picnic. Unbeknown to Lucius, Cassandra had also packed a bottle of wine.

"Look what we have here!" she said, holding it aloft and smiling.

"Well, we'd certainly better drink that," Lucius said, opening it and pouring them each a drink.

After the bottle had been quaffed, Cassandra sidled up to Lucius and rested her head on his shoulder. He, in turn, held a buttercup under her chin.

Chapter Nine

"Let's go back to the river. It's such a nice day, we can have a paddle," she said, playfully running her fingers through Lucius' hair. Standing, he reached out a hand and helped Cassandra to her feet, before both descended the hill, luxuriating on the panorama that lay before them.

"It's so beautiful here. It reminds me of that Johnny Depp film *Chocolat* – have you seen it?" said Cassandra asked.

"Johnny who?" Lucius replied.

"Sorry, I forgot that he won't even be born for another seventy-three years! He's an actor."

"An actor? Like Sir Henry Irving?" Lucius asked.

"Something like that, yes," Cassandra replied. "To think, I wasn't even going to visit your shop. If I hadn't been bored of staring at the same four walls – and going mad because of the pandemic sweeping the country – I might never have met you."

"Met me *again*," Lucius said.

"Yes, sorry – again."

"Life can change in an instant," Lucius replied.

The village was strangely silent as they passed through it, with only a few children playing games in the street.

"It's nice to see them out rather than sat at home on their Xbox," Cassandra said.

"Xbox?" Lucius asked.

"It doesn't matter," Cassandra said. "It's just something else from my time that's creating a generation that doesn't know how to talk to one another. Lucius," she added. "I feel a little tipsy."

Soon the lovers were both by the slow-flowing river. Occasional bushes and the odd tree stood along its banks. Spying a gap between one clump of bushes and another, Cassandra pulled Lucius between them.

"Guess what?" she said, kissing him.

"What?"

"I'm almost naked under this dress," she said, unbuttoning it and letting it fall to the ground. "See, I told you I was a little bit tipsy!"

"I love seeing you naked," Lucius said.

"Thank you" Do you think I have a nice bum?" Cassandra said, as she slid down her underwear and, turning, slapped one of her bare cheeks.

"Callipygian perfection, my dear," Lucius said, falling to his knees and kissing the cheek that Cassandra had just slapped. Sidling up to Lucius who, by now, had returned to his feet, Cassandra began unbuttoning his shirt with one hand and rubbing his groin with the other.

"That wine has made me a little frisky," she giggled.

"Me too," Lucius replied.

Soon, the two stood naked, holding each other close as flickering shadows of light and dark dappled upon them as the sun bounced off ripples in the water.

Cassandra led Lucius down to the water's edge and stepped in as Lucius followed her.

"I already feel like I've been here a lifetime," she said, kissing Lucius and gently massaging his manhood beneath the water. Again, she giggled as it stiffened at her tender touch.

"I want you inside me," she whispered coquettishly, straddling him and sliding down his rigid staff.

"Feels so good," Lucius gasped as the cool water splashed around them. Taking Cassandra's nipples between his fingers he gave them a squeeze, causing Cassandra to quiver in paroxysms of delight.

"Don't cum! I want to tease you - I want your balls to ache for me so much that you can hardly walk back to the shop! And then as soon as we get there, I want you to just bend me over and fuck me hard as you have to have me there and then for being such a tease and making your balls ache," she softly laughed.

"But I want to cum now," Lucius implored, sucking Cassandra's nipple, and looking up at her with his bright blue eyes.

"Too bad," Cassandra said, dismounting and masturbating Lucius beneath the waters of the cool rivers. "I love your big balls," she added, giving them a rub. "Want to go back to the shop and give me a good seeing to?"

Chapter Ten

Back at the shop, Lucius closed the door and strode toward Cassandra, kissing her passionately as she massaged his groin through the fabric of his trousers before unbuttoning them. It wasn't long before her nimble fingers began masturbating him. Now that he was fully erect, she turned around, lifted her dress, and bent over to expose her bare backside.

"Come on, Lucius, slide it into me," she said, looking around at him, widening her eyes and blowing him a kiss. "I've dropped my knickers for you – now this ass is all yours!"

Lucius took a hold of his penis and stroked his hand back and forth, lusting at the sight that awaited him.

"I love watching you masturbate – it really turns me on," Cassandra said, spreading her buttocks so Lucius could more easily slide himself inside her. She gasped as it entered her, his thrusts soon becoming so hard and deep that she had to steady herself by bending over the shop counter.

"Come on, Lucius," she said. "Give it to me! Teach me a lesson for making your balls ache" she added, reaching between her legs to pleasure herself. "I'm a bad girl and bad girls need to be taught a lesson!"

"Yes they do," Lucius said, playfully smacking her bare backside, then clenching his teeth in ecstasy, digging his fingers into Cassandra's backside and leaving red marks as he kneaded the flesh beneath them.

"See, I told you that you'd want me even more if I made you wait. Come on, fuck me, you dirty bastard! Use me! Call me a whore," she gasped.

"You like that, you whore?" he said, thrusting hard, before bending over Cassandra to mound Cassandra's exposed breasts and pinch her nipples so hard that she moaned with pleasure.

"I want you to cum inside me," she said. "Cum hard and deep - fill me up with your hot cum," she moaned.

Gasping, he brushed aside Cassandra's hair and kissed her neck.

"Bite me," she panted, as Lucius continued to thrust his engorged member in and out of his lover, biting the flesh of her tender neck where it joined her shoulder. "Oh God," she gasped. "Harder," she gasped, rubbing between her legs a little faster.

Lucius continued to pound and as he felt a wave of orgasmic pleasure shudder through Cassandra, he bit down even harder.

"Yes! Yes! Oh God, I've missed you," she gasped.

"You're incredible, Cass," Lucius said, watching as Cassandra turned, sank to her knees, and took his member into her mouth.

"I told you, I'm a very oral person," she said, licking Lucius' semi-erect penis.

"Sorry to bother you – are you open?" came a voice behind them.

Unbeknown to the lovers, in their frenzied passion, a local had been watching them the whole time.

"Give me a moment," Lucius said, tucking his manhood back into his trousers as Cassandra wiped her lips with her finger before covering her chest, and standing up so that her dress fell back down to her calves.

"Now, how may I help you?" Lucius said, turning to see that the local had left them.

"I hope he enjoyed the show," Cassandra said, laughing and taking a step toward Lucius to kiss him.

"How could he not with someone as beautiful you as the star performer," Lucius replied, wrapping his arm around Cassandra's waist, and drawing her near to him. "I know that I keep saying it but, God, I've missed you," he said, kissing her face.

Chapter Eleven

The next day, the two lovers once again awoke to the sound of birdsong outside the little cottage window. Cassandra gently pulled back the blankets and stepped from the bed to peek through the panes at the world outside, sighing with pleasure at the view of the woodland before her.

"What's the matter?" Lucius said, stirring from his slumber and sleepily looking about the room after his outstretched arm had sought Cassandra and found nothing more than the pillow on which she had lain.

"Nothing's the matter – nothing could be more perfect," she replied.

"Good!" Lucius replied, yawning, and stretching his arms as he sat on the edge of the bed. "What would you like to do today?" he asked.

"Aside from making love to you?" Cassandra teased, walking across the room to give Lucius a kiss.

"I was hoping you'd say that," he said, reaching around her and squeezing her bare backside before pulling her close and kissing her stomach.

"I may need to go back to the twenty-first century as I've forgotten my pill," she replied, stroking his face with her hand, and running her thumb across his lips.

"Pill? Are you ill?" Lucius asked, concerned that Cassandra was unwell.

"No, my contraceptive pill," she said smiling and running her fingers through his hair.

"They have a pill for it? My, how times have changed," he said.

"Well, we don't want to be using condoms, do we? I want to feel skin on skin!" Cassandra said coquettishly, leaning forward to kiss Lucius' handsome face.

"Prophylactics? They sell some vulcanised rubber ones in the village."

"Really? Since when? I thought that contraception was a real problem for nineteenth-century women," Cassandra said, a little dumbfounded.

"For about twenty years, I think," Lucius replied, looking around for his clothes. "I've not used them but a customer of mine likened them to trying to scratch your foot while you're still wearing a shoe," he laughed.

"Well, we certainly won't be using them then," said Cassandra, wrinkling her nose in mock disgust.

Lucius paced around the room, looking for his clothes, clothes he had thrown off in the heat of passion after the previous day's sex in the shop had progressed upstairs.

"Have you seen my boots?" he asked.

"Over there," Cassandra said, pulling on a shirt. "Have you seen my underwear?" she asked.

"Up there," Lucius said, pointing at the stained-glass lampshade that hung by a chain from the ceiling and Cassandra's underwear hanging from it.

"Sorry," said Cassandra, laughing at the memory as she climbed on the bed to retrieve them. "I still think it would be best if I head back to the twenty-first century and pick up a few things, my pill included," she added, stepping into her underwear before climbing down from the brass bed.

"Will you be safe?" Lucius asked, concerned that Cassandra's former partner may cause trouble.

"Why do you ask? Are you worried that I may not be able to find a way back here – and you?" she asked, her forehead creasing into a frown. "Maybe you can come with me," she added.

"Maybe," Lucius said, as they dressed.

After dressing, the two made their way downstairs.

"Will it be okay to lock up the shop for a few hours?" she asked.

"Yes, it will be fine. It's not as if I'm going to lose any customers, given I have so few of them."

"I remember," Cassandra said, interrupting Lucius and curtailing what he was going to say.

"I don't understand," he responded.

Chapter Eleven

"When I first came here you said you hadn't had a customer in years."

"*Years*? That was back in the future," Lucius replied. "Is that what happens to me?" he asked, looking sad.

"Don't you ever divine your own future?" Cassandra asked.

"No, definitely not. Imagine if I had done such a thing in the eighteenth century and found out I would have to wait another century for you to return to me. By not doing it, I could wake up every day and think 'Ah, perhaps this will be the day she'll return to me," he said. "Life has been very lonely," he added.

"Yes, but then I came back into your life," Cassandra said, brushing his cheek with the backs of her fingers.

"And brought sunshine back into it," he said, taking Cassandra in his arms and kissing her.

The two closed the shop door behind them and began the perilous descent through the ancient wood and down to the river. Within half an hour, they were back in the village.

"I parked my car in the twenty-first century as it attracted too much attention last time - when I parked it over there," Cassandra said, pointing across the river to Wales.

"They won't have ever seen a motorcar, that's why. It's going to take another four years before Evelyn Ellis imports a *Panhard et Levassor*."

"Yes, well mine's a Fiat," Cassandra said. "Hey, that's also French!" she added.

The two walked down to the ferry where the ferryman, once again, gave Cassandra a look made up of equal parts suspicion and fear.

"What's his problem? I've got Victorian clothes on today," Cassandra asked, leaning into Lucius in order she not be overheard.

"It's your face - I told you, he's a relative of the husband you had that murdered you a year ago."

"That's creepy," Cassandra said. "When you say it like that it makes me feel like I've come back from the dead."

The ferry bumped into the opposite bank and Cassandra and Lucius quickly disembarked.

"Lucius, what's wrong?" Cassandra asked, grabbing hold of his arm.

"We're leaving the nineteenth century – I'm getting older," he said, his hair beginning to grey and his skin to wrinkle.

"But you said that I had made you young again after I first saw you in the shop."

"I don't know," he wheezed. "I can't explain it - look at my hands!" he said looking at his wrinkled hands and the liver spots that now marked them.

"Go back! I'm only going for my pill – I'm sure I'll be safe. I don't want to lose you," Cassandra said, tears filling her eyes as she embraced Lucius and held him close to her.

"Nor I, you," he replied, his back beginning to curve into the stoop of age.

"Let me help you," Cassandra said, taking him by the arm.

"I'm sure I'll be fine when I'm back over there," he said, nodding to the far bank.

Cassandra guided Lucius back to the ferry and watched as he returned to more than a century before the moment they had parted, breathing a sigh of relief as his back straightened and his hair returned to black.

"I love you," she shouted, waving goodbye.

"Love you, too," Lucius replied, much to the scorn of a few passing dockers.

Cassandra made her way back to her car and changed back into modern attire. All the while she thought about how should she want to stay with Lucius, she would have to find the courage to say goodbye to the twenty-first century and her own time.

The drive back to the house she had shared with Simeon seemed to last an eternity before she drove into the street in which she had once lived, her heart pounding when she saw that Simeon's car was parked outside their former home.

Leaving her car unlocked, she quietly trod the path to the front door, annoyed that she would now only have a little time to pick up a few things and not have the time to change her passwords to keep Simeon from posting malicious things on her accounts.

Chapter Twelve

Cassandra tried to open the door as quietly as she could and, at first, assumed she had been successful.

"Who's there?" Simeon shouted from the living room. "Oh, it's you," he added, now that he stood by the living room door. "I knew you'd come crawling back to me once you had come to your senses," he said, as his lips twisted into a cross between a smile and a sneer.

"I haven't, I've just come back to pick up a few things," Cassandra said, smiling a triumphant smile back at him.

"What?" he replied angrily, the smile on his face quickly dissolving into a look of fury.

Cassandra moved to the bottom of the stairs and quickly climbed them before hearing Simeon's phone ringing.

"I can't talk, mate – the bitch is back," she heard him say. "I'll call you later."

Cassandra grabbed a few things and thrust them into a holdall. Suddenly, she was aware that Simeon stood on the landing, gazing at her through the open bedroom door.

"You can't leave me – we had a good thing going on," he said, taking a step nearer and blocking the doorway.

Without looking up, Cassandra continued packing, going back to her wardrobe for a few more things before responding.

"I've already left you - I've just returned for a few things. I'll soon be out of what's left of your hair," she said, looking at Simeon over her shoulder.

"Oh, yeah? You're not going anywhere - I won't let you. No one other than me would put up with your shit," he said.

"Fuck you," Cassandra replied. "No one tells me what to do," she hissed as she ducked underneath Simeon's arm. By now, now that he was attempting to block her exit by blocking the door with his hefty body, his right shoulder pressed against one side of the door frame and with his left arm outstretched, the palm of his hand pressed against the other side of the door frame.

As Cassandra passed him, he grabbed her arm, spinning her around and trying to force his open mouth onto her lips.

"No!" she said, pulling free of his grasp.

"We were made for each other," he protested. "I won't let you go," he added as Cassandra turned away from him and ran down the stairs. Quickly opening the door, within a few moments she was back in her car. Turning the key, only to hear the engine making nothing but a click.

"No, don't do this," she shouted, looking up to see Simeon running down the garden path toward her. Within a second, his hand was on the handle of the door on her side of the car. He tried to open it but anticipating such a course of action Cassandra had already locked it. In his unabated fury, he began punching the door's window.

Again, Cassandra tried to start the car and this time the engine roared into life. Slamming the car into reverse, she sped away from the house.

Cassandra drove through the narrow lanes back to Lucius at speed, glancing in her rear-view mirror every few seconds to make sure Simeon wasn't following her and hoping that he would let her leave in peace.

Parking where her car had been parked less than an hour before, she quickly made her way back to the ferry, forgetting to change into her Victorian attire.

"Yes? What's your fucking problem?" she shouted, as the ferryman approached and began eyeing her with even more suspicion than he had when she had taken the route earlier that morning.

"Nothing," the man said, shaking his head and looking at the river.

"Then take me over there," she said, pointing at the opposite bank and jumping on board.

A few minutes later she was back in the little village and the nineteenth century.

Lucius appeared, and ran toward her, rejuvenated, and vivified at having left the twenty-first century.

"Let's go for a drink," said Cassandra, closing her eyes in the warmth and security of his embrace.

Chapter Twelve

"And you'd better get changed," he said, aware of the commotion Cassandra's modern attire would cause them and which were already causing a few glances.

"Why?" she asked.

"They've never seen a woman in trousers," he explained.

"Oh God, really? I will get changed, as I've had enough of today, but I won't kowtow to what others expect of me. If they don't like me as I am then they can kiss my arse."

One drink later, and with Cassandra having changed into her Victorian clothes in the pub's toilets, they emerged and began to make their way down to the riverbank and back to the shop.

"Oh, shit, it's Simeon," Cassandra said, noticing a man crossing the river aboard the little ferry, his modern clothes causing as much interest as Cassandra's modern clothes had caused. "I don't think he recognises me in these clothes – it must be the hat," she added.

"Then act as if you don't know him. We shall deal with this when I've had time to think," Lucius said, taking hold of Cassandra's hand.

"I don't want the doorway to the nineteenth century to close and him and me to be both stuck here," Cassandra said to Lucius, trying to smile in the hope that what she was saying would be construed as something trivial.

As Lucius and Cassandra drew nearer to where the ferry had docked, Lucius leaned into Cassandra to speak to her.

"I didn't have much of a look of him that first day you came to shop but now that I have ..."

"What? What is it?" Cassandra said, breathing a sigh of relief as Simeon walked past them.

"Cassandra, he was your husband – the man that killed you."

Chapter Thirteen

Cassandra fell mute at the thought that someone that had once taken her life was now stalking her. Worse still, she had been a partner of his in twenty-first-century life. Almost paralysed with fear, it took Lucius to break the evil spell Simeon's presence had wrought upon her.

"We need to get back to the shop," he said. "I have a few ideas."

Cassandra felt too scared to talk for most of the walk back to the shop, turning every few seconds to make sure they weren't being followed. Finally, they made it home.

"Back home," Lucius said, as they reached the cottage, Lucius reaching inside his coat pocket for his keys.

"At last," Cassandra said, breathing a sigh of relief that she had reached what already felt to her to be her sanctuary.

"We'll work this out, I promise. We're going to face this together," Lucius said.

"Kiss me," Cassandra asked, putting her hands on Lucius' shoulders, tears filling her eyes as she kissed him. "I knew something would spoil it," she added.

"We won't let it," Lucius said, opening the door so that they could both walk inside and leave the world behind them.

Cassandra let out a sigh.

"Ah, I feel safe here - in this little cottage," Cassandra said, breathing a second sigh of relief. "Now I can talk again without having to look over my shoulder."

"So, we have a problem," Lucius said, as he locked the door and walked across the shop toward the velvet curtain that separated the rooms. "We don't yet know why he's here, nor do we know his motives. He is the latest incarnation of the man that killed you last year but even though only a year has passed since then, he's slipped into what you and he think of as the past and so despite being born a century after he killed you, he appears to be the same age as he was when he did it."

"It disgusts me that I didn't recognise him when I met him in the twenty-first century - and, worse still, slept with him. He's a cruel bastard," Cassandra said, dabbing her eyes with a tissue.

"From what you told me last year, he always was. When you and I were lovers and he was your husband, he had a reputation for violence. The trouble is, he's a coward and only picked on those he thought wouldn't fight back – women, children, and cripples. This village was – and is – a rough and lawless area that attracted many people that we might think of as outsiders. He quickly found out that there were people here that made a living from fighting and that he was no match for them."

"So, how did we – you and me, I mean, not him and me - meet?" Cassandra asked, sitting down at the table as Lucius poured them a drink.

"You came to me one day after he had hit you. You needed a salve for the bruises and the pain. As I have said to you, souls recognise one another and I knew as soon as I saw you that you were the one I had loved and lost in the French Revolution, a century before," Lucius said, handing Cassandra a glass of wine.

Suddenly, the noise of the shop door opening interrupted them.

"Hold on," Lucius said, quickly rising to his feet. Brushing aside the velvet curtain, he entered the shop.

"Where's the old man?" Simeon asked, looking around the shop.

"Old man?" Lucius asked.

"Yes - I was here last week with the Missus and she said she'd seen an old man with white hair here. She's been visiting him since and I want to speak to him," Simeon said, the quiet fury in his voice tempered only by the fact that Lucius was more toned and muscular than him.

"There's no old man with white hair here, I assure you," Lucius said.

Cassandra quietly rose to her feet and moved to the velvet curtain to better hear the conversation about her.

"The lying bitch!" Simeon said. "I can't believe a word she says."

Chapter Thirteen

"Is there something else with which I can help you?" Lucius asked, parting his arms, and gesturing around the shop with open palms.

"No. Is this village being used for a film or something? Everyone's in fancy dress."

"No, this is how we live. Is there anything else?" Lucius replied his voice calm after a thousand years of experience in dealing with objectionable people.

"I suppose not," Simeon asked, looking around the shop in disgust. "Is there a McDonald's anywhere near here? I'm starving."

"McDonald's?" Lucius asked. "There's a James McDonald in the village," he added, moving to the shop's door, opening it, then standing next to it and smiling at Simeon.

"What are you on, mate?" Simeon asked as he walked past.

"Floorboards, I believe," Lucius said, looking at the floor, before closing the door behind Simeon.

Lucius watched as Simeon stood outside for a few moments, apparently perplexed, and looking at the cottage in confusion, his simple brain trying to make sense of why the shop looked in a state of good repair today compared to the abandoned and overgrown state in which he had seen it the week before. Pulling the map that his father had given him from his pocket when he and Cassandra had first used it to find the place, there appeared to be a moment's elucidation on his face as he strode back down the woodland path.

"Thanks for that," said Cassandra, walking quietly across the shop floor to kiss Lucius' cheek and enjoy the sight of Simeon leaving them. "I'm glad he's gone. Do you think he'll be back?"

"I don't know. If he thinks you've lied to him then he's not going to have any idea where you are and that you might have said you were here but might be anywhere in the country. On the other hand, if he thinks you've left him for the man you told him about last week then he may return. He's a coward and a bully, so if he thinks there's an old man here that he can push around then he may return. Let's worry about that when ... if ... it happens, shall we?" Lucius said, returning Cassandra's kiss with a kiss of his own.

"I love how you take control of situations," she said. "Nothing seems to bother you."

"Thank you, but there are things that bother me," Lucius said.

"Such as?" Cassandra said, hoping such a fear was something she could assuage.

"Loneliness ... and losing you," Lucius said, holding Cassandra close and kissing the tip of her nose.

The two of them spend the rest of that day together, Lucius in his working apron preparing a few perfumes and Cassandra sat in the garden, enjoying the sunshine and birdsong, her mind on Simeon and whether or not he would attempt to spoil her happiness.

Chapter Fourteen

After an evening meal and a few more glasses of wine, the cares of the day seemed a distant memory.

"I've never wanted anyone more than you," Cassandra said, as the two lovers sat on high-backed chairs, facing one another. "Did you know we'd end up as lovers again when you told my fortune?"

"It wasn't a certainty, no. Life deals us a hand of cards but it is up to us how we play those cards," Lucius said, looking at Cassandra across the warm glow of the candles he had lit for them as day turned to night.

"I can see why in every life I've had, I've fallen for you," Cassandra said, smiling the smile of true affection at Lucius. "I've never met anyone else like you."

"And I've never wanted anyone but you," he replied, rising from his seat and walking around the table to kiss her, brushing her long hair from her face so that he could more easily see her expression.

"You're so beautiful," he said, leaning in for yet another kiss.

"Let's go to bed," she said, blowing out all but one of the candles, their flames dying until the room was finally illuminated less by candlelight and more by the pale light of the full moon as it cascaded through the leaded window.

In the bedroom, Cassandra lit a few candles from the one she had brought up the stairs with them and began to undress.

"Here, let me help you," Lucius said, standing behind Cassandra and unbuttoning her shirt, the two of them watching their reflections in a large mirror that stood in the corner of the room. As Cassandra's shirt fell to the floor, leaving her topless, Lucius cupped her pert breasts in his hand kissed her neck. Cassandra closed her eyes and sighed with pleasure before reaching behind her and stroking Lucius' groin, once again giggling with delight as it began to stiffen beneath her fingers.

"They're not too small for you are they, Lucius?" she asked, placing her hands on top of his.

"No, they're perfect."

"Here, let me undress you," Cassandra said, turning and unbuttoning Lucius' shirt and letting it fall to the ground in a discarded heap, as they had with her shirt.

Seductively, Cassandra tugged at the buttons on his trousers, looking up at him through her long, dark eyelashes and then back down at the light work her nimble fingers were making of unsheathing her lover.

"So big ... so hard," she chuckled, kissing him and gently masturbating him after pulling his erection from his britches.

Cassandra sank to her knees, and took his virile member in her mouth, slipping it in and out as she moved her head back and forth.

"God, I've missed you," Lucius said, holding the back of her head, the pleasure causing his hands to tighten around a bunch of hair.

"Oh, I like that," Cassandra said. "Pull it harder."

Lucius did as he was requested, gasping for breath as pleasure ran through him like a torrent.

"What was that?" Cassandra said, startled by a noise outside.

"I didn't hear anything," Lucius said. "We're in the middle of a wood so it could be a badger or a fox."

"Okay, sweetheart," Cassandra said, her delicate hands taking a hold of Lucius' bare buttocks to slowly rock him back and forth into her mouth as she looked up at him cat-eyed, her dark pupils glimmering in the candlelight.

After a few minutes of fellatio, Cassandra paused and again looked up at Lucius, her eyes looking more like those of a feline than ever.

"That wine has gone to my head, Lucius. I'm so wet," she whispered. "Want to feel? Or fuck me?" she added, touching her most intimate part and then bringing the finger to her mouth to lick it as she arched an eyebrow and then winked at Lucius.

"I'd be delighted," Lucius said, helping Cassandra to her feet and carrying her to the bed.

Chapter Fourteen

"I want to see your face this time," she said, lying on her back and opening her legs as Lucius knelt between her open thighs, slowly drawing his hand up and down his erection.

"I love watching you masturbate," Cassandra said. "Do you like watching me when I do it?" Cassandra asked, licking the finger on her right hand a second time before spreading her labia with a pair of fingers on her left hand.

"I also love watching you do it," Lucius said.

"Are you sure?" she teased, toying with her clitoris with the finger she had just moistened.

"More than you know," Lucius said.

"Fuck me," Cassandra said. "I need to feel you inside me."

Lucius rubbed the head of his swollen member up and down Cassandra's lips and then with one gentle push, slid himself inside her.

"Oh God, that feels so nice!" Cassandra said as Lucius ground against her, his pelvis pounding into the pelvis of his lover.

With one hand, he squeezed one of her erect nipples before taking it in his mouth and flicking his tongue all around her dark areola.

Each thrust brought him closer to orgasm but Cassandra, still rubbing her clitoris, was also close to a climax.

Lucius reached his hands underneath Cassandra, and squeezed her bare backside and feeling his erection slipping in and out, looking at Cassandra's beautiful face for signs of the pleasure he was bringing her.

"What is it?" she asked, after opening her eyes for a second and seeing that Lucius was looking at her.

"Nothing's the matter," he gasped. "I just love looking at you, seeing the pleasure on your face."

"I'm cumming," she said, bucking against Lucius' thrusts.

"Me too, he said," kissing her as he ejaculated deep inside her.

A few minutes passed as each lover caressed the other, exhausted in passion.

"Wow, that was amazing," Cassandra said, as Lucius rolled off, his chest heaving from the exertion.

"Incredible," he agreed, touching her face, and gazing lovingly into her eyes.

Just a few minutes later there was another noise outside.

"There's definitely something out there," Cassandra said.

"Yes, I heard it that time," Lucius said, moving to the window. "I can't see anything," after gazing into the darkness. "I'll take a look tomorrow.

Chapter Fifteen

The rest of that night was spent in a satiated stupor, each lover just a touch away from the other, their limbs entwined as they enjoyed the sleep only lovers can know.

The next morning, Cassandra awoke to see Lucius at the window.

"What is it, sweetheart?"

"There's a ladder up against the tree outside our window," he answered. "It's one of mine, but I didn't put it there."

"Was it there yesterday?" Cassandra asked, sitting up in bed and pulling the sheets around her, as though the thin fabric might afford her some protection.

"No, it wasn't," Lucius said, turning from the window and looking at Cassandra with a steely expression on his face. "That must have been what we heard," he added.

"Oh, shit - I bet it was that bastard, back again," Cassandra said.

"Well, if it was, he seems to have taken what he saw quite well," Lucius said.

"You mean last night?" Cassandra asked.

"Yes, after all, I don't know how I would feel if I saw you doing what we did last night with another man."

"Would you be jealous?" Cassandra asked, looking around the bedroom for her clothes.

"More than jealous," Lucius said. "I'd want to kill him."

"He's too cowardly for that," Cassandra said. "As you said, people like him only hit people they know can't - or won't - fight back."

"Time will tell, but I'm ready for him," Lucius said, sitting on the edge of the bed to pull on his trousers.

"Maybe that will be the end of it and he'll go back to the twenty-first century."

"Perhaps," Lucius said.

"You don't sound very sure," Cassandra asked, suddenly feeling as if Lucius was keeping something from her.

"It's nothing," he replied, tying up his bootlaces.

"Do you know something? Have you seen something in the cards?"

"Not in the cards, no," tossing a pair of braces over his shoulder and fastening them to his trousers.

"Then where? Lucius, tell me," Cassandra demanded, more out of concern for Lucius than curiosity.

"I used an Ouija board while you were away to contact a spirit who's helped me since the twelfth century. I think the noise we heard last night *was* your ex."

"Oh, shit," Cassandra said, as she found her clothes and began getting dressed. "I hope he enjoyed the show, the pervert."

"Not as much as I did," Lucius said, slapping one of Cassandra's bare buttocks and leaning into her to kiss her.

"Nor me!" Cassandra said, as Lucius blew her a kiss from the bedroom door and descended the stairs, the moment of tension seeming to have passed.

As Lucius unlocked his shop, Simeon was waiting for him.

"Where is she? I'd like to speak to her," he demanded.

"Who?" Lucius asked.

"Look, mate, I know what's going on between you and her," Simeon replied.

"Oh, you do, do you?" said Lucius, folding his arms.

"Yes. I saw you both - last night. I have it all on here," Lucius said, pulling his mobile phone from his pocket. By now, the sun was warming the shop and the smell of the various perfumes that Lucius had created were becoming heady and intoxicating.

"What's that stink?" Simeon asked. "It smells like a brothel in here."

"Well, you'd know," said Cassandra, holding aside the velvet curtains that separated the rooms. Neither Lucius nor Simeon had heard her bare feet on the shop's floorboards and both turned around a little startled at hearing her speak.

"I saw you both - last night. I have it all on here," Simeon said.

"All what, exactly?" asked Cassandra.

Chapter Fifteen

"You two - last night. I saw him screwing you and you sucking his cock. It's all on here," Simeon said, waving his phone at Cassandra.

"So, what if it is," Cassandra replied. "It's all over between you and me. I can do what I want, when I want, with whomsoever I wish – I don't need your permission."

"Says who? If you don't come back to me, then I'm going to send this to everyone you know," Simeon glowered, tapping his right index finger against the phone he held in his left hand.

"Everyone?" Cassandra asked. "Such as who?" she added, trying to remain calm. "My parents are dead, I've no job and only one friend," she said, then paused. "Do you really think that trying to blackmail me into coming back to you is going to work?"

"I'll post it online," Simeon said, shaking his head in disgust.

"And say what? That your ex-partner is cheating on you? I wasn't cheating on you - I told you, it's over."

"You won't be quite so cocky when all the world sees you," Simeon said.

"That will be a century from now, so I shall be long gone."

"What sort of bollocks are you talking now?" Simeon asked, turning to Lucius. "Take it from me, mate, don't believe a thing this woman says," he said to Lucius, pointing at Cassandra in disgust.

"Then why do you want her back?" asked Lucius.

"Why don't you post it!" Cassandra asked, calling Simeon's bluff. "This is the year eighteen ninety-one. You can't hurt me or publicly humiliate me as the time you want to post it is over a century from now," said Cassandra.

"Ah, fuck it," Simeon said, kicking one of the display cabinets before turning and walking from the shop, slamming its door behind him.

"I knew he'd be like this," Cassandra said, watching as Simeon kicked open the gate that led from the property into the dark woodland.

"What's he doing?" Lucius asked, squinting as if looking at Simeon's back was the only way to figure out the machinations of the feeble-minded.

Immortal Seduction

"He's trying to get a connection on his phone! Yeah, good luck with that," she added, as Simeon stomped off into the dense wood.

"I believe that this can now go one of two ways," Lucius said. "He can either catch the ferry back to his car, the twenty-first century, and then go back home without a problem," he paused. "Or he will start to age as the ferry crosses the river."

"How come I don't age when I cross it?" Cassandra asked.

"Every time is different and each time it's a gamble. It's not a dangerous gamble as all anyone needs to do is catch the ferry back and the process of ageing will reverse," Lucius explained.

"But if he can't get back to the modern age then he's stuck here - with us," Cassandra said, the horror of not being able to escape from Simeon having just occurred to her.

"Let's just see, shall we?" Lucius said. "If he can get back home, he's going to have a gadget that's been around for over a century so I don't think it's going to be something that will still work."

"I hadn't thought of that," Cassandra replied. "Sometimes technology letting us down is a blessing in disguise."

Meanwhile, on the riverbank, Simeon was making his way back to the village. "Bitch," he said to himself. Turning, he screamed it at the woodland he'd just left.

As Simeon arrived in the village, the ferry was just about to disembark.

"Hold on!" he shouted, jumping on board.

"I know you," said the ferryman. "You look just like the cousin of the other fella that usually does this job."

"Handsome, is he?" Simeon asked, puffing up his chest in conceit.

"Dead," said the ferryman. "They hung him last year for killing his wife."

"I don't blame him, she probably deserved it," Simeon replied, beginning to wince in pain as the ferry moved across the river.

"You alright?" asked the ferryman.

"No, do I look alright? My knees and back are killing me."

"It's not that, it's your hair and face."

"What's wrong with them?" Simeon asked, pulling his phone from his pocket, and taking a selfie. "Shit, what's happening to

Chapter Fifteen

me?" he said in astonishment as he saw a photo of what appeared to be the face of an old man staring out from the phone's tiny screen.

"Your hair is falling out and your face has aged about fifty years in two minutes," the ferryman said, pointing at the hair on Simeon's hoody and then to the hair on the floor.

"I can see that," Simeon said, rolling his eyes as if the ferryman's observation was obvious.

"Just saying," said the ferryman, his grimy face breaking into a leer. "You're still a nice-looking fella, though."

"I think I need a doctor – are there any in the village?" Simeon asked.

"Yes, there's one up that lane," said the ferryman, pointing back into the village. "If it's the clap you've got, then he's your man."

"Take me back," Simeon begged, grabbing a hold of the ferryman's arm.

"We need to get to the other bank, first. You're not the only one on board," the ferryman replied, pulling his arm free.

By now, Simeon was doubled over and losing his teeth. He sat down as the ferry landed and waited for it to make its return journey.

As the ferry's passengers climbed aboard and it started making its way back, Simeon looked at his hands. They were gnarled, wrinkled, spattered with liver spots, and had cracked and broken nails. As the ferry made its slow approach back to the village, the wrinkles began to disappear. By the time they had reached the bank on the English side of the Wye, Simeon was able to stand upright.

"Don't know what happened there," he said to the ferryman.

Chapter Sixteen

The day was a very warm one and feeling a little more confident that Simeon may have returned to the twenty-first century with a broken phone, Cassandra suggested that Lucius leave the shop door open to let in a breeze.

"*Oui, Mademoiselle,*" he said.

"Oh, stop it! You've never seen *The Addams Family*, have you? I never understood how hearing Morticia speak French could have such an effect on Gomez until I heard you!" said Cassandra.

"No, I've never seen them. Are they friends of yours?" asked Lucius.

"No, it's an old TV show."

"TV? What's that?" Lucius asked.

"It doesn't matter. It's a box that sits in the corner of the room that shows moving images."

"Sounds a bit boring, no?"

"*Oui*, most definitely *oui*, but that show was a great one."

Lucius pottered about his shop, making scents that nobody would ever buy and Cassandra, to keep him company, polished the wooden shelves and worktops.

"So, we first met two centuries ago in Paris?" she asked.

"Yes - although the days between then and now seem to have disappeared," Lucius replied, stopping for a moment to stare wistfully into the distance.

"And I was a courtesan?"

"Yes, you were, although after we met you gave up the profession. I think poverty drove you to it."

"I was poor?"

"Yes, a lot of people in Paris at that time were desperately poor," Lucius replied.

"Yes, I remember from school that revolutionaries used the phrase 'let them eat cake' to attack the aristocracy of the *Ancien Régime,* as it was a quote attributed to one of the ruling elite."

"And losing you is a tragedy that has haunted me for centuries. I have lost count of the times I have asked myself if having taken you out of poverty, is it my fault that you were then mistaken for a member of the aristocracy and killed by members of the *Montagnards*."

"Did you hear something?" Cassandra said, pointing to the open door and placing her index finger to her mouth to gesture for Lucius to be quiet.

"No - what was it?" he asked.

"I thought I heard footsteps," Cassandra replied.

"Maybe you're still a little worried about what happened earlier."

"Maybe," Cassandra replied, falling silent for a minute but after hearing no further noise, she continued.

"So, I was a prostitute and then, later, my husband attacked me for having an affair with you and was hung for it?"

"Yes, that's right," Lucius said.

"I knew it!" Simeon said, stepping in through the open door.

"God, you made me jump," Cassandra said, holding her chest and taking a few steps backwards. "Knew what?"

"That you had a past. Didn't mention online that you'd been a hooker or that you'd been married and had an affair with him," Simeon said, pointing at Lucius.

"So, you only heard the last sentence, did you?"

"For fuck's sake, don't tell me there's more!" Simeon said in disbelief.

"All you heard was me saying that I'd once been a prostitute and that my husband had attacked me for having an affair with Lucius."

"Who's Lucius?" shouted Simeon.

"He's Lucius," Cassandra replied, pointing at Lucius as he replaced his pestle in its mortar and fixed his gaze on Simeon.

"How much of this was going on behind my back?" Simeon raged.

"None of it."

"Why are you lying? I just heard you say it and now you know that I heard you you're denying having said it!"

"What you didn't hear me saying was that I'd been a prostitute two centuries ago and that I was reincarnated to a life here and

Chapter Sixteen

despite being married to a previous incarnation of you, I fell in love with Lucius and when you found out you killed me. That was one hundred and thirty years ago. We have slipped back in time to a year after you killed me and that's why people in the village think that we're haunting them – they fished my body from the river after you hit my head with a rock and threw me in the Wye. You were found guilty of murder and hung for it," Cassandra said as if she were talking to an errant child.

"Do you believe this crap?" Simeon said, wrinkling his nose as if he'd just smelt a noxious smell, and addressing his question to Lucius. "We're going home," he said, grabbing Cassandra by her wrist and dragging her to the door.

"Don't touch me, you bastard," Cassandra said, struggling to free herself as she punched Simeon in the back and kicked his legs.

"Get your hands off her," Lucius said, blocking the door. Neither Cassandra nor Simeon had seen or heard him move and the demand struck such fear into the immortal soul of the cowardly Simeon that he let loose Cassandra's wrist.

"Look, mate, I'm doing you a favour! You should be paying me for taking her off your hands," Simeon protested, throwing open his arms and looking at Lucius.

"Cassandra has made it very clear that she doesn't want to leave with you," Lucius said. "Until such a time as she says otherwise, there's nothing here for you."

"Well, that's it then," Simeon said. "If you're not coming back with me then I may as well end it all," Simeon said, looking back at Cassandra. "And it will all be your fault," he added.

"Oh, that's ridiculous. When you had me, you were vile and told me that you were only with me until someone better came along - now you've lost me you can't live without me!"

"Yes, make fun all you like but I loved you," Simeon said, wiping his eyes in the hope Cassandra would think he was crying. "I'm going," he said, walking past Lucius and leaving the two lovers behind him.

Chapter Seventeen

Lucius closed the shop door and took Cassandra in his arms, tenderly pressing his lips against her forehead. Tears began to stream down Cassandra's face.

"I'm sorry you have to go through this," Lucius whispered.

"I'm not crying because of him, I'm crying because of you," Cassandra replied.

"Me?" Lucius said, surprised at hearing the words.

"Yes. I've had three lifetimes of dealing with people like him but you're the only man to ever show me any kindness - and that's why I'm crying," she tearfully whispered.

"Oh, Cassandra," Lucius said, pressing his lips to her forehead a second time. "Whatever happens *we* will deal with it," Lucius said, then paused. "We're a team, so even if it's us versus the world, it will still be *us* versus the world, not *you* versus the world."

On hearing the words, Cassandra began to sob.

"I love you," she murmured.

"And I love you, too," Lucius replied.

"I don't know how long we've been stood like this but it's over an hour since I last looked at the clock when Simeon left," Cassandra.

"It's one of life's cruel jokes that a moment spent in paradise passes as quickly as a month in hell," Lucius replied.

"Lucius, I need to make one last return to the twenty-first century. I've made up my mind that I want to stay here with you but I should tell my friend, Anna, as she may be worried about me if I just disappear. She'd never met Simeon but I'd told her about him and how unhappy I was with him," she said, looking at Lucius and stroking his cheek with loving affection. "If I just disappear, she may think that he's done something to me."

"You do whatever you need to do, sweetheart," Lucius replied, rubbing his hand up and down her back, through the fabric of her dress.

"Right, I shan't be long," Cassandra said, giving Lucius a quick kiss and walking from the room and back to the bedroom to fetch her car keys. When she returned, Lucius was donning his work apron.

"I shall see you later," Cassandra said, blowing Lucius a kiss as she stood by the shop door.

The journey down the steep path now seemed less arduous than it had when first she had climbed it. Maybe she was getting used to it or becoming a little more fit with the exercise after being housebound for a year due to the pandemic lockdown.

As she walked alongside the river, her mind was on Lucius and the joy he had brought her. Before long she was back in the village. Dockers were already working on the river, loading barges with logs from the Forest of Dean. Thankfully, the ferryman that recognised her was not working that day and so she was able to travel across the river without issue. A few passengers seemed to look at her askance, as if recognising her as the woman that had been murdered the year before but, Cassandra told herself, they might just be thinking that she looked a little like that woman and that maybe that woman had a sister.

Back at her car, Cassandra quickly changed into her modern clothes. Thankfully, the car started and as she had not parked it in the nineteenth century the fate Lucius had predicted would befall Lucius' phone had not befallen her car.

The drive back through the Wye Valley was as beautiful as always, past cliffs and views down the Severn Estuary. Soon she was parking her car outside Anna's house.

Cassandra locked her car and walked the path to Anna's door. Anna hadn't been expecting her but that would be fine as she knew Anna was always pleased to see her.

Cassandra rang the doorbell and soon after Anna answered the door.

"Cass! Where've you been? I've been thinking about you," Anna said, giving Cassandra a hug and holding the door open so that she could enter.

"Wow, do I have a tale to tell you!" Cassandra said, following Anna to her kitchen.

"Coffee?" Anna asked.

Chapter Seventeen

"Yes, please – no milk."

"So, what's this story?" Anna asked as she waited for the kettle to boil.

"Remember when I was last here?"

"Do I ever!" Anna said, batting her eyelashes.

"And me saying that I wanted to be seduced?" Cassandra said, smiling and rubbing her friend's arm.

"I did my best, Cass," Anna laughed.

"Well, I went for that day out with Simeon, the following day, as planned, and we found this old place covered in ivy. It looked like a ruin but it was a shop – an apothecary shop – that hadn't had a customer in fifty years! We went in, and the shopkeeper was still there. The idiot didn't see him but I saw him. After we got home, dickhead and I started arguing and, I swear, I almost stuck a knife in him."

"Cass, you need to be careful! That temper of yours is going to get you into trouble," Anna said, surprised but not shocked, as she knew what her friend was like when her temper was roused and that she had never been one to cut fools much slack.

"It's fine, I didn't do it," Cassandra replied, flicking her hair over her shoulders. "Anyway, I went back to the shop the next day, on my own, and the man that lived in the shop read my tarot cards."

"Ooh, that sounds interesting. I'd love to have someone read mine," Anna said, heaping coffee into two mugs and pouring boiling water into them. "Did he forecast a lover for you?"

"I'm coming to that," Cassandra said, widening her eyes and nodding. "Well, I went back the day after he'd read my cards, and the old man I'd seen the day before had turned into a young man as I'd gone back to the nineteenth century!"

"What?" Anna said, almost dropping her teaspoon.

"Yes, I've spent the last week in eighteen ninety-one, with a man born in the eleventh century!" Cassandra replied, hoping her friend would share in her excitement.

"Cass, let's sit down," Anna said, drawing a chair away from her kitchen table for Cassandra to sit, then pulling a second chair from the table to sit in front of her friend. "Don't be offended, but this sounds a little bit …" Anna added, struggling to find the right word, lest the wrong word cause offence.

"And he told me that I used to be a courtesan in the eighteenth century and that in a later life he and I became lovers again but that I was murdered a year before I met him," Cassandra said, taking a sip of coffee.

"Cass, you and I are old friends," Anna began, "but this sounds crazy."

"I know! That cosmic ordering thing you suggested – where I had to ask the universe for what I wanted and I asked to be seduced – really worked!" Cassandra replied, still oblivious to the fact that her friend didn't believe her.

"And what does Simeon have to say about this?" Anna asked, leaning back in her chair, and rubbing her hands on the back of her head.

"He doesn't like it but now he's trapped there in the same year as me and I think he may be dead."

"Dead!"

"Yes - even if he isn't, you won't be seeing him again."

"Again? I've never met him, remember?" Anna said, the veracity of her friend's strange tale sounding more far-fetched by the second.

"So, this is the third life I've had since I met Lucius," Cassandra said, clapping her hands together and smiling.

"Lucius?" queried Anna.

"Sorry, I forgot to mention his name. The man that read my cards and with whom I've been living in the nineteenth century is Lucius, d'Orléans – he's French. He used to be a knight, and was a member of the *Rose-Croix*."

"Okay, Cass. Have you ever thought about counselling? I know a lot of people have struggled under the lockdown but what you're saying does sound," again Anna struggled to be tactful. "Odd," she added.

"I thought you'd be pleased for me," Cassandra said, looking crestfallen.

"You had a brain tumour when you were younger, didn't you?"

"What's that got to do with it?" Cassandra asked, her eyes widening with surprise.

"I just wonder if counselling might help you," Anna said, stroking her friend's arm in pity. "Why don't you consider it?"

Chapter Seventeen

"You don't believe me, do you?" Cassandra said, putting down her mug on a coaster.

"I'm sure you believe it's true, Cass," Anna said, trying to sound sympathetic.

"It is true!"

"What does Simeon have to say about it?"

"Oh, bollocks to him. I've just told you, you won't be seeing him again," Cassandra said. "He's stuck in the nineteenth century and threatening to kill himself."

"What was his surname?" Anna asked, trying not to show that Cassandra's tale had given her such a cause for concern that she was worried about his wellbeing.

"His name is Simeon Danton. Why? Do you think I've made him up as well?" Cassandra said, folding her arms.

"I'm just asking, Cass. It's only a small town and neither Andy nor I know of anyone named Simeon. Andy even looked up the name on Facebook and none of the people named Simeon that we found on there were saying they were in a relationship with you."

"Oh my God, you don't believe me!"

"Cass, calm down – please," Anna said.

"Don't tell me what to do," Cassandra said, beginning to feel angry with her friend.

"Cass, please."

"I thought you'd be pleased for me! I only came back to tell you that you won't be seeing me again as I'm going to live with Lucius in the nineteenth century. There's a chance the doorway between what we think of as that time and what we think of as today may close and so I won't be able to return – and, to be honest – I wish I hadn't bothered coming back today, now I know the reception that you've given me," Cassandra said, pausing for a moment. "I'm sick of the twenty-first century," she added.

"Well, I don't think many people are very happy at the moment, babe. We've all been shut inside for a year and it's causing us all a few problems," Anna said.

"Oh God, I'm telling you facts! I've not lost my mind, I assure you. You seem to think that the men in white coats need to come and take me away," Cassandra said, looking at the ceiling of Anna's kitchen as if seeking divine intervention.

"Cass, please think about counselling – I don't want you to do anything stupid," Anna said, reaching out a hand to her friend.

"Don't touch me! I thought I could tell you everything," Cassandra said, pushing her friend's hand away from her.

"You can, but I'm not a counsellor," Anna replied, trying her best to sound concerned but starting to feel a little scared that her friend had lost her mind after spending too long shut indoors.

"Look, when I had a brain tumour I was going back and forth to the doctors' for years and all I ever got was the same look of pity, disgust and impatience from them that I'm getting from you right now! Even after I collapsed and needed emergency surgery, not one of them apologised. As a matter of fact, I tried to explain to the neurosurgeon how ill I was feeling at the first consultation I had with him after the operation and all he did was look at his nails as I was talking to him and then tell me that the only thing that would help me would be fucking counselling!"

"How about mindfulness? That may help you," Anna persisted.

"Look, I have physiological damage," Cassandra said, letting out a sigh. "I've seen the scans so that's not me being a hypochondriac. It hasn't made me crazy or prone to imagining things! What it has done, is caused nerve damage. How is counselling going to help with that! That's like saying to someone with a broken arm that you're not going to put it in a cast but have a chat about it! I did psychology as part of my degree so the last thing I need is someone telling me to pace myself, write lists, and practice mindfulness! If you had arthritis, do you think counselling would help you?"

"It may be an idea, Cass. After all, he knows best," Anna replied.

"Right, I'm going," Cassandra said, rising to her feet.

"Cass, where are you going?"

"Far away from here – to the past!" Cassandra replied, moving to Anna's front door.

"Cass, please come back. I will try to get you the help you need," Anna said looking around for her phone.

"Don't bother – I'm going. Goodbye," Cassandra said, opening the door and closing it firmly behind her.

Chapter Seventeen

"Hello, police please," Anna said, having finally found her phone and telephoned for help. "I'm concerned about my friend. Yes, she's just been here and is saying some very odd things. I think she may either harm someone or harm herself. Her name is Cassandra Wyvern. Yes, I'd be happy to give you a statement."

"Unbelievable," Cassandra said, as she started her car. "Right, let's pick up a few things and get the hell out of here"

Cassandra then made her way back to the house she had once shared with Simeon.

"Ah, good! He's not here," she said to herself as she pulled up outside. "Time to pack a few suitcases. Twenty twenty-one can then kiss my ass goodbye!"

Chapter Eighteen

Cassandra finished packing her things and loaded them in her car. Looking around, she wondered if this would be the last time that she would ever see the modern-day.

The drive back to Lucius was a strange one as it had a finality to it and even though she was going to a place she hoped would be a happier one for her, she still felt like she was saying goodbye to an old friend.

She parked her car in Wales and changed her clothes. A car of young lads drove passed and one of them shouted a lecherous obscenity at her, throwing an empty cup from McDonald's at her, after seeing her removing her jeans.

"God, I won't be sorry to see the back of assholes like that," she said to herself.

As she waited on the riverbank, she breathed a sigh of relief to see that the ferryman on duty today was not the one that thought he recognised her.

On the far shore, she could see various labourers busying themselves loading a barge, smiling to herself that the streets, shops, and pub looked like something from a movie.

Then the thought that Simeon might still be in the village came back to her and her smile faded.

The walk back to the shop was one she should have enjoyed, given it was a new beginning for her but her suitcase was heavy and so the journey took even longer than usual. Every now and then, she turned her head to make sure she was not being followed.

She smiled as she passed the bushes near where Lucius and she had shared a passionate moment in the waters of the Wye.

As she gazed up the steep path into the wood, she wondered why Lucius had ever thought that a shop so hidden from view would ever do well, even though the path was beautiful and reminded her of something from a fairy tale.

"Lucius," she shouted, as she drew near the cottage. There, in the garden, Lucius was sat in the sun, next to his sprawling, poisonous castor bean shrub.

"Ah, Cassandra," he said, rising to his feet and coming to greet her. "Let me help you," he added, taking the suitcase from her.

"Well, I'm back! Did you miss me?" she asked.

"Of course," he replied.

"I went to see my friend but wish I hadn't bothered," Cassandra said, as Lucius opened the shop door.

"Why, what happened?"

"I told her what had happened to me - that I'd met you and that you were born in the eleventh century, that we had met twice before in my past lives, and she didn't believe me."

"I suppose it does sound a bit far-fetched when you say it like that," he said, wrapping a comforting arm around her.

"And she told me I needed counselling – and that really pissed me off, as I almost died because doctors would only suggest counselling and wouldn't listen to me when I told them how ill I felt," she fumed.

"Come inside," Lucius said. "I'll pour us a drink and we can sit out here in the sun," he added, picking up Cassandra's case and carrying it into the shop.

"A drink would be wonderful," Cassandra said.

"Hold on," Lucius said, opening a door to his cellar and descending its worn, stone steps. "Here we are," he said, returning with a bottle of wine. "Here we have a Chateau Margaux, seventeen eighty-seven."

"As mentioned by Poe in his *Thou Art the Man*," Cassandra said.

Lucius uncorked the wine and held open the door for Cassandra to return to the garden.

"Please, sit down," he said, gesturing to his chair. "I shall go and get myself another one," he added, handing Cassandra his drink.

Cassandra sat down and waited for Lucius to return. A minute or two later, he returned with his chair.

"This wine is wonderful," Cassandra said.

"I thought you'd like it."

Chapter Eighteen

"I love it," she replied. "But you know how naughty I can get after a drink," she said, giving Lucius a wink.

"Shame on you, Miss Wyvern," Lucius said. "You don't need a drink to be naughty with me," he said, laughing.

"Lucius, I have to ask, why do you have so many poisonous plants in your garden? I know the castor bean is deadly," Cassandra said.

"I find them fascinating," Lucius replied. "Take this one - Brugmansia, or angel's trumpet, is a member of the same family as deadly nightshade," he said, gesturing to plant growing next to him. "It's an amazing aphrodisiac but can kill you if you take too much of it - but an amazing way to die as it's pain-free. Even the cuttings from a pruned laurel hedge can emit fumes so toxic that to breathe them risks one falling into unconsciousness."

Wide-eyed at why Lucius had such an interest in deadly plants, Cassandra took another sip of wine and persisted with her question.

"So, why do you grow so many deadly plants? You even have opium poppies!" Cassandra asked. "I'm curious."

Lucius laughed and took a large sip of wine.

"It's not that I poison people, or add any of them to any of my medications or perfumes."

"What is it, then?" Cassandra asked, her curiosity piqued by the apparent reluctance of Lucius to tell her.

"I don't need a memento mori to remind me that life is short as for me it is not," he said. "But these plants," he added, gesturing to the plants in his garden, "remind me that nature is in control. Man is a vain buffoon if he thinks he can tame such a force."

Chapter Nineteen

Lucius stood up and took Cassandra's hand, helping her to her feet. The two then walked the short distance from the lawn and back to the shop.

"What is it? What's wrong?" Cassandra asked.

"Nothing, it's just that sitting in the sun is making the wine go to my head," he answered.

"I logged on to the ex's computer while I was there, and he hasn't logged on since he followed me here."

"That's a good thing, no?" Lucius asked.

"Yes and no. It means he hasn't uploaded the video he took of us," said Cassandra, pausing for breath. "But it probably means he's still here - and that means that sooner or later he'll be back."

"He's been here while you were away," Lucius said.

"Oh no, why didn't you say? What did he want?" Cassandra replied, leaning her back against one of the shop counters.

"He said that he wanted you back and that he wanted to speak to you. I told him that you weren't here and had gone back to the twenty-first century but I don't think he believed me. He said that when he'd tried to go back home, he had turned into an old man and couldn't even get off the ferry."

"How can we get rid of him? He's going to spoil everything," Cassandra said, lost in thought as she gazed at the sunshine streaming through the door, its rays like ghostly, gossamer fingers.

"He says that if you won't go back to him then he will kill himself," Lucius added,

"Well, that's up to him - I won't cave in to blackmail."

"No, and if he does kill himself then he has issues that go a lot deeper than you ending your relationship with him. Anyway," Lucius said, walking toward Cassandra who, by now, was sitting on the shop counter, "we now have each other," he added, lifting her hands from her lap and kissing the backs of her fingers.

"Yes, we do," Cassandra said, placing her hands on Lucius' shoulders, pulling him toward her and kissing him. "And I'm feeling a bit tipsy – and you know what that means," she added, blowing him a kiss.

"Cassandra, I can't go on without you. You have to come back to me," said a voice from near the door that startled both Cassandra and Lucius as neither had heard the owner of the voice approaching the shop. Both Cassandra and Lucius turned and there, staring at them, stood Simeon.

"No, Simeon, listen to me," Cassandra said, getting down from the counter. "It's over between us - I love Lucius," she added, pointing at Lucius. "When we were together you were horrible to me. You only want me back now because you wanted to be the one to end it and it's too great a blow to your vanity and ego to have a woman finish with you."

"That's bullshit! Are you coming, or not?" Simeon asked.

"No, it's over."

"I can't even get back to the twenty-first century," he implored. "I'm stuck here – in a place I don't know, with people I don't know – and it's all your fault."

"I didn't ask you to follow me," Cassandra said, turning to Lucius in exasperation. "You always do, this," she added, looking back at Simeon.

"Do what?" he asked.

"Gaslight me."

"What? I don't know what you're talking about," Simeon said, a look of disgust on his face.

"Try and sow seeds of doubt in my mind and try and have me question my memory or judgement."

"That's bullshit," Simeon said, slowly walking back and forth, like a bored caged beast.

"You did it to make me feel as though I was to blame for your unhappiness and that I needed you for emotional support as you were the only one that I could trust. Well, you underestimated me for if there hadn't been a pandemic sweeping the country then I'd have left you months ago."

"I followed you here because I love you," Simeon said, taking a step nearer to her.

Chapter Nineteen

"No, you don't – you followed me here because you're a controlling narcissist with a fragile ego. I know what you're like - even if I did come back to you, you'd be horrible again within an hour."

"So, there's a chance then? Cass, I've changed."

"No, there's no chance. I want to stay here," she said. "With him" she added, pointing at Lucius who, while still standing nearby, had stayed silent and let Cassandra and Simeon end their ties with one another themselves.

"Then screw you, you bitch," Simeon said, turning to leave.

"See, you haven't changed at all! Still throwing a tantrum because you can't have your way," Cassandra said, looking at Lucius and rolling her eyes.

Simeon didn't stop to listen and left, slamming the door behind him.

"Oh God, what did I ever see in that idiot!" she said.

"Twice," Lucius replied.

"Twice?" queried Cassandra.

"Yes – you were once married to him, remember?"

"Ah, yeah – and he murdered me," Cassandra said, the wheels turning in her mind as she now wondered whether history was once again going to repeat itself.

"Yes, he did."

"Do you think he'll try and do it again?" Cassandra asked.

"No, I don't think so. What's more, this time you don't live with him, you live with me," Lucius said, stepping forward to wrap Cassandra in his arms.

"What do the cards say?" Cassandra asked.

"I don't know, I haven't looked. Shall we see?" Lucius asked.

"Yes," Cassandra said, breathing a sigh of relief. "Shall we have another drink?" she asked. "I need to get out of this room for a start and a drink will help take my mind off it. Can we lock up for the day?"

"Of course – anything for you, sweetheart," Lucius said, walking to the door and locking it. He then returned to Cassandra and ran his fingers through her hair as he looked lovingly at her face.

"I must have come back to you a third time as we have something unfinished," Cassandra said. "I don't want a tragedy to take me from you again."

"Neither do I," Lucius said, kissing her.

"My legs turn to jelly when you kiss me like that," she murmured, closing her eyes as Lucius kissed her again. "I wish we knew we had the day to ourselves," she added. "I need you inside me."

"Well, we can always forget about the cards," Lucius replied, holding the side of her face with the palm of his hand, and stroking her lips with his thumb."

"No, we need to know what's going to happen," Cassandra said, letting out a sigh.

"Your wish is my command, dear lady," Lucius said, following Cassandra as she walked toward the back room, pulled aside the velvet curtain, and entered. "Oh, I forgot your suitcase," he added, spinning on his heel, returning a moment later carrying it.

"Yes, we don't want to forget that," Cassandra said, suggestively.

"That sounds intriguing."

"Good," she replied, as Lucius fetched the pack of tarot cards.

"Would you like to shuffle them?" Lucius asked, handing Cassandra the cards, and sitting down opposite her.

"Yes, okay," she replied, shuffling them, then handing them back to Lucius.

"Now, choose three," he said, spreading them out onto the polished tabletop.

Cassandra leaned forward and pulled one from the pack.

"Ah, the lovers," she said, breathing a sigh of relief and blowing Lucius a kiss.

"Would you like to choose another?" he said, smiling and blowing a kiss back.

Cassandra reached forward and turned a second card.

"Oh no, not again!" she said, looking at The Hanged Man card. "That's all I need."

"It doesn't mean that anyone's going to hang themselves," Lucius said, reaching across the table to give Cassandra's hand a reassuring squeeze.

Chapter Nineteen

"No, but with some lunatic running around threatening to kill himself then it's not the card I wanted to see, even if I'm not to take it literally."

"Do you want to choose a third?" Lucius said, giving Cassandra's hand another reassuring squeeze.

"Oh, I don't believe it!" Cassandra said, turning the card over. "Death."

"It doesn't mean death as we think of it but the end of one chapter and a new beginning," Lucius said.

"I remember but, again, what if it does mean what it says?" Cassandra asked.

"If it does, and Simeon does choose to end his life here in the nineteenth century, then that will mean he will have died before he was ever born," Lucius said.

"I don't follow you – what does that mean?" said Cassandra, her brow knitting in confusion.

"It will mean that he was never born and so no trace of him will exist. He will disappear from the memory of everyone that ever knew him."

"No way! Really?" Cassandra said, her jaw dropping in disbelief.

"Yes - he will have died a century before he was ever born so people in his own time won't even know that such a man ever existed," Lucius said.

"Some people think I'm already crazy," Cassandra said, thinking of what Anna had said to her about her needing counselling. "If I start talking about someone that never existed, they're going to think I've lost it."

"No, they won't," Lucius said.

"You don't know my friends," Cassandra replied.

"You won't mention him."

"I might, if the memory of the way he treated me plays on my mind."

"It won't," Lucius said. "He will never have existed for everyone – including you."

"That's so bizarre," Cassandra said, shaking her head in disbelief. "There may be thousands of people out there that had relationships with people and those people somehow slipped back in time, died there, and so were never born – and the people they had relationships with now have no memory of them."

"Yes, that's true," Lucius said.

"So, how will I remember the year I spent with him?"

"You won't have spent it with him as he never existed," Lucius explained.

"So, I may have met someone else?"

"Yes."

"Hang on a minute – if I'd never have met him, I'd never have gone on that day out with him, never come here, and never met you," Cassandra said.

"You and I were destined to be together," Lucius said. "However difficult the circumstances, love would have overcome them."

"Are you sure?" Cassandra asked, breathing a sigh of relief.

"I promise," Lucius said.

"God, I want you," she said, standing and reaching out to take a hold of Lucius' hand.

Lucius stood and walked around the table, picking up Cassandra's suitcase.

"Then I suppose we'd better go upstairs," he said.

Lucius let Cassandra go in front of him and followed behind her with her suitcase. As soon as Cassandra entered the warm room she turned around and passionately kissed Lucius, running her hands through his hair before pulling his head closer to hers.

Taking her hands from his hair, she slowly undid the buttons of his shirt until his chest was exposed. Kissing his neck, she crouched and looked up and him through her eyelashes as she licked his nipple, her left hand rubbing the growing bulge in the front of his trousers.

"Oh, Miss Wyvern, you have the most delicate touch," he said, groaning with pleasure.

Unbuttoning his trousers, she gently tugged them down before cupping his testes in her hand and giving them a rub.

"You like that?" she asked, as he groaned.

"Very much."

Sinking to her knees, she began to masturbate him, looking up at him to enjoy the pleasure on his face.

Chapter Nineteen

"Sit on the edge of the bed," she asked, removing his trousers, and tossing them to one side.

Lucius happily obliged, as Cassandra held his erection in one hand and looked up at him.

"Cass, that feels so nice," he said.

"I love licking your balls."

"And I love you licking them," he groaned.

Standing up, Cassandra quickly turned and hitched up her dress.

"No underwear!" Lucius said.

"I thought you'd like it," she said, sitting on his lap and wriggling as he reached around to massage her breasts through the thin fabric. "I've also brought something from the twenty-first century that may be fun.

"What's that, then?"

"It's in my suitcase - let me watch you play with yourself while I get it," she said, dashing to her suitcase and watching Lucius masturbate as he watched her.

"Here it is!" she said, holding a vibrator aloft.

"A dildo?" Lucius asked.

"No, a vibrator. I've always fantasised about having two men but I don't want to have sex with anyone but you. With this, you can use it on me and I can suck you and pretend both are you," she giggled, letting her dress fall to the floor.

"My God, I've missed you," Lucius said, still stroking his erection.

Within seconds, Cassandra was lying next to him on the bed.

"Want to see me play with it?" she teased.

"Yes, please!" he said, as Cassandra lay back on the bed and opened her legs. Switching the vibrator on, she began rubbing all around her groin, her free left hand massaging her left breast.

"Don't stop playing with yourself," she ordered. I want to put on a show for you – and know that it's turning you on so much you have to take yourself in hand!"

Moving her hand down her body, she parted her lips and began running the vibrator over her clitoris.

"Oh God," Lucius gasped.

"You like? Watch this," Cassandra said, bringing the vibrator to her mouth and sucking it. With the vibrator still wet, she quickly brought it down the bed. With two fingers on her left hand, she parted her lips and slid the vibrator inside herself.

"I have to lick you," Lucius said, leaning forward and licking Cassandra's clitoris.

"You can use it on me if you want. I want to suck you," she suggested, patting the bed for Lucius to lie next to her.

"Like this?" he asked, lying next to her.

"No, like this," Cassandra said, straddling his face with her open legs before bending forward and taking his penis into her mouth.

Lucius began licking Cassandra's clitoris as she performed oral sex on him, sometimes licking it, sometimes sucking it, sometimes running her lips up and down the shaft, sometimes taking it in her mouth and sliding it in and out of it.

Lucius slid the vibrator deep inside his lover, all the while licking her and savouring the taste.

"If you keep doing that, Cass, I'm going to cum," he said.

"No, not yet," Cassandra said. "I want to try something," she added, moving so that she now sat cross-legged on the bed, facing Lucius. "Give that to me," she demanded, holding out a hand for the vibrator. "I want to rub it over your balls when you're in my mouth."

With that, Lucius handed it over and Cassandra began rubbing the vibrator over Lucius testes as she sucked him.

"That feels great, Cass."

"Think you can hold on for a few minutes?" she asked.

"Only if you go slowly," he laughed, looking down at Cassandra as she held his erect phallus in her right hand and licked it as though she were licking an ice lollipop.

A few minutes elapsed with Cassandra taking things slowly, as Lucius had asked.

"Want to cum?" she asked.

"Yes – and I don't think I can hold back much longer," he groaned.

"Then cum inside me," Cassandra said, lying on her back.

"Sure," Lucius replied. "But you know you said you fantasised about two men at once?"

"Yes – what have you got planned?"

Chapter Nineteen

"How about me and the vibrator inside you at the same time?" he asked.

"We can give it a try," Cassandra said excitedly. "I'm going to feel pretty full what with a man with a dick as thick as yours *and* the vibrator – but let's give it a go!"

With her thighs wide open, Lucius eased the vibrator inside his lover, then slid himself in above it.

"Oh my God," Cassandra gasped. "Now fuck me," she added, frantically rubbing her clitoris with one hand as she leaned her head forward and pulled her breast toward her mouth to lick her nipple as Lucius thrust in and out of her.

"Does it feel good, you dirty bastard?" Cassandra gasped

"Yes!"

"Call me a whore," she said. "Is it buzzing against your cock and balls?"

"Yes, you whore" Lucius said, thrusting into Cassandra as deeply as he could.

"Oh God, I'm going to cum," gasped Cassandra.

"Me too," said Lucius, his breathing stopping for a moment before he let out a gasp, moving his mouth from Cassandra's breast to her mouth.

"I can feel it!" Cassandra said, pulling Lucius's head toward her to French kiss him.

"That was amazing," Lucius said, lying on top of Cassandra for a few minutes, before withdrawing and lying next to her.

"Thank you! I guess being a courtesan two hundred years ago taught me a thing or two," she said, giving a little giggle.

"Come here, you," Lucius said, wrapping Cassandra in his arms and kissing her.

"It's hot in here," she said.

"Yes, we're all wet and sticky," Lucius replied.

"Just the way I like it!"

The next few hours were spent blissfully naked, lying in the sun as it alighted on their bed.

"You've made me so happy, Lucius. I was lost until I met you," Cassandra confided.

"And you've brought me back to life," Lucius replied.

Suddenly, there was a noise outside.

"Oh God, not again," Cassandra said, sitting up in bed and pulling the sheets around her.

"Let me go and see," Lucius said, pulling on his trousers and quickly fastening them before pulling on a shirt.

"There, I heard something again," Cassandra said, getting from the bed and looking for her clothes. "Is it him?" she asked, now that Lucius was at the window.

"I'm not sure. I can't see anything that could be making a noise," he replied.

"Cassandra! Cassandra! Are you going to come back to me?" Simeon shouted. Only then was Lucius able to see him standing beneath their bedroom window.

"Yes, it's him. He's down there with a noose around his neck."

"Oh, for God's sake," Cassandra said, quickly getting dressed.

"If you don't come back to me, I'm going to kill myself," Simeon shouted.

"We'd better get down there and talk to him," Lucius said.

"This can't go on – I just want him to leave me alone," Cassandra said.

Within a minute, Cassandra and Lucius were downstairs. With the door unbolted, they ran around the front of the shop and turned around the corner of the house to be confronted by Simeon who, by now, had placed a ladder against a tree, climbed it, and fastened the loose end of the noose around a branch.

"So, are you going to come back to me or do I have to kill myself?" Simeon said.

"This is ridiculous – it's blackmail! If I came back to you, would I be coming back because I love you or because I don't want you doing this?"

"I can't live without you, Cass. Didn't I always treat you well?" Simeon said, raising his voice in accusation.

"No, you were horrible to me," she replied.

"You bitch!" Simeon shouted, losing his footing, and falling from the ladder.

"Lucius, do something!" Cassandra screamed.

Lucius raced toward the ladder and quickly climbed it.

"It's no good, I can't undo it," he said, reaching for the rope to pull Simeon back onto the ladder.

Chapter Nineteen

"He's turning blue," Cassandra screamed, reaching up, then jumping as if to support Simeon's feet.

Simeon thrashed about on the end of the rope as he struggled to breathe, clutching at the noose with his fingers.

Suddenly, he stopped moving and let out a guttural last breath.

"What are we doing out here?" Cassandra asked. "Whoa, who is that?" she said, pointing up at the corpse. "Quick, get him down."

"I don't know what we're doing out here. We were in bed and that's the last I remember," Lucius said, running for a knife to cut the rope by which Simeon had accidentally hung himself.

"But who is that guy?" Cassandra asked. "Is he one of the locals?"

"I don't know, I've never seen him before," Lucius replied. Quickly he cut the rope and Simeon fell to earth with a thud as Lucius descended the ladder and ran to the corpse, turning it onto its back.

"Cass, he looks very much like the husband that murdered you."

"But you said he'd been hung," Cassandra replied, rising to her feet, and backing away from the corpse in fear.

"It's okay, Cass. I can't be sure it's the same man. Let's go into the village and tell the police."

"Lucius, I'm frightened," she replied.

"It's okay, Cass – everything will be fine, you'll see," he added. "Nothing will come between us, I promise."

.

Chapter Twenty

Two weeks later, Cassandra's friend Anna Harris had a visit from the police to give her an update on her missing persons' report.

"Anna Harris? I'm PC Watkins. I've come to give you an update on your missing persons' report. May I come in, please?" said the fresh-faced policeman, as Anna opened the door.

"Yes, of course. It's been two weeks and I was going to call you and find out if you had an update for me," Anna said, beckoning the policeman to enter and closing the door behind him. "Please, come in and sit down," she added, gesturing to her sofa.

"Yes, sorry it's taken a while but people aren't always missing because something has happened to them – sometimes they just want a little time to themselves. We usually give it six days before we make any enquiries."

"That seems rather a long time," Anna replied, folding her arms and leaning back in her chair.

"Well, your friend's not a child and if she just wants to up and leave then that's her decision."

"I understand that, but I was concerned for her mental health as she was saying some very strange things when she last visited me."

"Yes, about that," the policeman said, looking at his notepad.

"What about it? Have you found her? Is she okay?" Anna asked, unfolding her arms, and leaning forward.

"No, we've not found her. In fact, the only Cassandra Wyvern we've been able to find died seventy-four years ago."

"That's ridiculous," Anna protested. "She was here just last week."

"How did she contact you to say she was going to visit?"

"She never did, she'd just turn up unannounced. We went to university together in Bristol, but she only moved to Wales about a year ago when she met some man online."

"Ah yes, that would be," the policeman began, before looking at his notepad a second time.

"Simeon Danton," Anna said.

"Yes, did you know him?"

"No, I've never met him. She'd only been with him a few weeks when the lockdown started. Why? Do you need a description?"

"No, it's just that we can find no record of anyone with that name."

"What? That's crazy!" Anna said, standing up and pacing around the room in agitation.

"I'm very sorry, Mrs Harris, but we can find no record of either your friend or her partner – at least, no one with her name in this area in the last seventy-four years – and no record at all of anyone named Simeon Danton."

"What! So they've both just disappeared and you're not going to do anything about it?" Anna queried.

"I'm sorry," the policeman said, rising to his feet. "Our enquiries indicate that the Cassandra Wyvern you knew – and her partner – never existed."

"That's crazy, they must have existed!" Anna shouted.

"No - I'm sorry. Maybe they were both using fake names."

"But I've known her for years," Anna remonstrated.

"I'm sorry," said the policeman.

"I'll see you out," Anna's husband said, having just entered the room from the garden and seeing that the policeman was anxious to leave.

"Thank you," said the policeman.

As the two left the living room, Andrew Harris shut the living room door behind them.

"I suppose I shouldn't tell you this, but the last year has been very difficult for her."

"I understand," said the policeman. "It's not been easy for any of us."

"Yes, she lost her mother and then she began obsessing about the past and how much nicer it would be to live then than now. She then started mentioning her friend a lot."

Chapter Twenty

"Ah, we can find no record of such a woman living around this area since nineteen forty-seven. Did you ever meet her friend?"

"No - Anna told me that she used to visit but it was always at times when I wasn't here. I'm not saying they're all a figment of her imagination but there's something amiss," he added.

"I hope that as the lockdown eases things improve for you," the policeman said, placing his hand on the handle of the front door now that Andrew Harris had removed his hand in order to talk.

"She's not well," Andrew Harris confided, as the policeman opened the front door and stepped out onto the garden path. "We've been told that the only thing that's going to help is counselling."

Printed in Great Britain
by Amazon